As a child, Lori Bank often spent afternoons with her grandmother in the Westchester family home. Her grandmother had emigrated from the Pale of Settlement in Russia in the early part of the twentieth century. Curious about her grandmother's childhood, Lori once asked what life in the settlement was like. Her grandma answered in a whisper: "The Cossacks threw babies in the air and caught them on bayonets. Who needs to remember?" Years later, imagined details of her grandmother's life and the history of the Pale of Settlement found its way into *Grandma Ethel's Braid*.

Lori Bank is an award-winning poet, essayist, fiction writer, and photographer, and the author of *There Is No Time* (2011), *The Lizard and Other Poems* (2014) and *Collected Poems of Lori Bank* (2020).

Her credits include The New York Post and Village Voice (photography), Primary Stages (company photographer), Brooklyn Graphic (arts reviewer), Chrysalis (poetry), Connecticut Review (essay), Conversing with Mystery-CD Anthology for Washington State Hospices (poetry), Sedona Centennial Poetry Contest (honourable mention).

To Dan Marshal

Lori Bank

# GRANDMA ETHEL'S BRAID

Assisted by Naomi Rose

## AUSTIN MACAULEY PUBLISHERS™
LONDON * CAMBRIDGE * NEW YORK * SHARJAH

Copyright © Lori Bank 2023

The right of Lori Bank to be identified as author of this work has been asserted by the author in accordance with sections 77 and 78 of the Copyright, Designs and Patents Act 1988.

All rights reserved. No part of this publication may be reproduced, stored in a retrieval system, or transmitted in any form or by any means, electronic, mechanical, photocopying, recording, or otherwise, without the prior permission of the publishers.

Any person who commits any unauthorized act in relation to this publication may be liable to criminal prosecution and civil claims for damages.

This is a work of fiction. Names, characters, businesses, places, events, locales, and incidents are either the products of the author's imagination or used in a fictitious manner. Any resemblance to actual persons, living or dead, or actual events is purely coincidental.

A CIP catalogue record for this title is available from the British Library.

ISBN 9781035815548 (Paperback)
ISBN 9781035815555 (ePub e-book)

www.austinmacauley.com

First Published 2023
Austin Macauley Publishers Ltd®
1 Canada Square
Canary Wharf
London
E14 5A

My thanks to Dan Marshall, Naomi Rose, and Anita Rosenfield.

# Table of Contents

**Prologue**   11

**Part 1: Russia Ethel**   15

*Chapter 1: Return to the Old Country*   18

*Chapter 2: Yeshiva Boy*   27

*Chapter 3: Odessa*   36

*Chapter 4: Peril and Sorrow*   53

*Chapter 5: Journey to America*   69

*Chapter 6: New Beginnings*   94

*Chapter 7: A Precarious Birth*   100

**Part 2: America Lillian**   107

*Chapter 1: The Bakery*   110

*Chapter 2: Playing*   113

*Chapter 3: Writing*   117

*Chapter 4: Like No Other Grandma*   123

*Chapter 5: Bennie and the Car Wash*   130

*Chapter 6: FDR*   140

*Chapter 7: Hair Care*   148

*Chapter 8: As They Say in the Museums*   153

*Chapter 9: Cleaning Out Grandma Ethel's Room*   162

*Chapter 10: A Day of Celebration*   177

| | |
|---|---|
| *Chapter 11: From Another Century* | *183* |
| *Chapter 12: To Shul or Not to Shul* | *190* |
| *Chapter 13: Seder at Merri's House* | *195* |
| *Chapter 14: Life at Forty* | *202* |
| *Chapter 15: Ruthie's Denouement* | *213* |
| *Chapter 16: Benny at the Hospice* | *218* |
| *Chapter 17: Caprice* | *227* |
| *Chapter 18: Grandma's Demise* | *236* |
| *Chapter 19: A Riddle Solved (Partly)* | *241* |
| **Epilogue** | **247** |

# Prologue

The year when Ethel was ten, the early spring was both beautiful and terrifying. She saw the white narcissus, flowering between patches of snow. From the river, bathed in sunlight, she heard the thunderous, staccato cracks of winter ice breaking apart. It went on for days, and the river soon threatened to overflow its banks and flood the village.

Friday came and Shabbos was drawing near as the waters rose and spilled into the lanes around the wooden houses. It was time to bake the challah when the village council decided all should ascend to the roof of the synagogue and wait there for the coming of the evening prayers. They had no time to do more than improvise bundles of food and coverlets. With these they climbed the small rise to the synagogue and ascended to the roof using ladders that were kept in the storage room. Most of the congregation mounted easily to the overhanging roof that would serve as their balcony beneath the oncoming night. But the Rabbi, an ancient man, had to be pushed up from behind and pulled up from the top like a sack of potatoes. When he got to the roof, he addressed them saying, "God will forgive, this once, and perhaps even rejoice in our unusual Shabbos celebration, out beneath this firmament, so set in the sky during the six days of creation. Such a work God has wrought."

How funny, thought Ethel, to see the men rock precariously back and forth on the roof in the rapture of their evening prayers, calling forth the beginning of God's holy time upon the face of the mundane: Sabbath, the time He descended to gather up all into His kingdom, His time on the earth for blessing and celebration.

"Why do we live near the river?" The children asked as night came on, "if the spring thaw can send water to the door of our home and make mud pools of our dirt lane?"

"Because," the mothers answered in a tone of finality that tolerated no argument, "no one else wants to live here. Besides, it makes the land fertile."

On the roof, Ethel felt far from the earth and close to God and His Angels. Closer than in the daily chores that ruled their lives, except on Shabbos, when God's Time reigned supreme. Workday life was a small world, so small that it fit like a little ball in one of God's sleeves, or under his cap (if He too wore a yarmulke). To be a part of God's glittering sky for one night was to be in the realm of the eternal, not lost among the day's struggles.

Mama said quietly, so Papa would not hear, "Look, see, tonight God's wife lights the Shabbos candles," as she pointed up to the heavens. After a time, the children saw the stars flickering in the deepening blue sky. They laid back and watched God watching over them.

"Shush, shush," all the mothers said to their children. Slowly the drowsiness of night came over them.

So, too, Ethel was falling asleep when she felt something jab her. She turned away from her family onto her right side and saw Jacob Brody lying next to her. Even in moonlight, there was no mistaking his copper-coloured curls that glowed like a halo around his head.

Without a moment's hesitation, and with her eyes shut, she poked him back. Then, she heard him giggle. Cautiously, she looked back over her shoulder toward her family and saw Mama hadn't stirred from where she lay wrapped in a black shawl with Chaim, not a year old, couched upon her breast.

Jacob opened one eye as Ethel peered through her lashes, the lids slightly raised. Suddenly, she startled him by opening her eyes wide. They laughed, trying not to make a sound, and that caused them to gasp for breath. No one nearby stirred. Their eyes sparked with the joy of outwitting the adults.

One by one, all lying upon the roof were going limp like heavy sacks of grain. The sound of breathing grew louder as the minutes passed, punctuated by snorts and coughs, and ragged snoring filled the night.

A muffled crack, like distant thunder, came from the river where the ice was splintering and the water flowing. Mama shifted her body, rearranging Chaim along her side and curled around him, settling down once more to sleep.

Jacob and Ethel went on talking with their eyes that curved up at the outer corners like smiling lips. "Look," he said in a faint whisper, shifting from his side to his back. He reached up his arm to the sky, pointing hard, finger waving. Speckles of stars were coming into focus like white granules of sugar sprinkled on the kitchen table after circles of cookie dough had been put in the oven to bake.

"Lion," he said, still pointing at the sky.

"Lion?" Ethel asked, searching above.

"Here," he said, and took her hand in his, tracing something in the heavens. "The lion of Judah," he said as he guided her hand. For a moment she saw nothing, then the head and four legs, a tail with a burst of silver threads. She had seen animals like this carved on silver Sabbath candle holders. So those were lions! God's lions, keeping the flames of God's time aloft for the evening that came on in their home.

After showing her, Jacob did not release Ethel's hand. They fell asleep, arms entwined, hands eventually falling open, away from each other's grasp. Many years later, Ethel realized that was when she fell in love with Jacob.

In the morning light they forgot their secret words, turning away from one another, toward their families. People were beginning to stir and wake. She heard elders coughing, babies crying for morning milk from the breasts of their mothers, working men grunting until they remembered it was the Sabbath and they needn't rise early. Mothers soothed their little ones as the sun rose and came to rest on the eastern horizon.

The morning light revealed muddy pools of water and the deep impressions of cartwheel ruts on the lanes between their houses. The men recited the Sabbath morning prayers and, later as the sun set in a blaze of orange light, the evening prayers. Then, they went slowly backwards, down the ladder, and took planks and long boards from the storeroom to make paths back to their homes.

# Part 1
# Russia Ethel

Along the Russian-Polish borderlands
a glistening, frozen river flows
secretly beneath the cold.
Wooden buckets filled from stone wells
or iron cisterns, hauled each day
stand waiting to be used.
Grandma's hand unlaces the golden braid
wrapped tightly like a crown
over the crest of her brow.
Unlaces the strands of her days
into one shimmering field.
Drenches it with water, soap, chamomile, and honey.
Then sits beside the window in the sun.
Fridays, the shtetl home grows lighter each hour,
gathering in the holy time.
Mother and daughter face each other
braiding together the strands of challah,
calling back and forth the names of those who are gone.
Gently they hold the sweet loaves in their hands,
sealing in the love,
binding the generations to the flourishing earth,
so darkness of forgetting not befall them
and dishonour those who brought them through the living chain,
offered each seventh day to God.
In America, Grandma Ethel wears
her gold hair free,
cut off at the chin.

# Chapter 1
# Return to the Old Country

Lillian, the youngest grandchild, found Grandma Ethel on the floor of her bright yellow bathroom, part of her bed-sitting room off the downstairs of their spilt-level ranch in suburban Westchester. She was conscious, but unable to get up. Ruthie, Grandma Ethel's daughter, saw the half-eaten Almond Joy with the wrapper still on, the empty coke bottle, and the piece-de-résistance, the still-uncorked bottle of Cherry Heering on the end table of the convertible bed-couch. Grandma's rhinestone-studded prescription sunglasses, the only glasses she owned, lay on the other end table as if watching the unfolding events from a detached posture.

Was it another minor stroke? Or had Grandma overindulged during the night, reached the bathroom in a dizzy state, attempted to sit, and fallen? With no blood on the yellow tiles, they hoped she had slid down without much trauma. Ruthie went to call for an ambulance while Lillian sat on the floor with Grandma, assuring her help was coming and she'd soon be okay.

Grandma Ethel's voice was faint, like all the wind had been knocked out of her. She was confused about where she was and why she was there. Even so, she raised her big-lidded Bette Davis eyes to 17-year-old Lillian's face and, in Yiddish, called her *a gitteh meydl, a zeeseh meydl*—"a good girl, a sweet girl."

When they got to the hospital, Grandma was wheeled through the Emergency Room quickly and into the adjacent intensive care unit as Ruthie filled out papers and explained Grandma's recent health history to a nurse. After the orderlies transferred Grandma from the gurney, they raised the sides of the bed to make a crib so Grandma couldn't fall out.

Minutes passed; Grandma opened and closed her eyes. She scanned the ceiling, then looked in Lillian's direction, then Ruthie's, over by the nurse's desk. Grandma was saying something Lillian couldn't make out from the foot of the bed.

"What is it, Grandma?" Lillian asked as she put her hand over one of Grandma's.

The words came slowly and faintly. She laboured to breathe deeply between each one. "You must…love…one another." She paused, "that's the only thing…that matters…you must love." Having delivered her momentous words, she closed her eyes and seemed to rest. Lillian watched Grandma's chest rise and fall for a few minutes, then went to see if Ruthie and the nurse were finished.

When Lillian looked back across the room, Grandma's eyes were staring at the ceiling, then scanning the room, closing for a moment, and then looking back up at the ceiling. As Lillian watched, she was reminded of the biblical Jacob who had watched angels passing up and down the ladder from earth to the firmament above. She imagined Grandma Ethel shuttling back and forth between heaven and earth, not knowing where she belonged.

\* \* \*

Ethel Smolens née Kaplan no longer lay in the safety of her hospital bed. She was no longer in Westchester county, or even America. No longer in the seventh decade of the twentieth century for that matter. From the time she had fallen while trying to clutch hold of her bright yellow bathroom sink, she had called out for help from inside a whirlwind in which she found herself spinning. Finally, it transported her back to a village along the banks of the Dnieper River in Imperial Russia.

She was three years old, sitting with her Zaide, noticing for the first time one of his hands. It was not like the other hand, nor her hands that she examined as they rested in her lap. Mama had recently taught her to count using her fingers and even her toes. Looking at Zaide's hand, she began to wail in anguish and fright.

"What is it, what is it?" Mama said as she ran in from the garden where she was digging up turnips. Right away she understood that Ethel had been showing Zaide all her fingers and counting each one out loud, when he had lifted his hands so she could count his, too. Suddenly, something Ethel had never noticed before came into focus. One of Zaide's hands was a monster. Thumb, pinkie, and ring finger were there, but what had happened to the other two? Stumps like worms that writhed without heads.

"Your fingers, Papa! She's frightened."

"Nothing to be afraid of," said Zaide, smiling at his granddaughter as best he could. "I lost them when I was a little boy, no older than you."

This only made Ethel wail once more as Mama picked her up and started to carry her back and forth in the kitchen. Mama banged on the old cooking pot and sang a little song about a brave little girl who did not cry. When Ethel was quiet again, Mama tried to explain what happened to Zaide's fingers. That Great Grandpa had really saved Zaide's life. The wicked Czar Nicholas was taking all the Jewish boys into the army. Without those two fingers, Zaide wouldn't be able to hold a gun and shoot. So he wouldn't have to leave the family and become a soldier for bad Czar Nicholas.

"Sometimes," Mama continued, "you must make a sacrifice for a greater good. Even the patriarch Abraham was ordered by God to sacrifice his son, Isaac. This won't happen to you, my little muffin. Girls are spared such trials by Czars and God. Here," she said, and pinched a crumb or two from the corner of the honey cake that had been cooling on the sideboard, and popped it into Ethel's open mouth.

Now she was older. Maybe six. Her mother was showing her how to take the kitchen pail of food scraps outside and throw its contents to the Christian peasants' pigs that roamed the village. Ethel was afraid of letting them near her, with their powerful bulk and snorting noises.

"Here," her mother said, and threw some of the remains of the last few days far into the alleyway between the *isbahs*, the wooden huts of the Jewish quarter. All the pigs scurried over.

Ethel was given the pail to throw the remnants into their midst. She was to get back into the house after rinsing the pail with water scooped from the rain barrel next to the front door. Glancing at the foraging pigs whose mouths and snouts were caked with mud, her mother said, "Etalah, my little one, this is why we do not eat pigs!"

Now Ethel was older and her days revolved around learning the household duties at her mother's side. She could cook, although in a plain manner, not having shown much interest or natural inclination. Her mother left her to complete cooking tasks that seemed to Ethel repetitive and uninteresting. Sometimes, she rolled out and cut dough for egg noodles, one strip after another.

Often, she would be left the odious task of plucking the feathers and soaking the chicken in its bath of salt after the unlucky bird had been killed for the Sabbath dinner. And whenever there was an irregularity in this honoured chicken—a blotch on its skin, or a gash in its leg, or its insides looked unusually bloody—Ethel and her sister Anna would take the chicken in question to Rabbi Zalman.

Was this a chicken properly slaughtered by the ritual slaughterer? Was this a righteously Kosher chicken? Was this chicken blessed? Did this irregularity mean—God forbid—we would have to discard this prized Sabbath chicken, get a new one, pluck it and salt it, prepare it and cook it, all before sundown when the Sabbath would begin and work was forbidden?

"What's wrong with this chicken?" Ethel once blurted out when the Rabbi questioned a chicken's fitness.

"This chicken," the Rebbe replied with a thoughtful expression as he examined the pot in which the chicken had been transported, "this creature in question wasn't thinking straight when it was killed."

"Chickens can think? What was it thinking?" Ethel asked the Rebbe, surprised to learn that other of God's creatures had the capacity to ponder and surmise.

"That," replied the Rebbe, "I do not know. I cannot read minds, even of a lowly chicken."

"But, what do you mean, Rebbe?" Ethel persisted. "What might it have been thinking?"

"You are a silly girl," the Rebbe replied. "Why, it thinks chicken thoughts. What else could it think? It's a chicken."

"Oh," Ethel said, abashedly, noticing that the Rebbe had a fine manner of not answering a question. It left her feeling upside down, with all the blood rushing to her head. Her cheeks would flush and she would feel momentarily embarrassed.

"This was a very confused chicken," he added thoughtfully.

After a moment or two, Ethel's curiosity got the better of her and she asked, "What could it be confused about, I mean, considering it's a chicken kind of confusion."

"I told you, I don't know, but…" Here, his voice trailed off and then he said softly, "perhaps it wasn't expecting to die so soon. That can make one quite confused."

"Yes," Ethel said, wondering what the Rebbe meant by this remark. He looked rather wistful, stroking his long, snowy beard.

"Chickens don't always die quickly, as you know," he said. "Sometimes they run around in circles, even after their heads are cut off, not knowing where they are or what has happened to them. This creates a confusion because the chicken doesn't know if it's alive or dead."

Ethel tried to imagine how it might feel with her body one place and her head another. She found it quite perplexing.

"Rebbe," she said after a moment, "does one know when one is dead?"

"I don't know," answered the Rebbe. "This is a great puzzle, even for a Rebbe. This is why when someone dies, a person from the burial society stays with the deceased and recites prayers, to help the person find his way to God."

"Oh," she said, looking down at the poor chicken in the pot and wondering at the distracted look on Rabbi Zalman's face. Gee, never before had she learned so much from a dead chicken, she thought to herself. There was an uncomfortable silence during which she felt Anna tugging at her from behind. Anna had grown impatient and had been amusing herself by first balancing on one foot, and then on another. She would soon be too restless to contain herself, and this brought Ethel out of her reverie.

"So, Rebbe," Ethel said, "can we eat this chicken for Sabbath dinner?" She was eyeing the sun, framed by the Rebbe's study window where it seemed perched to descend into the afternoon hours, bringing them all too soon to the end of the day.

"Yes," said the Rebbe. "One can now eat this chicken," as he murmured inaudibly a prayer and blessed this humble creature who had inspired so much speculation and discussion.

Of all the Sabbath chickens discovered to be confused in one way or another, there never was one that could not unconfuse itself with the help of a prayer or two. Never did Rabbi Zalman declare a chicken inedible, and for that they were most grateful.

"Just don't bring me a fish," the Rebbe said. "In such a question as that, I would be floundering."

Ethel's and Anna's education was not completely neglected. Between her mother's marketplace stall for milk, cheeses, and vegetables from their garden, and her father's job overseeing the forest of a local estate, they had enough money to send the two girls to cheder to learn to read Yiddish and a speckle of

Hebrew. The girls' *melamed* was not a bright teacher, but he was able to instruct them in the basics.

Right off while learning the Bible, first in Yiddish, Ethel found she could not make heads or tails of God's universe. The Bible said things like, "In the beginning," and Ethel's lively mind wondered what there was *before* the beginning. Before me, Ethel reasoned, was my brother Samuel. Before him, my other brother, Issac, may he rest in peace. Before my mother and father, Bubbe Sarah, and Zaide Elias, and Bubbe Miriam, and Zaide Samuel. And they too had mothers and fathers and sisters and brothers.

And, where had God lived before the beginning? And what was He doing?

When Ethel started to ponder these questions and told the *melamed* what was on her mind, he said, "Such a silly girl. So, you want to question God, do you? Why don't you wait until you're a little older and have some knowledge in that brain? You know that brain comes from God, too."

But this did not stop Ethel from wondering about creation. First off, how could God fashion the earth if there was nothing? If you're going to make something, you need something to make it from, Ethel reasoned. To make a chair, you need wood; to make a pot, you need metal; to make a broom, you need straw.

To this, the *melamed* said, "God can make things from nothing, like a magician."

But, Ethel thought, magicians use tricks. Even my brother Samuel's hands can go so fast in a confusing way that he makes a groschen disappear from his palm and come out of his mouth. Surely God was not doing tricks, or was He? Did the world pop out from behind God's palm or out of the end of his sleeve? And since we're made in the image of God, does that mean He looks just like us, or, um, like Papa only bigger, much, much bigger? Is He stretched across the heavens from one end to the other?

But the *melamed* said there was no end to the universe.

So she started wondering about that. Beyond our house is the lane. Beyond our town is the rest of the Pale of Settlement. Beyond the Pale is Odessa. Beyond Russia is what? Poland and other countries and beyond these is the wide ocean, and America. Ethel hoped someday she would see America, filled with the people of all nations, trying to have a better life with unimaginable freedom and opportunities. Now, what was there beyond the world? The sun, the moon, the stars?

From this thought, she was brought to thoughts of Jacob on the roof of the synagogue. He understood far more than she could ever hope to; he would know the answers. But boys and girls in the shtetl were mostly kept apart until they were of marriageable age. All she could do was think about him and listen to the village gossip.

Jacob was studying with the Rabbi and hoped to go to Yeshiva in Vilna, so good and smart a student that he was. Already, he could argue forwards and backwards, from one side of a Talmud page to another. Rabbi Zalman jokingly called him *Pilpul*, or pepper, after the method of disputation training he would formally take up in the Yeshiva.

Jacob would be a Rabbi, that was certain. And she knew he would be a Rabbi whose words would light up the souls of his congregants like the stars that evening on the roof of the Synagogue lit up the night sky. The night two years ago when they had slept, arms entwined, waiting for the waters of the Dnieper to be soaked up by the softening earth of the spring thaw. Her family could not offer a dowry worthy of such a man. Surely he would have a great future and be a prized husband to any girl from a rich family.

Ethel knew Jacob had a religious mission. His youth and energy would be able to keep the people to the traditional ways and sow the seeds for future generations. So many were emigrating and scattering across the globe to Palestine, England, America, and elsewhere. Many were leaving behind their faith, and disappearing into lands that swallowed them up. Surely Jacob's fervour could hold together communities.

As he turned twelve, Jacob's copper curls that stuck out beneath his cap were accented by a newly sprouting beard. His hair was like the outward flame of his roiling spirit, which, as manhood approached, grew even more serious. His speech could soar to heaven and back to earth to speak God's words: God's vision for His people, who could see no end to their poverty and toil.

The lives of Russian Jews were vulnerable to continual disruption. The laws that governed Jews changed from year to year, and with each new czar. When one generation began to thrive, the soldiers would bring yet another edict, exiling them from their present circumstances, requiring them to sell everything they owned in a matter of days, and leave behind houses, livestock, land, and the whole fabric of their communities.

Over and over, they had been moved from one place to another and squeezed out of thriving cities to be imprisoned in the Pale of Settlement. This was the western land (annexed from the division of Poland), which substantially increased Catherine the Great's Russia, but caused the perplexing "problem of the Jews." The Jews had once been thriving Polish citizens with many rights and successful occupations.

However, from the time of the annexation and onwards, the Jews were viewed with different eyes. The ruling elite feared they would corrupt the Christian peasants' natural virtue and contaminate Russia like a moral pestilence: It was said these "foreign people, these Jews" would kill Christian children to use their blood in the making of the Passover matzos and kill Christians to drink their blood as wine in their Sabbath rituals. This rampant slander, the blood libel, was periodically voiced and intermittently went dormant.

For Jacob, the Hebrew letters of the Torah were like little flames illuminating God's meaning, God's desire, God's laws and guidance for His troubled people. But in the space of one night, in only a few moments, all of that was altered. The Czar's soldiers returning to the southern steppe came riding through the shtetl, and Jacob's heart and fate were changed forever when his sister was killed by the Cossacks.

Jacob's father, who had been traveling for business, returned, and was distraught with grief and rage. He could no longer see a future for himself in the traditional ways. He pulled up all roots in the village and took his family to St. Petersburg. There, he put Jacob into one of the Crown schools, meant to assimilate the Jews into Russian society and eradicate their religion. Jacob's father was determined to forsake the God of his ancestors, if such a God would allow the butchering of an innocent child, as his had been cut down.

Jacob was nearly thirteen when his family left the village. Ethel watched him leave with his family in a wagon piled high with their possessions. The flames of his copper hair and beard were in stark contrast to the sadness of his countenance. His father had spoken, and Jacob was to obey.

As Ethel watched them depart, Jacob's pale, freckled skin seemed to glow in the light of the morning sun, despite the doleful apparition of his face. At that instant, Ethel's love for him grew even more than before. When Jacob saw Ethel, the light trickled out of his eyes like sand down an hourglass. Then, the wagon passed by and Jacob turned his back on the village. With resignation, he faced the road ahead of him.

Ethel heard Jacob's family was doing well, his father a prosperous wine merchant in their new home in St. Petersburg. However, they faced the daily possibility of expulsion and the ever-present heavy yoke of additional taxes levied against Jewish businesses. By all accounts, Jacob's life was progressing. He was preparing to enter the University in St. Petersburg, under the small quota allotted to Jewish students. Perhaps he would find a teaching position in the Crown schools, or a professorship in literature, having mastered the Russian language. The God of his ancestors lay shattered by the death of his sister. As it was, he was lost to Ethel. She tried to forget him.

Time passed and by now Ethel's Papa and brother Samuel had left for America. They were working to save money for the family's passage and a nest egg to support everyone until they found work in the new land. To make more money, Mama enlarged the milk and vegetable business at their market stall. All the children helped make sour cream, buttermilk, and cheeses to sell.

Mama was away from early morning till night. She wanted to rescue her mother's Sabbath pearls from Izzy the moneylender, so she made a small payment every week. These pearls had gotten Papa and Samuel all the way to America across the Atlantic.

Ethel could not imagine so large a body of water with shores one could not see in a glance. She had heard it took two weeks or more to cross this ocean, which was salty as tears. Mama's pearls had carried Papa and Samuel a long way from home, a great distance from the rest of the family.

# Chapter 2
# Yeshiva Boy

Four years after Jacob's departure, Ethel's family still waited for the letter from Papa telling them to sell everything and come to America. Recently Papa had found permanent employment in a factory rolling tobacco into cigars, and Ethel's brother Samuel was now working as a carpenter in the building trade. Surely in the next few months they would save enough for the passage over for the rest of the family.

By this time, Ethel was sixteen. She was finished with girls' cheder, able to read and write in Yiddish, and to recite prayers in Hebrew. As the eldest girl she took over all the household duties while Mama minded the market stall, selling vegetables, eggs, and dairy products. Ethel got her sister and brothers off to school, did the cleaning and laundry, tended the vegetable garden, milked the cow, and made cheeses.

This morning Mama had left early. It was Mama's custom to rise before dawn to do the first milking of the day, stock the stove with wood, light it, and get the evening meal set into pots. Dinner foods simmered for hours, making the house fragrant with the smells of stews or soups, seasoned with spices and vegetables, and rounded out with noodles, groats, or potatoes. All day the aromas saturated the air and set everyone longing for dinner hours before it could be eaten.

Today Mama had put up beef *flanken*, an extravagantly good cut of meat. She had traded Abramel the butcher one week's worth of eggs and milk plus two honey-almond cakes for the delicacy. It was a dear price, but Mama thought one should splurge now and then. Besides, they were rich in eggs and milk even if otherwise poor since they no longer had Papa's income from overseeing the Rukovskys' timber forest.

Poor was poor, but Mama was sure they would not starve. They always had vegetables and cheese to trade, and she could transform any less-than-spectacular meat into a lavish stew. Somehow Mama could cut stew meat into so many pieces that it seemed everyone's bowl was filled to overflowing.

Before she left for the market stall, Mama asked Ethel to bake *lokshen kugel*, a tasty noodle pudding with raisins, for dessert. She wanted to top off everyone's dinner so they felt filled to the brim and able to last till the next evening meal. All day long they survived only on milk, black bread, and a piece of herring.

Ethel groaned. "Mama, it's laundry day! I don't have time to make noodles."

"So, rice *kugel*? The rice practically makes itself."

"I'll try," replied Ethel.

With that Mama had to be satisfied and left for the market.

Later that afternoon, while Ethel swept out the house, she heard a knock at the door; an unusually faint knock, unlike the sonorous ones she was used to hearing. She thought perhaps it was their neighbour Yentle, come to borrow some flour or eggs for a dish she was making for dinner. When Ethel went to the door, she found a boy with sidelocks, dressed in the garb of a religious man: a black caftan with green silk sash, and of all things on this hot day, a fur-trimmed hat. *He must be a Yeshiva boy*, she thought.

It was customary in *shtetls* to help out a boy studying to go to Yeshiva with a meal or a night's lodging. Every family had the honour of helping out, but not the onerous task to care for the student more than one or two days. This one seemed particularly young. Innocence showed on his face like the early morning sun on the surrounding hills. Ethel thought, *he must be at least thirteen and Bar Mitzvahed if he is dressed in such clothes*. Ethel had little experience with boys outside her village, and she thought maybe somewhere else in the Pale of Settlement he was not such an unusual sight.

"Yes," Ethel asked, as she stood in the doorway.

"Might I have a drink of water? I have been on the road since early morning." He never looked directly at her, but slightly askance as religious boys are instructed to do when speaking to girls, so as not to be stirred by physical attractiveness.

*He is well-mannered*, thought Ethel. She showed him into the kitchen. Off came his fur-trimmed hat and underneath shone a beautiful yarmulke embroidered with gold and silver thread. *He certainly wears nice garments. Perhaps*, thought Ethel, *they were parting gifts from the people of his village.*

"Are you headed for Odessa?" Ethel asked expectantly as she put a cool glass of water before him on the kitchen table. He picked up the glass and sipped the water slowly and deliberately while the question hung in the air between them.

"No," he finally replied, as he set down the empty glass. He stood saying nothing more. Ethel looked at him as she waited for words of explanation.

"Then Vilna?" She asked. He made no reply, but stared off to the side and nodded his head slowly.

"What is that cooking on the stove?" He asked, not at all shyly, and added, "It smells good."

*Oh, so that is it. He is hungry too*, thought Ethel.

"Had you nothing to eat today?" She asked sympathetically, thinking how helpless men are, so in need of womanly assistance to keep them alive from moment to moment.

"Nothing but a dry piece of black bread before the sun came up."

"I'm sure my family and I would like the honour, a religious student as you are, to have you dine on some of my mother's splendid beef flanken and vegetables, and maybe a bit of kasha. Perhaps you will make a prayer for my father and brother, labouring in America? They hope to bring us over soon, so we can all be together again."

"I do not pray to receive things from the Almighty," he said hesitantly. Then he added energetically, "but I understand the nature of your request and will be happy to make prayers for your family."

This satisfied Ethel. She took the ladle from its hook on the wall and measured out a modest bowl of food. She made sure to give him some meat, but not so much that would deprive a family member.

Ethel set the food before him. He sat quickly, rinsed his hands with the bowl of water Ethel provided, said a prayer under his breath, and commenced to eat the hot food as rapidly as he could without burning his mouth. Then, Alya, the family's dairy cow, began to bellow from the shelter in the backyard, anxious to be relieved of her afternoon milk.

"Yes, yes I'm coming," Ethel called from the doorway.

"Excuse me," she said to the Yeshiva boy. "Take your time. I'm sure the stew will add energy to your steps. And here," she said, pouring out a small glass of cherry brandy, placing it on the table.

"Thank you. I am grateful for your generosity," he said, pausing only a moment from his eating, and nodding in Ethel's general direction.

"Alya," Ethel said in a tone of admonishment when she got to the shed, "please be patient." The cow had continued her incessant mooing, which was unusual because Alya had never before seemed so distressed. Ethel sat on the stool and wondered if Mama had skipped Alya's early morning milking before heading to the market stall. Seeing one milk can was gone, Ethel abandoned that possibility.

Throughout the chore, Alya continued her mooing and even flinched from Ethel's touch. "Be happy you are a dairy cow," she scolded, "and not one bound for market." But Ethel could never stay irritated at Alya. The cow's big moony eyes, heavily fringed with light-coloured lashes, would look soulfully back at anyone's gaze, as if she were not just a dumb creature. If animals had souls, Alya had a big-hearted one. Ethel slowed her milking and took extra care as Alya was acting so irritable. *And why should an animal not have her better and worse days like people? Troubled with physical ailments as well as moods?* Ethel thought.

Her mind drifted back to the Yeshiva boy, her vague hopes for America, and finally, as always, to Jacob. She wondered what his fate had been, whether he was at university. Whether he had an exciting and varied life in St. Petersburg. Had he found love? Was he at this very moment married with a family of his own? People all around her were growing up, going away, and making their lives in the world. Soon she too would be bound for America.

When she entered the kitchen a little while later, she was surprised to see the Yeshiva boy was gone. On the table were two empty bowls and two brandy glasses. *What's this?* she thought at first, but soon surmised that Zaide must have come in from his afternoon walk and helped himself to an early dinner. She checked his room and there he sat in his rocking chair, eyes closed, dozing. She wondered if he had met their guest and perhaps talked a few minutes about Torah, something Zaide loved to do. Ethel closed up the house and went out to do some errands. She met her brothers and sister at *cheder* and brought them home.

When they returned, Mama was seated in the small parlour asleep and snoring. She woke from her catnap as the children marched in and got ready for their supper. They ate their stew heartily. As in fairy tales, it had miraculously stretched and filled each bowl to overflowing. A loaf of black bread enabled everyone to sop up each precious morsel.

Ethel went to check and see if Zaide wanted some kugel and raisins. There he lay, stretched out on the bed sleeping. She did not disturb him.

"What a day!" Mama said, as she began to clear the supper dishes.

"Sit," said Ethel, and picked up the plates herself. "What? Something unusual?"

"Everything," Mama said. "Alya's morning milk curdled. Unheard of! Someone returned four eggs with cracks in them. Another three came back with red spots on the yolk. God forbid word should get out I sell bad eggs and milk. Our livelihood would dry up like that!" Mama snapped her fingers to emphasize the swiftness of such a catastrophe.

"We had a visitor," Ethel said to distract Mama from brooding about her calamities.

"This day does not bode well," said Mama, anxiously. "I stopped at Selma's to get an amulet and some herbs. No harm warding off the evil eye."

"The visitor," said Ethel quickly to reassure her, "was a Yeshiva boy, finely dressed, but hungry and thirsty. On his way to Vilna. He said he'd make a prayer for Papa and Samuel."

"Why didn't he go to the Study House or the Rabbi?" Mama asked.

"I don't know. He seemed in a hurry."

"Did you let him in?" Mama asked. "Was Zaide in the house?"

"Alya was making a fuss, I had to milk her, Mama," Ethel said. "You had to see him. Gentleness shone from his brow like a halo. He hardly had the sproutings of a beard. If Zaide met him in the kitchen, I'm sure they debated Talmud passages. Maybe that's why Zaide went to bed so early. Tired from conversation. If they met at all, I'm sure it was fine."

"Still," Mama replied, admonishing her daughter, "with so many people on the roads these days, you can't be too careful. He could have been a little thief, all dressed up to fool you." Mama got up and went to peek in on Zaide for a moment and came back satisfied.

"Here," she said, "help me tie this amulet to the door."

Ethel steadied the kitchen stool as Mama climbed up, sturdy as a mountain goat, to attach the charm. Mama spat three times and put bundles of herbs in the rafters at the four corners of the ceiling. Ethel did not share her mother's superstitions, but she thought about having left the Yeshiva boy alone in the house with Zaide and thanked God nothing seemed amiss.

A heavy rain that night made the morning the air smell fresh and clean. Mama was up before dawn, rattling her pots in the kitchen. The sound drifted through the house and invaded Ethel's dreams.

*She was walking on a road through a forest of pine and cedar. Thunderclaps assaulted her ears and filled her with fear. The sharp smell of pitch pierced her lungs as she laboured for breath. The path she was walking on dissolved, and was lost among the towering trees. She could no longer see the sky. She could no longer tell one direction from another, or how to get out of the woods. Suddenly, high above her on the limb of a tree, a dark form with wings burst upwards in a flash of light and disappeared.*

Ethel woke abruptly, clutching her blanket, feeling she had witnessed something not of this world, and it cast a shadow over her heart. After a time, the troubling dream faded from her mind. She got up, dressed quickly, then went to wake her brothers and sister to ready them for *cheder*. As usual, three-year-old Avrom could not get his shoes on. Ethel bent down to help him.

"I saw him," Avrom whispered into her ear. "I saw him, I saw him," he chanted in a singsong fashion, and tapped his fingers playfully on the top of Ethel's head as she finished helping him into his shoes.

"Who?" Ethel asked offhandedly as she pulled him into the kitchen for a glass of milk and a poppy seed roll that Mama had left them for breakfast. But Avrom would say no more.

Ethel stuffed buttered black bread sandwiches into the children's pockets for lunch. She hurried them out of the house and pulled them all in a line, holding one another's hands. When she turned to leave them at school, Avrom began to cry. She bent down to wipe his face, told him what a big boy he was, and to mind the *melamed* and learn his lessons well. But the boy's tears broke from his eyes once again. Ethel fished in her pocket, found a few dried raisins, popped them quickly into Avrom's mouth, pushed him through the door, and turned away without looking back.

The sun had been up nearly two hours by the time Ethel reached home. She noticed Zaide wasn't awake yet. He was sleeping restfully. She put on the stove a huge pot of water hauled from the cistern. What with the making of the kugel and the visit from the Yeshiva boy yesterday, she had not done the laundry. There was no putting it off today.

After hanging the clothes on the line, Ethel went ins inside to check on Zaide, to see if he was up and hungry. To her surprise, he was gone. Ethel wondered if he'd eaten. Nothing was out of place in the kitchen. She worried, since he'd retired so early the night before, whether or not he was well. He was in his eighties, but energetic enough to go on walks to the edge of town where he had a berry patch from which he loved to eat.

Something about his absence struck a chord in Ethel. No one had spoken with Zaide, nor he to anyone else, except perhaps the Yeshiva boy, since yesterday afternoon. She would go to the Study House and the Rabbi to see if Zaide was there.

But he was nowhere to be found in his usual haunts. Worried, Ethel hurried off to the market to find Mama. Mama was already upset.

"Rifke, that gossip, stopped by just a few minutes ago," said Mama hurriedly. "You know *her*—what happened to who, who happened to what, and on and on. Then, she finally tells me that Zaide was seen on the bridge heading out of town, engaged in talk with a boy finely dressed in a caftan. I say to her 'no, not possible. Zaide takes his walks in the other direction.' But she insists her boy Shlomo saw them headed west, out of town, engaged in lively conversation. Now that makes no sense," Mama said, panic and confusion on her face.

"Maybe it does," Ethel said. "Zaide must have run into the Yeshiva boy while on a walk. Probably they were discussing Torah and Zaide walked along to keep the boy company."

"*Oy vey*," Mama cried out, "He'll get tired and lose his way. God forbid anything worse! We better search for him." Mama, who could not be calmed, left the stall to sound a general alarm for help.

Ethel went at once to trace the route Rifke's son had mentioned, west out of town. She hoped to find Zaide somewhere along the way, safe and sound. After all, what could the boy gain, thief or no. Zaide had nothing of value to offer him.

As she crossed the bridge out of town, a peasant's wagon passed her on its way to the marketplace, carrying a lamb for sale or slaughter. Her halting inquiries were pushed aside with a brusque "no" and an annoyed shake of the head. The young man seemed indignant, as though Ethel had needlessly wasted his valuable time. The encounter cast a pall of gloom over her.

She hastened on. With each passing step, a feeling of apprehension grew in her chest. *Oh, why did I let that boy into the kitchen? Why did I not send him to the Study House?* If anything happened to Zaide, she would bear the sorrow like a mark upon her soul. Her mind lit upon Jacob's sister, barely a few months old, who had been so horribly cut down in all her innocence. Ethel could not fathom a God who let such things take place. She knew it was wrong to think that way, but she could not help her aching heart that now saw the iniquities of the world around her, even in her little village.

Wheat harvesters worked in the fields as she passed. No one she asked remembered seeing an old man and a young boy. But then, they were taken up with mowing their crops and might have easily missed them.

Along came a peasant who nodded his head vigorously and responded to Ethel's question, "*Da, da, da,*" clicking his tongue with each sound. His words cheered her. Once more she felt hopeful that soon she'd come across Zaide, pleasantly passing the time with the Yeshiva boy. Or else, walking slowly back to town. Ethel walked quickly now for another twenty minutes with no sight of anyone, and a strange darkness seemed to settle over her.

Abruptly, she came to the towering forest with its ancient copper beech trees. Their deep purple leaves swayed in the late afternoon breeze with a hushed rustle. She was now so far from town she knew she would have a taxing walk back. For Zaide, it would have been nearly impossible. *I must go on*, she told herself, *in case he is a little farther along the road.*

Then she saw him. He was seated on the ground, his back leaning against the grey trunk of one of the copper beech trees. She called out, but he did not look up. Was he dozing in the late afternoon sun, tired out from his ramble? When she arrived at the spot, she saw his closed eyes and purple berry stains streaking his white beard, dripping down onto his chest. The Yeshiva boy's green sash was tied loosely around his neck. She shook him gently but he did not awaken.

Ethel dropped to her knees. "Zaide, wake up, I will help you home." But he did not respond, and she cried out convulsively, "Please, oh please, wake up Zaide, wake up." But Zaide remained as silent and still as a stone.

The men of the *chevra kaddisha,* the burial society, brought Zaide home late that afternoon in a horse drawn cart. He was placed in the burial house to await funeral preparations the next day. A congregant sat up all night, as was the custom, reciting religious passages and prayers so Zaide's soul would not be afraid and lose its way back to God.

The next morning, the men said they could find no mark upon Zaide's body and nothing seemed amiss. They believed it must have been his heart. His body was washed and cleaned with fresh pitchers of water, and shards were placed upon his closed eyelids. The loose white robe, the *kittel*, in which he'd been married so long ago was wrapped around him. It would now serve as his burial shroud. They placed him gently in a plain wooden coffin with a branch of myrtle by his side, so when the Messiah came Zaide could dig his way out and be reunited with all his loved ones and ancestors in Jerusalem. There, everyone would live eternally before God.

At the funeral in the small Jewish cemetery the sound of earth hitting the wood echoed dolefully in the waning afternoon light as Mama threw the first handful onto the coffin. She could not stop her tears, which fell down her cheeks and stained her chest with dark spots. The children bore it as best they could, with stricken and confused expressions, trying to fathom where their beloved Zaide had gone. Avrom cried out because his Za-Za was being shut away in a box, all alone, without anyone to hug or kiss him as Avrom was frequently wont to do. Ethel could not stop the thought that she was somehow to blame.

Elderly as Zaide was, Mama had hoped he would make it to the new world of America with them. He was the last leaf of that ancient tree that had come before the present generations. The family's dead ancestors lay scattered, like winter leaves, all across the Pale of Settlement, wherever the Jews had been forced to live under the various and contradictory edicts that regulated their movements.

"When we are gone," Mama said, "there will be no one to visit Zaide's and Bubbie's graves."

"They will be together, always," Ethel said quietly, to quell her mother's and her own tears.

"Yes, side by side in death as they once were in life for more than seventy years." Mama anticipated the roots of that venerable tree would be yanked out of her heart when they left for America.

That night, after all the others had gone to bed, Mama turned to Ethel and said softly, "What a miracle of life you are, Etalah, you saw him face-to-face," and kissed her eldest daughter upon the forehead.

"Saw who, Mama?" Ethel asked, confused and a little frightened.

"The Angel, my child. The Angel that came to gather up Zaide. May you not see him again for a long, long, time."

Despite what anyone might say about Zaide's advanced years and failing health, or Rifke's boy Shlomo having seen the Yeshiva boy, Mama insisted that the stranger had not been an ordinary mortal, but the Angel of Death, dressed up to fool the living.

# Chapter 3
# Odessa

During the first decade of the twentieth century waves of pogroms—violent "mass actions" aimed at massacring Jews—spread through the Pale of Settlement, hitting large cities like Kishniev and Odessa as well as small towns and villages. How these came to happen was explained by different theories. In Kishniev, a young Christian boy was found dead during the Passover and Easter week. Rumour spread that Jews had killed him in holiday ceremonies and used his blood to make Passover matzos. Some thought the pogroms were started by government secret police. No one knew for sure. But they spread like a pestilence.

In the towns, groups of unidentified men with clubs and sharp farm tools rampaged through the Jewish quarter. They smashed the windows of shops—butchers, tailors, tinsmiths, jewellers. They ransacked stores, stealing what they could carry and dumping the rest onto the streets. They dragged merchants out and beat them. Drunk with the bloody violence, they moved from one street to the next. Eventually, they broke into houses, looting, raping, maiming, and killing. They desecrated synagogues with thunderous destruction, stealing Torahs, altar ornaments, ivory Torah sticks, gold and silver candelabras, all consecrated to God.

The pogroms went on for days while the authorities, nowhere to be seen, did nothing to stop them. Only when news of the pogroms spread outside of Russia, and a clamour of outrage rose from western countries, did the government order the local police to quell the rioters.

It was several years after these events that Ethel's Papa and brother Samuel had gone to America. Like many of the shtetl inhabitants, the Kaplans felt nothing was left for them in the old country except their poverty. While Papa and Samuel worked many jobs in New York to raise money for the rest of the family's passage, Mama busied herself securing the needed emigration papers. Russia didn't want her Jews, but the officials made it difficult for them to leave.

Finally, when Ethel was sixteen, the money arrived. Papa and Samuel had steady employment. They had rented a three-room tenement apartment on the lower eastside. The whole family could squeeze in and make do. Mama, Ethel, and the children made a little celebration, shadowed by the knowledge that many hardships still lay ahead.

When the time came, Ethel went to Odessa to collect her aunt, her father's sister, who would travel with them to America. Nothing kept Aunt Miriam in Russia any longer. Her husband of fifty years, Max, had been brutally killed in the Odessa Pogrom years before. All her children were grown and gone. Two lived in the Pale of Settlement, hoping soon to emigrate as well, and three others had left: one going to Palestine, one to England, one to America.

Aunt Miriam planned to join her youngest daughter's household in New York and see her grandchild for the first time. Another child was to be born soon. Aunt Miriam doted on her youngest daughter, but doubted the girl's maturity; she anticipated a grandmother would be well-needed as the household expanded.

When Ethel arrived in Odessa, Aunt Miriam was selling off the contents of her house. She told Ethel how surprised she was at the swell of emotions that moved through her as her belongings diminished each day. So much had accumulated. So much had been handed down from one generation to the next.

Almost all the things of value had come to her though Max's family and held some remembrance of him. The hand-painted bone china, the porcelain vases, the cut crystal, the holiday silver. They would have to be left behind. In any case, she needed to sell them and consolidate her money for New York. She did not want to be a burden to her daughter's family. She only wanted to be another pair of hands and another heart to share their lives.

She confessed she felt that each day she was folding up her life, folding it up ever smaller to fit into this journey to a new land. She knew it would never unfold again in the same way. All that had grounded her in memories, both joyous and sad, would be gone.

Surprisingly, nothing seemed more precious than the scarred wooden bowls, the mixing and chopping utensils that carried the marks of three generations of her family. They had been used to make matzo brie and borscht, gefilte fish and horseradish, chopped liver and potato latkes, cherry blintzes and honey cake—all the foods that had nourished them and helped them celebrate the holidays.

These foods were made, each of them, with special ingredients from family recipes and with cooking and baking tricks perfected and handed down by generations of grandmothers, mothers, and daughters. Their household could not have been a treasured Jewish one without them.

What was more full of a mother's love than the daily nourishment that had passed her children's lips? How better for a mother to express her caring than to have provided for their growing bodies?

As if they were magic talismans that could transport the generations of the old country to the soil of the new, Aunt Miriam selected a wooden bowl—small enough to hide inside her under bloomers—and a wooden spoon, radiating a potpourri of spices from sauces, gravies, stews, and soups, to take with her on this longest and final journey of her life.

While Aunt Miriam was busy concluding her affairs, Ethel ran errands and did the daily marketing in the Jewish quarter. One day, searching for fresh horseradish to complement her aunt's gefilte fish, made the "Odessa way," Ethel happened upon a café. Ensconced at a large table out on the sidewalk were ten or twelve young men and women arguing robustly, voices raised, hands in motion, fingers jabbing to emphasize the arguments that were flying back and forth across the table.

Some listened silently, sipping from glasses of hot tea, nursing bowls of scarlet borscht and sopping it up with large chunks of black bread. In the midst of it all, Ethel suddenly recognized a face with a coppery beard, with curls to match sprouting from beneath a Russian cap. Jacob. She had not seen nor heard of him for four years. Ethel stood off to the side, trying to catch her breath, stunned. She had thought him lost to her.

As Ethel drew nearer, she saw one of his companions, a woman, older than herself, well dressed in high-laced boots and cape, listening raptly to all of Jacob's animated words. He was talking about class and society and a great change that was poised to happen in Russia. The same passionate Jacob; only the cause was completely different and held no sway with religion. His flame-coloured beard shook with agitation, as he went on talking of world truths and historical forces all coming together with people's minds and desires.

Finally, he fell silent. Timidly, tentatively, Ethel approached him. She was aware of her country clothes, of her dirndl skirt and embroidered peasant blouse that seemed so unsophisticated and out of place here in Odessa. She feared he would not recognize or even remember her. But she was wrong. As she approached his chair, he looked up, distracted, just coming out of the absorption that his words had spun around him, and his eyes widened upon seeing her face.

"Etalah?" He said in disbelief. "Is it you? The little girl I used to tease so mercilessly?"

"The same," she replied, "but no longer so little."

"Indeed not," he said, standing to greet her. He warmly clasped her hand in both of his, peering into her gem-like grey eyes that had always mystified him. He stared as though looking deeply into a well, trying to fathom something. The whole table was now absorbed with inspecting Ethel. She flushed with embarrassment, her face glowing as red as the bowls of borscht on the table.

"Here," he said, "sit, I'll get another chair, you must join us. I want to hear how you come to be in Odessa."

"And I, the same for you," she replied.

Soon the table broke into smaller, intimate conversations of two or three. Only the woman on the other side of Jacob followed their words in silence.

He had been in school in St. Petersburg when, without reason, the authorities had suspended his enrolment. He thought perhaps they found out about his political activities, his meetings to form a students' Bund affiliate. The socialist party was slowly growing and spreading its influence into Russian society. It was being closely watched by the State, which had likely infiltrated its ranks with government agents.

Without his university enrolment, he could no longer legally stay in St. Petersburg. Even in Odessa, it turned out, he had no residency papers, and constantly had to evade the eyes of officials. So far, he had been in the city four months and was helping to organize socialist activities and disseminate the movement's literature and ideas.

"In this port, new ideas enter Russia from all over the world. The possibilities here are immense for social change and understanding. Even the officials are more accommodating because of the diversity of the population and are not alarmed by activities that might be investigated elsewhere."

"Still, Jacob, you are in danger of being discovered without residency papers."

"And you?" He asked after hearing that Ethel had come to Odessa to see her aunt.

"You are right," Ethel said laughing with embarrassment. "I am in the same pickle, until I leave."

"And when will that be?" He asked, peering into her eyes once more as if looking for something.

"At least another week, as far as I can tell."

"And?"

"And possibly longer."

"Well then," he said, grasping Ethel's hand with affection, "I must play the host and show you the great city of Odessa. And tell you about this new vision of society, like no other yet in history. Truly great possibilities are before us."

"Yes, I would like that."

Suddenly, the woman, who had been silent, stood up abruptly and said her goodbyes to the table. She turned to Jacob. "We will continue at another time," she said, "when your friend has left Odessa."

"Or before," Jacob replied in a serious tone. "Let us not fall behind in completing our article and getting it printed."

"Whenever you are free," she replied, then left the table and strode down the street with a purposeful gait, leaving Jacob to attend to his guest.

"Marta is invaluable to our cause. She has helped many of us to survive while we work for change. The movement here could not go forward without her."

"I'm glad to hear you have such support," replied Ethel, although she felt somewhat downcast at Jacob's praise of this woman who was not only beautiful and well dressed, but a woman of ideas *and* action. Nothing about herself could compare with this woman who obviously had a close working relationship, if not more, with Jacob. For the moment, however, she was gone. Ethel did not stay much longer. Jacob arranged to meet her early the next day to show her around Odessa.

The next day, Ethel was a bundle of excitement. The two met and strolled down the wide avenue of Preobrazhenskya Street, eventually leaving the Jewish quarter of Moldavanka behind. All of this was completely new to Ethel. The air was filled with the scent of acacias and the white blossoms of regal chestnut trees that rimmed the squares and lined the avenues all the way down to the broad harbour.

Along the water, the businesses were a jumble of nationalities. They passed a shop selling South American coffee and another Indian spices. A German butcher shop displayed a dozen different kinds of sausage. A store of spirits and liquor sold Jamaican rum, Malaga wine, and French champagne. In the harbour were ships from Newcastle, Marseilles, and Port Said. Along the side streets were warehouses filled with American tobacco, oranges and pomegranates from Jerusalem, dates and figs from the Arabian Peninsula, Chinese and Japanese silks, olives from Greece, and French cheeses. The aromas radiating from these places were as heady as a trip around the world.

They stopped by a shop overflowing with fruits. Jacob took Ethel's hand and placed an orange in it. "Smell," he said, and lowered his head. As Ethel bent over, the sweet, light aroma like that of a flower became strong. Jacob squeezed the skin of the orange as he held it aloft. Oils, sharp and bitter, sprayed onto Ethel's lips. Then he stuck a thumb into the top, broke the orange open, and gave her a handful of crescent pieces like the moon. Laughing, she struggled to eat them. The juice dripped onto her cheeks and down her chin. He plucked a purple fig from a stacked pile and broke it inside out with his fingers.

"Here," he said, and plopped a piece, full of tiny seeds, into her waiting mouth. They shared the sweet, sticky brown lozenge of a date that came, Jacob said, from palm trees in the Middle East. He told her they were like no other tree she'd ever seen, with circular fringes of long, slender green leaves like the edges of a prayer shawl.

"Bananas," he said, "from Africa," with bright yellow skins the colour of sunflowers. He ripped one out of its pliant case, revealing a firm yet soft fruit that tasted like chunks of sweet cream. Ethel was so full she began to protest, but Jacob picked up a red pomegranate. "This last you must see," he said, and broke it open. A handful of rubies shone in his palm. He gave her a section and she tasted the jewel-like fruit. The inside of her mouth puckered with tartness that made her suck upon her own tongue.

After tasting the fruits of Odessa's markets, they walked for a while. Then they stopped and sat on a bench in one of the city's tree-lined squares.

Jacob asked Ethel about news from their village. Not much had changed since his years growing up.

"Anyone with means to leave has done so," she assured him. "Papa and Samuel have been in America four years. The rest of us are leaving in a few weeks."

Jacob became quiet after she spoke, "And you want to leave?"

"They're my family. No one will be left in the shtetl," she replied.

"Do you know great changes are taking place in Russia? A new society is struggling to be born. Changes that can deliver the impoverished from lives of virtual slavery. Changes that can bring a genuine sharing of power and wealth. A true caring for one another."

"I did not know this," she replied, shaken by his insistent words.

"Wouldn't you want to be a part of such a movement? A reorganization of society like none before? With each person contributing according to his abilities, being assured his needs would be met?"

"I don't know," Ethel said quietly.

They fell silent and walked back to the café in the Jewish quarter.

"Would you like to walk again tomorrow?" Jacob asked, smiling. "There is much we can discuss."

Ethel's heart lifted. "Yes. I would like that."

The next day Ethel and Jacob met at the café. The market square around them bustled with activity. As they sipped from glasses of hot tea and took bites of black bread and raspberry jam, Ethel listened to Jacob. He said changes had started to come about in Russia, new ways of living that beckoned from the West. In fact, a great new world, different from the one that had gone on for centuries, was poised and ready to develop.

They got up and walked through the quarter. As Jacob talked, Ethel thought he seemed blind to the earth under his feet. Ideas burned in him. Burned him so deeply. His mind was like a smelting furnace.

Instead of God, Jacob now dreamt of freedom. The freedom to own land, to go to university, to travel through the Ukraine to Moscow without permits and residency papers. The God of his fathers was the god of the old, the weak, the blind. They could not see what was so obvious—their history was tied like a rope around their legs. Antique prayer rituals were blowing away like smoke before a great wind. A wind of ideas, clearing away thousands of years of suffering. What had been the Jews' great sin? No homeland, no home. If they had been expelled from the Holy Land for some reason, for some spiritual crime, they had paid it back over and over again. *Haskalah*, the great Jewish movement of Western learning, like the European Enlightenment, was now sweeping across the continent to burn away the old ways of living.

Yet, that was only part of a great story poised to unfold in Russia. A new Russia that belonged equally to everyone: merchant, tradesman, and farmer alike. "Already we see burgeoning unions and associations for workers of all vocations here in Odessa—the shop clerks, the carters, the tailors, the butchers, the dairymaids, the midwives, and even the doctors! A new Russia without royalty, without political oppression. One with a new type of government for all people."

"I can see you are devoted to this new society," Ethel murmured. Jacob hardly stopped talking to acknowledge her words.

"I want to help bring this new society into existence. It requires educating the masses about what is possible if great numbers of people—far greater than any government or army—leave behind the old inequalities. As things stand now, each person is trapped in an entrenched culture, limited by poverty or oppression or both. The social fabric must be torn to be sewn aright."

These words frightened Ethel. She said nothing and continued to listen.

"Each of us has the inalienable right to have a share and be supported, protected, cared for, according to our needs. Russia must now strive to be free of all prejudice, with each person as a friend, a companion, a compatriot in vision and in work."

As all this tumbled out of Jacob, Ethel could see how it had taken over his soul. He seemed to have found a purpose that used every part of himself—intellect, heart, will, strength. Ethel thought this new purpose defined him as if he were still wrapped in a prayer shawl, rocking to and fro in synchronous pulses of union with God.

Ethel wondered how she, a mere woman, could be of equal importance to him as such a mission. She realized she couldn't. She could only join with Jacob and live in the same danger of discovery by the authorities. It would be a difficult life. And if this vision never materialized? If Jacob died fighting for it? What would she do? Cut off from the sinew of family and the possibility of creating her own? There was no room in Jacob's world for a normal life.

Ethel had found Jacob and lost Jacob, all in one breath.

She still felt he was her other half. The sight of him stirred her to a passionate place where life was a precious gift. She felt joined to him in some silent way beyond words. Yet, she craved the normal loving life that he seemed to have foresworn. Could she resolve this contradiction?

Ethel wasn't sure if Jacob felt their bond as strongly as she. Was he just revisiting old tucked-away feelings he may have had when they were children in the shtetl? Then, one late afternoon, they were taking a walk together when Jacob impulsively grasped her hand and pulled her down upon a bench facing the harbour. They were sheltered under a sweet-smelling acacia tree that had strewn its tiny yellow seeds and blossoms upon the ground at their feet.

He turned toward her and undid the pins that held her braids in place. They cascaded down over her shoulders. Ethel had not stopped him, but held her breath as he told her how her golden hair dazzled him like the sun, the sun flashing on a dove's white wing in the early morning sky.

Ethel in turn reached out her hand and touched his copper-red curls. In one swift movement he took off his cap and laid down next to Ethel, slowly lowering his head until it was cradled in her lap. She knew he'd given her time to protest, but she said nothing and reached out her hand to touch his face.

He took the ends of her braids and rubbed them over his cheeks, his eyes closing slowly as if concentrating on the feelings stirring in him. The two stayed like that, quietly, no words coming between them as the warmth of his head spread through Ethel's body. Opening his eyes, he took the end of one braid and placed it against his lips and sucked upon it for a moment.

"Ahh," he said, "sweeter than honey cake sprinkled with almonds. Sweeter than manna falling in the desert. I do not think I will taste anything sweeter upon this earth, no matter how long I shall live, my Etalah."

And in that moment Ethel felt proud and happy and complete.

As evening was coming on, they roused themselves and got up to stroll the streets of the harbour and watch the water darken. Suddenly red and purple clouds burst forth as the sun sank its flaming ball into the Black Sea. They walked the broad avenues of towering chestnut trees heavy with the smell of blossoms, still busy with the day's buzzing of nectar-collecting bees, a mesmerizing hum that vibrated the senses. They continued to walk and soon the full, prodigious moon rose and passed slowly up the inverted cup of the star-speckled sky.

The moon's light silvered over the world they shared, erasing the gold of the sun. It silvered over the trees, each drenched in infinite sparks. Silvered the branches and the leaves swinging softly in the evening breeze. Silvered the bark of the trunks, down to their roots.

Turning toward Jacob, Ethel saw the moonlight had sketched each feature of his face with memorializing silver. His clothes, his limbs, his torso, too, reflected the radiant moon. Even the copper of his beard and the tousled copper curls from beneath his cap did not escape the moon's effect.

Extending a hand to Jacob, Ethel saw the same effect upon her outstretched arm as they strolled across the city that was fast going to sleep. And she knew, walking in that silver light, she was dipped in eternity and would walk forever with him, no matter where her life would take her.

For nearly a week they walked each evening, wrapped in the moon's scintillating net. It cast over them a veil, delicate but deeply felt. Their arms now encircled each other as they walked. One current joined their limbs, one current animated their bodies, one current of force melded them together. Where on this earth could they walk like this forever? Silently, Ethel thought how impossible their situation, and wondered how temporary their union.

If only she and Jacob could survive on the moon's nourishing light. It was like soothing milk, a sweetness that comes from the mother's full and ample breasts, waiting to succour new life.

For a time, this moon reassured her that their bond could never break. In its light she felt a rightness that no country, no history, no political event could shatter. Ethel knew she might never find this feeling again in the haphazard wanderings of her young life.

Finally, as the nights passed, the moon waned and eventually disappeared. They were nourished by darkness. The unearthly light that had filled their souls like wine was gone. The darkness whispered that they had only stolen away for a few days from real life, from practicality. For just a while longer, Ethel tried to believe they might see their paths united in the light of ordinary day. But that was the sword point of reality: they had no life in the light of ordinary day. There was no place for them unless they went back to the Pale of Settlement. Ethel knew, though, that Jacob would never succumb to the defeat of his dreams.

When the blackness of the new moon took hold of the night, Ethel and Jacob continued to haunt the neighbourhoods of Odessa. Darkness shrouded the evenings despite the yellow lamps shining from windows. The two wandered aimlessly like homeless children, lost. Together they belonged nowhere.

On one of those nights, Jacob told Ethel about his infant sister, killed at the hands of Cossacks years ago in the shtetl. Instinctively she knew his heart had been cut into pieces and had never healed. After hearing him speak, she understood the source of the fire burning in him that fuelled the passion of his beliefs. She understood his yearning for Russia's history to be erased by a new society, healing the pain of those who had been wronged.

They sat down on a bench facing the harbour and listened to the water lap against the rocks below. Jacob sat apart from Ethel as though trying to distance himself from his words and the story he was telling.

On that fateful day, Gittel, his second youngest sister, was out in front of their house sewing. She was doing intricate handwork and wanted to take advantage of the last light of the sun, as the afternoon shadows had grown dark inside their kitchen. She was only seven, but already better than her mother at embroidering with gold and silver thread the festive aprons that all the women, Jew and Gentile alike, wore on their separate holidays. Those aprons brought a good price in the market stall her mother stocked with spools of thread, needles, kerchiefs, and shawls.

As she worked, Gittel was also minding her baby sister until their mother returned home. To make things easier, she had placed the baby in the sewing basket when she went outside for more light. The baby slept serenely in the open air.

Dusk was falling. One last apron, needing only a few minutes more to finish, kept her bent upon her task. She had almost completed her handiwork when a sudden clatter of horses' hooves at the far end of the lane startled her. Fast upon this came the sound of breaking glass and the singing of drunken voices; an obscene song, a few of the words familiar to her. The Czar's soldiers, Cossacks, had come down upon the village without warning. They were probably traveling to the eastern steppe from the border wars between Russia and Poland.

Gittel could see these were not men, but animals, drunk with blood, riding with leather boots and metal spurs clicking, their coats soiled with death and dirt. In a moment the riders were galloping down the lane between the two rows of wooden houses. They brandished rifles with bayonets that glinted sharply in the last vestiges of light. Terrified, Gittel got up and ran inside, leaving all her things behind her, and was quickly herded by her sisters and Jacob into the root cellar below the mud floor of the kitchen.

Can a child think at a moment like that? As soon as Gittel came to rest in the safety of the cellar, she knew what she had done. Her sleeping sister in the basket with the sewing things had been left outside. She made her horrified confession and Jacob scrambled up out of the cellar intent upon retrieving the baby. The basket was only a foot or two from the front door. It would only take a moment. But it was already too late.

When Gittel had run for the house, she jostled the sewing basket waking the baby who began to cry. Unattended, the cries became louder and the soldiers, rampaging down the lane, heard her. This sound inflamed them even more. They wanted to get this baby in their filthy hands. To them, it was a noisy rag, not a child who wanted the comfort of her mother's breast as she felt the cool night coming on.

One of the soldiers stopped and dismounted. "You forgot something, eh?" He yelled to the dark windows of the house. Inside, Jacob drew back instinctively from the door. He bit his tongue so hard to stop himself from crying out that his mouth filled with blood.

He could not step back to the small plank that covered the hole dug in the earthen floor where his sisters lay hidden. He could not move forward into the street to meet the soldiers. A bitter surge of nausea moved up from his stomach into his throat, but he swallowed hard. In a few moments, he crept forward to the unshuttered window and stood there, covered by darkness. The last traces of day were nearly gone from the lane; dusk was over and night was coming on. No lamps were lit in the neighbouring houses as the neighbours, too, waited, praying for the ransacking soldiers to leave.

Jacob watched the soldier pick up the sewing basket and begin to swing it slowly, carelessly, like a peasant woman returning from the fields with a load of turnips or potatoes. The Cossack swung the basket higher into the air, and sang something that sounded like a lullaby, as if rocking the baby to sleep. But soon, the baby began to howl, frightened by the increasingly jerky, wild motions that had taken over the basket. The soldier broke into peals of guttural laughter.

More soldiers on horseback came down the lane. They were singing in raspy voices a marching song with their own words, mocking dead Czar Alexander I, who had given lenient reforms to the Jews. The soldiers stopped their horses every few yards, yelling and cursing into the darkness, swinging their rifles, knocking over potted plants and breaking the precious window glass of the houses.

Then one of the mounted soldiers heard the baby's cries. He watched the basket tossed higher and higher. The sound of the baby's screams tore through the air and this horseman, drawn as if by a magnet, positioned his rifle, the bayonet gleaming. He dug his boot heels into the sides of his horse and charged upon the basket, knocking it out of the air.

Jacob was watching it all. His body had become numb, as if it had vanished. He seemed to see as though from the roof of the house. It was as if he knew exactly what would happen. He could see it. Only, the horror down in the lane was taking so long. There was so much distance between him and what was happening. He could not make his body work.

The soldiers were like puppets he had once seen in the marketplace with large sticks and clubs stitched to their palms, slapping the other puppets in the head and across the back, laughing and howling. The sound of the bayonet hitting the basket jolted him upright, and he saw the basket fly across the lane and settle along the wall of the neighbour's house as the soldier began charging upon it, over and over. The baby's frantic screams turned to shrieks. Jacob could see the gleaming blade of the bayonet drip dark and oozing blood as the soldier pierced the basket again and again.

After a time, the baby's cries subsided. The men did not linger, but rode down past the houses, swiftly out of the village, going south with the night wind.

Jacob, still frozen, imagined animals with glittering eyes hunting down their prey. Wolves with pink tongues and shaggy winter coats, descending upon skittering flocks of chickens that crooned in terror and grief and ran in circles, not knowing what to do.

The baby was dead when they found her out in the lane. She was cut to pieces like the scraps of cloth she lay among. The blood had drained out of all the slashes and wounds on her tiny body, turning her clothes crimson and soaking the basket. They buried her the next day, blood and all, because the Rabbi said she would need every part of her for resurrection upon Judgment Day when the Messiah would finally come.

Sounds of water breaking against the stones of the harbour wall seeped back into Ethel's awareness. She reached out for Jacob's hands. They were cold and lifeless. He would not look at her. For a long time he said nothing, but wept. Then he said he had murdered his sister because he had done nothing to stop the soldiers. Ethel realized this was how he felt in his soul. Witnessing the savagery and hearing the baby's death cries had cut out most of his heart. That evening, and the following days, Ethel fed him parts of hers. She fed him first one piece, then another. Barely a woman, she thought she had enough to give away like that. Later, she would find out she was wrong. She would find out she only had half a heart left to love another.

Over the following week, Ethel contemplated her intertwined fate with Jacob, feeling she could not leave him. Her aunt was nearly finished selling off what remained of her home in Odessa. In three days' time they were to leave for Ethel's village. A momentous decision faced her, the greatest of her brief sixteen years. Perhaps it would be the most important one of her entire life, setting her on a course of action that would make for inalterable consequences.

On their last full day in Odessa, Ethel was seated at the kitchen table sipping tea, trying to calm her nerves. She was in anguish, unable to decide whether to stay in Odessa, living a subversive life with Jacob—whose heart she could not separate from her own—or go with her family to America. She was to meet Jacob at the cafe´ that afternoon, possibly for the last time. Tomorrow she and her aunt were to leave the city.

Aunt Miriam came into the room, crying into a handkerchief, and sat down opposite Ethel, who gave her a strong glass of tea from the samovar.

"What's wrong?" Ethel gently inquired.

Aunt Miriam could not speak for a few moments. "As I am preparing to leave Odessa, memories are flooding over me. I must stop looking backward, or be turned into a pillar of salt tears without end."

"You will get past this," Ethel said to comfort her. "Soon you'll be on the way to America and reunited with your daughter."

"I know," Aunt Miriam said, sighing heavily, "I know I must not dwell upon what happened to Max or I will be cut off from God. Maybe not the God of the Bible—who knows His ways except the great rabbis—but the God that is here," and with that, Aunt Miriam took Ethel's hand and placed it over her own matronly bosom. Then, she placed their clasped hands on the kitchen table between them. She could not go on without her hand clinging to Ethel's.

"It started when a Christian boy was found dead in a field of a small village," began Aunt Miriam. "Suspicion fell on the Jews. The rumour was his blood had been used in Passover rites. Riots broke out against the 'Jewish barbarity.' The officials did nothing for days while the peasants murdered and destroyed property."

"How can people believe such things?" Aunt Miriam asked, wiping her eyes. "Like a wildfire, violence spread to nearby villages and towns." More tears welled up in Miriam's eyes. Ethel gently held her aunt's hand as she spoke of the Odessa Pogrom that took place nine years ago.

"We had been hearing reports from other places for nearly a week. We kept to ourselves our fears of such an outbreak here," she said. "The less talked of, the less chance we thought of a similar calamity in our beautiful Odessa. Our sophisticated Odessa, filled with cultural life and world renowned for trade, was not like the rest of Russia's backward villages and ignorant rural populations. 'No,' we thought logically, 'it cannot, will not, must not happen in this city.' The authorities would take precautions. They would not wish the city or its reputation to be marred by such an occurrence. When it did happen, some said the police and governing body were taken by surprise." Her aunt made a derisive cluck of her tongue. "All I know is they did nothing to stop it for nearly three days."

Aunt Miriam closed her eyes as if resting; then she continued. "It was after sundown at the beginning of Shabbos. The men were at synagogue. I don't know where the fighting and looting broke out first. Probably in more than one neighbourhood. Mobs of men spread out with their weapons, wooden clubs and iron tools—shovels, rakes, scythes, implements easily at hand to the peasants. In the marketplace they attacked bystanders, overturned carts, and shattered the windows of the stores lining the square. Then the looting began in earnest: Dry goods stolen from the general stores, butcher shops ransacked and emptied of meat, tailor shops raided for cloth and sewing machines, jewellery stores picked clean, furriers plundered. And everything inside the stores broken, smashed, defiled. Used like privies. Excrement and urine covering the counters and floors."

For a few moments Aunt Miriam could not speak. Ethel gave her another glass of tea. Fresh tears formed in her eyes. As if compelled to tell the rest of her story, she went on.

"The looters moved deeper into the Jewish quarter and began breaking into houses. Such uproar! The news spread from one block to the next. Jewish men began to gather to protect the streets as best they could, using whatever weapons they had at hand. When they came to the synagogue, our bold Jewish men were brought low by the sight of the worshippers who had been dragged out and beaten in the streets. Even—God should have forbid!—the Torah taken. The sacred parchment, that not even the rabbi can touch without a Torah pointer, was cut and torn into ragged pieces. Not even the most skilled scribes could resurrect that Holy Scroll. The writings of God's thoughts were scattered by the wind, the bright flames of His wisdom, as if extinguished, lay in the gutter."

"The Rabbi survived despite a severe beating, but he was never the same. His mind was left in shambles and all he could do was babble like a distraught child, a transformation terrible to look upon after a lifetime of brilliance and learning."

Here, Aunt Miriam looked down at the table as if unaware of her surroundings. Her eyes moistened with more tears. Ethel could see her aunt struggling to relieve her pain.

"How did you escape?" asked Ethel as she leaned in and gently squeezed her aunt's hand. Ethel knew Aunt Miriam and her daughters had come safely through the horror. Uncle Max was the only death in their household.

"Tatyana," said her aunt with great love and warmth coming into her eyes, "Tatyana our maid saved us. The news spread to the Christian outskirts of the city and Tatyana and her brother came in a wagon full of barrels and burlap sacks. For all eyes to see, only a Christian peasant's wagon transporting goods out of the city, back to their farm. No one stopped or even approached them. Her brother, Alexi, brought the wagon to the alley behind the house and Tatyana knocked at our kitchen door."

"Quick, there is no time to lose, the streets are dangerous," she said. "You must get away from here." We had been gathering food and water to take with us down below in the cellar.

"We must get you away," Tatyana urged. "You cannot take the chance of being found."

"But where will we go?" I said, too fearful to leave.

"I have an idea," said Tatyana, "Come, we must hurry."

"With that, I put my life, and Rachel and Sarah's, into the hands of our servant, who had been part of our family for over twenty years. My heart told me to go with her."

"And where did she bring you?"

"Such a smart woman she was. To outwit the Angel of Death, she put us among the dead! She brought us to the Christian cemetery! We hid all night behind the gravestones, blessing them for our protection."

"All forms of love are upon this earth, residing in the breast of all nations. Tatyana risked danger that day to rescue us. Her humanity shone forth. She did a mitzvah out of her love. To this day I keep her and her family in my prayers, and will always."

"After two days, Tatyana returned with the wagon. Some looting was still going on, but the authorities had begun to fan out across the Jewish quarter and make arrests."

With the heart-breaking story of Jacob's sister fresh in her mind, Ethel's courage to hear the rest faltered. All she knew was that Uncle Max was killed in his shop. She didn't know the details. But Ethel could see Aunt Miriam being carried to a new crest of emotion by her memories. A keening wail burst forth from Aunt Miriam as if God were squeezing her heart and she could not breathe.

"You needn't go on if it is too painful," Ethel said as she reached out to embrace her aunt across the table.

After a few minutes, Aunt Miriam said, "Leaving Odessa has reawakened the memory of the savagery that befell Uncle Max." She rubbed at the tears flowing like a river down her cheeks.

"Your Uncle Max must have been late setting out for the synagogue. Perhaps he heard the looting that had begun in the Jewish market and decided it was safer to barricade himself in our clothing store. I pray he only stayed for this reason and not to safeguard the property. But a roaming band, filled with blood thirst, broke the door down and overran the shop. He had nowhere to go," she shrieked in horror, as if seeing the scene before her. "I cannot wipe out of my memory how he looked when we found him. His eyes open, his mouth agape, and…and a metal spike driven through his head! All around him a sea of blood." At this pronouncement, her aunt broke down and sobbed. Ethel slid her chair next to her aunt and embraced and rocked her while they both cried.

"A man," Aunt Miriam finally continued, "who had no angry bone in his body. A man of peace. A good husband and virtuous father who worked hard all his life."

Now Aunt Miriam began to breathe deeply. "I shall leave this dreadful memory behind and remember him always for his loving, kind, and respectful ways. A leader in the community and a good man, I am sure, in God's eyes."

"Yes," she said, "here in my heart where wisdom and pain are joined, God will usher in his illumination. Blessed be He, Creator of the Universe. I only regret leaving this city because I will not be able to visit his grave. But each holiday I will tell him how his family is doing and that he must not worry. We will be joined once more in God's sight soon enough."

# Chapter 4
# Peril and Sorrow

Late that afternoon, with thoughts of the Odessa Pogrom filling her head, Ethel left the house to meet Jacob. On the way she wondered how she could survive if she remained in the city with no residency papers nor means of support. She had no idea how Jacob managed, although his needs were meagre. Still, he had to eat and rest his head each night.

What was she to do? Did she want to work side-by-side with Jacob, helping to bring his grand vision, no matter how long delayed, into fruition for a new Russia?

As soon as Ethel reached the square of the Jewish marketplace, she saw people congregating on the sidewalks and in the doorways of shops, clearly agitated. Her aunt's recounting of the pogrom flashed through her mind once more, but the shops she passed seemed intact. She overheard bystanders talk of the authorities cracking down on people without papers.

"Where did this happen?" Ethel asked insistently, "Where?"

"Over on the east side of the square. At the café."

As soon as she heard this, her breathing became rapid and a force she could not describe propelled her forward.

When she reached the café the outdoor chairs and tables were overthrown, the doors to the restaurant closed, the windows smashed. Glass was scattered over the sidewalk. Ethel stood surveying the destruction and looked hopelessly at the empty street. She spotted three or four caps in the gutter, soiled and crushed. She could see no sign of Jacob and his comrades. Piles of horse manure lay about, filling the air with stench.

*Mounted authorities must have run down upon them*, Ethel guessed. The soldiers had never caused any destruction before, even when arresting or apprehending possible renegades. She stood, planted, unable to move. She did not know what to do except gather what information she could on the street. Formulating in her mind a route back to her aunt's, she circumnavigated the marketplace, afraid she too might be stopped and arrested because she had no residency papers.

Ethel turned her back on the devastation and suddenly saw Marta at the edge of a nearby building. The woman signalled to her. Ethel's heart began beating again and soon she reached Marta's side.

"Was Jacob arrested?"

Grimly, the woman nodded. "Yes. There's not much time. All the men here, with or without papers, were taken. They have never done that before."

"And what about you, Marta?"

"My papers are all in order and, because I am not listed as a Jew, they declined to arrest me."

"I thought…"

"No, only my grandfather. I have slipped out of their net."

*So, Marta's stylish airs, her clothing, are a result of a privileged background.* Ethel had once thought of Marta as a rival for Jacob's affection. Now she surmised Marta had been helping them all, without concern for her own danger.

"Something must be about to happen. They likely took the men to prevent any resistance in the area. You should leave. There may be wide-scale violence, not just to the shops and market, but throughout the quarter."

Ethel stood paralyzed. Her words came slowly to her lips. She did not think Marta knew about the intimacy between Jacob and herself.

"I can't go," Ethel said. "Not without knowing Jacob's fate."

Marta minced no words. "He has no papers. He will be held, imprisoned, likely sent north. There is nothing you can do."

"And," Ethel asked, "what will you do?"

"Eventually I'll be able to find out what has happened to him and the others. I'll go to the work camp. The guards are amenable to bribes. They can make the prisoners' time easier."

Ethel now faced a reality she had not, until that moment, fully understood. The possibility of it had been a distant threat, at some remote time in the future, if ever. Her life had suddenly halted. She had neither residency papers nor money. Jacob's fate could become hers. She could fall into the hands of the authorities. In all likilihood, Marta would be the one who could rescue Jacob, or at least soften his fate.

In a desperate voice Ethel said, "You must write me."

"Yes," Marta said, nodding.

In her heart Ethel knew how futile that might be. If she returned to her village, the family's journey to America would shortly be underway. If she chose to stay, where would she live, how would she survive?

The two women embraced. Silently, Ethel prayed Marta could save Jacob from a brutal fate. In a blur of shock, she realized she had to get off the streets. If rioting broke out, she and her aunt would have to hide or flee the city.

On the way back to her aunt's, Ethel was haunted by visions of Jacob—sent to the labour camps in the north, or tortured and possibly murdered. What did the life of one troublesome Jew mean to these police? It meant the world to her!

She wondered if she might be able to stay with Marta until they could find out more about Jacob's fate. Would that endanger them all? She did not know. There was so much she realized she did not know. Ethel thought her idea worth a try and nearly returned to the marketplace to find Marta, but decided she must get back to her aunt's house. Aunt Miriam could have heard of the arrests and might worry. Tonight, she could sort out the things she could do.

When Ethel arrived home, news of the young Jewish men taken in the marketplace had reached the neighbourhood. As far as anyone knew, all was quiet and no other disturbances had happened. They did not know what to think. Aunt Miriam, fearing further disruption in the Jewish quarter, wanted to leave Odessa as soon as possible. She said she did not want to remain another day. Old memories, scenes of carnage, had surged back into her mind. She vowed to leave by the next afternoon and sent a message to secure the wagon that would take them out of Odessa.

Ethel, beside herself with grief and fear for Jacob's life, secretly wept.

Her night was full of fitful starts and awakenings that, near dawn, released her into an hour of unrestful sleep. A nightmare image of Jacob's coppery curls and beard drenched with blood woke her. She got up, dressed quickly, and slipped out of the house. She did not want her aunt to know where she was going. Aunt Miriam knew nothing about Jacob or his friends. Telling her would just alarm her.

In a blast of courage she did not really feel, Ethel made her way back to the marketplace. Mounted police were stationed at each corner of the square, which froze the blood in her veins. They made no move to stop or question her. Ethel seemed just another person opening a shop or heading to work.

She had a difficult time finding the address Marta had given her. It was off an alleyway between two close-set buildings at the edge of the Jewish quarter. Although it was still quite early, she knocked at the door and rang the bell repeatedly. If anyone was inside, her efforts to rouse them failed. With sinking spirits, she slipped a note under the door. Perhaps someone would find it and give it to Marta.

Disheartened, Ethel found her way back to her aunt's and slipped quietly into the house. It was still before breakfast. Just then, Tatyana arrived at the back door, entered the kitchen, and cast a questioning eye at Ethel's outdoor attire. The servant realized the girl had either gone out at an early hour, or perhaps had been out all night. Whatever Tatyana was thinking, she kept it to herself. Ethel made her way back upstairs to divest herself of her shawl and kerchief and re-emerged from her room as if she'd never been gone.

Tatyana reported that the city was quiet. In the Jewish quarter people were still wondering whether life would continue as normal, or whether a second police action or other violence might erupt. Aunt Miriam was bustling throughout the house, telling Tatyana they were to leave that afternoon and the furniture buyers would arrive to pick up the items that had been sold.

Aunt Miriam gave Tatyana many beloved objects in remembrance of their years together. "To leave so much of our life here makes me sad," she said, "but to give these things to you, Tatyana, brings gladness to my heart. I will never forget how you saved my family." Years of connection, love, and complex emotion surged through the room as the two women embraced. Then they separated, regaining their everyday composure.

With little hope of leaving the house without her aunt noticing, Ethel realized she must risk enlisting Tatyana's help. On the back staircase off the kitchen Ethel overtook Tatyana. Her heart pounding, in a hushed voice, she asked if a note could be sent with a messenger who was to wait for a reply. Ethel explained she must tell a friend she was leaving Odessa today. She pulled an envelope from inside her sleeve and held it out to the servant with shaking fingers. It stayed there between them.

"I...I don't know if I can..."

"Please," Ethel said in a whisper, sorrow beginning to choke her throat.

Tatyana stood weighing her loyalties. She had been young once, yet she hesitated.

Ethel tried to press coin into the woman's palm, but the servant refused it.

Finally, Tatyana replied quietly, "I'll do my best," then hurriedly ascended the staircase to answer her mistress' call for assistance from the second floor.

Ethel waited in an agony of anticipation for nearly two hours, not knowing if Tatyana had been successful or had even fulfilled her request. Finally, Ethel descended the back staircase and found Tatyana in the kitchen preparing the noonday meal. Without saying a word, the woman retrieved a note from her apron and slipped it into the pocket of Ethel's dress. In trepidation Ethel climbed the stairs to her room, knowing her heart's desire might be shattered by what was written on that piece of paper. As she reached the landing, her aunt surprised her.

"You will be ready after lunch?" Aunt Miriam inquired.

"Yes, of course," replied Ethel, her throat tightening with tension. The message in her pocket was like a hot stone, scorching her.

Slowly she opened the door to her room and went in. When she heard Aunt Miriam walk down the staircase, she pulled the paper from her pocket. Struggling to breathe, she opened it.

The message was not from Marta, but from an unidentified person. It said that Marta had left the city and there was no forwarding address so the missive could not be sent to her. "All I can tell you," read the note, "is that Marta is gone." Ethel collapsed upon her bed and began to sob. The pain of her predicament sank deeply into her soul. She now knew no one in the city who might give her lodging or help her learn Jacob's fate. She was utterly on her own.

After a time, her sobs subsided. Thoughts flooded her mind. Perhaps Marta had heard what the police were planning and she had to flee for her own safety. Perhaps she had to go into hiding. Whatever the reason for Marta's sudden departure, her circumstances must have been dire for the sudden change in plans.

The whole situation brought home to Ethel how fleeting life is. How, within an instant, all could be lost. She suddenly felt much older than her sixteen years. A feeling of weariness overcame her as she tried to figure out what to do.

Tatyana knocked on her door to announce the noon meal. Ethel excused herself, saying she wasn't feeling well and needed to rest for an hour or two if her aunt did not need her. Tatyana offered to bring up some tea but Ethel declined, saying she would be fine.

This was a ruse. Ethel had decided she would go back to the market square and see if she could find any of Jacob's friends. The whole trip would take less than an hour. With luck, she could make it back before her absence would be noticed. In any case, she must take the risk. She could not leave Odessa without attempting to find out more.

Ethel covered herself with a shawl and stole down the back staircase, slipping out the kitchen door. She walked briskly down side streets toward the marketplace, eyes fixed upon the pavement. As she walked, ideas floated through her mind. Perhaps she might ask Tatyana for lodging, although the servant's home was an hour walk outside the city. Or, Tatyana might know of someone in the city who could put her up for a few days. Whoever sent the note about Marta might be a close associate, willing to aid her search or offer housing.

What could she do for money? The café came to mind. She would have no trouble taking on the duties of a waitress. Then an idea that did not depend upon the good will of others came to her. Why hadn't she thought of it sooner? She could sell her hair! Surely a wigmaker would pay well for this golden prize. One day she and Jacob would laugh about the rescue financed by her thick, wavy locks. They could tell the story to their children. Yes, as she hurried along everything seemed possible once more—Jacob's safe release and a future for them both.

What about residency papers? How could she solve that problem? Was there a way to enlist her aunt's help? Surely her aunt would know what might be possible. She might even offer her own papers, now that she had no need for them. Then one more idea presented itself, something that made Ethel cringe with disgust yet offered an easy solution. She could register as a prostitute. Young Jewish women hoping to live in a city would sometimes do this. She would have to find out more about what this entailed, and whether she had to provide evidence of some association with a brothel. The thought scared her, but less than the thought of losing Jacob.

As she arrived at the Jewish market square, she slowed her pace and observed the activity of the streets and shops. The market square was subdued, as if no one wanted to attract any undue attention. The sounds of lively shoppers bargaining with gusto over the price of a chicken were not heard this day. A hushed quiet seemed to have descended upon the quarter.

Mounted police surveyed the streets, and one officer on foot was posted near the corner where the café stood. The restaurant had reopened its doors despite the broken windows, and people were inside eating lunch. The smells of herring and black bread, potato latkes, and smoked whitefish wafted out along the street as Ethel passed. She cast a glance through the shattered windows, trying to see if anyone familiar was inside. She did not know if by approaching anyone, she could cause them trouble. Without thinking, she turned and walked into the restaurant.

The waitress brought the traditional glass of strong tea and a lump of sugar to hold in the mouth and sip the tea through. The warmth of the liquid relaxed Ethel's stomach, bound up in knots since she saw the police. The room was crowded. When a middle-aged man came in, he asked Ethel if he could share her table. Without a word she nodded, and he sat down.

"You must eat something with your tea," the man said. "You're pale. Do you not have any money?"

Ethel realized she had been up early and had eaten nothing that day.

"I'm fine, I just need tea to refresh me, then I'll be on my way home."

"And where is that?" The man asked in a conversational tone.

"Not far," Ethel replied evasively. Her stomach muscles were tightening again.

The man ordered soup and the waitress brought it with several pieces of black bread. He offered one to Ethel and she thought it best to accept.

"There was a big commotion at the café this morning. Some people were taken. Did you hear?"

"No," she lied. "I came to do an errand. What was it?"

"Oh, the usual, Bund members. A thorn in the side of the authorities. Propagandists. Police swept down upon them like birds of prey upon little sparrows. Most had no papers so they were hauled off."

"What will happen to them? I'm only in Odessa visiting a relative," she said. She quickly realized she should not divulge any information and silently reprimanded herself.

"It's a fair guess you're not from Odessa," he replied, smiling. "Your clothes. I hope your papers are in order, for your sake. You never know what can happen from one moment to the next." He paused.

"Yes, of course!" Ethel replied quickly.

"Carry them with you?"

"Always." Her stomach churned. The man's questions felt intrusive. She wasn't sure what to make of them. Was he simply making conversation, offering advice to a peasant girl who may not know how to take care of herself in the big city? Or was there something behind his politely probing questions?

"What will happen to those they took?" She asked, to deflect the conversation away from herself, and in hopes of gleaning some useful information.

"Hard to tell where they'll end up. For a while, jail. If a case can be made against them, such as activities to threaten the Czar or subvert the government, they'll be sent to a work camp."

"Siberia?"

"Possibly."

"For how long?"

"Three years, seven years. Depends upon their activities. But no matter how long, many succumb to the harsh conditions—the insufficient food, the gruelling work, the below-zero temperatures."

"Have you been?" Ethel asked, knowing she was treading upon delicate ground. The man lowered his voice and said conspiratorially, "To look at me you wouldn't know. I was once a young man with a great passion for reform."

"Of the political sort?"

He nodded. "All kinds, social, economic, political. Now I just follow what is happening. My subversive days are over."

Ethel began to feel comfortable with him and thought to enlist his help more directly. She asked several questions. Why was the Bund not outlawed? How did it spread its ideas? Who were its members?

"I see, young lady from the countryside, you have perhaps a passion for change, too?"

"Not exactly," Ethel replied cautiously. "So much is going on in a city like Odessa. I wish to learn more about the people who live here. More about the world. My village is a lovely place, surrounded by field and forest. Yet, everything has been the same for hundreds of years so I sometimes feel a hundred years old." This made the man laugh and Ethel laughed in response.

"The way some talk of a new society that is coming, you would think great changes are in store for Russia."

Ethel held her breath, waiting to see if the man would say something about current politics, but he simply continued eating his soup and looked as if he were waiting to hear what more she would say.

She took a chance and asked, "If one wanted to learn more about these matters what would one do?" She hoped he might tell her how to find Jacob's organizations and how to approach them without bringing notice to herself. Even, maybe, how to find out Jacob's whereabouts.

Suddenly, however, he signalled the waitress, paid his bill and said he was late for an appointment. "It was nice to meet you...I forgot to introduce myself, I'm Dimitry." He held out his hand to Ethel and said, "And you are?"

Ethel could not think fast enough. At the last moment, she settled on her sister's name. "Anna. I am Anna."

"Well perhaps, Anna, we will meet again at the café? Like old friends?"

"Perhaps," she answered, smiling, and shook his outstretched hand. And with that, he disappeared out the door, turned to the right, and walked out of sight.

Ethel's time was running out. She knew she must head back home or risk the discovery of her absence. Still, she wanted to go once more to Marta's address and see if she could find anyone.

She rose, and as she turned around to take her shawl off the back of the chair, the waitress signalled from the kitchen doorway. Ethel walked to the back of the restaurant with a sudden feeling of hopefulness. Did the waitress recognize her as a member of Jacob's group of friends? Did she know anything about his arrest? Could she perhaps guide her to the right people to contact?

With an expressionless face the waitress told Ethel to follow her, then turned abruptly and led her through the kitchen to a back door off an alley.

"I think you should leave this way," the woman said, glancing at the door.

"Why? What's wrong?" Ethel whispered, frightened.

"The man at your table," she asked hesitantly, "did you know him?"

"No," Ethel answered.

"From now on," the woman said, "it is better if you do not speak to people you do not recognize. You understand?"

"Yes, I think so," Ethel replied. "I know you, though," Ethel hurriedly added. "What will happen to those taken yesterday morning? Please, you are my only hope."

The woman looked down at the floor, then up again at Ethel's expectant face. "It's too soon to tell. Even the authorities probably do not know what will be done with them. Held and questioned for sure."

"Will the authorities hurt them?"

"It is better if you do not think about these things."

"But I must find out," Ethel insisted.

"Come back tomorrow," the woman said. "I'll tell you whatever information I've heard. I do not promise anything. Now go."

When Ethel emerged from the back door of the restaurant she found herself in a maze of alleyways that went behind the shops and buildings of the marketplace. Confused and disoriented, she kept turning to her right, but could not find her way out. For a time, she feared she would never find her way back to her aunt's, much less to Marta's. At the intersection of several alleys, she stopped for a moment and spun around to look at her surroundings.

Suddenly, she saw Dimitry, the man from the café, standing at the end of one of the passageways, talking with a police officer. A chill went through her. Why had she spoken to him? Why had she asked about contacting those political groups? She felt foolish for trusting him because he was friendly and sympathetic. The waitress had been suspicious, and rightly so.

Before she could collect herself, Dimitry looked down the alleyway where Ethel stood and a jolt of awareness registered in his body. He and the policeman began running toward her.

In a panic Ethel hurried down one of the other alleys. She zigzagged from one passageway to another until she was out of breath. Glancing over her shoulder, she saw her pursuers were nowhere in sight. But looking around to get her bearings, she realized, with a sinking sense of dread, she was again at the back door of the restaurant: She had travelled in a circle. Not knowing what else to do, she ran into the kitchen.

The waitress was loading her tray with dishes, lifting it with one hand over her shoulder when she saw Ethel standing there panting and frightened.

"You must go," the woman said sharply. "You are not the only one at risk. You will endanger others."

"I can't go out there," Ethel said, looking at the doorway to the alley. "That man will arrest me, I've no papers. Please let me stay for a few minutes. I must catch my breath."

The waitress lowered her tray and went over to a storage area near the back of the kitchen. "Come," she said and sat Ethel down amidst a pile of wooden barrels, then took a burlap sack and tossed it over Ethel's crouched form. On top of that she placed open bundles of onions, carrots, and beets. Even in her frightened state, the sharp smell of the food registered in Ethel's brain and she felt faint. She had not eaten since the night before. The waitress resumed loading her tray and went to serve her customers.

In through the alleyway door came the policeman. "Have you seen a young woman come by in the last few minutes?" The cook and kitchen help looked up and shook their heads, then returned to their chopping and stirring.

"She is wearing a blue shawl," he said. They continued their tasks without answering and the officer, angered by their silence, said gruffly, "Stop what you are doing."

"I asked if you saw a young woman in a blue shawl."

"No," replied the cook, standing at attention.

"No," replied the two kitchen helpers.

Suspicious and unsatisfied, the policeman looked around the kitchen. He walked over to a pile of burlap sacks containing buckwheat groats, lentils, and rice. He stuck his baton down the open bags and slapped hard at the sides of other sacks piled around them. Nothing moved. Eventually, he gave up his search and stationed himself outside the back-alley doorway.

Soon the waitress came into the kitchen, rummaged in a cupboard and pulled out what looked like rags. These she threw into the corner where Ethel was hiding. Then she tapped her heel three times on the floorboards, and went back into the dining room.

Ethel slowly lifted the sack so she could see what had been dropped near her. In an instant she grabbed the items and slipped them over her clothing. Now what was she to do? Another minute or two passed with only the hissing of the pots on the stove.

"Here," the cook said to his assistants, "help me pour off this water." He and the others lifted a huge pot of bubbling liquid, took it to the doorway and poured it in the alley.

"Watch what you're doing," the policeman yelled as the hot water went flooding down the stones of the back street and over his shoes.

In that moment Ethel knew she had her chance. She slipped out of the kitchen into the dining room. Heading for the front door, she noticed the customers' coat rack, swiftly filched a hat, and left the café. No one had noticed. Tucking her hair tightly under the cap, she pulled the brim down over her eyes. She looked like a young workman, all traces of her true identity hidden. A policeman was on the corner watching people come and go. Ethel walked as quickly as she could past him without running. She was out of breath but dared not slacken her pace. *Now, I must try Marta's once more.*

Finding her way quickly to the right avenue, she turned down the side street to Marta's building. But an uncontrollable shock went through her when she spotted Dimitry lounging across the way, newspaper in hand, as if reading. He glanced up just as she managed to turn on her heels. Slowly something roused his senses, and in a moment he was walking down the narrow street after this strange male figure he had glimpsed.

It occurred to Ethel that the authorities may have had Jacob's group under surveillance and may also have known of her association with them. Dimitry obviously knew Marta's address. Perhaps that was why Marta had had to leave so abruptly.

At a distance Ethel's disguise might fool Dimitry, but she dared not turn around. She would try to lose him by crisscrossing avenues and ducking in and out of shops.

As she turned down a crowded boulevard toward the harbour, her route seemed a perverse reminiscence of the day Jacob guided her through the various neighbourhoods of Odessa. She passed the cheese shop, the spirits store, the fruit and vegetable grocery. Looking quickly behind her and not seeing Dimitry, she stepped into a tobacconist's where, in her male attire, no one would find her out of place. She lingered in the shop inspecting smoking pipes and rebuffed the sales clerk's inquiries as to assistance.

After a few minutes she glanced cautiously through the shop window. She made out the figure of her pursuer moving swiftly down the sidewalk, heading back in the direction of the Jewish market square. There was nothing left for her to do but pray for an undetected return to her aunt's, and hope Dimitry did not know where she had been staying. She cautiously stepped out to the sidewalk and, after 20 minutes, was back in her aunt's neighbourhood.

Making her way without incident, she felt relieved. When she rounded the corner to her aunt's home, without warning, a mounted policeman loomed up before her. Her scalp prickled with heat. All she could do was walk by as calmly as possible. He did not stop her—the disguise was working.

Just as she reached her aunt's house, however, he called out, "What is your business in this neighbourhood?"

She turned around and lowered her voice as much as possible and said, "I'm the butcher's boy. I made a delivery to 220 on the next street."

The policeman looked Ethel over for a minute, then said, "Don't loiter."

"No, sir," she replied and continued down the block. Had she fooled him? Her limbs shook in fear. Did the authorities know where she lived? Or was the policeman on a routine patrol through the quarter? Then she heard the sound of the horse's hooves recede and fade away.

What was clear was that without a disguise, Dimitry would recognize her. Perhaps the police would as well. With a fearful and sinking heart she slipped around the corner into the alleyway behind her aunt's house and reached the kitchen door.

Tatyana was busy washing the dishes from the noonday meal. Her eyes popped open as she saw before her a stranger, a young man in torn and dirty clothes. She stifled a cry of alarm as Ethel whipped off the cap that hid her golden braids. "Please," she whispered, "do not tell my aunt."

Tatyana caught her breath as she made the sign of the cross and said, "It is none of my concern. You leave in an hour. Your aunt is attending to a few details."

On the table were pieces of challah. Ethel grabbed the bread and dowsed it with honey from a pot on the counter. *This last sweetness will mark the end of my days in Odessa. The sweetness of my love with Jacob. The only one I shall know on this earth.* By the time she reached her room at the top of the staircase, the morsels of bread were devoured.

Exhausted, she fell on her bed and wept. Would the authorities come to the house and arrest her? She did not know. All she knew was that it was dangerous for her to remain in Odessa. The desire of her heart was destroyed. She lay in a state of shock, adrift upon the inexorable currents of circumstance, a sea of historical events she could not overcome.

Later that afternoon Ethel took her seat next to her aunt as they rode out of Odessa in a hired cart. Until they made it into the countryside, Ethel feared she would be stopped and arrested. But all went quietly without incident. No one questioned them or asked for travel papers.

As the cart droned on, Ethel had to confront the finality of leaving Odessa behind, of leaving Jacob behind. She felt as if she were dying, her heart bursting into flames and turning to ash. Summoning all the self-possession she could muster, she hid the grief that was spiralling through her and bit down on her tongue.

Aunt Miriam was distracted, too, by a grief that broke over her in waves. She was leaving behind all she had known of happiness—the memories of when all her children were growing up and her husband Max was still alive. She felt the roots of her existence cut out from under her. Crying quietly from time to time, she thought how scattered her family was—two children in the Pale of Settlement, one in Palestine, one in London, one in New York. Never would they be a family again, and in all likelihood, they would not see each other again in this life. They were forced to wander through God's world, separately, until He would make for them a homeland once more.

After two and a half days, aunt and niece arrived safely in the shtetl. Mama devoured them with kisses. Ethel covered her grief with excuses of tiredness and the onset of her woman's time. She managed to stay in bed for a day, but had to rise with a pretence of renewed vigour or Mama would ply her with more household remedies. By the following day, Ethel was so sick of chamomile and raspberry teas she never wanted to swallow them again.

In hopes of some privacy, Ethel rose on the second day and went to the mikveh to ritually cleanse herself. She pretended to wash out blood from old rags. Eventually, she would have to explain away her real monthly by blaming it on the excitement of the trip.

For the next ten days, Ethel helped settle the household affairs while Aunt Miriam minded the stall in the market and Mama went about selling the remaining flock of chickens, the dairy cow, the house and its furnishings. Outwardly, Ethel did all she could to appear calm. Inwardly, she was in turmoil, caught in the rush of a river of emotion overflowing its boundaries like the violent flood of a spring thaw. Each day she waited to receive word, even if bad, from Marta. Those days were her *Gehenna*. They wore upon her nerves as she watched letters arrive from America and from the steamship line with details of their trip and what to expect on the train ride through Germany to Bremen.

In the relative safety of her family's embrace, a great struggle was going on in Ethel's soul. The road back to Jacob was blocked at every turn she'd undertaken. She feared returning to Odessa, feared her capture by authorities in that city. She came to understand she did not want to be on her own and face brutal crackdowns, or a country in the throes of change. Neither in Odessa nor in the shtetl. Could an historical upheaval cover the streets of cities and villages with blood? The blood of Jews and Gentiles alike? Ethel thought it doubtful that centuries of Imperial rule could be overcome by ragtag groups of individuals.

Could old religious and class animosities be dissolved? Could engrained hatred and prejudices be conquered in a land of hundreds of historical slaughters? For Ethel, the landscape lay soaked in ancient blood.

For these ten days, Ethel felt ill over the intractable choices she faced. How could she silence her heart's cry for Jacob? How could she go back to a multitude of perils and believe she might elude them? She did not want to live a life drenched in fear and constant threat, risking capture and incarceration every time she ran an errand. By week's end her mind was worn out. If only she had never spoken to that man, Dimitry, who was obviously connected to the authorities, perhaps a secret agent of the Czarist regime. He knew her and probably knew of her ties to Jacob and his comrades. Maybe she had always been a target and the conversation in the café only hastened the inevitable.

One night, Ethel dreamed of Jacob kissing her hands, her eyes, her lips. Then she saw his face transfigured by a death mask, a skeletal landscape of emptiness surrounding them. She woke terrified. In the early morning her limbs were paralyzed with fear, as though she were nailed in a coffin, her arms and legs unable to move. Her dormant childhood asthma gripped her chest. She had spasms of breathlessness when she was unable to get air into her lungs. The village midwife gave her herbs, but breathing remained difficult. During the day she tried to live as though time did not exist and she would not have to choose.

The selling off of their old life eventually came to an end. Her family was ready to depart. Surely something would save her from an impossible decision that cut her in two. Nothing did. Yet she felt as long as she was not on the boat, there was hope.

Never sleeping more than a few minutes at a time, Ethel woke on the final morning to a sombre, grey dawn. Everyone was in a bustle of excitement while she threw up, her stomach churning with the meagre repast of black bread and herring. She ran to the outhouse to relieve her bowels. Swallowing her urge to be sick again, she packed the remainder of their food stock for the trip: smoked fish, loaves of black bread, kasha, kugel, honey cake, potatoes, carrots, onions, celery.

When all was ready, Ethel climbed into the cart alongside her family. In three or four days they would reach Minsk, where steamship tickets were waiting for them at the office of the Red Star Line. As they rode out of the shtetl for the last time, Ethel burst into tears.

"Etalah," Mama said in surprise, "surely you will not miss our dilapidated *isbah*, that hovel the icy wind blew through in the winter, and rain poured through in the summer? I promise you won't miss our old life. We are going to America! A new life will start and, *halivai*, would that it should happen, you'll meet someone and get married."

This made Ethel weep more as little cries, so long bottled up, escaped her lips. Mama hugged her tightly. "Enough now. You'll make yourself sick. In a few weeks you'll be a new person with a new life."

Tears flowed down Ethel's cheeks as they rode through the countryside. A black bell tolled in her head. Each mile she travelled away from the village cut her heart to shreds.

Suffering and exhausted from lack of sleep, she could not solve the dilemma plaguing her: How to have a life with Jacob that promised happiness. Looking back in later years, she realized this was the moment she began to relinquish her dream of him. She wanted a life of safety and fulfilment, simple joys, everyday sorrows, family and children. Not one of historical struggle, resistance and confrontation, jeopardy and lurking tragedy.

Not knowing what to do, Ethel stretched out her legs in the back of the wagon amidst family, leaned against Mama, and fell into a fitful sleep.

# Chapter 5
# Journey to America

For the next week of travel in the crowded wagon, Ethel subdued her grief.

The first part of their journey took them over rough roads and hills they had to climb on foot to spare the horses. Fortunately, the weather was good and the days were filled with early summer sunshine. Chaim and Avrom played guessing games with Anna.

"Where is America?" She asked.

"In Minsk," said four-year-old Avrom.

"No, stupid head," said Chaim, who was eight. "The tickets are in Minsk."

"I know," said Avrom, "America is across the sea."

"What is the name of the sea?" Anna asked.

"The Black Sea," said Avrom.

"No!" Chaim cried. "You don't know anything. That's Odessa, where Ethel went to fetch Aunt Miriam."

"Okay little prophet, do you know the name?"

"The Atlantic," said Chaim proudly. He did not tell them he had listened to the letter his friend's father had sent from America, which told about the journey.

Ethel was half following the game, half slumbering in the morning warmth. At the mention of Odessa, she was thrown back into the cauldron of emotions she had suppressed for the past few days. She wondered if this was a sign. If she only knew for certain the right choice, perhaps she would be at peace. The world around her told her nothing certain, and her mind and heart told her two different things. *If I do not make a clear choice, how will I live a true life? Letting circumstance drag me along is not living freely.* Perhaps, though, a deeper part of her knew she had already chosen. She only needed to be sure.

On the fifth day of their journey the family rejoiced in reaching Minsk. Everyone, however, was surprised at the plight of the town. The streets and sidewalks were crowded with the destitute, the sick, and the dying. All were starving. Most pitiful were the families with children. They looked haunted and forlorn.

Parents pleaded for morsels to give their little ones; anything that could be sucked on to quell the children's hungry cries. For them a slice of bread given by a stranger was a gift from God. At first Mama gave food to some of these, only to create a horde of the hungry around her. She had to stop.

How many of these impoverished ones perished on the streets of Minsk no one knew. The local council, unable to chase them from the town, had the dismal task of carting away the dead each morning to pauper's graves.

When the family reached the offices of the Red Star Line, the scene was chaotic. Crowds of people vied for places in the long lines that snaked around the building. Company employees policed the queue as fights broke out with people pushing and shoving in an attempt to get a better position.

Through the first day, Mama, Aunt Miriam, and Ethel took turns keeping their place in line while Anna and the two boys remained at a rooming house. By the time the office closed for the day, they had moved a quarter of the way to the front of the building. At that rate, it would take them another three days. That wasn't enough time. They had to make the evening train the day after tomorrow.

Overnight as they stayed to safeguard their spot, Mama decided to break the rules. First, she fed the patrolling steamship staff one piece of honey cake after another. "From your mouth to God's ear," she said to each one of them and winked. In the darkness with people dozing on the ground, she quietly moved up in the line.

Sometime before dawn, she turned the corner of the building and could see the last guard at the front door. She made her way to him. "Have you tasted my honey cake, *tatteleh*? It's world famous," she added as she winked and handed him a piece.

"I don't like sweet cake," he said and scowled at her.

"*Nu*? Maybe your family? I have a whole cake here waiting for a few hungry stomachs."

"Get back in line where you were."

"You have a missuhs?"

"What if I do?"

"Well, she has dark hair or light?"

"What's it to you?"

"Maybe, I thought, she might like this?" Mama pulled out of her hair a lovely comb set with garnets. "It compliments any colouring. Real silver and real stones. I imagine it's worth ten, maybe fifteen rubles—in case it's not to her taste, that is."

"Eh," said the guard.

"Feel the weight of it," Mama urged. She forced it into his hand.

He looked it over and then abruptly slipped it into his pocket. "I'll ask her," he said flatly.

"*Mazel tov*!" She said and laughed.

"Now get back in line where you were."

In the morning Anna arrived with the boys and saw their much-improved position in the line. When she heard the story of the lost comb, she began to cry. Anna often borrowed the hair ornament as the deep red tones of the garnets set off the auburn highlights in her hair. She had hoped to inherit it one day as a keepsake from her mother.

Mama, though regretful of the loss, mildly scolded her second daughter. "*Shaineh maideleh,* my beautiful girl, no more tears for such a trifle. In America, you'll have half a dozen combs, a different one for each day of the week!"

By the end of the second afternoon, despite the front door guard's refusal to help, the gains Mama had secured during the night brought them into the Red Star office. Only a few more minutes and the tickets would be in their hands.

Finally, Mama reached the purchasing window and was about to ask for the reservations when the clerk said a perfunctory, "Sorry. Closed for the day."

"*Gött in Himmel,*" Mama lamented under her breath, "God in Heaven," she repeated. Fate had intervened. She was superstitious, yet believed in making her own fate. The last train would be leaving tomorrow for Bremen. They would have to be on board to arrive at the boat on time. Who knew what bribes others might use to get to the ticket window before them? Who knew if the tickets were properly held?

Assured by the solemn young man at the door they would be let in first the following day, she decided to secure their place. Mama shocked the family by pulling her Sabbath pearls from beneath her shirt. Turning to the young man, she promised him the necklace if he let them enter first in the morning. But he would not receive them now. She would not make the same mistake she had made with the disgruntled guard.

Everyone thought Mama had lost her necklace to pay for Papa and Samuel's passage to New York. But she had redeemed the pearls from the broker in the village before they left. A great victory. Ethel understood in a new light Mama's unrelenting zeal to wrest every kopeck out of the market stall, out of the sale of the animals and the house. Now this treasured heirloom would be lost forever into the hands of a stranger in Minsk. That night Mama let Ethel wear the pearls under her blouse so Anna would not become petulant. She was always jealous of Ethel's birthright to them as oldest daughter.

In the evening the whole family waited outside the steamship office, determined no one would get ahead of them. Toward midnight as the air cooled, people huddled together and fell asleep.

When morning arrived and the office opened, the young man came out and escorted the family to the purchasing window, making good on his promise. Ethel unclasped the pearls from her neck and handed them to Mama. With a look of utter dejection, Mama dropped them into the man's hand.

In a few minutes they would be in possession of the "golden" tickets, with time to spare before their noon departure. Mama waited patiently for the window to open. Finally, the clerk appeared and she stepped up to the counter, asking if he had their reservations.

"Yes," the agent said. "I have five tickets."

"No," Mama replied, "six." The sixth person was Aunt Miriam. Perhaps her reservation had never been held. "Yes, yes," Mama insisted. There was the letter from the company. The reservation in question was for six. It was in writing.

The clerk said the money to hold them had only been enough for five. The price of steerage had gone up since the reservation was made. Without notice. That was that. Sorry. "Hurry up and decide," he said briskly. "Do you want the five? There are plenty of others who want them. If not, step aside."

In defeat Mama nodded her head and bought them. What were they to do? They could not leave Aunt Miriam in Minsk.

On the street the family gathered in a circle to consolidate their warmth. The day was raw and threatened rain. If they wanted to make it to Bremen they would need to leave at noon, or, at the latest, that evening. All were in shock and disbelief. How could they go without their dear aunt? Yet they could not miss the departure of their boat.

At this turn of events, Ethel's internal conflict returned. Was this another sign that she was not meant to go to America? She could relinquish her place to

Aunt Miriam. And then what? Wander the streets of Minsk among the destitute? Beg for money to hire a cart to take her back to the *shtetl*? Where could she stay? With neighbours? Then what? Return to Odessa? Her makeshift plans broke down whenever she was faced with the prospect of returning to that city. Yet all trace of Jacob led back there. A cold sweat came over her and she was unable to breathe. If only she had the courage to act on her heart's desire. But she remained silent.

For over an hour the family waited outside the steamship office, asking if anyone had a ticket to trade. Then Mama spotted the agent who had pocketed the pearls leave the building and walk down the block. "Come on," she said, "he is our one hope."

The fellow met up with a woman in front of a restaurant. After a few moments they went inside. This woman wore rouge, powder, and so much finery as to seem a confection rather than a lady. And Mama knew, a lady she was not. Under ordinary circumstances she was the kind of woman Mama would not acknowledge.

The pair sat down at a table near the window. Through it, the family could see the agent and lady talking animatedly. The woman closed her eyes and then the clerk leaned across the table and fastened the pearls around her neck.

"A sacrifice," burst from Mama's lips.

With squeals of delight the woman fingered her new necklace and began looking at herself in the glass of the restaurant window. She only seemed to see her reflection there, and not the scene outside—the family huddling close for warmth, gaping at the restaurant diners enjoying their feasts. Every once in a while, Ethel would catch a glimpse of herself and the family's reflection, sad and miserable as they waited with little hope to solve their crisis.

Somehow, Mama drew courage from the scene. She said that often success and failure were only a hair's width apart, so long as one did not give up—and trusted the Almighty.

She drew Aunt Miriam aside and asked her for the jewellery she was carrying, which was pinned beneath her skirts for safe keeping, out of sight of any authorities' inspections. Everyone converged around Aunt Miriam to allow for her modesty, while Mama rummaged through the silk pouch that hung suspended from their aunt's undergarments.

"What about these?" Mama said, not exactly asking a question but making a demand.

"Well, yes, all right," replied the disconsolate aunt. Mama had wrested from the bag a pair of earrings, large water-drop-shaped pearls with gold filigree.

"Good!" Mama said, "but not enough," she added with a note of realism. Then Mama spied something that would likely be irresistible to any woman, and especially the kind that sat inside the restaurant already wearing Mama's Sabbath pearls.

"Oh, no," moaned the aunt, more in sorrow than as reply to Mama's question. In Mama's palm sat a ring with an emerald, not so small as to be insignificant, and not so large as to be showy, but brilliantly green as spring grass, and just as delicate in design.

"Weigh the choices in your mind," said Mama. "America, with its streets paved in gold, bestowing upon you, for a little bit of effort, a lifetime of abundance. Every kind of food you could desire, pickles, herring with *schmaltz*, lox, white fish. You can eat honey cake every day if you like, apricots and plums, peaches and oranges, pineapple and cherries. Every brandy you can imagine, and other cordials to whet the appetite. The newest styles in clothing and finery imaginable. Your choice of living in city or country. The seaside or mountains to visit. A horseless carriage and electric lights. Hot and cold running water right inside your kitchen. And the sweet smell of indoor plumbing!"

"All of this," she said, with the ring sitting modestly in her open palm, "in place of a little trinket. A lovely trinket, of course, but paltry in comparison with what it is going to buy you."

"It's not that," Aunt Miriam replied with tears coming to her eyes. "Max gave it to me for our anniversary."

"Oh," said Mama. "I didn't realize." And she began to place the ring back into Aunt Miriam's pouch.

"No. You're right," Aunt Miriam said in a quiet voice, "what woman could resist such a lovely thing. It is our best hope. I will think of it as Max sending me to America. A gift I know he would want with his whole heart, to see me settled in a new land." She took the ring from Mama's hand and kissed it goodbye, then placed it back in Mama's palm.

At that moment the woman in the restaurant got up from her seat, possibly to get a better view of her new pearls, to see how they graced her neck and set off her dress and hair. The woman started to walk away from the table. Mama acted quickly and entered the restaurant. A man stopped her and inquired something, which Mama waved away with her hand. Then she pointed to the lady in question, who passed into the back of the room and through a door. The man, with a scowl, directed Mama out of the restaurant. With lightening quickness, she walked around the back yard and disappeared from sight.

Five, six, seven minutes or more passed and all waited in suspense. Finally, Mama emerged from behind the building, a look of deep concern upon her face. "We must wait now until 6:00," she said, "and we shall see what magic this woman can weave. God forgive me for such a bargain as I have struck."

"You have done it out of love and God will not punish you for this," said Aunt Miriam. "It goes on the accounting of my soul, not yours. Any rabbi worth his wife's 'golden coins of chicken fat' in her Sabbath soup would say the same. Don't grieve, dear sister. The angels are made to plead the case for such a thing as this."

The family saw the woman return to the table, Aunt Miriam's earrings dangling from her ears. The lady appeared supremely happy at the way her day was playing itself out and had another prize to win if she delivered on another bargain by that evening. All made a prayer that God, Who works in unknown ways, might deliver Aunt Miriam from this crisis and save the family in its journey to a new life.

The cold of the day had settled into everyone's bones and they now had several hours to pass until the appointed time. They wandered down the main street of Minsk and found a woman roasting potatoes over a small fire. "Here," Mama said, handing the woman some coins. She piled everyone's cold hands and numb fingers with this food that did double duty, warming their hands for a moment, then warming their mouths and bellies.

The family plied Mama for details. Uncharacteristically, she closed her mouth and would not divulge the bargain transacted with the questionable lady in the restaurant. All they surmised was that it had something to do with the emerald ring.

Nearing the six o'clock hour, the family returned to the steamship office and waited. If they did not leave within an hour, they would miss the train to Galicia and from there through to Bremen and the German port that was their destination.

At a few minutes to six, the lady appeared strolling down the street in a fine coat. She made no sign to the family. Mama and Aunt Miriam did not acknowledge her. They looked in bemused wonder as her gentleman friend let her into the office. He drew the shades, locked the door, and extinguished the lamps. The office was swallowed in darkness. On the street the day was coming to an end. In a few minutes the streetlamps were lit, casting a thin veil of light upon the nearly deserted avenue.

As the family waited in the cold, they could hear the clock tower chime out the quarter hour, then half, and then three-quarter hour. The station lay at the other end of town and some minutes' walk away. If they did not start out now, they would miss the train.

"Etalah," Mama said, "go, and take the children and Aunt Miriam. Find the stationmaster and tell him your mother has been delayed. If I do not arrive, do not get off the train. I will meet you in Bremen, God willing!"

Mama undertook responsibility for solving the problem because their dear aunt was no longer robust. Under normal circumstances the walk to the station took ten minutes, but their aunt could not walk fast. She would never make it in time for the train if she awaited the outcome at the steamship's office.

When the family reached the station, they found the train was due in eight minutes. Ethel and Aunt Miriam, though out of breath, lost no time in finding the stationmaster. In a solicitous but business-like manner, he explained that the departure of any one train could not be compromised without affecting all other departures. Indeed, the entire line. They must trust to Providence for their assistance because he, unfortunately, could not help.

The dire nature of the situation gripped Ethel as if a hand were pressing upon her throat and squeezing her breath out of her. How could they proceed to the port town without Mama? How would they find her amid the crowds in a large city? No sooner had these thoughts gone through Ethel's head than she saw a small circle of light down the track, moving closer and closer toward the station. The great roar of the engine and its whistle filled the air. Ethel's heart began to race. The dark metal beast, like some ancient dragon breathing fire and smoke, was soon screeching to a halt before her.

"Go, Aunt Miriam," Ethel said. "Get seats for yourself and the children. I'll wait here till the last moment."

Ethel paced the platform, straining to see if Mama was coming down the avenue. All was dark and empty. The people had finished disembarking and boarding. Only one or two were scattered at the far end of the station. Soon even they were gone. Something had to be done in the next moment for the conductor was clearing the doors of passengers and seeing that all were safely on board. The whistle was pressed to his lips to give the all-clear signal. Ethel could think of nothing else to do, so she screamed and fell forward halfway between the train and the platform. She secretly wedged her foot in a small gap between the two and began to cry in pain.

The stationmaster ran out from the waiting room. Together with the conductor, the two men converged upon Ethel nearly at the same moment.

"What foolery is this, young lady?"

"No," Ethel cried, her face red and streaming with tears. "I've gotten my foot caught. Here," she said, and lifted the hem of her dress a little above her ankle, further than was necessary, to draw their attention to the outline of her leg. Ethel felt some power fill her with bravado and exhilaration. Maybe it was the effects of having watched the lady from the restaurant gather those jewels by bestowing her smile upon a man. Or maybe it was her female ingenuity bursting forth at the moment of greatest need. Whatever it was, she had fallen and conquered. She felt her heart beat with excitement. The two men tried to extricate her foot, but Ethel winced and made small cries in response to all of their attempts.

"Can you slip your foot out of your shoe?" asked the conductor, who was perhaps familiar with this type of mishap.

"If you loosen the tie," she said, blushing with modesty.

"Yes, of course. If I may?"

"Indeed," she said, "it is the only way."

As delicately as a doctor, the conductor untied the lace and spread the shoe apart at the ankle. Ethel pulled her foot out gingerly and sighed with relief. The shoe took a bit more work. By twisting and turning it this way and that, he succeeded after a minute or two.

"Now," he said, "We must get you on board. Do you think you can stand?"

"With your help I am sure I can," Ethel replied, smiling up at him. "Oh, oh, oh," she murmured as they raised her up.

"We will get you to your seat," he said, "and once I've made my rounds, I'll bring a compress for your foot."

"Thank you. Thank you so much for your kind help," Ethel replied.

The stationmaster and the conductor eased Ethel up the steps. As she shot a last glance back at the street, she saw Mama climbing out of a carriage in which sat the lady in question, smiling and waving a goodbye as if she were the Czarina.

Mama boarded the train just behind Ethel and exclaimed, "What *meshugass* is this? What has happened?"

"A little mishap, but all is well," said the conductor. He left Ethel at her seat and, as Mama bent down to examine the foot, Ethel winked and whispered, "Did you obtain the ticket, Mama? Whose carriage was that?"

Mama drew herself upright, seeing Ethel was not really in pain, and said, "Do not ask me about this unfortunate incident anymore and I will not ask what you've been up to." She finished off her speech with a pointed expression. Ethel was left wondering why the "incident" was "unfortunate" and for whom? Mama turned to Aunt Miriam in the next seat over and smiled and handed her the precious steamship ticket. They looked at each other with tears in their eyes and then hugged warmly.

After three days and nights of travel they reached the German border. There, the train abruptly stopped. For an hour the passengers waited. What could be the delay? Would the Germans extract a tax for crossing into their country? Would people be sent back for some arcane bureaucratic reason? The Germans were known as sticklers for regulations.

Mama had a foreboding. Quickly she went over minute details. Did they have enough money? Were the Germans concerned about emigrants wandering the cities destitute, a burden on their government? Did they have too much money? A target for easy extortion?

Uniformed officials entered the car and began inspecting travel documents.

"Let me see your papers," Mama said to Aunt Miriam. She could find nothing amiss. Then she took another look and saw the problem. The hard-won steamship ticket was not made out to Miriam Bialostok, the Aunt's married name, but to Miriam Kaplan, her maiden name, the same as the family's. The ship's manifest probably listed her as Kaplan, too. Surely the authorities would check this against the name on the emigration documents.

Soon the two officials reached them. They spoke neither Russian nor Yiddish, though some German was intelligible to Jews. First they checked the family's papers, then asked for Aunt Miriam's. The men noticed the discrepancy. They repeated the same question, getting louder and more aggressive each time. Tears came to Aunt Miriam's eyes. She did not know what to say. Mama, always quick to remedy any emergency, repeated the Yiddish word for sister-in-law, "*shevegerin, shevegerin.*" They turned to Mama and told her to shut up. Again, they asked Aunt Miriam the same question in German. Their patience gone, they took the ticket and motioned her to get up and come with them.

Suddenly a man in the seat behind the family interrupted. "Pardon, pardon," he called out in German. The officers turned toward him with menacing looks, but the man continued to speak. He translated what Mama was telling him in Yiddish: Aunt Miriam had joined the family to travel to America; when they made the reservation for the steamship, they forgot to provide her married name, so they were all made out to Kaplan; that was her maiden name; she was the aunt.

The two men conferred with each other for a few minutes. One appeared to accept the explanation. Finally, the other looked with annoyance at the full train car, then nodded with icy correctness. He handed the ticket back to Aunt Miriam.

"Stupid Jews," he said as they proceeded down the aisle. Aunt Miriam and Mama each quietly exhaled deep sighs of relief.

Another two hours passed and the train still did not move. Mama and Ethel grew increasingly uneasy. Then uniformed soldiers with rifles appeared at the head of the car. An officer spoke in short, clipped sentences. His men went down the aisle motioning for everyone to stand up and follow them. With misgivings, the people disembarked. No one dared disobey. One man who reached for his luggage was sharply yelled at and his hand slapped.

Outside, the men and women were separated into two groups. Avrom began to cry as he and Chaim were taken away from the rest of the family. Mama bent down to hug and kiss them, and said soothingly, "Everything will be alright. You must be my brave men and do as you are told. Chaim, hold your brother's hand and do not let go."

The train passenger who had helped with the officials saw the two boys standing alone. He walked over to them and took their hands. He called out to Mama that he would watch over them.

*An angel*, she thought. *Now at least they will not be alone.*

At that moment, orders were shouted and each group was forced into a line. They were marched several blocks to a building that had other lines of people, from rag-tag to nicely dressed, looping around the yard. The soldiers ignored all inquiries. It was unclear whether their silence reflected a language barrier or was simply a matter of policy.

Anxiety among the travellers grew. They inched their way toward the building's entrance. The door shut sharply at 12:00, then reopened exactly at 1:00. Their slow progress continued. As the afternoon wore on the old, infirm, and young grew tired and sat down on the ground. Immediately the soldiers ordered them back up. By late afternoon, Mama, Aunt Miriam, Ethel, and Anna reached the door and were finally inside. They saw that Avrom and Chaim, with help from the stranger on the train, had also arrived inside. Stocky German women and burly men bustled the females and males off to separate holding rooms.

Now the travellers lost hope and feared they would be incarcerated. Another wave of shock went through them as the attendants, half speaking in German, half pantomiming, instructed the captives to disrobe. Many kept on their undergarments but were forced to remove even these modest coverings. The matrons collected all the clothing. Shame from their nakedness flooded through the women and children. They felt helpless and vulnerable.

The Germans shouted more orders at them. The women cowered; it seemed that none of them understood German. The matrons continued to shout and finally pushed them through a door, herding them in groups of 40 into a large room equipped with showerheads and drainage grates. Without explanation, the matrons opened large, handheld hoses and sprayed them down with a foul-smelling liquid. The travellers were then allowed to wash themselves in the showers. An hour later their clothes, damp and smelling of the same fumigating chemical, were returned to them. From the odour of the spray, Ethel concluded that this harrowing event was to ensure that no one with typhus would be let into Germany.

Decades later, when reports of the shower-rigged gas chambers came out at the end of World War II, Ethel remembered with a shudder this episode from her journey to America. The emigrants, naked and ashamed, had feared for their lives at the hands of Germans. With the Holocaust, Germans brought those fears to ghastly reality.

All in all, it took a day to perform these precautionary measures against disease. The travellers boarded the train late that evening and were soon on the way to Bremen.

During the long train ride the following day, Ethel had nothing to take her mind off her sorrowful imaginings. The unrelenting sound of the tracks clicked away as if counting the increasing distance she travelled from Russia and from Jacob. Would she never again see his eyes filled with love, never stroke the curls of his copper hair, never lay her hand like a nesting dove inside of his? Was he facing a sentence of punishment, a broken life in the Czar's prison, or a brutal work camp in Siberian cold and desolation? Or, worst of all, did he lie beaten and dead? That night Ethel hardly slept, her mind careening from one blood-soaked image to another.

By morning she realized she could not continue in her anguished state. Should she tell Mama what happened in Odessa, ask for money or a piece of jewellery she could sell along with her steamship ticket, and return to Russia? Otherwise, she must relinquish her love and shut off the part of her that bled anew with every memory.

She could not do either. Her desperate mind finally hit upon a compromise. She would go to America, get a job, and do all she could to find out what happened to Jacob. Hoping for the best, she could send money to ease his difficulties. This might accomplish more than if she'd stayed without residency papers in Odessa.

Late that afternoon the family arrived in Bremen. A cold, grey fog descended upon them as they made their way to the port, Bremerhaven, on the Weser estuary. Though still ten miles from the North Sea, the harbour seemed huge. So did the ship. Ethel thought of giants in a children's story.

As the clouds turned to rain, the fog dissipated and Ethel saw the name of the ship painted on its prow: "S. S. Freedom." The huge letters seemed a sign for her and Jacob. Perhaps both would ultimately be freed by her choice of America.

Ethel stood dockside with her family. Chaim and Avrom ran up and down unable to contain their excitement. The enormous ship let go a loud blast of its horn to signal boarding. German soldiers were stationed nearby to maintain order. Avrom looked afraid of them. "Will they send us back?" He asked Ethel. "I don't want to go back. I hate the Czar," he whispered in subdued tones. "He eats little boys."

"Chaim," Ethel said sharply. "Stop filling Avrom's head with tales."

"Zaide said the soldiers stole Jewish boys. He said they swallowed them up," replied Chaim.

"Avrom," she said. "We are going to America. Remember? Over the ocean. Far from Russia and far from the Czar's soldiers."

With that, Avrom became quiet and docile, clinging to Mama's hand as they got in line.

Ethel stared at the gangplank as she waited to board. Could a few steps change the course of her entire life? Take her to another continent, another country, another future? Most of all she wondered, with a heart-stabbing pang, how a few steps could bring an end to her heart's desire, her love for Jacob.

Those steps would take her away and entomb her heart. Yet she wanted a future that promised safety and freedom.

As she climbed the ramp, she promised herself she would not go forward in halting half-steps. If she boarded, it would be with a firm resolve. She would never stop loving Jacob, but she could not help him now. He was lost to her as if he had died the day he was arrested. Her passage across the ocean would be a goodbye, a commemoration, and a sitting *shiva*. She would need her strength to face the challenges of a new life. Stopping her thoughts of Jacob would take a harsh discipline she would need to exercise for the rest of her life. She would need to sear her bleeding heart shut, cauterize it with a branding iron of will.

When the steamer finally departed and went out to the north Atlantic, Ethel thought once more she had made the wrong decision and would not survive the crossing. The sea heaved, and below deck the people were stacked on wooden shelves like dishes as the waves constantly jostled them. Ethel felt she would break into pieces that could never be put back together. The one room for relieving oneself filled more and more as the trip progressed. The stench was *Gehenna*. At night Ethel and other stricken passengers vomited each time a swell hit the hull.

Though the weather remained stormy, Ethel stayed on deck as much as possible. The miles of sea were boundless; grey waves and grey sky stretched in all directions. She could not get her bearings. Jacob was lost. Whatever they'd had in Russia was speeding farther away from her every moment. Her old self was slipping away like a discarded garment tossed onto the boat's foamy wake. It shrank into the distance and grew heavy as the dead weight of the water pulled it under.

Day after day the sea washed everything away. Ethel came back slowly. One day she noticed the sun, another day the spray upon her face. The salt invaded her lungs, as if she were breathing again after years without air. She had only a part of her heart, yet she knew she had enough of it to keep her alive. The rest, she believed, would never grow back.

By the second week of the voyage, the family had fallen into a routine. Mama and Aunt Miriam tended to the boys on deck, weather permitting, as they played games of tag and coin tossing with other children. Anna had found a group of girls her age who sat together, sewing and playing cards, fixing each other's hair, talking and wondering if the boys in America would be as annoying as those in Russia. Ethel, her head throbbing with the roll and surge of the sea, sat by the railing. Her stomach hadn't settled. In the afternoons, a few musicians gathered together and played klezmer music for an hour or two. A sad-faced Romanian, whose violin wept and shrilled and danced its tunes, made the old cry and the young sway in rhythm.

One morning near the end of the voyage, Ethel felt particularly sad. She stood at the railing wanting to ride out the waves in peace and solitude. Watching the water curl and foam, her mind played over early memories of her childhood in the *shtetl*. Unbidden thoughts of Jacob as a boy surfaced, a time before the world had taken over and brought its tragedy to them. She breathed in the salty air, as tears skimmed down her cheeks, falling to the water below. She remembered something she had once heard the rabbi say: one's sorrow, released into the ocean of God's Being, lost its sting and became one with all creation. The good and the bad blended and cancelled each other, so all that remained was God.

Lost in these thoughts, she heard a voice say, "You stare at the water so deeply. Such sadness? Such regret?"

Ethel turned and saw beside her the young man from the train at the German border who rescued Aunt Miriam and watched out for Avrom and Chaim. She thought she had seen him on the docks in Bremerhaven, but had lost sight of him when they boarded. Trying to regain composure, she smiled softly.

"It is a lot to lose one's home. I know. I make a habit of losing it every few months." He laughed quietly.

Straightening up, Ethel wiped her eyes and blew her nose.

The man went on in a talkative, friendly tone. "I know why you stare at the ocean. You were once a mermaid. Now you have been born on land. Your eyes," he said, smiling into her face, "are grey like the sea, and deep. You are a natural wonder come to tread the earth in human form."

Despite her sadness, Ethel laughed. *He is full of himself*, she thought.

"You like to tell stories? Do you compliment all the girls in this way?"

"No," he said solemnly. "You are the only one I say such a thing to. Forgive me. I am too forward. My name is Philip. Philip Smolens. From Smolensk, of course."

"My family is in your debt. We never had a chance to thank you."

"Your gratefulness is a bounty I will treasure," he said with an exaggerated bow.

Ethel could not tell if he was play-acting. "Truly," she said, "Your kindness and courage were admirable."

At this he smiled and dipped his head.

Ethel suddenly grabbed her stomach. She was afraid she might be sick again.

"Are you all right?" Philip asked solicitously.

"Yes," she said, swallowing. "My stomach. If I eat anything, I feel ill. If I don't eat anything, I feel ill."

"Ah. You need the seaman's trick," he said, taking something out of his pocket. It was a piece of matzo. "Better than soda crackers to settle your stomach."

Ethel took the matzo and began to nibble it, feeling relieved.

"More? I have more. Enough to get you through the next few days, until we reach New York."

"Have you been a sailor?" Ethel asked between bites.

"No. I have been many things. A tinsmith, a tailor, a wine maker, a wheat merchant, a carter of crates and boxes on and off ships. So, yes, I have been on many vessels but not a sailor."

"Were you ever a scholar?"

"No. You have got me there. Never a studier."

This pleased Ethel. He was full of life and playful as a child. She couldn't imagine him studying. His sonorous voice filled her like the wind filled a sail. It was the first time she had felt alive since she left Russia.

"Are you stopping in New York? Traveling on?" He asked.

"No. I mean yes, stopping. My father and brother came over a few years ago. They found a place big enough for all of us."

"The lower eastside?"

"Yes."

"Me too," he said. "I'm staying with my brother on Orchard Street. He found me a job driving a wagon, making deliveries."

"Oh, Orchard Street is where my father lives."

"Look at that," he said. "We are already neighbours. May I come visit you sometime?"

Ethel felt her heart contract. She did not know what to say.

Three days later the S. S. Freedom entered New York harbour. Grey weather shrouded the harbour for the next two days as the steerage passengers waited on board for the final ordeal of their trip—entry to Ellis Island. They could not see the "mountains" of New York. They could only see the kerchiefed and capped heads of the people around them. They stood in a mist, their clothes drenched in droplets of water as if the air were crying tears of exhaustion and relief that they had accomplished the impossible. They were, of course, all hungry, having eaten only watery broth and mouldy bread for 14 days. They were all exhausted, needing to sleep on beds that did not pitch and roll with the waves of the sea.

On the third day the weather cleared. Before their astonished eyes sprawled the great city—its tall buildings, its lights and streetcars, its horse drawn carriages and motorcars. Nearly within reach its people walked and ate, worked and slept as they hoped to do. When Ethel saw the Statue of Liberty she knew, somehow, she would survive in this new world.

An official arrived on a barge to take them to Ellis Island. The ship's officer handed over the manifest that listed their names and ages, countries of origin, ultimate destinations, vocations, whether they could read and write, and anything else known about them. America wanted useful citizens, hard workers who could take care of themselves and be of help to the country.

When they arrived on the island, they were directed into a line that snaked its way from the landing dock to a forbidding brick building with turrets, towers, and metal spires, reminding many of the oppressive governments they had fled. Everyone was heavily laden with belongings. Some struggled along a step at a time bearing suitcases and even dragging trunks. Bundles tied with string or rope rode upon the heads of others, while in the arms of many were baskets and boxes, sacks made of cloth or leather, feather quilts and pillows, tins and pots and pans. Whole families wore layer upon layer of clothes, some for everyday work, some with beautiful embroidery for what they hoped would be festival days and celebrations once again.

They knew they could be sent back if the doctors found the dreaded trachoma spots on the insides of their eyelids or if they breathed heavily, a sign of a heart ailment or lung disease, or if they walked with difficulty or were crippled. But sent back to where? To what? Did their villages still exist, overrun with soldiers? Would they have to go back to a land of famine and disaster? Or unrelenting poverty? Even the most fortunate among them had nothing to return to. Their houses and belongings had all been sold. What if one family member was singled out because of some illness? Would the family remain and see the beloved grandparent or child returned alone to the old country and to catastrophe? The journey had cost these families too dearly for all to return. Who would go back with the excluded ones? Some families would have to face these tragic decisions within the next few days.

When the immigrants finally entered the main building, they found to their amazement the amenities of a small city. Inside were restaurants, a post office, a hospital, a bank, a railway office, baths, a laundry, courtrooms, offices for aid societies of different nationalities and religions. Arrivals could check their boxes, trunks, and baskets in a checkroom, though most held onto their belongings for fear they would be stolen or lost. Mostly these things were worthless, but they were all the people had left from centuries of ancestors.

One flight up was the Great Hall, a huge two-story high space with tall windows that streamed down sunlight onto their upturned faces. Here the immigrants waited on benches until their turn came to mount the grand staircase that went up to the third floor's balcony off of which were the examination rooms. If they made it through this final test, a new world would open before them. This staircase would be a climb to freedom, opportunity, achievement. And it was not only a staircase of dreams, but one of laws that would grant them the right to live as they chose in safety and peace.

But on that third-floor balcony, outside the examination rooms, stood white-coated men with forbidding expressions, who gazed down relentlessly at the flood of forlorn humanity. As Ethel sat with her family, in the Great Hall, waiting their turn to climb the stairs, she watched others ascending. Some struggled to reach the upper balcony. One walked noisily with a leg dragged up each step. Would that make him a burden on the state? Another breathed heavily, gasping for air, and resting every few moments. Would he be barred admittance? Ethel knew a cough could be a sign of pneumonia or tuberculosis. She watched apprehensively as those afflicted immigrants reached the landing, were quickly pulled aside, then had letters chalked upon their chests. They were led off somewhere, and Ethel could no longer see them. Realizing the climb up the grand staircase was the beginning of the examination and selection process, Ethel sank down inside herself with dread. She soon noticed how dry her throat was. The air was filled with the smells of hundreds of people from foreign lands, along with their dirty, dusty clothing and belongings. She gasped. Exposure to the unhealthy air combined with anxiety was beginning to trigger her childhood asthma.

Just at that moment the family's turn came to ascend the stairs. Trembling, Ethel rose from the bench and began climbing. Nervousness overtook her and her breathing came in short, jagged bursts. Her heart rose into her mouth, beating wildly. She swallowed hard and tried to make the rhythm of her breathing slow and even, so none of the white-coated doctors up on the balcony would see her panting. In a moment of apprehension, she looked up at the landing and one of the doctors looked directly at her. She did the only thing she could at the moment; she stopped, held onto the railing and breathed as deeply as she was able. Her actions did nothing to loosen the gaze that had fixed upon her like an iron clamp. As she reached the top step the man made his way to her and drew a letter "L" in chalk on her chest. He brought her to a nearby bench and motioned her to sit. Suddenly, he was called back to his post and left Ethel alone. Her mind raced with thoughts of the worst possible outcome—her journey ending in failure, her admittance prevented at this final door. What would happen now? She sat rigidly in a terror that numbed her body.

If anyone had asked her to rise and follow, she surely could not have performed that simple command. But it wasn't just anyone who did ask her to do this. It was Mama. Her shrewd expression was sizing up the situation. She made Ethel stand up quickly and take off her coat. Mama grabbed the garment with such ferocity Ethel was nearly knocked down onto the bench. In a matter of seconds, Mama turned the coat inside out and ordered Ethel to put it back on.

"Suck on this," Mama said, handing several honey candies to Ethel. She popped one in her mouth and felt a soothing calmness relax her chest. Then Mama pulled her over to a line of women where Anna and Aunt Miriam stood waiting to enter one of the nearby rooms. That no one in authority had seen the ruse was probably due to the profusion of people now mounting the stairs. A flood of humanity crested the steps every ten or fifteen seconds.

Female attendants staffed the room they next entered. In their hands they held buttonhooks. What was this? Ethel wondered. She watched as the immigrants' eyelids were rolled up to check for the spots of trachoma that would bar their entry.

As her turn neared, Ethel fidgeted nervously in anticipation of the metal hook. Mama noticed and said in Yiddish, "stop jumping out of your skin, little cow, and take the touching hand as a help to unburden your teats." Ethel began to laugh and this relaxed her. She remembered their cow Alya's moony expression after milking, and she breathed deeply, ready for her eyelids to be raised.

After the eyelid test the women were subjected to more inspections—for measles, chicken pox, scarlet fever, other illnesses—and to more questions.

"How many tests can there be?" sighed Anna, who was tired.

"Look alert," replied Mama. "They are checking to see if you are dim-witted."

Individuals were singled out and asked to complete puzzles, count backwards, do arithmetic, or select happy faces in a picture.

Last of all, an inspector asked them, "Do you have jobs?"

"Yes." Mama replied. "We all have jobs," although they did not.

Finally, the women were sent to the Hebrew Aid Society. After receiving a bundle of clothing, bedding, and linens they were directed to a waiting area of benches hemmed in by a metal fence. They checked for the boys, but did not see them. After a few minutes, Mama spotted Chaim coming towards her. Her voice broke out, "Where is Avrom? What has happened? Why is he not with you? Tell me! Tell me!"

"They took him," blurted out Chaim as he reached Mama's side. At this news Mama—exhausted by the day's momentous events, the weeks of travel, the months of preparation, and the frustrating nearness of this final goal—fell back on the bench, silent for several stunned moments.

Ethel stepped forward and bent down to talk to Chaim. "Tell me what happened? What did the man say to Avrom?"

"Said nothing," Chaim insisted. Mama slowly rose to her feet, ready to go back to the Hebrew Aid Society for help. She kept mumbling, "No, not possible, not possible." Her hand clutched her chest as if she were unable to breathe.

"Mama, Mama," they heard a voice call out.

All turned to see Avrom, guided by an attendant, skipping jauntily along, whistling.

"So, this is America?" Avrom said as they stared at him in silence. "They look and look at my eye. They poke it with their fingers. Shine a light. Call one, two, three doctors. Make me bend my head, like this and this." Avrom tilted his head to show them. "I say, 'not my real eye, accident, not my eye.' Then they understand. So, this is great America!" Avrom whistled again. Everyone burst out laughing.

Mama took his head in her hands to scold him. "You should have told them right away, you troublemaker. My heart nearly stopped. Pity your poor Mama next time. If I weren't so happy, I'd give your little *tush* a smack!"

Now they were all together and had their papers. They had made it to America. They sat down on the benches to wait for Papa to come get them. After half an hour Mama said to Ethel, "Maybe he has mistaken the date. Maybe he came two days ago, while we were still on the ship. So now he doesn't hurry. He takes his time. What if he thinks we missed the boat?"

"Rest, Mama. Close your eyes and rest. We'll all watch for him," Ethel said.

Everyone quieted down, even the boys, who had been playing with their coins clacking noisily on the wooden benches.

Late afternoon slowly drew to a close. Ethel thought perhaps they would have to go in search of Papa. Make their way to Orchard Street, not knowing how to get there. They'd come this far not knowing the way, and they'd arrived in America. What were a few more miles? Ethel prepared to go to the Hebrew Aid Society for directions.

As she turned to tell Mama, a melodic greeting, "Mama, my *Yiddisher* Mama," rang out from somewhere nearby. "Here we are, here," came the words from behind the metal fence at the back of the room. All eyes turned toward the voice. Then they saw the small man slightly stooped, with flecks of grey in his beard. From glittering eyes, a flood of tears poured down his face. He reached for the handkerchief in his jacket pocket, took it in his hand, and wiped his face. "My *Yiddisher* Mama, *meine kinderlech*, my sweet, sweet children." He wept openly as the family gathered around, fingers intertwined with his between the links of the fence. "So long, so long without you," he said and gulped down more tears.

Next to Papa stood a giant of a stranger. They knew it must be Samuel, but his broad frame and muscular arms amazed them. When he left Russia, he had still been a boy. Now he was a man. But he was still the same Samuel—everything was lightness and mirth. He laughed loudly and kept breaking into English, forgetting he must speak Yiddish to his immigrant brothers, sisters, and mother.

Papa bent down to talk through the fence to Avrom, who clung to Mama's skirt. The little boy shied away from this stranger.

"Is this my *boychik*, all grown up? It's me, your Papa!" He said with a huge smile on his face.

Avrom, less than a year old the last time he saw Papa, didn't remember.

Papa took from his pocket a piece of chocolate-covered halvah. He gave it to Avrom, who devoured it in silence.

Papa gave everyone else a piece too. They all savoured the sweetness of the moment and laughed over Avrom's bashfulness.

Somehow the family found its way outside. Samuel took the baskets, bundles, and suitcases as if they were of no consequence, little things weighing nothing. Papa led them to the ferry. It was a short ride, just a few minutes. Then they were on firm ground again. The young ones ran ahead following Samuel.

Mama walked along with Papa. She was uncharacteristically silent. She said to Papa, "Twenty-eight years since our marriage vows and I don't know what to say. I feel like a stranger. For the past three years I would turn to speak to you, as if you were still by my side, to tell you about my day. Now you are by my side and I don't know what to say. It feels like a dream."

"No dream," Papa assured her gently. "We are in America, *Mamaleh*. All we hoped and worked for. It is before us now. Wait. Wait till tomorrow; you will wake up from the three years of a dream that passed both fast and slow. Now we will live in freedom. The rest will come day by day." Then Papa announced, "We will take the streetcar," as proud as if it were his invention. He dispensed coins to each of his children, winked as he gave another to Aunt Miriam, then took Mama's arm. He strode ahead to the corner. Avrom jumped back in fright when the trolley came barrelling down the street, whizzing close to where he stood, ringing its shrill bell. Everyone hopped on board except for Avrom, who was lifted up the steps holding tight to Mama's hand. There were only a few vacant seats. Mama settled in one, Avrom on her lap, and Aunt Miriam squeezed in next to them. The rest took their chances holding poles and straps. They swung this way and that in a dance of movement with jostling stops and starts. The trolley threatened to crash into buildings or sidewalks before rounding corners at the last possible moment. They travelled through the business area with buildings as big as the transatlantic steamer ships. The streets were crowded with people leaving their jobs.

When they reached the edge of the lower east side, they got off and began the walk to their new home. They came to Grand Street where ladies were parading by in the latest fashions.

"We look like greenhorns," Ethel said as she cast a critical eye over her peasant clothing, the traditional embroidered blouse and dirndl skirt. "Mama look," she called out. "They're wearing dresses with tailored shirts on the top."

"I see, I see," said Mama.

"No shawls or kerchiefs, real hats with feathers." Mama did not seem impressed.

The family turned off of Grand Street and onto Rivington where the sidewalks, and practically the whole street, were crowded with push carts. They had no space to walk more than single file. The vendors assumed if you were dressed in Old World clothing you had just arrived and were in need of everything they sold. One called out, "Get your new pot, Mrs., to cook up your delicious Friday night chicken. This is just the right pot for the job!" Another said, "Get your brooms, aprons, and scrub brushes here, for scrubbing coal dust off the walls after you dump the coal scuttle into your stove." The family passed wagons selling fresh fruits and vegetables, carts with breads and rolls, others with poultry and eggs sitting on top of blocks of ice. Everything was Kosher, if you believed the vendors who tried to waft their foods under the noses of passersby.

Then they came upon another cart. Ethel cried out, "Look, they're selling… women's things." Anna laughed shamelessly. Women's unmentionables were spread out for anyone to see: The slips and corsets that the new fashions required; woollen hose, and silk underthings that not even your husband should examine.

Papa turned onto Orchard Street and stopped in front of a tenement building. Along came an organ grinder to serenade them on the sidewalk. Papa proudly gave the man a penny and he played something unrecognizable but jolly. Down the block the boys caught a glimpse of an acrobat juggling balls. They wanted to run over but Papa gave them a stern look. He cleared his throat and announced that this building, 33 Orchard Street, was their new address. The family smiled and neighbours sitting on the stoop gossiping cried out, "*Mazel Tov*!" They all braced for the climb up four flights.

"Look," Papa said, "Indoor plumbing." He pointed to little closets on each floor. The hallways were dark and sombre. Babies were crying, people were arguing, children were shouting down to a dreary little courtyard where more children played games dressed in raggedy clothes.

"Here we are," Papa said as he opened a door with a key. In the shtetl there were no door keys. Before them was their new home in their new country. Everyone stepped in slowly. The first room was the kitchen, but it was really an all-purpose room. Mama sat down at the wooden table to catch her breath. Right away Papa said, "Come, here, look. There are more rooms." Only the first and last had windows bringing in natural light. All the rooms were grey, with paint peeling off the walls and embossed tin ceilings that echoed the footsteps of the upstairs neighbours.

"Yes," Mama said to Papa. "I see." She made her way back to the kitchen.

Papa went on showing her all the modern conveniences. An icebox for keeping things cold. "You buy a new block each day from the iceman," he said. He pointed to the gigantic coal stove that was bigger and better than their old wood stove. "No wood chopping," he said with triumph in his voice.

"Yes," Mama replied. Tears were cresting her eyes, falling down her cheeks.

Avrom went over to her. "Mama," he said. "What hurts?"

Papa could not stop. "Look Mama," he said with true amazement in his voice as he walked over to a sink at the back of the kitchen. He turned the spigot and out came water. "No hauling, no rain barrels. A twist of your hand."

"I see, I see," she said as she dried her tears with the handkerchief Papa shyly offered. Another burst of tears came over her.

Ethel stepped forward. "Some tea, Mama? You'll eat something and rest. Your energy will come back." She turned to Papa and related how difficult these last few weeks had been for all of them. "Samuel, quick, go down and buy some cooked potatoes from the carts. Better if you can find some honey cake."

Samuel knew exactly what to do. He flew down the stairs and headed into the hordes of vendors. The human sea parted miraculously to make way for this giant of a man. When he returned a short time later he had cake, potatoes, corn on the cob, seltzer, and a pint of cherry brandy.

Ethel had made tea. She cut the food into portions for everyone to eat. She added brandy to Mama's tea and to Aunt Miriam's, then poured a glass for Papa and one for Samuel. They raised their glass or cup and shouted, "*L'chaim.* To Life!" This was their first day as a family after three long years of separation. Papa cried quietly as he kissed the top of Mama's head.

Ethel, Anna, and Aunt Miriam bustled about setting up benches with linens for sleeping on. They put Samuel and the boys into one room, the girls and Aunt Miriam in another, leaving a room for Papa and Mama with the feather bed. Everyone was grateful the day was over and they retired for the evening.

Mama slipped into bed while Papa undressed. They lay side by side for a while. After a few minutes Papa asked, "Can you sleep?"

"No," answered Mama. "Too tired."

Papa laughed. "Me, too."

"I can't believe we're here. We made it through every year, every obstacle."

They were quiet for another few minutes.

"It's like our wedding night—again," Papa said, laughing.

"Oh, you," Mama replied. "Go to sleep."

"You'll get used to America," he said.

Mama started to cry. "It's not that."

"What is it, little one?" He leaned over and put one arm under her head.

"Bubbe and Zaide. There is no one to visit them and leave a little rock on their headstone to show they are not forgotten."

"You'll light a *Yahrzeit* candle each year."

"Not the same," Mama replied.

"I know. I know." Papa gathered Mama up in his arms. "We won't forget them. In God's eyes they are not lost. We will carry them in our hearts for the remaining days of our lives."

"Yes," Mama murmured.

They fell asleep holding each other, and drifted into wordless dreams of their America. A new world would begin tomorrow.

# Chapter 6
# New Beginnings

Two weeks after their arrival in New York, Ethel found she could not bear the stifling heat and overcrowded tenement streets teeming with immigrants from around the world and lined with pushcarts. People were constantly hawking their wares; the tenement stoops were overrun with screaming children, the sidewalks bustling with men and women trying to make their way to and fro. The streets, heated up with the summer weather, did not cool off even in the evenings. The dumbbell apartments had few windows, so at night many people brought their pillows and bedding out on the fire escapes to sleep.

The air was never fresh as it had been in their village in Russia. Nothing grew nearby, no trees, no plants, no bushes. There was no soil. To breathe the air on that poor immigrant's "balcony" was like breathing recirculated air expelled from the lungs of 200,000 bodies sequestered in a 20-block radius. There was only one saving grace: a clear blue morning sky, cut in small strips above the streets and the tiny alleyways. And, at night, the sparkling crystal of the stars was almost visible.

The family's apartment felt cramped. Their little *isbah* in the *shtetl* had been small, too, but there they always had fresh air. Too much of it in the winter. Here the apartment air was almost as stale and odorous as the street air and the apartment was almost as noisy and chaotic as the street. The little boys were always underfoot; Avrom cried and Chaim sulked. Anna, too, was cranky. Mama seemed harried and confused, as she never had in the village where everything was familiar. She snapped at the boys; she snapped at Anna; sometimes she even snapped at Ethel.

Ethel could stay busy helping Mama, but she decided to look for a job. She needed to get out of the apartment sometimes. And some extra money would be helpful. And, she felt, with a twinge of sadness and a dollop of guilt but also a surge of resolve, that it was time to embrace this America. Time to set the past aside. Jacob was a hole in her heart that would never heal, but the way to honour him was to make the most of the freedom he would have wanted for her. This was a new land, and she swore to become a new person. A person with a future, not just a past.

When she shopped for Mama, who hadn't caught on to American currency, Ethel made discreet employment inquiries in the shops along Orchard Avenue and among the stalls and pushcarts that lined the avenue. But before she found a job, she found something else.

One morning a resonant voice called out to her, "My little mermaid!" She turned to see Philip Smolens, the young man from the ship, the young man who had rescued Aunt Miriam and watched over Avrom and Chaim on the train at the German border. Ethel's heart leapt.

"Philip!"

"Call me Phil. We're in America now." He strode toward her. "I told you we'd be neighbours! Right here on Orchard Avenue."

"You're staying with your—um—brother, was it?" Ethel hated how hesitant her voice sounded.

"My brother, yes." He gave her the building number. It really was only a couple of blocks from her family's apartment.

"And you're—um—driving a wagon, making deliveries?"

"You have a wonderful memory." He laughed gaily. "I'm flattered. But the wagon job turned into something else. I'm still making deliveries, but now I'm—" he paused dramatically and spread his arms wide—"driving a TRUCK."

"Just think," he continued, "A month ago I'd never even seen a truck, and now I'm driving one. Isn't this America something?"

Ethel noticed, and liked, that Phil looked American. No *yarmulke*—or skullcap; no *peyos*—the long sidelocks of hair that hang in front of—or behind—the ears of Orthodox men. Did he have them on the ship? She couldn't remember. But it didn't matter. What mattered was now, and now he could be any young American man trying to impress a young lady on a busy sidewalk.

"So, you drive—what? All over New York?"

"Oh, much further. Boston, Providence, Buffalo. I'm gone for a week at a time. Next month they're going to start me on a Chicago route. Two weeks."

Ethel had never heard of Buffalo, and driving a truck to Providence sounded vaguely sacrilegious. But this was America; sacrilege didn't matter so much here.

"Can I see you? This evening?" Phil almost begged. "I have a few days off between routes. Could we—take a walk or something?"

"Yes, I'd like that."

When Phil called at the apartment that evening, the little boys were thrilled. Avrom hugged his leg and Chaim shook his hand American style. Aunt Miriam almost cried. Mama explained to Papa what Phil had done for them on the train, and Papa greeted him effusively. Samuel turned out to know Phil's brother. The little apartment played host to a love-fest.

Ethel rushed Phil out the door. She was glad to see him and wondered what this might lead to, but she didn't want pressure from her family. She wanted to do this at her own speed. Phil might be a good man, but he wasn't Jacob.

Ethel's speed, however, turned out to match her family's. Phil might not be Jacob, but he was a good man. Ethel had too much to forget, and she wanted her new life to start immediately.

That first night, Phil spoke of his dreams. A big family. A better life than anything Russia could offer. He didn't speak of God. He didn't speak of the past, except as a foil for the bright future. Ethel approved. She even caught a bit of his exuberance, if only a pale shadow. Could she too make a new life in this land? A new life without the constant ache in her heart? Could Phil, such a fountain of optimism, help her do this?

On their second evening stroll, Ethel experienced some hesitation about a relationship with Phil. All she could think of was Jacob. The memory made her cry. She tried to hide the tears from Phil, but he saw them and misinterpreted them. He apologized and said he didn't mean to rush her. So she tried to reassure him. They ended up in each other's arms. Ethel hadn't exactly intended this, but she found it eased the pain of missing Jacob.

On the third night, Phil asked her to marry him. He wanted to marry the American way—no marriage contract, no family, jut a city hall license. This informality suited Ethel. She folded herself into Phil's embrace. Since his embrace eased her pain, maybe this marriage would ease the pain as well. She nodded and cried. He mistook her tears for tears of joy.

But even as she stepped haltingly toward a future, Ethel realized she would not slip so easily into a new life. It was Jacob's heart that beat for her in Phil's broad and powerful chest. It was Jacob, not Phil, she embraced. She finally realized that night how thoroughly she was possessed by Jacob's love. It was a love that did not seem to die, but like a fire from the burnt shards of her heart, sprang up anew whenever she turned toward happiness.

It was that night, too, that Ethel's taste for liquor began. Phil had a silver brandy flask in his pocket and he encouraged her to drink from it. As the brandy's warmth flowed through her body, sweet memories of Jacob's love flooded her heart. She drank, then and for the rest of her life, to savour that unearthly sweetness. But, like many another drinker through the ages, she found she could not hold onto the feeling she craved. As the sweet memories evaporated, she would flare in anger.

Although she cherished the memory of Jacob's love, she also began to resent its claim on her. She wanted to be free—not free of Jacob himself, but free of the duel between her past and her present. Jacob might live in her heart forever—she prayed so—but she would shake a drunken fist, that first night and ever after, at the God who created such a pure and undying love and then prevented its fulfilment.

The next morning Ethel woke with a renewed resolve to plant roots firmly in this new soil. She was determined to water and feed her new existence with every ounce of her strength and will. Thankfully, she had been sent a distraction: a husband-to-be. Phil wasted no time in whisking her off to City Hall. Within a week they were married. Mama and Papa were thrilled, mostly. They liked Phil well enough, and they were glad to see Ethel's fate settled. They were a little disconcerted to miss the traditional wedding celebration and to know nothing of their in-laws. Still, as Papa said, "This is America. Things are different now."

Together, the family decided that since Phil was away on his truck route for a week or two at a time, the newlyweds would live at Mama and Papa's apartment for the time being. They saw no good reason why Ethel should be left on her own for such long periods. Life went on as before. Ethel continued to help Mama in the apartment, and she continued to look for employment. This eased Ethel into her marriage without much disruption from her former life, and without much guilt regarding her parents.

But perhaps it eased her into her marriage *too* easily? She hadn't really gotten to know Phil. On the rare occasions when he was home, he seemed like an awkward guest rather than a family member. When he related an adventure from his travels, Mama and Papa looked blank—they could no more imagine Buffalo than Timbuktu—and Ethel's laughter sounded forced. Soon enough Phil stopped relating his adventures. While Ethel bantered comfortably with Mama and her little brothers, and even with Papa, she trod on eggshells with Phil. And Phil said less and less.

Phil's silence affected their intimacy as well. Endearments turned to grunts, and embraces turned from tender to mechanical.

Ethel wondered how Phil would relate to her if he came home to her only, rather than to a clan of in-laws. Would he be his old ebullient self? Or would he be even more sullen with no observers to modulate his behaviour? But then, she thought, W*hy should he see my family as a burden? Even if he'd rather avoid them, what kind of a weakling can't roll with a few punches?* She had certainly rolled with worse punches than that.

Ethel realized, with sadness and guilt, that Phil was relieved when he could get away on a trucking run. She also realized, with sadness and guilt, that she was relieved as well.

But she had a new life to embrace, a new Ethel to forge in this miracle of a new land. If her love for Jacob couldn't stop her, whatever she might feel for Phil certainly wasn't going to stop her either. During Phil's absences she redoubled her search for work, and she soon found a job in a clothing store on Orchard Street, a few blocks from home. She took to sales work readily.

One day, the owner's wife, Bella, pulled Ethel aside and told her to try on one of the store's shirtwaist dresses.

"Why?" asked Ethel, surprised.

"Because you have a good figure and the customers will admire the dress on you," Bella said matter-of-factly.

Ethel obliged her.

"Stand in the doorway," Bella urged the girl.

At first, Ethel felt self-conscious, but she soon forgot herself as she enjoyed the fresh air and a view of the pushcarts and crowded sidewalks. Her first customers, a mother and daughter, came right up to her and asked where she bought the dress she was wearing. Ethel studied the women's hair and dye colour before she selected dresses to show them, and she chose dresses that complemented their colouring. Mother and daughter both cried out in delight at how the garments flattered them. Ethel sold a dress to each of them and Bella was ecstatic.

From that day on, Ethel arranged to work on commission instead of a straight salary. She knew she was taking a chance, but it offered the possibility of a much larger paycheck, unlimited by the number of hours she worked.

As time passed, Ethel saw she had a knack for selling just about anything. She always made sure to match the dress colours to the customer's colouring, as well as to the woman's particular type of figure. Bright colours for well-proportioned girls, more understated ones for those with lumpy figures. She knew, too, how to coax the shy ones and build their confidence, how to flatter the secure or vain into displaying themselves even more, like strutting peacocks showing their tail feathers. The women overspent, but went away happy and satisfied just the same.

With her extra commission money, Ethel bought small presents for Mama, who told her to put it aside for savings. But Ethel had watched her mother do without nice things over the years, so she couldn't resist surprising Mama with something special every week or so.

"You'll be needing that money for a family, maybe," said Mama with hope in her voice. To everyone's pleasant surprise, once this was said out loud it promptly came to pass—Ethel was pregnant a month and a half after her nuptials. Her pregnancy barely showed, so over the next four months Ethel kept working. During that time, she put her money aside for the coming baby, buying all the little things that would be needed.

Phil was more than pleased. He wanted a big family and the sooner it happened the better. He took on more work, driving longer trips. Ethel didn't mind much. She was in a pleasant, dreamy state of mind, showing the glow that is often seen in pregnancy. She was carrying so big and low by the seventh month that Mama expected a boy for sure. Phil anticipated a son.

But the biggest surprise happened when the delivery was premature: the baby arrived at the end of the seventh month. Phil was away on one of his ten-day trips and Mama thought it just as well. Men, according to Mama, were helpless when it came to childbirth. They didn't know what to do with themselves. They got underfoot. They were no good in a crisis. You ended up babying them. As it would turn out, the birth was an ordeal and Mama was glad she and the midwife were left alone to do the necessary work and handle the emergency.

# Chapter 7
# A Precarious Birth

"The baby's just in a hurry to become an American," Mama said laughing when Ethel's water broke that morning. Ethel was not prepared for the sharp pains, although the doctor at the Henry Street Settlement had scared her, saying she'd never be able to carry the baby to term. If that miraculously happened, he had pronounced in a rising voice for emphasis, "You'll never be able to deliver it alive." Her pelvis was too narrow, he'd said.

*Well*, thought Ethel, *he'd been wrong about carrying the baby*, although she wondered if carrying it only to the seventh month showed that he had a point.

Mama said many women had borne perfectly healthy babies even in seven months. Hadn't she done it twice? She didn't mention that those children had eventually succumbed to typhus one winter. Ethel could not help thinking perhaps their constitutions were weak because of the early births.

Still, this birth was happening this morning. The baby was insistent upon coming into the world. Ethel felt she had a fighting chance, a good chance, so long as that doctor wasn't consulted. Mama agreed; she sent for a local midwife who had a reputation for delivering miracle babies.

Henriette, a stocky German Jew, arrived with not only her bag of herbs, but also a small doctor's kit of instruments. "I never use," she told Mama, "unless baby or mother at risk. Only v'onetime," she added, but did not elaborate.

"Thirty-year experience," she assured Ethel and Mama. "And tricks from the Old Country. Success ninety-nine time out of v'one hundred." She practiced strict hygiene for herself, the mother, and anyone else attending.

As the morning drew on, Henriette made Ethel as comfortable as possible, put down clean linens, and took out an hourglass that she set upon the table next to the bed.

"When you count 20 pains the hour, send note, I vill come immediate." Then she left, leaving the address of another mother whose time was near.

The day wore on slowly. Ethel's first hour passed with only five pains, but they were sharp and hard along her lower back. Mama helped her to sit halfway up with the aid of pillows, but the intensity of the pains continued. Mama made Ethel cups of raspberry tea in hopes of easing the muscle spasms in her back.

Nothing seemed to help. After several hours, her pains were coming ten to the hour, but still in the small of her back, not in her belly. Mama foresaw a long night ahead and prayed the midwife would not go to sleep, exhausted from her multiple rounds of patients.

Mama sat in the chair next to the bed and dozed off and on for several more hours, massaging her daughter's back and belly between catnaps. Now it was after one o'clock and the pains were coming every few minutes, still focused in the back. Mama quickly sent for Henriette and succumbed to her fear that something was not right.

True to her word, the midwife took only fifteen minutes to appear. She washed her hands well and Mama boiled water for hot compresses. Henriette began to examine her patient. Ethel's cervix was dilated and the midwife was able to insert four fingers into the opening. However, she could not find the baby's head, which should have presented itself.

"Vere ist the pain?" Henriette asked, in a severe tone of voice.

"My back," Ethel replied, fearing something was wrong.

"You should have sent note many hours before," replied Henriette. She began palpating Ethel's belly. She could feel the bulge of the baby's head and feet, not in the inverse position, but horizontally across the abdomen. The midwife hurriedly inserted her hand as far as she could. She tried to grasp the baby and manoeuvre it into the correct position while using her other hand on Ethel's belly to help move it externally.

Ethel groaned with pain and nearly stopped breathing.

"Continue breath," Henriette ordered. "Short inhale, long exhale. Push!" No matter what the midwife tried, she could only reach the baby with her fingertips and these quickly slipped away from their goal. She stopped her efforts and opened her bag, explaining she would have to use an instrument. "Baby out ov reach."

At this pronouncement, Mama suddenly cried out, "No!" She had heard bad stories about these kinds of births, which could damage the baby's head, producing an imbecile, or could cripple the child's feet. "I will not let you," Mama shouted loudly at the midwife, startling her and Ethel.

"Danger to vait," Henriette warned. "Coot be tear or cord around throat."

"Turn Ethel over and onto her knees," Mama said in a commanding tone.

"If you t'ink you do better, go ahead," Henriette snapped back. She stood stiffly with her arms crossed over her chest.

"Please," Mama said in a conciliatory tone, trying to get the midwife to help her daughter into this strange position. "I saw it done in the *shtetl*. If it doesn't work, use your instruments."

While Ethel positioned herself on her hands and knees, Henriette instructed Mama to massage her daughter's abdomen, pushing downward in long strokes where she felt the bulge of the baby's head. Meanwhile, the midwife inserted her hand into the birth canal, trying to reach the head internally. After a few minutes of struggling, Henriette said, "Cannot vait longer." She began to wash her instrument in the pot of hot water beside the bed.

"Ohhh," Ethel suddenly cried out. "He's moved." She could feel the downward pressure at the opening of her womb. "I think he's…ready now," she cried out from pain and happiness.

"*Mazel tov!*" said Mama. "What does he call it, that Mr. Einstein, gravity? Gravity!"

Henriette was sceptical. She slipped her hand halfway in and could feel the baby had repositioned itself and the head was pressing down through the birth canal.

Ethel was guided to sit back against the pillows.

"Push! Breath, breath," the midwife instructed with annoyed expression on her face. "Greenhorn vrom the Russian *shtetl*," she slurred under her breath.

With widening eyes Ethel gasped and then froze at the sight of the baby's head, richly adorned with rose-coloured hair, poking out from between her bent knees.

"Oh, oh, ohhhh—" came the cry from Ethel's throat. She was astonished, and at the same time focused on the pain between her legs. How could such a large head get through the small doorway of her body? She felt she would break in two from so much pressure. Then a shoulder came through. It was streaked with blood and a glistening web of fluid. Ethel wanted nothing more than to be relieved of the searing pain that had taken control of her body. With the baby halted half in and half out of her body, she tried to focus on the sense of amazement. How had she created a living thing, another human from *his* seed? What was this power of the female body in partnership with a man? How did a moment of pleasure burgeon into this: a creature so helpless and small, in need of love and protection, but one day to take its rightful place as another human being on this turning globe.

"Rest," commanded Henriette, puncturing Ethel's delirious musings.

"What? What is the matter?" came Mama's instinctive response. She dropped her daughter's hand, leaving her side, and went to see what was happening at the foot of the bed. Too quickly, she saw it: a slow but steady trickle of blood. The baby, only half born, was large for seven months.

"Here," the midwife said to Mama, handing her a clean piece of cloth, "Hold against it. I vill take care in v'one moment," she said pointing to the problem.

The determination in Henriette's voice hastened Mama to take her position, halting the flow of crimson drops.

"What's wrong?" cried Ethel, looking at Mama.

"Shh, shh," Mama said, in a soothing voice. "Just a little bleeding, nothing so unusual. Listen to what Henriette tells you."

"Folloh v'hat I say—inhale, v'one, two, t'ree. Big belly, like balloon. Exhale, push downward like relieve bowel. A little dance, a waltz—v'one, two, t'ree, in; v'one, two t'ree, out. Goot, goot."

As the baby began descending, the bleeding increased. Henriette seized the moment to pull the other shoulder through and in an instant the rest of the body followed.

"A girl," cried Mama, "it's a girl! Who knew! So big you would think it must be a boy."

Quickly, Henriette took the child and began rubbing her between the folds of clean linen. Then came the cry, loud and long, announcing itself. "I am, I am," the baby was saying. "You cannot stop me. I welcome myself into the world."

Both Mama and Henriette looked towards Ethel as her face blanched white and she went unconscious.

"Etalah! Etalah!" Mama cried.

"Vainted," came the midwife's reply. "Look in bag, smelling salt. Take brandy. Rub lip."

While Mama struggled to bring Ethel back, Henriette laid the baby down on the bed and went to see how badly torn the young girl was. The blood oozed out of her in a slow line of drops, not so fast as when the baby was pushing through.

Henriette thought she must hurry and put in a stitch or call a doctor within the next few minutes to stop more blood from being lost. She scrubbed the blood away with alcohol whose smarting pain caused Ethel to jump and open her eyes.

"Goot," Henriette said. The midwife opened her bag to bring out a needle that looked suspiciously like a fishhook and thread like fish line.

"No, Mama, no," Ethel cried out at the sight of it.

"Stay still," came the midwife's sharp voice. After a moment of inspection, though, the blood slowed of its own accord. The tear appeared to be superficial and not the feared emergency.

"It's okay, Etalah," Mama said, as she watched the blood dry, "miracle of miracles you are still in one piece. The bleeding has stopped."

At this encouraging pronouncement, Ethel released the pillow she had been clenching and, for the first time, focused on her baby girl. "Oh, my little one," Ethel said, reaching out her hands for her infant. "How you scared us. You are a fighter," she said with pride as the baby settled into her arms. *And so much beautiful red hair like his, she said to herself as she stroked it.* "Look at the heartbeat at the top of your head," she cooed with wonder.

"That is fontanel," Henriette said, and admonished Ethel. "Cranial bones not grown yet. Do not touch."

"No, of course not," Ethel, a bit cowed, replied to the bossy midwife. She felt like kissing every part of her beautiful baby—her eyes, her nose, her lips, her forehead, each finger of each hand, the chubby little thighs and dimpled knees, and every perfect toe.

"Give baby to mother. She'll vash her *mit* varm vater," Henriette said, looking at Mama and nodding. "Ethel, I vill show you how to breastfeed."

"No need," Mama said, "I bore twelve children and I never had any problem feeding them. Etalah will be the same."

"Instruction *ist goot*," Henriette said, implacable.

So, Ethel listened attentively to the midwife's directions to massage the breast and squeeze the nipple to get things started, to alternate breasts, and to give the baby time to explore the bosom when not feeding. If she was getting sore to let the baby suck on Ethel's pinkie for a while. Sometimes that was enough to satisfy the infant. And, if all attempts failed to get the child started, to put some honey on the baby's lips and some on the nipple. That usually did the trick. (Later, Mama told Ethel cherry brandy on the lips and on the nipple never failed).

When Phil returned from his truck route to Boston a few days later, he looked down at the little girl with distant eyes. He had wanted a boy and everyone had assured him that the way Ethel was carrying promised one. He seemed disappointed and cold to his baby girl. Despite this, Ethel was wholly taken up with her new motherhood, fussing over the baby every moment as well as resting and healing. Phil acted as if he was being neglected. When his time off between trips was over, he seemed relieved to get back on his route. He would be gone for two weeks to Chicago.

*Gött in Himmel*, Ethel thought after Phil left. *God in Heaven!* What she had suspected had come to pass. A piece of Russia had made it to the new world. What she thought was irrevocably lost had been resting in her womb, waiting to emerge.

Jacob would always be with her.

\* \* \*

# Part 2
# America Lillian

In America, Grandma Ethel wears
her wild, gold hair free
cropped short at the chin.
Her gold braid, an heirloom like a jewel,
lies abandoned in the bureau drawer.
She clipped it from her neck after she left Minsk.
Now it is nearly forgotten. She calls it her "rat,"
confusing the children of the house
who try to make it come alive
with wooden hangers and innocent cries.
In America, Grandma puts old sorrows away
in drawers of ancient forest wood
that gleam and whisper in the night
like wind through leafless branches singing
of old loves, a dark river, and the southern steppe.

In America, new generations sleep
beneath dry, unslanted roofs,
dreamless under their clean sheets.
Their hands and minds exhausted from the day's work,
almost a peasant's life of toil—
making, selling, haggling, surviving—
though now the days revolve around success, not Shabbos.

\* \* \*

# Chapter 1
# The Bakery

A memory. It is Friday morning. I am Lillian, and I am five. I'm going with my daddy for cookies and *challah*, the special braided bread for *Shabbas*.

When we enter the bakery, my daddy comes to life and lifts me up to take the ticket out of the metal mouth of the ticket machine. He lets me pick out cookies. He lets me sniff the fresh-baked bread, which makes me feel warm and snuggly. He buys me a Charlotte Russe and then laughs at the face I make when I taste the cherry. He grabs the stem of the cherry, pops it into his mouth, and twirls it like a cartoon villain twirling a moustache.

Loaves of *challah* cover the end of the wooden counter. They are braided like Grandma Ethel's hairpiece. She says it was her braid when she was a girl. She calls it her "rat," and keeps it in a dresser drawer. Miriam and Samuel, my big sister and brother, sometimes dare me to poke the "rat" with a hanger as they pull open the drawer and run laughing and screaming from the room.

No way is the *challah* like an old rat, though. It's beautiful and it has meaning. Its braids remind me of my family, each of us separate in a way, yet all tangled together and always next to each other, no matter what. I want to hold the loaves to my face and breathe in their sweet smell, the way I breathe in my mother's smell when we gather on Friday nights.

And there's even more to the *challah*. In Sunday school I've learned that *challah* has been part of the story my people for thousands of years. When we eat *challah* today, we feel part of our people as they loved and struggled and suffered through all that history. I see my own family's small braid as one strand of a bigger braid, entwined with the twelve tribes of Israel and all the Jews who came after them.

Our trips to the bakery change as I get older. The cookies all start to look the same. The Charlotte Russe tastes too sweet. And my father seems to be farther and farther away from me, hiding in his own quiet dark space. His face no longer lights up when we walk into the shop, and now that I am seven, I'm too big for him to pick up. Absentmindedly, he draws a ticket from the machine himself and stands quietly until our turn comes. He does not ask me to pick out the cookies we will buy and does not offer me a treat to eat. He just gives his order to the woman behind the counter. His face seems blank.

*Why is he so sad when he is with me?* I wonder. I no longer seem able to make him smile. His sadness makes me feel helpless, turning the pit of my stomach into a painful knot. The pain has grown familiar to me. It is the same pain I feel when my mother screams at my father, who recedes more and more into silence. *Somehow, I must be able to make him happy again*, I think. Yet I cannot.

When I am nine, I have an idea on the way back from the bakery that I think might make my father happy. I'm looking out of the front seat passenger window, hypnotized by the sight of telephone poles marching past the window frame, marking a beat like a metronome. Suddenly, I think, *Time occurs when you have a succession of individual moments.*

I turn to my father to tell him what I realized. I feel proud to have figured out something he might respect. Excited, I take my finger and draw straight lines like telephone poles on the car seat between us. I say something about time being a bunch of marked off moments, one after another. That you need these individual moments to have what everyone calls "time," like the second hand on the clock passing over the individual dots of seconds. *Did I explain it right?* I wonder. I don't know, but I think so. Or at least, my father will help me make it right.

When my father turns his head to look at me, I see that his eyebrows are pinched together at the bridge of his nose as if he smells something he doesn't like.

"What's that supposed to mean?" He says, not a question but a challenge.

My brain freezes behind a wall of sadness. My discovery is a monster. The air goes out of my lungs as if I've been punched in the chest.

A moment later I try again, but my words turn to clay in my mouth. With effort, I draw the telephone poles again with my finger on the car seat that separates us. And, in a false note of triumph, I say, "See, that's how you get time."

He turns to me, his eyebrows still pinched together, and in a mocking tone says, "Sure it is."

I sink down, down, down, like a falling elevator. I have been standing on a heap of garbage. A little kid, with big, stupid ideas. I suddenly feel ashamed, but I refuse to cry. Later I think, *it was a good idea.* I did not deserve his scorn. Coals of anger solder beneath my sadness.

It is the last trip to the bakery I remember taking with my father.

# Chapter 2
# Playing

It is a dreary winter day and I am six—almost seven. I am playing in my pink bedroom. It is joined to my parents' room by a connecting bathroom. I am playing with my Barbie doll. She is everything I am not. She has blond hair and blue eyes. She has a perfect body—with breasts. She also has lots of clothes that I and other girls across America collect. A new adventure blossoms with each new outfit.

It is Christmastime, so I imagine Barbie going to New York City in her fur-trimmed blue suit and fur coat, to see the festive store windows. Although we are Jewish, my mother buys and decorates a tree each year and places gifts under it for Christmas morning. Often, she takes us to the city to see the holiday decorations. She says she doesn't see why we should miss out on all the fun. But we're not supposed to let on to our neighbours. Even the tree gets smuggled into the house after dark.

Next I change Barbie's outfit to a white sweater and short black velvet skating skirt. I put tiny white ice skates on her feet so we can go skating under the stars at Rockefeller Center. For dinner, I put her in a burgundy satin evening dress with long sleeves and we are off to the Rainbow Room. My father once took my mother to the Rainbow Room, but I don't know when that was. A long time ago, I think.

My daydream is broken when I hear my parents' bathroom door open and someone go in. It is my mother and she is crying. The sobs come in powerful bursts, then let up for a moment, then break out even stronger. The sound is like a jagged piece of metal scraping over the sidewalk, only I feel it inside my chest. My stomach falls like it does on an elevator. Alarms ring in my head. I don't know how to stop the crying. I don't know how to stop the pain in my chest. I sit on the floor and listen, my Barbie forgotten.

The loud sobs go on for a few more minutes, then finally subside. I hear my mother return to her bedroom and climb onto her bed. She blows her nose and cries again, this time more softly. I feel I must save her from this sadness. I must lift her out of the deep hole where she has fallen.

I search my room for something to bring back her happiness. I open a dresser drawer that has several sparkly tiaras. I can't remember how I got them. Probably they are hand-me-downs from Miriam. I doubt my mother would want to wear a tiara. They are for kids.

I open the sliding door of my closet and search along the back wall where I find my box of favourite things. I am hoping for some magic charm from a fairy tale that is strong enough to stop the Evil Queen and rescue the good girl and make everything turn out right. One at a time, I pull things out of the box. I find a dusty, crumbling butterfly wing. That won't do. A glittery giant coat button like a big jewel. No, not good. Then, I find it—a huge shiny pin in the shape of a four-leaf clover. I hope this will change everything and bring my mother good luck. I wrap the pin in coloured tissues tied with a pink ribbon.

Now comes the hard part. I have to cross the sea of green bathroom tiles and enter the dark room on the other side of the door where my mother lies crying. There is a push-pull inside my chest. I can't breathe. It's the way I feel in the pool when someone pushes my head under. I'm afraid I'm going to sink, hand-in-hand with my mother, into some place with no bottom and no air.

Finally, I push myself through the bathroom and knock on the door. I hear my mother blow her nose. She calls out in a low voice, "Yes, sweetheart, what is it?" I half open the door and stand there, waiting. My mother sits up and swings her legs over the side of her bed. "Yes Lillian, what is it?" She asks. She sounds far away. She blows her nose again.

"Here," I say, as I walk over to her side of the bed and extend my hand.

"What's this?" She asks. She picks up the tissue-wrapped present as if it has fallen from the sky.

"For you," I say, not sure if I'm doing the right thing. I do not want to upset her.

"Oh," says my mother, beginning to understand. "Let's see what's inside." She unwraps the tissue and looks quizzically at the clover pin that shines softly in the darkness of the room.

Seeing my mother doesn't recognize the significance of the shape, I say, "For good luck." A mix of shame and sadness seems to flutter across her face.

"It will bring good things," I say, trying to reassure her.

"Yes, uh huh, pumpkin," she replies and smiles dimly. "Thank you, sweetheart. How about we watch a movie?" She flicks on the TV and lies back down on the bed.

I climb in to keep her company although my stomach is still tied in a knot. But soon we are in another world, a '40s Hollywood melodrama with steely-eyed Barbara Stanwyck or relentless Joan Crawford, struggling to make their lives work despite the odds.

My mother spends many other days in the bathroom crying. When she does this, my father is downstairs in the living room listening to music on his hi-fi, or reading with a book in his lap. Does he know? Does he hear? I'm not sure. Sometimes my mother yells at him and slams doors. Other times she screams she will never come back and runs out of the house and drives away. All the while my father sits in his living room chair, quietly reading. He answers my questions without looking up and says my mother will be back soon enough, in an hour or two, or maybe three.

I am not sure she will come back. I stand guard at the window in the front hall, letting the music from the hi-fi flow over me, making the wait bearable. I am sure if I do not stand watching the street my mother will never return. I hear the echo of her words, "You won't see me again. I will stay away forever." A dark pit opens up in my chest as I try to imagine life without her.

As I grow up, I see that she also screams at Miriam and Samuel and Grandma Ethel. Not to mention department store clerks, waitresses, and supermarkets cashiers. I'm never sure when she will start fighting or what will set her off. So I am anxious and watchful when we go out.

Despite the danger to store clerks, the most hurtful fights stay within the family. More and more my mother confides in me, explaining how everything will improve when my father or Samuel or Miriam or Grandma Ethel comes around and behaves properly.

After some fights, she takes me with her. We go on long shopping trips, all the way up Central Avenue to White Plains to look for bargains at Alexander's. Sometimes we go to the neighbouring Saks and get gloves for Grandma, or a scarf for Miriam, a wallet for my father, or a shirt for Samuel, and have them wrapped in boxes with ribbons. Afterwards we catch an early supper at a local diner. My mother says the others at home can take care of themselves.

When she has a really bad fight with my father—who hardly raises his voice, which makes her fight even harder—she takes me with her to see the stately homes in nearby Connecticut. Connecticut is the Promised Land. One day we will all live in Connecticut, in a white house with green shutters or one made of stone with statues and pillars. All the houses have expansive, shade-dappled lawns. Driveways are lined with towering oaks or sycamores. Flower gardens peek out from the back or sides of the houses. Seeing these estates seems to soothe my mother. She starts to talk about how good everything will be in a few years. Will everything be better? I don't know what to believe anymore. I just try to enjoy the scenery.

Then, when I am twelve, something happens. It is one of those afternoons when no one else is around. My mother is taking a nap, but I hear her crying on and off.

As I come into the room I see she looks especially sad, sitting on the edge of the bed. I ask, "What's wrong?"

"Nothing, sweetheart," she replies and tries to smile.

"What's wrong?" I ask again, almost begging for an answer.

My mother glances away from me for a second. Then she says, "I guess you're old enough to know this." She lowers her voice and says, "Your father, he's been fooling around."

I am so stunned by what she says I'm not sure I've heard her right. "Fooling around?" I say in confusion.

"He's seeing another woman," she replies.

My mother has finally given me a real answer, but all I want to do now is stuff the words back into a dark hole. Instead, I ask in a doubting, almost angry voice, "How do you know?"

"Because," she replies, lowering her voice again and glancing down as she speaks, "he hasn't touched me in months."

I feel like I am going to be ill. I know what sex is. It is all mixed up with forbiddingness and shame and embarrassment. My stomach turns and nausea rises up to my throat. I swallow hard and my mouth tastes bitter. I say nothing. I have no words, no reply, no way to defend myself from this revelation. I can't do or say anything to make this right. I can't help her. I can't help myself.

# Chapter 3
# Writing

After my mother's revelation about my father's infidelity, when I am twelve, my relationship with my father changes.

My father had always been the one to champion my talents. (In some ways I am his child and Miriam is my mother's.) My father and I had many activities we did together. Early on we invented a game called twiddle-the-dial. He twiddled the knob of his hi-fi receiver and stopped at different stations playing different musical styles: Mozart or Bach, Elvis or The Stones, maybe a girl group like the Shangri-La's. Then, I would dance in a way that matched the music: arabesques or leaps to go with classical tunes, Charleston or boogie-woogie to period music, and expressive movements to go with free-style jazz.

Music has always been a way to dance out my feelings. I translate music and emotions into movement and am transported to a place inside myself where I feel whole and happy and oblivious. Nothing can compare to the joy of putting physical expression to a kaleidoscope of musical sounds. It is like painting the air with the colours of the notes, creating shapes and motions that are incandescent flames or moving sculptures. I am good at it. I know this because my father would ask me with the wide eyes of surprise how I learned to dance all those different styles. He was wowed by the fact that I pick up steps by seeing them on TV or in the movies.

When I was seven, my parents had a fight over the dancing. My father said I was talented and should be given lessons. My mother fired back, "and what about your other daughter, she's talented, too." I was in the corner of the living room, behind a couch, listening and wanting to disappear. I felt like the cause of the discord between them. Worse, somehow, I was causing pain for the sister I loved. The fight ended in a stalemate and a cold silence sprang up around the issue. Neither my sister nor I took lessons.

For the past few years, my father has been my writing and literature teacher. In fact, my mother instigates this. "You know how much he loves to read," she tells me. "He's just better at that stuff than I am."

Although he's only finished high school, my father loves words and is a voracious reader of the classics, and the not-so-classics, too. (Later in life he admits he has a taste for second-rate English novels with atmospheric weather.) When he is home, he's usually ensconced in his reading chair, reading with relish. Like a kid collecting bottle caps or baseball cards, he collects new words and proudly shares them with us. He pronounces them slowly, syllable by syllable, rolling the sounds around on his tongue while his eyebrows bob up and down with delight.

Sometimes, he even spins out a short story and reads it to the family. Once, he enrols in an adult education writing class at the New School in Manhattan. This doesn't last long. He quits after the instructor reprimands him for not doing the assignment.

When he reads over my compositions, my father talks to me about the mysterious placement of commas, which allow the reader and the work to pace themselves in rhythms of pauses and breaths. Writing is like a fine wine to be savoured and lingered over, to be tasted on the palate and lips, the words exploding full in the mouth, articulated for flavour and shades of meaning. The words are sounds that affect the body and mind, creating impact, eliciting moods and feelings. This is what literature does. It is not merely flat lines on a page. It entrances. Literature takes me on a journey of experiences far beyond my real life and world. It is a journey that takes me both into and out of myself.

Writing is my favourite activity. My best school marks come from my compositions. I fall into a deep place inside myself when I am writing. Despite my joy in dancing, I am changing. I am becoming a self-conscious, shy, bookish adolescent. I now disappear into the secret corner inside my mind where I can experience a new world without the screaming fights that roil my stomach and clench my chest.

With my mother's startling disclosure about my father—which I have no way to verify—I begin to feel as if I am the other woman, too. Like the one my mother says exists in the outer world. I fear that I steal my father's affection away from my mother and sister; that I am somehow wrong being who I am and doing what I do, hurting those I love. My father's attentions to me begin to feel intrusive, even sexual. When we interact, he shows a delight he does not have when he is with my mother.

Sometimes, after I am already in bed, he comes into my room to kiss me goodnight. I pretend I'm asleep as he coos in my ear, "Lillian, little Lillian, give me a kiss. Are you sleeping? No, you're not sleeping." But I am too old to be kissed goodnight, I think to myself. The sound of his voice makes my skin crawl. Makes me hold my breath for fear he'll touch me with his lips. I decide I will no longer play twiddle-the-dial for his amusement. I will tell him I am too old for such a stupid little game. That I am too mature to have him correct my English assignments. Next year I will be in junior high and will need to be responsible for my own work, without any help from him. Otherwise, it would be like cheating.

As I edge away from a joyful relationship with my father, he in turn seems both sad and angry with me. He starts to make fun of my body. One day he overhears my mother and me talking about "training" bras. All my friends are buying them.

"What do you need a bra for? To train what?" He says over Friday night chicken. (Thankfully, Miriam and Samuel are out.)

Instantly I close down and go silent, not saying what is on my tongue—*mind your own business, stop intruding on my privacy.*

"Now, now, hush up and leave the girl in peace," my mother admonishes.

But he continues to tease me, "Not flat as a board, but I'd say they're not even the size of walnuts," he laughs.

"Bennie!" my mother says, raising her voice. "Stop it!"

"Maybe the size of grapes or cherries," he continues.

My mother yells at the top of her voice, exasperated, "You're impossible! Shut up this instant!" She turns to me and says, "Did you ever hear such an idiot? He's impossible!" as if I were a disinterested party. Then, she continues in her high register, threatening and pleading all at the same time, "You're going to scar her for life. Let her be!"

Finally, I can't stand it anymore. I bolt from the kitchen and the ensuing commotion, run upstairs, and lock myself in the bathroom, crying.

*I will never speak to him again*, I swear to myself. I will ignore his presence from now on. I will hide my just-beginning-to-blossom body under oversize shirts and bulky mohair sweaters.

Perhaps my father's ribbing is like salt in a wound that started years before. I recall another time: I am six and we are taking a ride in the country. We stop at a pond in the woods off a dirt road. I have to go number one and my mother says to just slip off my dress, crouch down a little, and do my business there in the pond. My mother holds my dress and I do what she says.

My father, who has been taking 8-millimeter pictures of the scenery, turns the camera on me, naked, peeing in the pond. When I realize what he is doing I start to cry and try to hide myself as best I can, wrapping my arms in front of my chest and collapsing into the water. My mother screams at the top of her lungs, "Bennnie! What's the matter with you? Stop it! Now!"

My father says I've nothing to show, so what's the big deal? Then, he pans the camera over to my mother as she continues to scream and yell, her face contorted with anger.

She stays disgruntled for most of the day, ignoring my father. He laughs it off. He doesn't seem to understand what the big stink is all about. He thinks it's funny.

Perhaps worse than that incident, months later on home movie night the footage turns up on the screen, despite the promise my mother made to destroy it. I am witness to the horror, now immortalized on film. I have to watch the look of shame overtake me as I hurriedly try to squat in the water, and then I have to watch my mother on the warpath, yelling and gesticulating, nearly spitting with anger—which seems almost as embarrassing.

The darkened room explodes into laughter and someone whistles. I run out of the room, go upstairs, and lock myself in the bathroom. Tears of humiliation sting my cheeks. I cannot believe I have had to suffer the same insult again. I cannot believe these are my parents. Some part of my love for them breaks off like a splintering block of ice and is lost to me. I think to myself that they must be imposters. That I must not be their child. My real parents would never act like this.

A few minutes later I hear my mother on the other side of the bathroom door. She says, "Lillian, I will cut up the film. I will destroy it. You know your father is an idiot. You don't have to worry, sweetheart. I will take a scissor and cut it up."

But as far as I know, she does nothing that night. The family continues watching home movies while I retreat to my room. It doesn't matter anymore. I no longer trust what she says. Forever afterward, impromptu movie nights fill me with dread; my stomach buckles into a knot as I watch, afraid I will have to witness the same humiliating scene again. I feel powerless.

When I grow up, I will wonder why things had to be so difficult. I realize Ruthie and Bennie were more like children than adults: Ruthie having tantrums at home and in public; Bennie wilfully throwing his weight around to embarrass and thwart others. At almost every family occasion, fights erupt. For some reason my parents cannot take joy in a birthday or graduation or award ceremony without reliving some hidden patch of their own childhood disappointment or pain, which then erupts into discord. It makes me wonder about their parents.

Did Bennie and Ruthie ever feel loved and appreciated? Life back then was harder. My grandparents had to make a new life in a new land and were wholly taken up by surviving. My parents were children in the Great Depression and that must have been a deprivation, a childhood without the safety and protection of their innocence. A life of difficulty. A life of lack.

In later years I spend a lot of time in analysis trying to figure out the past. I lie on the couch, the doctor often silent as I tell my embarrassing stories. The doctor is a sympathetic listener, but the therapy is really nothing but expensive moral support. Over and over, I dissect my history, continuing to feel confused, irrationally guilt-ridden, and wounded: taking on my parents' shameful betrayals as if I am the cause of their behaviour. I feel like damaged goods, black and blue with psychological bruises. After many unfruitful years, I give up on the couch. It never changes my personality or my unsatisfying life.

I go on to other short-term therapists who do respond to my stories and say helpful, eye-opening things like, "Your parents weren't your parents. They had sibling rivalry with you." "Your sister took on the authority role because no one else was in control." "Your brother rebelled because of all the projecting going on."

And me? The good girl, mother's helper, without any needs of her own. The lost child, wanting to be left alone, ending up the loner.

Eventually, I stop trying to succeed as a freelance writer. Turning a lifelong hobby into a job, I become a professional photographer. I am no longer the person in front of the camera, but the one behind it. A career opens before me doing headshots, theatre stills, weddings, Bar Mitzvahs, sweet sixteens, magazine work, along with my own fine art photography. I am frequently included in group shows garnering good reviews.

My fine artwork focuses on street photography featuring people from all social strata. However, I make my specialty the homeless, and I include snatches of dialogue and descriptions of the people I somehow coax into emotionally disarming portraits. They feel listened to and, even if just for a moment, their lives have meaning again.

I guess I see myself in them. Somehow cast out of the satisfactions of ordinary life, with no partner to complement me, no children to nurture and love. The thought of a permanent relationship fills me with dread. The idea of being part of a family again, even my own, is like contemplating torture. I did not survive the dynamics of my family. How can I build a healthy one for myself?

Besides, in the later part of the twentieth century, society's expectations of women change. It's now okay to pursue a career in lieu of marriage and family. I enter the workforce at the time of the Feminist Revolution, *MS* magazine, and Gloria Steinem.

Even in my thirties, I still don't know how to have a successful relationship with a man—I always find myself with someone who pushes my buttons—but I know how to be a successful photographer. I know how to control the camera, the lights, the subjects. People trust me; I look so young and unassuming they relax and reveal their emotions through their faces and postures. Looking for the moment when their souls hover before my eyes, I chat with them like an old friend, and listen to the stories of their lives.

Sometimes I recite lines of poetry to them, not Shakespeare or Donne, but Frost for his poignant wisdom and Dickinson for the luminosity in everyday things. Flashes of their inner selves flicker across their faces. Like dropping a pebble down a well, the visual echoes of who they are come back to me, crisp and resonant. I capture these with my camera.

If the subject is subdued, unable to forget the camera, I share stories of Grandma Ethel. What a cut-up she was even in old age, dressed to the nines, cracking Mae West jokes, flirting with any handy male. People love to hear about a spirited woman. Someone who likes to celebrate herself—not unlike Whitman. She is my role model as a successful career woman. I like to think she would be proud of me. Though I'll never be a colourful personality like Grandma Ethel, I hope to live as fully, in my own way, despite my solitariness. These many years after her passing, she is still a guiding spirit.

# Chapter 4
# Like No Other Grandma

When I am small, I take my Grandma Ethel for granted. She's Mom's mother, and she lives with us, and that's that. But, when I'm a little older—eight or nine—I start to notice that she's pretty darned interesting.

Grandma Ethel isn't like any other Grandma I've met in our Westchester, Lincoln Terrace, Jewish neighbourhood. She doesn't cook, bake, knit, crochet, sew, or keep extensive photo albums. She has rhinestone-studded sunglasses. She wears flaming red nail polish and large pieces of jewellery—the real stuff as well as the costume kind. She chain smokes Kent cigarettes that arrive by delivery boy from the neighbourhood candy store that also keeps her in chocolate bars, salted nuts, and Dentyne gum—the kind that supposedly freshens your breath.

Mom says Grandma has the immigrant instinct for making the most of everything, no matter what. When she gets dressed up, her arthritically clawed hands—she was stricken in her forties—are usually adorned with oversized rings, jumbo golden charm bracelets, or wristbands like serpents grasping their tails in their mouths. When she goes to an affair—a wedding or Bar Mitzvah—her still elegant neck sports gold-set gemstones, necklaces of topaz, sapphire, aquamarine, or her favourite multi-strand pearls with the ruby clasp. She loves to wear pastel-coloured flowing scarves, kid gloves, custom-made felt hats, cashmere sweaters, her mink stole or the full-length coat, both in champagne, which set off her blond hair. Oh boy!—one of Grandma's expressions—does she know how to accessorize!

Despite her arthritically deformed feet, which require specially made open cut shoes, all my sixth-grade girlfriends think Grandma is the coolest thing on two legs. She strolls out of her bed-sitting room, waves hello with a red-finger-nailed, cigarette adorned hand, rolls her tremendous smoky grey eyes in a silent greeting, and smiles mischievously all the way through the downstairs playroom to the kitchen for more ice, a frosty cold ginger ale, or a bowl of strawberries and sour cream.

My other Grandma, whom we called "Bubbe," was the inimitable old-world cook. She produced a steady stream of chopped liver, made the old-fashioned labour-intensive way. She made crispy noodle or rice puddings baked to a scrumptious gold hue and dotted with sweet raisins. Years later, Daddy memorializes them by saying no one could make them the same as his Mama. Along with this she also made "exquisite pot roast," which Ruthie swears was cooked to the consistency of shoe leather. But when I am eight, Bubbe passes away in her sixties, from colon cancer, while Grandma Ethel, despite her reckless ways, lives on.

Grandma Ethel embraces contradictions. She eats an Almond Joy, a Milky Way, or a Three Musketeers with one hand, and health food with the other. She extolls the use of chamomile tea for everything from upset stomachs to lightening your mood as well as your hair. She eats avocados to keep her skin smooth with only slight "folds," as she quaintly calls her practically non-existent wrinkles. She puts wheat germ on her yogurt, or into her buttermilk, both of which she says have beneficial bacteria.

She splits open a peach or apricot pit to eat the bitter seed inside that she claims gives you long life, but later turns out to contain poisonous laetrile. She drinks pickle juice upon occasion for fermentation bacteria, eats salted watermelon rinds for God-knows-what reason, and regularly downs V-8 juice for its vitamins and minerals. She also likes beautiful fruits such as pomegranates and persimmons, just for the look of them, although she swears they are healthy, too.

None of these habits get in the way of her regularly downing Coke or ginger ale, eating candy or nuts, and constantly puffing on her cigarettes. These she forgetfully lights one after another, putting them in one of the ubiquitous ashtrays, so sometimes you find three or four lipstick-smeared cigarettes burning all at the same time. Walking into Grandma Ethel's room is like strolling into a dense fog.

Grandma Ethel divides her time between the television and phone calls about selling off her remaining lots of property on Long Island, where she made her fortune over the decades as land there became increasingly popular for suburban housing developments. She often shows me her day's list of activities that she makes out in the morning. This consists of favourite TV shows—reruns of *I Love Lucy*, and game shows like *Beat the Clock*, or *The Price Is Right*, or *Queen for a Day*—alternating with her "telephone appointments" with real estate agents.

"See," Grandma says, pointing to her yellow legal pad list inked in red pen, "I cross off as they're done, that's how you accomplish things." She smiles broadly at me as I nod my head in agreement. Yet I wonder about the meagreness of her day-to-day existence.

If Grandma Ethel decides she has holed up in the house for too long, she takes one of her lavish vacations. Over the years she travels to many places on top-of-the-line cruises—she won't get on airplanes. In the '30s she goes to Cuba, in the '40s Bermuda, in the '50s Haiti and the Dominican Republic, and the '60s find her on the Mediterranean, going to Italy, Greece, and Israel.

When I am seven, Grandma Ethel lets me pack the big, metal ribbed, dark green steamer trunk several weeks before her departure on one of her extended vacations. Bennie goes down to the storage area of our sprawling basement to retrieve her old-fashioned trunk from under a pile of Samsonite luggage next to the makeshift room for the current sleep-in maid. More likely than not, that room is vacant. A sporadic succession of young black maids comes up from the South, but they usually leave within a couple of months, tired of the never-ending fights and slamming doors of our tumultuous household. Ruthie's erratic instructions leave most of them dazed and confused. (One even went so far as to tell me that my mom wasn't exactly well, but declined to elaborate any further.)

After dusting off the trunk, Bennie pulls it up the basement stairs, hitting each step with a resounding clunk. He enters Grandma's room with it jokingly carried on his bent-over back, calling out in hawking, old-world peddler style, "Beads and baubles for a *shaineh maideleh*, beads and baubles." Grandma responds by lifting her shoulders seductively up and down, perfectly timed with a huge roll of her dawn grey eyes, up to the ceiling and down again, ending with pursed lips and a thrown kiss.

Grandma is a shameless flirt. She flirts with all males of the species, no matter their age. Attention and compliments from the opposite sex are her lifeblood. She never shies away from telling a dirty joke, in euphemistic terms, in mixed company. Not until years later does it dawn on me that none of her flirting has brought her love.

Once the steamer trunk is lowered into its spot in the middle of the room, Grandma ceremoniously hands the key to Bennie and he does the honours of jiggling the lock open, prying back the claw-like hardware clasps, and opening the standing trunk at a 45-degree angle. The musty cellar smell releases into the smoke-filled air of the room. I pull out the flat wooden hangers that lock in place, as well as the drawers, to air them out on the sill of the recently opened window.

To my mind, the inside of the trunk is like a gigantic jewellery box, lined in a fading blue-grey satin brocade, embossed with fields of flowers—stalks of gladiolas, bouquets of roses, lilies, and round blossoms of chrysanthemums with their big pom-poms. These last are like the gigantic mums that we buy each year for Grandma's birthday. They are always bright yellow, with pencil thin rows of petals that curve in toward the half-hidden centre, crooked little pinkies saying, like Grandma herself, "Come, come here, smell and admire me. Sip my sweet nectar, you beautiful butterflies and amorous, zigzagging bees."

Out of Grandma's bureau, I fetch pink satin sachet bags that smell of lavender and roses. I place one in each drawer of the trunk, and one in the zipper compartment in the bottom, which holds Grandma's open cut shoes.

After everything is aired, I put onto the hangers the colourful daytime dresses and exquisite evening wear with embroidered bodices, or glittering beads in neatly patterned sprigs of flowers, or sparkling sequins exploding into fireworks of design. Each fancy evening dress has its accompanying jacket in case the nights are cool, and sometimes her champagne mink stole goes with her, too.

I love packing Grandma's jewellery into silk bags that roll up and are tied with a ribbon, keeping the gold chains and necklaces from tangling, the earrings from sticking to one another, and the bracelets from twisting in snags. Each past trip has its signature piece: from Florida a gold starfish brooch encrusted with pearls; from Bermuda a bracelet watch with opal studded cover; from the Mediterranean a pearl ring; from France a long three-strand pearl necklace with ruby clasp; and from Israel a gold, braided charm bracelet, studded with tiny sapphires, rubies, emeralds, and pearls. The bracelet has Hebrew words on each gold charm, but I can't decipher them because I don't go to Hebrew School.

"You especially like pearls, Grandma?" I ask when I notice the abundance of pearl jewellery—earrings, necklaces, brooches, and rings.

"Yes," says Grandma. "Every Friday night your great Grandma Sarah dressed up with a strand of pearls in preparation for the Sabbath. She called them her Sabbath pearls. And I should have inherited them, but instead, they bought passage to America for our family. If it wasn't for those pearls we wouldn't be here talking," says Grandma. She looks at me, searching my face for something she doesn't seem to find there. Her eyes grow moist, yet she smiles as if she feels both pain and happiness at the same time.

"Grandma, was it Russia or was it Poland?"

"Who knew," said Grandma, "You went to bed it was Poland, you woke up, it was Russia! The soldiers were always riding through, going or coming from one border war or another." Her smile fades now and she looks down at her clawed hands.

"What was it like?" I ask, imagining a town with dirt streets and wooden stores and houses, like the cowboy westerns on TV. For a while Grandma says nothing. Then a shadow crosses her face. "Who needs to remember such things," she says quietly. Then, under her breath, "They threw babies in the air and caught them on bayonets." She shakes her head slowly, stops talking, and won't say any more. After a time, she picks up the TV guide, turns on the set, and searches for a show to watch.

"How about my husky boyfriend?" She says, rolling her eyes, as she tunes into *Perry Mason*.

Grandma loves the swarthy lawyer who rescues and victoriously defends the wrongly accused innocent client. She likes the sound of the theme music's jazzy saxophones: daa-ta-da, daa-ta-da. As she shrugs her shoulders in rhythm to the music, you can picture a mink stole sliding down her arms.

"Sure, Grandma," I reply. "He's the cat's meow." She laughs.

Often, Mom fights with Grandma Ethel before one of her particularly luxurious vacations. Grandma gave Mom and Dad a lion's share of her money to buy our Westchester land and build the big house we all live in now. But, despite Grandma's generosity, Mom is increasingly critical of the way she spends her remaining money on vacations and fancy trinkets. Mom looks at such things askance, as if they were morally unacceptable. Grandma's life attitude, on the other hand, is neatly summed up in her oft-repeated advice to us grandkids, "Dahling, if it makes you happy, do it!"

Often, especially when a vacation is looming, Mom bursts into Grandma's room unannounced. She decries the smoke-filled atmosphere. She says it's ruining Grandma's health, and the grandkids' health too, if Miriam, Samuel, and I happen to be with Grandma watching one of her favourite night-time TV shows, like *Gunsmoke* or *The Fugitive*. And if Mom catches everybody in the process of devouring an Almond Joy or a Three Musketeers bar, she decries the unhealthy effects of that, too. Mom rants and raves about Grandma Ethel's way of living and then storms out of the room.

Before one vacation, I hear Mom screaming in Grandma's room at the top of her lungs. I'm sitting in the overstuffed reading chair in the adjacent "playroom." Mom bursts out of Grandma's room, banging and flinging the door wide open as she exits. Grandma is following close behind, yelling, "Get out of my room! Get out of my room!" She is padding along in an old pair of Dad's slippers.

Grandma stands in the doorway of her room a moment, turns to me as if to an audience and yells in disbelief, "She's telling me what to do! She thinks *she's* the mother." Then Grandma yells at Mom's receding figure, "You're not the mother, I am." And with that she shuffles back into her room, slams the door and locks it.

For some reason, that seems to puncture Mom's war cry. She turns to me looking sad and defeated, and says in a low voice, "She likes to go away so she can drink undisturbed."

This comes as a shock to me. I've only seen Grandma happily tipsy after a glass of champagne to celebrate New Year's. But a few years later, I discover what Mom says is all too true. Grandma takes Miriam, Samuel, and me to Florida with her for two weeks. She is to stay on for another month after we leave. The night the plane is to take off, however, a whopping big snowstorm hits the northeast and all the airports in New York are closed. Our flight is cancelled and rescheduled for the next day. We trudge back outside to the steamy, sultry, Miami streets, suitcases in hand, and take a taxi back to the hotel. When we arrive, Grandma is happily watching a TV show, her words all slurred.

Grandma has ordered room service, but the linen covered cart and the platters and dishes, covered with metal tops to keep the food warm, are untouched. A bottle of wine is uncorked and nearly empty. Alongside it sit miniature bottles of Scotch and Brandy with twist off tops. Wry smiles pass back and forth between Miriam and Samuel. I go in the bathroom and start to cry.

For a long time that night I can't fall asleep. I worry Grandma Ethel might hurt herself more when we leave tomorrow. Although she often seems to enjoy life, I sense that some deep underlying pain must be driving her to lock herself in a room and drink as if she were alone in the world.

One time I'd overheard Mom and Miriam discussing Grandma Ethel's marriages—plural. This was news to me. I knew about Grandpa Phillip and their divorce. But it seemed Grandma had married three times before she was fifty: a gambler, a real estate charlatan, and a drinker. For some reason, I don't think she is sad about *them*. I think something hurt her before them, and that's why she picked them. She picked them from some painful place inside herself. A place that's buried deep. A place nothing—no jewellery, no furs, no fancy cruises, no other men—can touch.

I'm too young to know what to do about this kind of hurt—though I see it all around me in my family. It is too much for me. That night in the hotel, I silently cry myself to sleep.

# Chapter 5
# Bennie and the Car Wash

My dad's a smart guy but he goes from one business to another.

"When things start to take off, so does Bennie," my mom says to me. "He's got that fear of success thing."

She cocks her head, studying me for a moment and adds, "You've got a little of that, too." Then she continues, "You don't know how I have to fight those cockamamie ideas of his. We could've been in the poor house a hundred times." She clucks her tongue and a 'can you believe it?' look comes over her face.

I feel her worry, but my mom's confidences are unnerving. I'm never sure what to believe. That our world can split apart on Dad's whim? That he can't be trusted? That Mom is single-handedly holding our lives together?

My brother Samuel says, "Dad's a maverick with an inventive mind. Only, he lacks discrimination and can't tell what is brilliant from what is plain off-the-wall. Once an idea lodges in his brain, he can't let go. He's just as stubborn and illogical as Mom." Coupled with the fact Dad can't work under anyone else without getting contentious, this makes him a tricky provider.

However, Mom never gives up on the genius part of him. "He just needs the right setting for his talents. Then with me by his side, we can fight 'til the cows come home and we'll still make it big."

I'm struck by Mom's realistic characterization of their relationship—that it's one of contention. But it's not until my teens that I see it completely: The fighting glues them together; the more they fight the more they stick to each other. It's so illogical it boggles my brain. I don't yet understand that thwarted passion can find another path.

When Mom and Dad first met, he owned a T.V. sales and repair shop. There he could tinker and make things light up, bleep on and off, flicker and sizzle to his heart's content. After the war, the larger outlets and chain stores took much of his business. He was newly married, and though Mom, big as a battleship, worked as a bookkeeper until Miriam was born, the shop didn't bring in enough for a growing family. Eventually, they sold the business.

For a few years, Dad worked at a tiny ad agency in Manhattan. However, the stresses of an ad agency, as well as the stresses of working under a boss, aggravated him so much he developed an ulcer. For a while he kept the thing under control with turquoise blue bottles of Maalox. The bottles were lined up on his side of the medicine cabinet like toy soldiers ready for battle. And a battle it was!

Missing the whole point of hierarchical structure (or, perhaps, not missing it at all), Dad couldn't stand anyone else having final say over his artfully worded creations. When Mom asked why he was fired, he said, "We had artistic differences. Let's leave it at that." Mom responded by clucking her tongue. "I told you it wouldn't work. Cooped up in a 2' × 2' plywood office describing a bottle of Anacin isn't for you."

Mercifully, they didn't fight. Dad receded into an English novel and blasted the hi-fi so loud it sounded like screaming.

The thing is, Mom's right. Dad likes to work with his hands as well as his head. He wants to figure things out and also to get his whole body involved with a problem. He likes to grab hold and have control of concrete things. He likes to cut, pour, screw, mix, chisel. He's descended from a line of wood carvers; maybe he's inherited their aptitude, but has to search for ways to express it.

Now, after the advertising fiasco, and with Mom's urging to "find a more active job" where he doesn't sit at a desk all day, Dad looks around and settles into a position with a house renovation business: aluminium siding, attic refinishing, porch extensions. He's a working partner, but he's not exactly into the physical side of it. His role is more conceptual. Dad looks at the house, talks with the owner, designs a plan, and gives an estimate. Still, the products of his imagination come to life before his eyes.

For six months or so, Dad seems content. He's whistling more around the house. Then his usual pattern prevails: He doesn't like his partners in the company. They aren't giving him the bigger jobs. It's unclear if they don't like his work, find him difficult to manage, or really are withholding the plum jobs. From what I can overhear between Mom and Dad, he's silently smouldering. He doesn't talk to his bosses. He just grows angrier and angrier.

Around the time his ulcer kicks up again, Mom has an idea. With Grandma Ethel's financial backing, they're going to look for an investment property to build a house on and sell for a big profit. As Mom always says, "Your dad can build anything." His experience with the renovation company will serve him well. They scour the newspapers for a likely lot for sale. Every Sunday, Dad, Mom, and Grandma Ethel ride around to various prospects. I go along for the ride.

Grandma sits up front wearing her rhinestone shades, puffing on a lipstick-smeared cigarette, looking like a bored movie star or gun moll. She's the moneyman. Mom is the realistic dreamer. She sits in the back seat, leaning forward, or peering out the window. All the while, her hands poke the air as she gesticulates energetically and schemes—half out loud, half to herself—about the suitability of the properties. Dad's the chauffeur as well as the monkey wrench. He throws in his two cents when he doesn't like the lot. He describes all the construction disasters that can come from that particular piece of real estate because of its shape, size, or location. Mom replies they're still at the planning stage. The more ideas they knock around and the more lots they consider, the more likely they'll find one that will be their "ticket."

"To what?" Dad wants to know. "A white elephant? Your ideas are grandiose."

I can't figure out who's right. Mom does have an inflated idea of home décor—consider her hodge-podge of antique styles in our sunken living room. Dad seems to see a glaring flaw in every lot and location.

Finally, after a month of Sundays, Grandma point blank refuses to get back in the car. She's firmly ensconced in her room. Why, she wants to know, should she listen to their endless bickering? She'd rather be watching the Sunday news programs, *Meet the Press* and *Face the Nation,* where real issues are analysed and discussed. "When you find what you're looking for," she says with annoyed disgust, "let me know," and turns back to her TV.

My parents continue to go out each Sunday for property hunting. Mom is hell-bent on actualizing her financial dreams. Dad digs in his heels nay-saying. One time a fight erupts.

"She doesn't know anything about house building. What it costs, what it takes in knowledge, time, and labour. She's unrealistic." Dad's directing these comments at me. I'm in the back seat, bearing witness. His driving—swivelling his head around, taking his eyes off the road—makes me as anxious as the role of compatriot he's forcing me to play. Suddenly he stops the car and turns around to address me further.

"Your mother has a screw loose. A couple of months after we marry I know something is wrong with her. We go to see a psychiatrist."

Mom doesn't say anything. She bites her lip and looks as helpless as a child of three. Her face crumples.

"His diagnosis is borderline personality," Dad says.

I don't exactly know what that means. I wonder if he does. In my naïve brain it simply sounds like being on the edge of a breakdown.

So I think to myself, *let's be careful to just never push her over the edge.* Dad's passive-aggressive button-pushing frequently does this. But as I grow older, I see she has these reactions with a lot of people, even total strangers. Dad never says if the doctor suggested some way to help her.

It's not until I'm an adult that I come to understand the disorder. At that time, my psychiatrist tells me the term describes a person with a fragile ego. Daily stress that most people can cope with is destabilizing, eliciting emotional outbursts. Three kids in five years is a big stressor, financial uncertainty is another stressor, and my father is an ongoing stressor. However, my mom doesn't have certifiable breakdowns. Somehow, she has enough psychological coherence to rebound and turn herself right side up, over and over again. She never gets help, which as an adult I mourn.

When my psychiatrist explains the disorder, my adult self wonders <u>why</u> Mom is destabilized by ordinary stressors. Is it because of a traumatic stress when she was young? Maybe she has something like post-traumatic stress disorder. As much as I loved Grandma, I can't help suspecting the home she made for Mom may have been at least a little, shall we say, chaotic.

On the other hand, surely Grandma was the one who'd be entitled to some PTSD. At a tender age she experienced poverty, trauma, loss, the harrowing immigrant journey. Maybe all that destabilized her, and kept her from being fully present for Mom?

After my father's revelation I, like Grandma Ethel, decide not to get back in the car on subsequent Sundays. So it comes as a complete surprise when one afternoon Dad comes back to announce that they bought a carwash! Of all things! He tells me this as he sits down on the edge of their bed, unlacing his shoes and putting his feet into his black plastic bedroom slippers with the synthetic red lining that looks like squashed tomatoes.

"Yessiree," he hums as he slips his thumb into one shoe and the rest of his hand into the other, and bears them aloft to the closet. Then he bends down and slaps them onto the wooden floor with an emphatic bang.

*What?* I say to myself. *A carwash?* "Are you going to run it?" I ask with distaste.

"No, no, no," he says practically singing.

I can't understand why he's so delighted.

"There's a manager. We're just buying it."

"Oh, gee." *How can he be so happy? It's such a messy business.* As an eleven-year-old becoming aware of social status, I feel a growing sense of mortification. Dad starts whistling Shostakovich's *Fifth*, which repeats itself endlessly.

"Yes indeedy," he says, cutting short the whistling. "We're going into the carwash business. Isn't that something? Wait 'til you see it! It's in the Bronx."

I'm in shock. I am slumped on the floor in the corner of their bedroom trying to imagine how I can tell my clique of girlfriends what my father is doing for a living. Owns a carwash, yuk! In the Bronx, yuk! Dirty cars and unskilled workers, yuk! Here we are living in this middle to upper middle-class neighbourhood populated with accountants, dentists, retail storeowners. Not working class. And now my parents own a business that employs manual labourers!

I feel scared, too. I sense my parents have embarked on a venture about which they know nothing. I fear they have no idea what they're getting themselves into. However, at the moment Dad is happy as a loon. He starts in again whistling Shostakovich.

Two weeks later my apprehensions materialize. The manager throws a fit. Dad has given him some "suggestions" on organizing the workers into three-man drying teams so they can do important "detail work" to give the car a glowing finish.

"If you think you can do a better job, do it yourself," the manager snarls, and those parting words click into place in Dad's consciousness. I overhear him talking to Mom. Of course he can do it better. He has a whole slew of ideas! Being the boss suits him to a "T." He wouldn't have to answer to anyone. Silently I add, "except Mom." The thought of that strikes fear in my heart.

Despite my worries, I eventually realize Dad has found his element. He is in love with the equipment. To him it's an assembly line of toys: rotating scrub brushes, hot and cold-water rinses, and air blasting blowers—which I have a hunch remind him of his decibel-blaring hi-fi. If there's one thing Dad knows and likes, it's machines: you always know where you are with a machine; either it works or it doesn't; either you fix it, or you don't. There's no ambiguity, no doubt. For Dad, machines are puzzles to solve. Not work, but a kind of play for his active mind. And as my mother says, he can fix anything.

The carwash becomes a kingdom of machinery that Dad rules. He is the one to turn on the switch in the morning and turn it off at the end of the day. He has peasant workers he likes to order around, organize, train, and oversee. The carwash makes Dad the king of the realm. In fact, they name it "The King's Karwash, where you always get the royal treatment."

The carwash is located in the Pelham Parkway section of the Bronx. It's surrounded by loads and loads of apartment complexes—i.e. people who have no way to wash their own cars—as well as two major hospitals—i.e. doctors, nurses, and medical staff who don't want to wash their own cars. They provide a steady stream of customers because the Bronx is a dirty place where cars get coated with grey smudge.

And as we soon find out, in every nearby ethnic neighbourhood people take pride in their chrome-trimmed, white-walled, spoke-wheeled symbols of prosperity and upward mobility—no pun intended. These people, bless them, are the bread-and-butter customers of the carwash business. They lavish love, attention, and money on their cars. They want every service possible: hot wax applied after the last rinse, all mats taken out and steamed, ash trays emptied.

One of these big spenders lets Mom know he runs numbers in the Bronx. According to Mom, he's sweet on her but respectful that she's married. (I guess even gangsters have their scruples.) He says if anyone gives her a problem—the customers, the workers, even the police—she should let him know. She's not exactly sure what he'd do, but she's obviously flattered. Of course, she never takes him up on it. "Wouldn't want to give anyone cement shoes," she says, laughing.

Soon the carwash becomes the family's raison d'être. It is not merely a livelihood, but also a collective faith that harnesses us body and mind to the Great American Dream.

"No, you can't go out with your friends this Saturday. We need you at the carwash."

"But it's Memorial Day Weekend!"

"Do you know what it's going to be like at the carwash? Unless it rains, God forbid, which will not help you anyway since you want to go to the beach."

The car wash is open 363 days a year—closed only on Christmas and New Year's Day. It is open 10 hours a day, except it closes at 2 p.m. on Sundays—unless cars are still lining up, because a customer is never turned away. We are the only kids we know who pray for rainy weather, because no one washes a car in the rain. Rainy days are the only days off for Mom and Dad. However, Dad usually goes in because there's always something to fix, or a new piece of equipment to install.

Saturdays and Sundays are the busiest. Samuel, who's thirteen, is expected to sacrifice his weekends off from a fancy private school (which we can afford, thanks to the carwash!) by manning a steam gun. Miriam, or "Merri," as she now calls herself, is fourteen and, to put it politely, hell on wheels. She won't sacrifice her youth and beauty to that place of dirty cars and dirtier workers. Not even over everybody else's dead bodies. Despite my qualms about manual labour, I am commandeered on Saturdays to do the odd jobs that make a carwash run. At age eleven I find I still have a tomboy streak that kicks in and makes the tasks weirdly enjoyable.

The business is built up on constancy of service—day in, day out, one year after another—and consistency of results. Dad's impeccable perfectionism, delivered with a sting of rebuke, sees to that. Although he causes workers to quit regularly, his attitude pleases the customers. Dad's philosophy: You have to provide a scintillating service, cars that sparkle, chrome that gleams. And you have to provide things carwash customers don't usually get: hot wax, steamed mats, ashtrays cleaned, dashboards wiped clean of dust. Not to mention the unique "free" bonus: windows washed on the *inside*, making them crystal clear. Because how else could you call your car really clean? Who else offers such a service? Nobody! Mom and Dad cover all the angles and corner the carwash market in the Bronx. No other establishment offers as much as they do, does a better job, or stays open as many hours and days of the week.

The carwash is the one and only success of my parents' rocky coupledom, except perhaps for us. For this reason (as well as the fact they are children of the Great Depression), they lay down their lives in order to "provide, provide." Ostensibly they do it for us kids. I say "ostensibly" because, for all the expensive clothes, summer camps, teen tours, cars, and colleges, they are happiest to spend their time at work rather than with us.

Money becomes the currency of their love. Each day they eagerly go to work to embrace the one and only way they seem able, unequivocally, uncontentiously, to express love.

I do not understand this until I am much older. At the time, I cannot fathom their willingness to dedicate themselves to such unrelenting toil, 10 hours a day, 6 2/3 days of the week, year after year. It reminds me of indentured servitude in the American colonies, which I am studying in school at the time. You sell yourself body and soul for a stipulated number of years, after which you are finally free to have a life. Yet the bargain often seems like it has been made with the Devil. He exacts more interest than you expected: The moments of your life are running out; your children are growing up without you; you are growing old.

However, at this moment in our history, Mom and Dad are reeling with euphoria. They are busy improving the gravy train for the next five years. The cash is pouring in and is immediately poured back out again on new equipment—better brushing machines, more powerful blowers, stronger conveyor belts. The walkway for the customers becomes filled with candy, soda, and coffee-tea-soup dispensing machines. The walls are lined with car air fresheners in the shapes of evergreen trees, little fuzzy poodles, and foam dice.

Chairs and a settee allow the customers to relax and safely watch through a glass wall as their cars are soaped, rinsed, and dried. Despite the professional aura of the business, my parents still run it like a Mom and Pop store. They lend the workers interest-free advances on their meagre wages, cover their N.Y. state employment taxes, and hand out frozen turkeys at Thanksgiving. Mom gives free vitamins to her poster child of the month. I guess Dad's rebukes figure in as parental guidance.

Eventually, when all aspects of the car washing process are tweaked and everything is routine, my parents, slightly bored, look around for other ways to increase income. They settle on a car rental business. They run the concern out of the carwash office and lease a vacant adjoining lot to hold the fleet. This keeps them occupied for a few years until they decide to open a car body shop in the building next door. Once that's successful, they are again restless to channel their energy into another project.

They take a long hard look around and realize they want to build their own super-duper, state-of-the-art carwash. On land they own, in a structure they build according to their own specifications: a giant of the carwash industry, a colossus. So, they go to the bank and mortgage the family home. After some scouting around the Bronx, they select a lot down the block from the first carwash—they've already got a legion of loyal customers in the surrounding area.

In a matter of months, they are digging the foundation. For twelve more months, Dad bounces back and forth between the old carwash—which is the cash cow supplying the resources—and the new one. Mom handles the daily grind of running the King's Karwash each day, only calling Dad, or rather screaming at the top of her lungs over the phone, when there are emergencies.

Fourteen months after the inception of their plans, the new carwash opens: A roaring, block wide, lip-smacking monolith that stands astride the corner of Webster Road and Morris Park Avenue. It is Vulcan at his forge—heart pumping electricity, lung bellowing air, stentorian booms of cacophony, all belching with water and dirt. It vibrates with washing, sloshing brushes, and tornadoes of hot wind.

It is chock full of the newest innovations in the industry—the scratchless faux chamois scrubbing machines, blowers that move along with the car instead of remaining stationary, and the "magic" chainless conveyor belt that requires no hooking or unhooking. It is floor to ceiling equipment, men, soap, steam, chrome, and glass. And, God bless them, the constant line of unwashed cars.

Right off, the new carwash breaks the previous records for a daily car count—over 300 vehicles on a Saturday. The cars move through quicker and come out cleaner. More engine steams are done, and more Simonizes, too. The coffers are overflowing. A weekend grosses $5,000, a weekday anywhere from $800 to $1,200. Mom and Dad are as happy as if they birthed a new baby. Their dreams have taken shape and come true.

By this time Merri is out of college, Samuel is in his last year, and I am a senior in high school. Grandma Ethel is generously footing the bill for college tuitions. So, although Mom and Dad are paying for housing, books, allowances, and cars, their costs are substantially decreasing. This would seem to be the moment when life is so full you ought to stop and breathe, and take it all in. And Mom and Dad do. They run the new carwash for a while, satisfied with their success. But it is like the story of the red shoes, which the ballerina can't take off; she has to keep dancing day and night, night and day. There are always new plans.

Six months after the new carwash opens, they have another project. They buy the old carwash building and divide it into four commercial rental units. They don't have the day-to-day labour of running it; they only need to maintain the building and collect the rental checks. In the next fifteen years they do more of the same. Always, somehow, doing it the hard way—buying the land, building the units, renting them out. Always with plenty of work for them, morning 'til night. Working as hard as the peasant stock from which they are descended.

Over the years, they often dispense with holiday celebrations and family vacations, miss summer camp visiting days, overlook parents' weekends at colleges. They make money hand over fist, bless them; they build businesses and develop real estate. All for us, the kids, to leave us a legacy, a future, an enduring security. The business gives us everything. The trouble is, for all those years, we have a business instead of a family.

It isn't 'til years later that, despite my bitterness over their distorted version of the American Dream, I can acknowledge their sacrifice. They had poured every ounce of their waking and dreaming lives into the black hole of material desire, the dripping maw of America, but it had been their attempt to arrive at a Promised Land. Like Moses and the tribes in the desert, their parents and grandparents had escaped from generations of virtual enslavement in Russia.

Like Moses, Bennie and Ruthie would see Jerusalem from the hillside, having driven themselves to their great moment, but would not be allowed to enter. They were the way, the bridge, the faith, the denial, the fear, and the hope. The worry and the attainment. The old branch lopped off so the new one could push up and flourish. They had fulfilled the dream that came over in steerage. They had fled the hands of death so we, the new generations, could spring up young and strong.

Yet the milk and honey of this new Jerusalem was barely to touch their lips before the breath of life, like a white dove, fluttered in release and receded into the blue distance of heaven. Now aged 80, they had only a few months earlier sold the last operating carwash. First Ruthie, overtaken by a stroke, goes in and out of the hospital while Bennie becomes her devoted caregiver. Seven months later, confined to her bed, she expires. Then Bennie, diagnosed with heart failure, declines slowly over nine months, and dies.

In some ways, at the end, I feel I was just like them, not truly able to voice my love in all its dimensions. I suffer the regret of opportunities missed. I see this mostly in hindsight, finally an adult and no longer the lost, grieving child.

# Chapter 6
# FDR

When I am thirteen I enter junior high and my view of adults starts to shift. Especially teachers. I get introduced to a survey course on American History, mid-sixties style, with a lot of patriotism and flag waving. We're still reciting the Pledge of Allegiance every morning in homeroom. No one's protesting yet or smoking pot.

For the first time, I realize teachers are just people with their own idiosyncratic opinions. Not quite under her breath, Miss Walsh, the history teacher, makes snide comments about FDR (whom she calls Mr. Roooosevelt). This FDR is the president Grandma Ethel waxes celebratory over whenever he's mentioned on TV or in company.

During one of her class presentations Miss Walsh goes off half-cocked in a rhapsody of opprobrium about how, since Mr. Roosevelt, the country has gone down the wrong road, how he led us to this impossible state where people think they deserve money for nothing. How it leads to more and more spending. An enormous debt on top of which we are all living and that will someday crash us back into a depression that will make the 30s look like a picnic.

"How," she wants to know, "can a household not go under with such goings on? It's fiscally and morally irresponsible." The future generations will one day pay the price. Maybe even *our* generation, because Mr. R's innovations have mortgaged us to a future of disastrous consequences.

I am so confused I don't know whether to laugh or cry. So, when I go home, I ask Grandma Ethel what she likes about FDR Her big eyes light up and her smile becomes contagious.

"Everything," she says. "Just about everything. He never let anything stop him, even the polio that crippled his legs. You know he wore heavy iron braces?"

That's something I didn't know. The history book shows him seated behind a big desk, like any regular president.

"Good looking, too," Grandma adds with an admiring glint in her eye, as she lowers the volume on the TV. "But it comes down to confidence, trust, security, jobs. He was a man of tremendous energy, and he knew how to be a leader and take action. Hell of a lot of charm, though. Of course, that doesn't get you far if you can't deliver. Here's a story for you. When he took office, during the Great Depression, there was a run on the banks—people were terrified. The very day he was sworn in, he said 'The only thing we have to fear is fear itself!' People listened, people believed him. Within just a few days he got an emergency bank bill through Congress. Then he got on the radio and told us the banks are safer places for our money than under a mattress. People believed that, too. They redeposited savings back into the banks and brought the run on capital to a halt. Now that's quite an accomplishment, to rescue the entire economy in a week!"

Grandma reaches for one of her cigarettes, lights it, and takes a puff. Puts it back down in the ashtray and continues.

"All Hoover did was chummy-up to the millionaires with their industries, practice laissez-faire government."

I look at her quizzically.

"Just means you don't do a damn thing except give industries tax breaks. The fat cats get fatter and the ordinary people grow poorer because of pay cuts." Grandma reaches for an ice cube out of her ice bucket and rattles it into a glass. I pour out ginger ale for both of us. I think to myself Grandma's a more exciting teacher than Miss Walsh. More energy. More enthusiasm. More colourful language filled with slang phrases that border on the poetic.

Grandma takes a long sip of her soda and goes on. "He was calling for a 'New Deal' for the average American. He had a snappy way of naming things. The man flew by the seat of his pants. Tried this and tried that until he found something that worked. Had a bunch of eggheads nicknamed the 'Brain Trust' who fed him ideas. He got Congress to pass legislation for Social Security, child labour laws, minimum wages, unemployment insurance, the 40-hour workweek. He came up with the WPA, the Works Progress Administration, which eventually employed several million people. They built and repaired roads and bridges, schools, tunnels, dams for generating electricity.

"Why, they electrified areas of the South where the poor folks hadn't entered the twentieth century. But you know what's most remarkable? Those were the ideas of his Secretary of Labour, the first woman ever to be appointed to the cabinet, Frances Perkins. She only accepted the job on condition that he endorse these legislative innovations and send them to Congress. Which he did! And we have them today. They make up the fabric of our working lives and government. He was a powerful man who could take his cue from a powerful woman with great ideas."

"That's a better history lesson than my teacher gave. I've learned more about Roosevelt from you in five minutes than a whole hour in class." I beam at her and realize she's on a roll; she isn't half finished singing the praises of FDR.

She picks up her cigarette, which has burned down to a long ash that falls carelessly into the ashtray.

I snuggle back into the corner of Grandma's couch and wait patiently for more.

"When the war came, that's the Second World War, he kept our morale up. Told us to plant 'victory gardens.' Food was rationed by then, along with gasoline and a lot of other things. Ever hear of Rosie the Riveter?"

I shake my head, curious.

"Women had to do the jobs the men who went to war left behind. Had to keep the tanks, jeeps, guns, planes, and boats coming. One of the reasons we won over the Germans was because, in the end, we had the military supplies to keep our fight going and they didn't. Rosie was the iconic woman on a poster to encourage women to work in the war industry. FDR knew how to motivate people to work hard for the principles of democracy. We are all living proof of that, this country of immigrants living together, making a life in freedom."

She took a sip of her soda, then blew her nose.

"Anything you didn't like?" I ask, wondering if she's a total FDR freak.

"He had his faults, too."

"Like…"

"They were drafting Negroes and segregating them. There was so much prejudice, although the Negroes were bleeding like everybody else. The entertainer Lena Horne—what a beauty—found when she was singing for the soldiers that the German prisoners were seated behind the white troops and the Negro soldiers were way in the back of the audience, in last place, behind everyone else, though they were fighting and dying for our country, too. The injustice of it rang her bell in a painful way. Second class citizens, behind even the enemy. It shocked her soul."

"Guess Roosevelt didn't want to challenge the way things were."

"No, he didn't seem to. But you know who did?"

I shake my head, wondering what would come out of Grandma next.

"*Eleanor* Roosevelt! She championed the rights of the Negro people. At the time, FDR couldn't get an anti-lynching law through Congress. Southerners wouldn't let it pass. Lynching was going on. Lynched Jews, too. Cross burning and all that horror. There we were, sort of in the same boat, not accepted as real Americans with the same rights."

Absent-mindedly she picks up a tissue and finds the lighter under it. She gets a cigarette started then puts it down in the ashtray. A curl of smoke wafts up around her. Looking dreamy, with her attention drifting, she says, "In the '20s I used to go up to Harlem to the Savoy Club. All of us mixing and enjoying ourselves. Together without problems. I loved the Negro music. Josephine Baker's reedy tones, and that gravelly voice of Louis Armstrong, sounding like whiskey over chunks of ice clinking in the glass. I danced my feet off all night. Years before the arthritis hit."

She looks down with a grimace at her shoes. "Yes, we'd go uptown to Harlem and drink our gin out of teacups because it was Prohibition. Don't tell your mother."

"Sure, Grandma," I say. "My lips are sealed."

I start getting a little hungry. It is after five, but Mom and Dad won't be back from work for a couple of hours. So, I open Grandma's candy drawer and find an Almond Joy.

"Want some?" I ask.

"No, *Maideleh*. I had strawberries and sour cream earlier. You know," she said, refocusing, "that man sacrificed his life for his country and for the world. Without his leadership who knows what would have happened in World War II. Hitler was overrunning Europe and the Jews. Hate breaks out over and over again throughout history. I'm sorry to say it to you, dahling. Maybe your generation will be different. I'm sure America will save us from that catastrophe happening again, here. Don't you worry about that," she adds, wagging her finger gently in the air.

My thoughts flash back to a documentary I saw on TV when I was nine. Footage of Auschwitz. Piles of skeletal bodies being taken on carts to the crematoriums. Images of broken eyeglasses and abandoned shoes. I had bad dreams for months. I realize Grandma is speaking.

"There's some evidence FDR might have known the Germans were imprisoning and killing the Jews. It's unclear how much he knew in '42. Jewish leaders came to the White House to talk to him. Nothing could be done. He didn't have troops in those areas."

"Do you think he was prejudiced?" I ask tentatively.

"Maybe a benign kind of prejudice. If such a thing exists," she says wryly. "He had his attention elsewhere in the war. But I don't think he knew the extent of the atrocities or the millions killed."

I think to myself, even those who do good can fall grievously short. My sense of the complexity of people enlarges. The world is changing before my eyes and I don't know if I like this loss of clarity. I don't want to give up my right to be angry or to ascribe blame. Growing up is more than I bargained for. I want the world to change and people to change. A rebellion starts churning in my gut.

"Anyway," Grandma says, "FDR had his hands full fighting the war and his health was failing—heart trouble. Never let on, though people around him could see it near the end. He just kept traveling overseas to meet with Churchill and that villain Stalin—what a piece of work that man was. Eventually took over one country after another and slaughtered millions of ethnic people. We didn't know the extent until decades later. Good thing we left Russia when we did," she says and winks at me.

"Can you open the window for me, *Bubeleh*?" she asks, pointing. "I keep meaning to ask your father to take a look."

I go over to it and find it a little hard to raise. "It's sticky," I say, but I get it open. A fresh breeze wafts in, clearing some of the lingering smoke.

It's spring and the luscious scent of blazing pink azaleas fills the air. Grandma takes a couple of deep breaths, then plunges back into her narrative.

"In the end it wasn't Eleanor by his side but his long-time mistress Lucy…Lucy…something or other. Though it wasn't talked about in the press, everyone knew about her, even Eleanor. He gave up his life. His health was ground down to nothing by the end. Churchill and he, like blood brothers, waging a war against the worst sort of dictator, one who's out of his mind. And that's how Hitler died, denying the truth of his failure. He and his mistress, Eva Braun, supposedly took poison. Never found the bodies. Relegated to oblivion as far as I care."

Grandma's attention goes back to the muted TV. One of her favourite shows is on, *The Fugitive*. How she loves to root for her honest, misunderstood hero, trapped by circumstance, hunted by authorities. She makes no effort to put up the volume.

"Did the Depression affect you, Grandma?" I ask, wondering about it because I am reading *The Grapes of Wrath* in English class.

She is slow to answer. "Not as much as other people," she says. "I had already bought real estate out in Riverhead, Babylon, and Deer Park on Long Island. Back then, you could buy a piece of land for a song. You only needed the imagination to picture its possibilities, to see it flourish in your mind's eye. Developing the land—getting the roads, utilities, water lines, and schools built—now that was a whole other undertaking. Because of the Depression, all of that came to a halt. With that work stoppage, the lots my partner Rudy and I sold didn't turn out to be the communities we'd advertised. Got into some trouble for that."

Grandma looks sheepish for a moment or two.

"I…well anyway, it couldn't be helped. But the important thing was that the land was still there after the Depression broke. That's the thing about land, it can't get up and go anywhere. Eventually my real estate holdings became extremely lucrative. Back then, money really did grow on trees. You just had to stretch your arm and reach for it. It was like a game and if you knew it was all a game and you played it well, you could win. Green leaves for the taking."

I marvel at Grandma's philosophy. It's so different from my parents' drudging work ethic. Grandma makes money and enjoys herself at the same time. But I also wonder what kind of trouble? Four years later, after her death, I learn about the scandal from Mom. At the moment, however, I don't ask Grandma to explain. I decide to tell her about Miss Walsh.

"My history teacher seems to have it in for FDR She doesn't like him or the programs he started."

"Must be a Republican," she says. Then continues, "You know I hear it on *Meet the Press* and *Face the Nation*, how he never got us out of the Depression. Supposedly the war did. They might be right about that. But some even go so far as to say instead of curbing the Depression he contributed to the length of it. That's what's called specious reasoning. There's no way to know if it did or did not. You can't say it would have ended sooner without the New Deal. Just because the events are coincident doesn't mean one is causing the other."

"Huh," I say finishing off the last bite of my candy bar. "Coincident?"

"Going on at the same time. Say I'm talking loud and the TV is on. Is the TV causing me to talk loud or am I just a loud talker?"

"Turn off the TV and see what happens."

"Very smart," Grandma laughs.

"I think FDR was a caring, compassionate president who wanted to help people."

Grandma smiles at me and says, "A smart girl and kind girl. Yes. The New Deal may not have conquered the Depression, but I think it did some other things just as important. For the first time it seemed Washington, D.C. was fighting for the common man. It was actively supporting its citizens. This gave people hope. It strengthened their belief in the government. It gave them the strength to persevere in difficult circumstances."

"Boy, Grandma, that'd make a great essay question on an exam."

Grandma smiles. "You have to realize that the several millions who were employed in the programs were helping others to a better life. They built schools to educate the young, roads and bridges to make commerce easier, faster, cheaper, dams to generate electricity for people and industries. In the Flood of '37, thousands of the Civilian Conservation Corps were put to work when the Ohio River flooded the Ohio Valley. They rescued victims, set up levies, helped repair roads, houses, and hospitals. Same thing with the Hurricane of '38 when a lot of the Northeast was devastated. What he did impacted the whole fabric of the nation. FDR did his best and that was a fair piece of work for a world economy that had plunged into darkness."

"He has my vote," I say.

Grandma nods a few times, pleased.

I glance at the clock—it's close to six. Mom and Dad should be home soon with rotisserie chicken and knishes from the Deli—it's Friday, we always have chicken. And since it's Friday, no homework is due tomorrow.

"I saw a show on TV," I say, "about Dorothea Lange. Didn't she photograph the poor during the Depression?"

"Oh yes," Grandma says, her face animated again. "FDR also gave work to the actors, artists, and writers to contribute their talents to the country. Perhaps that aspect of the programs was controversial. But why should a creative person not benefit like any other? We don't live by bread alone. We live by roses, too. When you go into some post offices in the city, you see the wonderful murals painted by artists back then. Showing beautiful depictions of people and landscapes: Wheat fields in the midst of harvest time, children learning in schools, factories with smokestacks chugging away, cityscapes with skyscrapers, all framed by the dawning sun on one side, the setting moon on the other. The whole life blood of a nation."

I am feeling the thrill of Grandma's eloquent outburst go through me when I realize she has suddenly gone silent and is looking at her TV guide. That is all she will ever say about why she loved FDR Certainly it is enough to support her opinion of him. And it is far more than I had learned from Miss Walsh. I am wowed by Grandma's range of knowledge and her sophisticated way of thinking.

I realize on that day that she has known, done, and achieved more in her life than I have ever glimpsed before. For me, it is all too transient a glimpse. Grandma seems spent afterward and even a little disoriented. But it all makes me wonder at the depth and breadth of her life, spanning Russia and America. I wish she would speak in similar detail of her life in the Old Country. I wonder what happened there, whether it was too painful to revisit.

Because of that talk with Grandma, I decide to do my history paper on FDR, but I only get a B minus. I can't help thinking the grade reflects some of Miss Walsh's prejudice against the handsome man who caught Grandma's heart and imagination. "Not sufficiently objective," Miss Walsh writes. It makes me realize how opinionated teachers can be. Just like everybody else. Teachers come down a peg in my heart. No longer founts of knowledge but complexes of personality. I feel as if I've lost my innocence. And I don't like it.

Grandma has somehow been an agent of change in my psyche, for good or bad. At age thirteen I am leaving childhood behind. The loss of innocence seems to be speeding up in my daily life, and it begins to colour my view of my mother and father. I find myself holding their words and deeds up to the light of day, and often to silent ridicule.

# Chapter 7
# Hair Care

When I am fourteen, I become acutely embarrassed by my mother's hair. It is red, stiff, and shaped like a box—sort of the Jackie Kennedy pillbox hat look. Even for the New York suburbs it's a bit off. You don't want to get too close because it feels like sandpaper and smells like insect repellent.

The rigidity of it reminds me of those Teutonic, horned helmets worn by Wagnerian sopranos. Maybe because Mom's in the high octaves at least once a day, if you get my drift. Someone always needs to be screeched at, according to her way of looking at things. Usually my father, or Merri, or Grandma Ethel.

To avoid conflict, I make sure I do everything right. Exactly as Ruthie asks. When she has a fight with Merri about a chore Merri doesn't have time for or refuses to do, I volunteer my services. I guess you can say I'm the sacrificial virgin. One time, Merri can't find her fountain pen for school—some Parker executive gizmo. She starts fighting with me to get mine. Ruthie gets aggravated. She asks me to please give up my pen for the sake of peace.

I feel I've no alternative but to surrender. So I do. I'm seething inside because I'm a budding writer and my pen is sacrosanct. Doesn't Mom know this? Doesn't Merri? The worst thing is, I don't know if I should blame Merri or Ruthie. So, I blame them both and in my heart I swear I'll resent them forever.

Ruthie started dying her hair red when she was pregnant with me. I know this because I asked her. She says she dyed it to restore its original colour. She swears that her hair was chestnut red in childhood but darkened as she got older. With her sea green eyes and pale, lightly freckled complexion, the story rings true. Anyway, I was the third kid in five years and I guess she had to do *something* to brighten up her life.

I don't think Ruthie was happy about that pregnancy. I don't think she wanted another baby. Once when I was fighting with my sister over a sweater she borrowed, lost, and wouldn't replace, she said that I was an "accident." Ruthie's "mistake." I thought I knew what she meant.

So, later I ask Ruthie. Putting down the *New York Times* crossword puzzle she's doing in bed, she looks up, surprised. She glances at me over her glasses and asks, "Where did you get such an idea?" Then laughing she adds, "If you were a mistake, you were the best little mistake that ever happened to me." And she gives me one of those hugs that hurt your shoulders.

I can't tell if she's kidding. A few months later, my sister tells me the whole story. Before she became pregnant with me, Ruthie had an illegal abortion and got ill from it. She was afraid to have another abortion, so instead she had me.

Ruthie's hair wasn't always abhorrent. A wonderful photo of her from the forties was taken just before she got married. Mom's posing on her side on top of a picnic table. She's leaning on one elbow, her body half raised up, a wave of hair sweeping softly across her cheek. She's clad in one of those bathing suits that frame the bosom in folds of drapery.

Everything in the picture is flowing—hair, bosom, curving hip—and she's smiling like an enchanting mermaid. Her eyes, though, are half questioning, as if she's not sure she can trust something. Probably my father, who is the photographer. This must be during their three-month whirlwind courtship, when they hardly knew each other and everything was still flowing.

Actually, I may have inherited that flowing hair from Ruthie. Only it's impossible to tell because of that thing she calls her hairdo. Nice hair runs in the family. When someone compliments me on my beautiful hair I say, "Thank you. My Grandma Ethel gave it to me." I don't have that succulent, honey coloured hair she has—mine is a deep, bittersweet chocolate. I do have the shine, the thickness, the texture, the flow of cascading waves that Grandma says men loved to touch.

In one photograph of Grandma from 1914, the year she arrives in America, she's standing in a group of cousins at a summer beach cottage. Her hair is like a luxurious crown, large and full, pinned up on the top of her head. Shiny and satiny even in the sepia tones of the picture, her hair glows. In another photo, from the '30s, it's short and beautifully coifed, thick with waves, and radiating light.

I recall the golden braid of Grandma's girlhood hair that now lies abandoned in Grandma's dresser drawer. When I was little, I used to sneak a peek at it whenever the coast was clear. Its rich colour has survived the years largely intact.

Grandma, who carries herself with confidence (to put it mildly), has never dyed her hair. I wonder if she wishes Ruthie could be strong enough to believe in what Nature gave her. But if Grandma harbours any such sentiments, I never hear them.

Ruthie's hair colour is a rich Hollywood red. She has her own special formula—two parts Clairol Copper #53 combined with one part Flamenco Nights #8. I've dyed it for her every once in a while, since I turned twelve, whenever she can't squeeze in an appointment at the hairdressers. Sixteen-year-old Merri refuses, saying she's washed her hands of it.

I remember how proud I felt the first time Mom asked me. I mean, she trusted me. But it's really a nerve-wracking job. The dye is so toxic that an accident could blind Ruthie. And an accident could easily happen, because the smell of the dye makes me dizzy. But I do what's expected of me.

What bothers me most about Ruthie's hair is the stiffness. Each night she sprays it with a new layer of Aqua Net. She goes to bed and gets up with every hair in exactly the same place. It sits on her head like some kind of foreign body.

Sometimes between salon appointments, the pill-box-hat-thing on top starts to lean to one side. I've walked into the bathroom and found Ruthie struggling to get it straight; a rat-tail comb stuck under one side, like a carpenter's level. But often, it's lopsided.

Ruthie has a tantrum if anyone hugs or otherwise embraces her and, in the process, disturbs her coif. She squints her eyes, her mouth widens in a grimace of pain, and she yells, "Stop! You're messing my hair." Oddly, it's not vanity or egotism, but more like some self-protective reflex. Her affection and closeness are layered over with veils of fearfulness and avoidance.

I don't know how my father deals with her. I can't imagine how they get "enmeshed" without disturbing her hair in some strategic way. I wonder at what point my mother's hair became a bulwark against my father.

Even when I was young and hopped into bed with my mother and father, she would be sleeping corpse-like on her back, her hands cupped over her belly. These days I don't think she can sleep in any other position without getting her hair messed up. One summer on a teen tour to England I visited a zillion cathedrals and I recognized that pose on those marble effigies laid out to honour the dead.

In later years, Mom's hair becomes so thin you can easily see through to her scalp. I wonder if all that dye somehow ruined her hair. I wonder if, despite my thick locks, I face the same future.

I'm sorry to say the sight of her baldness gives me shivers. She doesn't seem to mind it. I suggest she see about a hair replacement weave. Proudly, she shows me the hairpiece one day and asks me to help her put it in. I decline.

"Never fear," she says. "I'll have the hairdresser do it." She promptly makes an appointment and the next time I see her it looks pretty good. Still, however, she has that box-like hairdo. Somehow, she never changes her look with the times.

Her personality does change as she ages. She mellows and becomes able to regret some of the ways she mothered. One birthday she presents me with an expensive, shiny, golden pen. She says she shouldn't have made me give mine to Merri that day I was in junior high and my sister couldn't find hers and fought with me. Ruthie knew I still dabbled with writing poetry. Knew, some way only a mother can, what would pierce my heart with forgiveness.

Ruthie also tells me the story of her abortion. It is a heartrending tale of days of bleeding and pain. The passage of a bloody mass, depression and fever. Six months afterwards, despite contraception, "one-two-three, I'm pregnant again. It must have been God's will," she says to me, smiling, with tears in her eyes. Then she leans over and kisses me on the forehead.

Days before she dies, she is agitated. She apologizes for not protecting me as she thinks she should have. She goes so far to say, "God should have never given me children."

I dredge up from my soul all my old sorrow, anger, and resentment, and I call upon the love that is coursing through my veins to help me relinquish the difficult emotions still embedded in my heart. Realizing that I am only a speck in the life of the universe, a sense of humbleness overcomes me. I grapple with the angels to give me the words that will release both of us from everything that is not love.

I tell her, "You always did the best you knew how. If you regret anything, let it not pain you. If you are worried about anything, know you have my love and forgiveness, completely, freely. If such a thing is needed, know I forgive you for whatever you did or did not do. You gave me the blessing of life, and for that I am eternally grateful."

This seems to calm her. I bend over and kiss her on the forehead. She closes her eyes, her features relax, and she is once again able to rest.

# Chapter 8
# As They Say in the Museums

The whole thing starts several months after my fifteenth birthday, on a gentle spring day. Warm showers drench the branches of young trees, turning them to glistening ebony, and new leaves are bejewelled with drops of water that magnify, as if in miniature, the eternal force of Nature Herself. On that idyllic day I go with Ruthie to see the nose doctor.

We sit in his Park Avenue office—a plush suite of rooms with gold trimmed French Provincial double doors leading to a Ladies Room here, an examining room there, an overflow waiting room over there—for what seems like an eternity. Looking around, I begin to notice something that, at first, strikes me as odd. The office has at least three, maybe four, perambulating nurses, clad in glowing white body-hugging uniforms and fetching little nurses' caps. Every one of them is drop-dead gorgeous.

It can't be a coincidence, I reason. Maybe he did their noses and they're eternally grateful? But, if their noses were done, I can't tell and I am pretty good at spotting fixed noses. The women are perfect, like my Barbie doll that lies abandoned at the back of my closet. They have perfect oval faces containing perfect features. Perfect bust lines and perfectly proportioned hips. Perfect curvy calves and slender ankles. Even perfect high arched feet, stuck into stylish white pumps that are perfectly clean, with nary a scuff or mark.

For all my fifteen years of going to the family doctor back in Westchester, Dr Gordon always had a fiftyish, clodhopper-wearing, tough-as-nails, iron-faced nurse-receptionist. I thought it was the way nurses looked because of the life-and-death nature of their calling. The nurses in this office look like ones on the TV soaps, *As the World Turns*, *Edge of Night*, or *General Hospital*.

Dr Panelli has done a zillion noses. He is famous for them. And, of course, he did Merri's nose three years earlier. In fact, Dr Panelli put Merri's before and after photos into one of the albums that are piled high in all of his rooms. Needless to say, Dr Panelli will not express an interest in *my* photos, either before or after. If he does, I don't think I want to be his advertisement. It is strange enough seeing Merri's photos in the waiting room. Am I supposed to live up to her example, follow in her footsteps, adopt the same profile?

Even to this day, Ruthie insists that when I was six, I got my nose banged and broken. We were traveling out West on a vacation, so the story goes. At a motel swimming pool some boys were roughhousing and threw another kid into the water right on top of me and Merri, bashing us into the side of the cement pool. So, according to Ruthie, the reason Merri and I have to get nose jobs is to *fix* our noses. We really were born with lovely noses.

Honestly though, I can't recall ever having a different nose. Too big, too bony, and too bulbous at the tip, sort of a zucchini with a bump in the middle. Maybe the actor Jimmy Durante was cute and funny, but a girl with a big proboscis isn't. She gets made fun of. And she'll internalize the teasing. She'll decide that her nose really is big and ugly. She'll feel ashamed. Even her girlfriends will be awkward and embarrassed and will avert their eyes.

When we're finally in the examining room, Ruthie and Dr Panelli greet each other like old friends. This is *my* appointment, but I seem to be superfluous. They talk about Miriam, how beautiful she looks, what college she's in, and so forth.

While continuing to talk with Ruthie, Dr Panelli motions me to sit down. He starts measuring my face with one of his hands like an artist assessing the composition of a painting. After a minute or so he commands me to tilt my head back and then, surprise of surprises, he looks up my nostrils with a little instrument that has a tiny light at the end. Dr Panelli is only tunnelling into the caverns of my nose, but I feel as embarrassed as if he were looking up my vagina with its new curly black hairs.

Within a few moments, he makes an astonishing pronouncement. He says that my nose has stopped growing and therefore I can have my operation this summer. I am speechless. Every other strategic part of me has just begun to sprout. How does he arrive at this startling conclusion? I have no idea. I guess I'm supposed to feel grateful and ecstatic, but all I feel is bewildered.

Ruthie, however, is happy enough for both of us. She wants me to be as pretty as I can, as soon as I can. She tells Dr Panelli that at college Miriam has been voted Sweetheart of Alpha Phi Pi, her boyfriend's fraternity.

Dr Panelli looks my face over and, for the very first time, looks straight at me and asks, "What kind of nose do you want?"

Now this might sound odd, but up until that moment, I hadn't thought about it in any concrete way. The only thing that pops into my mind is that I don't want Merri's nose. Everyone else loves her nose. It has a loop, a small upward tilt at the end, that people call a turned-up nose. It isn't my sort of nose. During the pause while I am thinking, Ruthie rushes in and says, "She wants a turned-up nose like her sister's."

"No!" I say, turning directly toward Ruthie. "I want a straight nose." In my mind I can see Greek sculptures at the Met. A Greek statue of a woman with wavy hair piled high on her head and a nose so straight it is the continuation of her brow. *That is a nose. That is strength. That is unassailability*, I think to myself. *Who could question or doubt me if I had a nose like that?*

Dr Panelli glances down at the floor for an instant, looks up, winks at my mother, and then looks back at me. I look directly at him and repeat, "I want a straight nose."

Ruthie smiles and laughs offhandedly, as if she knows better in this situation, and interjects again, "Like her sister's."

*It's hopeless*, I think to myself. I'm afraid I have lost. I have no idea what kind of nose this man is going to give me. I look at him beseechingly, shake my head and say once more, "I want a straight nose." It won't be until months later, when the bandages come off, that I will see who has won.

In mid-July, a few weeks after school is out and all of my friends have left for sleep-away camp in Maine or Vermont, or the really lucky ones have gone on a teen tour of the Grand Canyon, I go down to lower Manhattan and check into the Ear, Nose, and Throat Hospital. It occurs to me I'm nearly back on the Lower East Side where my grandparents and great grandparents lived after they got out of steerage on some transatlantic steamer in the early 1900s. They had made their escape from the wave of bloody pogroms in Russia where they eked out their living in a no-man's land of poverty, prejudice, and centuries-old border wars.

*Gee*, I think to myself, *all I have to contend with is becoming a pretty American girl. A knife in my nose, but thanks be to God! not in my throat.*

I go into the hospital the evening before my operation. Everything feels surreal, like I'm in an episode of *Twilight Zone*: I've checked into a dreary hotel with shabby furniture and I find I can't leave. The windows are nailed shut. The door is locked from the outside. Men and women in white come in, but I can't go out.

When I finally fall asleep, surprisingly, I don't have a nightmare. Just the opposite. I dream of an Amazon bird with the most amazing Technicolour plumage—sharp turquoise, lime green, deep sea blue, crimson, and a bright, lemon yellow. It perches outside a room that's very high up with a set of windows open like French doors onto a balcony. But there isn't any balcony. There's only a huge drop down into a canyon. The bird perches on the threshold and won't hop inside. I think to myself, *It has wings. It's supposed to be free.*

Of course, it is a bird with a big nutcracker of a beak like mine.

The next morning a nurse comes in with a couple of pink pills in a white paper cup. She turns quickly on her heels, tosses a gown on the bed, and tells me to "Poot it on, yeah."

I put on the gown—sort of a sheet with slits in all the wrong places—and sit on the bed to wait. I feel like I'm going to be executed and all my time has run out. I've arrived at that unimaginable moment, my death, and there is no escape, no reprieve. The truth is, I'm a coward: I can't handle physical pain. It makes me feel like I've done something wrong, and I'm being punished by God. I realize that in a few hours I will be in excruciating pain. Worse, someone's going to change my face! Oh God, this is awful!

By now I'm really weirded out. I get up and go into the bathroom to look at "me" in the mirror for the last time. I start interrogating myself.

"What are you doing? What are you doing?" I say out loud.

"I haven't any time left," I reply. "They're coming to get me. I've already taken the pills." A sense of impending doom, tinged with desperation, engulfs me. Everything has been set in motion. I can't stop it, even if I want to. And the worst part is: I don't want to stop it—I want to be pretty! As pretty as I can be. Even if it's only half as pretty as Merri. The real trouble is I don't feel I have much of a choice. Either way I know that inside I'm going to feel just the same: Eyes too big, nose too big, hair too big, all hung on this face that's too puny.

I don't linger over this revelation; an orderly is drumming his knuckles on the door. "Yes, I'm coming," I call out from the bathroom. Before I exit, I turn for a moment to leave my old reflection in the mirror, but like a yo-yo on a string, it silently slips back into my heart. I become calm and resigned to my fate.

Standing in the doorway is a little brown man. He croons at me in island rhythms, "Hop you up, Missy" and points to this banquet table on wheels. Now

I feel like I've smoked a joint. I climb up onto this thing, and he tells me to lie down and adds with a wink, "No sittin' you up Missy when I drivin'."

Suddenly, I'm moving through space at a tremendous speed while flat on my back. It's a novel sensation. "Gee," I say. "I've never seen the ceiling move this fast."

Things feel vague and watery. I'm floating and detached, like it's a movie. It's *Frankenstein*! No—*Bride of Frankenstein*! I'm going to be married. But first I need an operation because, tsk-tsk, I'm not alive yet. In the operating room the doctors will levitate me through the ceiling, up into a huge thunderstorm. Zigzagging bolts of lightning will strike me. The monstrous me will be transformed, and then some big lug will fall in love with me.

*Bam.* A pair of swinging doors crash open and I'm plunged into an extremely well-lit room.

"Are you sleepy?" asks this towering, Boris Karloff sort of guy, as he bends down within an inch of my face. His breath caresses my cheek. My mouth won't open; I can't get my lips to work. Mercifully, he doesn't wait for an answer. He begins to say something about an injection. I don't catch this; it doesn't matter, I'm out like a light.

Sometime later, I'm in a waking dream state. My eyes won't open and I can hear voices; a deep, mature one on my left and a higher, younger one on my right. The voices are talking back and forth. Whole sentences are beyond me, but once in a while I catch words like "good" and "more, more." At intervals, the mature voice commands me to "swallow." The whole time I can feel a lot of pressure between my eyes. Something like a mallet hitting a wooden ball, a pounding.

A while later, I see red roses bleeding onto a green lawn and a huge flash of gold light, like the sun in Florida. Finally, the voices stop.

Dissolving out of some vast grey landscape, I begin to wake up. I must be dreaming. A second later, I realize, *No, I'm in the hospital. This is real*. And with my returning consciousness comes the pain. I've never felt this bad in my whole, short life. I can't swallow because my tongue feels like broken glass. I can't breathe through my nose. My nose is bandaged and I can't feel where it's located. My whole face throbs.

My eyes begin to focus and I can see Merri standing next to the bed. She says, "Here, open" and flips a chip of something into my mouth. Ice, it's ice. I feel slightly better, but not much. I plead with her to give me water. "They told me not to," she announces firmly without elaborating. In my state I can't imagine why and I don't ask. In a cracked whisper, I plead again and offer a future massage. Merri considers this, her eyes moving back and forth with lowered lids for a second. Surprisingly, she doesn't bargain. With hesitancy in her voice she says, "Okay, but I'm not supposed to."

She picks up a plastic pitcher from the metal nightstand a few inches from my head and pours the water into a small paper cup, adding a few chips of ice, her alibi. She lifts the cup to my lips and for a moment, I'm plucked from the jaws of hell. My alphabet soup of a brain miraculously finds, "the quality of mercy is not strained. It falleth like the gentle rain from heaven." My sister has become an angelic Maid Miriam.

A moment later, my jumble of metaphors dissolves like dirt on a window sprayed with chemicals: I don't feel so good. My whole system is in revolt. My stomach is quaking. Molten fluids are surging up from the pit. I hear Merri scurry for the plastic ice bowl, which reaches me, almost in time. I hear a loud "ugh" escape from her lips. She rings for help and when the nurse arrives with an aide in tow, they quickly size up the situation, take the brimming bowl from Merri's hands and, in an annoyed, bustling silence grudgingly change my bed covering and nightgown, which is souring with yellow spittle.

Merri goes away, but returns momentarily with another bowl of ice and resumes her vigil, responding to each whispered "please" by slipping a succession of ice slivers into my parched mouth. For the first time in a long time, probably since Merri became a teenager, I feel close to her. She tells me Mom will be in at evening for visiting hours, after a full day at the car wash.

I feel grateful and warm towards Merri. She suddenly becomes Florence Nightingale—that is, until she starts jabbering at me: How she's been through this herself—something I'm already aware of; how I'll go through a lot of pain—something I've already found out; and on and on. Her voice is blasé, like she doesn't actually recall how it feels. Three years ago might as well be three centuries. Or maybe she's trying to get me to focus on the good stuff that's to come. As far as I'm concerned, she has a funny way of doing it.

"Kind of feels like somebody's been bouncing a football on your face, huh? Doesn't it?" She says brightly.

My only reply is a strained, "Please!" Immediately, she responds by slipping more ice chips into my, by now, frozen mouth which is feeling oddly hot and burning. It dawns on me that absolute cold and absolute dryness are surprisingly similar sensations.

"Just think," she continues energetically, her eyes widening, "in two weeks the bandages will come off. You'll be black and blue and bloodshot, but after six or seven more weeks of that, the swelling and bruises will go down, and then you'll be gorgeous, just like me. Aren't you happy?"

At the moment, I am finding this happiness hard to imagine and, as my mouth is full of ice, I can only reply by widening my eyes in response.

I am not at all surprised that the next few days are worse. I can barely sleep. It's summer. It's hot. It's New York. And I'm on bustling, commercial 14th Street: honking cabs and trucks, people yelling all day and all night. This is before the era of climate-controlled buildings. I mean, there's no air conditioning. The big, wooden framed windows open up nearly to the ceiling. I could walk right out onto a rooftop without stooping, if I could get up and walk. It doesn't matter though. I can see from the bed the only things out there are brick, blacktop, concrete, tar, and, oh yes, soiled metal exhaust fans that are constantly running and sound like taxiing airplanes. Nothing out there can give the body or mind any relief. Not a shade, not a breeze, not a living green thing. I can't sleep and the hours go on and on. I imagine this is what eternity feels like.

More than that, I realize something has happened to me, and I don't want to close my eyes. I don't want to let go because I don't know what I'm letting go of anymore. I'm not sure if I haven't left a part of me in that operating room. I don't mean the little piece of flesh and bone. Part of me is gone, only I can't figure out what. I feel anxious, rootless, and at times delirious.

In my calmer moments, I think about Grandma Ethel. She didn't have her nose done, and she was a celebrated beauty and still is even in her 60s. She's sexy, out-spoken. Her nose isn't gorgeous: Too fleshy and bulbous at the tip, and the nostrils a bit cavernous. But she doesn't think that. She had nothing bad to say about nose jobs but I wonder if she finds them silly, or even distasteful. Like rejecting a part of who you are instead of embracing it.

Three weeks after the operation the packing comes out and the bandages come off. My eyes are black and blue, like I've been punched in the face, a lot. The blood vessels in my eyes are broken and inflamed, red and spidery. This is why I'm not able to go anywhere for the summer.

Ruthie's and Merri's reactions to the finished product are mixed, probably because the product is, too. Ruthie says little except, "ooh" and "aah," when it's first unveiled. Later, she says I'm prettier than I've ever been, that I'm a lovely young lady. Merri, on the other hand, thinks the tip is too bulbous and lacks the slender effect of hers. She thinks I should ask the doctor for an injection in the tip of my nose to draw out fluid in order to bring down the "bloated look" and make it thinner. Or better yet, I should have the whole thing redone right away to get it perfect. "Don't lose your courage by thinking it over." Needless to say, I do not follow Merri's instructions in this instance.

By my last check-up, Dr Panelli seems uninterested. I think he thinks it's a so-so job, too. I imagine he traces the results back to the confusion over what nose to give me. The way his eyes always perk up whenever Merri is mentioned makes me think he agrees with her and with Ruthie's advice at our first meeting. Everybody, except me, seems to know what's best for me.

And what about my reaction? How do I feel about the nose? Not only do I not know who I am, I don't know who the person in the mirror is. Inside, I'm still looking out from the same place. I'm fifteen though, and I find out quickly that it gives me a decided advantage, superficially, with teenage boys. The return to school in September, however, makes me nervous. I mean, I have a different nose; aren't people going to say something? As the day approaches, my embarrassment grows. What am I going to say, my parents bought me a nose during summer vacation? Instead of eight weeks at Camp Tall Pines, or a membership at the Copacabana Beach Club?

And you know what? Most of them really don't care. They only say, "Gee, it looks great." Of course, they are mostly Jewish. I mean I don't have to face a group of "*goys*" (as Grandma Ethel would say). And the guys, they *really* don't care. If I now look cute, I now am cute. End of discussion.

After six months pass, I am used to seeing myself in the mirror and become content, even a little happy. I feel this way because I now have something that isn't exactly me; something I can hide behind. I know that whatever people say, they aren't getting to the me *inside*; they're only getting to the me on the *surface*. As any teenage girl does, I become skilled at posing, wearing this barrette and that sweater. I mean, you learn how to present yourself to the world. You try on all different ways of looking. I was handed a mask to play with just in the nick of time. Only thing is, I can never take it off.

Years later, whenever I hear people talk about the cosmetic surgery this or that celebrity has undergone, I begin to cower and withdraw. I'm not sure whether their remarks are innocent or whether they are taking potshots at my "fake" nose. I have a perfectly valid claim to this nose, I silently defend myself. It is "on permanent loan," as they say in the museums.

My parents worked so hard to give us all the things they never had growing up during the Depression. They worked non-stop to give us the right clothes, the right nose, the right teeth, the right education, and someday a beautiful wedding. I guess they were trying to make us so secure that not this land, nor any other, could expel us, murder us, or imprison us. Enough money, possessions, a house and land, could perhaps buy all the security that might be needed. My parents didn't say this. I doubt they thought it. We knew it before we spoke our first words. We breathed it in with our first gasp of air and fed on it with our first nourishment. It is in every cell of our bodies and holds together all of our history at the end of the twentieth century, at the end of 2,000 years of running.

# Chapter 9
# Cleaning Out Grandma Ethel's Room

I am seventeen and Grandma Ethel passed away the previous fall. It takes Ruthie a year before she tackles clearing out Grandma's room. But eventually she enlists my help with sorting Grandma's personal items.

Grandma's drawers and closet hold things that were never seen by any eyes but hers. And even she may not have seen them for decades. She has a closet full of clothes dating from the '30s, when she began taking cruises, all the way up to her sequined gown worn to Sammy's Bar Mitzvah. I expect to find Grandma's antique golden braid in its bureau drawer, but it isn't there. When I ask Ruthie, she just shrugs.

Of course, Grandma's closet contains a few minks—one champagne-coloured full coat with shoulder pads from the '40s, a little dark half-cape, a stole, and some whole minks with fake eyes and noses worn clipped around the shoulders. They are all visible in a cache of photos that I retrieve from the back of the closet. I discover the photos in a box fashioned like a miniature steamer trunk. Along with them are some letters and a few pieces of inexpensive jewellery that must have held some sentimental value.

Ruthie takes on the task of sorting Grandma's "real" jewellery, to be split between Merri and me. "This long strand of pearls I'll have made into smaller necklaces for you two," Ruthie says as she continues assessing what to do.

"Look," I say at periodic intervals, showing Ruthie photos. "One of you and Uncle Max as kids. Him with knickers and you in a sailor suit and, oh my gosh, a Buster Brown haircut."

"Ugh, how I hated that haircut," Ruthie says emphatically.

"Look how decked out Grandma is in this one." I hold up the photo. Grandma sports a fur wrap and a wide brimmed hat; an old-fashioned pocketbook hangs from her wrist. Suddenly I focus on the whole scene, "A chauffeur, Ma?

Grandma had a chauffeur?" In the background a man is seated behind the wheel of an open car wearing livery and a cap.

"Yeah, we lived in Seagate for a while, a gated community, very hoity-toity," Ruthie says, laughing, then looks a little sad. "Why don't you put those photos into one of our albums," she suggests.

"And the letters, too?" I add.

"Yeah. You'll be literary executor! Read through them and see if they contain embarrassing stuff." Ruthie laughs, a schoolgirl's nervous giggle.

"What do you mean, Ma?"

"Nothing, nothing," Ruthie replies absently.

The letters I read are mostly from friends, one business associate, and Grandma's other grandchildren, Uncle Max's daughters. They are mildly interesting. None contain startling, off-the-record family secrets. So, what the heck is Ruthie referring to?

That night Ruthie spills the beans on Grandma. I'm in the kitchen while she's overcooking a roast for dinner. Dad loves it cooked to the consistency of shoe leather. Mom always promises she'll take ours out while it's still pink and put the rest back in for Dad. Somehow, she always forgets. This one looks like it's halfway to Hell.

"So Mom, what's Grandma's scandal you were so mysterious about this afternoon?"

"What?" Ruthie asks buoyantly, with false surprise, "you didn't find any scandals in your grandmother's past?"

"Well, I haven't gotten through all the papers yet, but so far nothing, except some more neat photos."

"Let me see," says Ruthie, motioning me to take them from the quaint little steamer trunk box and hold them up. Ruthie's hands are still basting the sacrificial roast.

"Here's one with her dressed as a flapper—long beads, cloche hat, short hair, short skirt, and raised teacup. I wonder who took the photo?" I say out loud, curious as to the development of camera equipment at that time. Then I notice Grandma's standing in front of a table that must be in a nightclub. *Oh*, I think, remembering Grandma's comment about drinking "teacup" gin somewhere up in Harlem with a racially mixed crowd. Since Grandma's drinking is no secret, I don't think this is what Ruthie means.

"That's probably Uncle Bob who took the photo."

"Ma, who's Uncle Bob?"

"Oh, he wasn't really our uncle, although we didn't realize that at the time. Grandma would introduce us to someone and tell us to call him—"

"You mean she had boyfriends? When you were little?"

"Something like that," Ruthie says. "Through high school. After that I moved out so I don't really know who kept her company."

"Did your friends know? Were you embarrassed?"

"Well, as I got older, I wouldn't bring friends home anymore."

"Did the boyfriends live with you?" I ask, thinking I'd discovered the really big scandal.

"Sometimes," Ruthie says quietly.

"Did that upset you?" I ask, as Ruthie isn't saying much.

"No," Ruthie says. "I grew up fast. I could handle myself around men. You done guessing?" She slides the roast back in, careful not to slosh the grease over the sides. Then she closes the oven door, letting it slip from her mitt at the last second so it slams shut.

"Another twenty minutes," she declares, and walks over to the sink as I roll my eyes to the ceiling. Nothing is going to save this roast.

"The clinker," she says matter-of-factly. "Your Grandma was in the clinker for a year on account of a real estate deal."

"Jail?" I ask. "What did Grandma do that got her sent to jail?"

"Her real estate partner left her 'holding the bag,' as they say. He skipped the state. So they charged her with false advertising with intent to defraud. The prosecutor was trying to make a name for himself. He was running for county attorney and used the case to get publicity. You know, tough on criminals, protection of the people, that sort of thing." Mom licks the gravy off the spoon and drops it in the sink. "He just loved the fact that she was a divorcée career woman which, of course, back then, meant loose woman with no morals."

Ruthie puts up hot water for instant mashed potatoes, and brings a large bowl of "Styrofoam" potato flakes to the kitchen table. The dinner vegetables will either be frozen or from a can. I don't think I ever set eyes on a fresh vegetable until I grew up and moved out of the house.

"I don't understand." I say to Ruthie when she gives me the potato flakes to stir as she pours in the boiling water. "How did they defraud people?"

"It wasn't really her fault," Ruthie sighs. "When she started in real estate, she was learning the ropes from a broker who had bought up acres of land out on Long Island. You know for two centuries it was farmland with cows and potato fields? He went so far as to make Grandma a junior partner, which was quite something. In exchange, Grandma was to handle all of the land transactions. He would do the rest. This was in the late '20s, when no one saw the potential. The idea was to build whole communities and sell plots for homes. The advertisements promised neighbourhoods with all the modern amenities, including paved roads, sewer systems, electric lines, hospitals, and schools."

"Then the stock market collapsed, the Depression hit, and local governments had no money for development. The people were left with land and nothing else."

Finished with the potatoes, Mom takes a sip from a cup of tea left over from the breakfast dishes. She makes a sour face, puts it down, fidgets with the teabag and gets up to put more water on to boil.

"Want some tea?" She asks.

"No," I reply, my attention riveted on the story. She sits back down and continues.

"You see, the land ads were placed in a lot of immigrant newspapers to entice those who were making it in America and wanted to move out of the city to neighbourhoods with people like themselves. They were left up a creek without a paddle, so to speak. They organized and brought their complaints to the local district attorney. He decided to prosecute for deceptive advertising and failure to meet the promises made by the real estate agent, who—ta-dah—was your Grandma. Her name was on all the legal paperwork for the sales, and she was good at her job."

The kettle whistles and I jump up to get it and pour some water for "old tea," as Ruthie likes to say, reviving the breakfast tea bag. (I wonder if this is some weird frugality left over from the Depression.)

"What about her boss?"

"He, as I said, left her holding the bag and skipped town. Went over the state line to, I think, Pennsylvania, where no one knew him and just began again. It really was a travesty of justice, but the prosecutor wanted to make a name for himself and go into politics. Grandma—femme fatale, morally suspect divorcée—got convicted. Besides," she says, "it all turned out like the ads said, it only took a few years."

*If it was the Depression*, I think, *it could have taken eight, maybe ten years.* Was Ruthie being ironic? A ghost of a smile goes across her face, but I don't know what to make of it.

"What did you and Uncle Max do? Where did you live?"

"With your great aunt Anna. What a chip on her shoulder! Grandma paid her well to take care of us. Max and I were *persona non grata*, second-class citizens, her servants. I grumbled a lot but I had nowhere else to go. I had literally two dresses for school—one for the wash and one to wear. She should have given us some of the money from Grandma, but she held onto all of it. She complained it hardly covered expenses for the two of us, made a stink about all the extra work she had to do. Which was a lie. I did the work. I shopped for food. I did the laundry, cleaned the rooms. I never felt so badly treated in my life."

"How old were you?"

"Just going on sixteen."

"Did you visit Grandma in jail?"

"Yeah."

"Was it strange, did it upset you?"

"Well, I'm a tough cookie," Ruthie says with a laugh. "Your Grandma wasn't to blame. Just caught in a raw deal. But you know, that's how she got her start."

Ruthie pauses to take a sip of her tea, which is probably cold by now. She makes another sour face, but I don't even bother to ask if she wants a new teabag.

"Well, her boss left her with valuable real estate and the legal right to make transactions. In another ten years, the development of the land was well under way and that nest egg launched her into real estate big-time. She'd sell a lot, then invest in more land. She could see the coming of the suburbs in relation to New York. When the towns started to incorporate, she knew she'd hit her jackpot. A steady trickle of sales kept her going until the G.I.s came back and everybody wanted their own home. Also, main streets for shopping were developed and Grandma had some valuable pieces in prime locations. The cards had finally come up in Grandma's favour and she was set for life when it came to money."

"Grandma married three times?"

"Yeah." Mom says, and says no more.

(I don't find out until later the real estate swindler is her second husband.)

"You know what they say, lucky in cards, unlucky in love. Sorry to say, she eventually settled for a drinking partner."

Ruthie puts the mashed potatoes in the oven to keep warm and sits down again. She rummages through the box and plucks out a photo.

"Look. Grandma must have just arrived in America." It's a group photo with about fifteen people in three graduated rows in front of a house with a large wraparound porch. A big sign up above the porch reads, "Bloom Family Cottage by the Sea."

I spot Grandma Ethel, front and centre, in the second row, wearing a shirtwaist dress with a tie. Her lovely hair is piled luxuriously on top of her head.

"Is your dad in it?" I ask, gingerly. My grandfather was never mentioned when I was growing up, as if he were a forbidden subject. I didn't want to make Ruthie sad. Once the estrangement happened, he dropped from sight, and took no part in a relationship with her.

"No," Ruthie says as she scans the photo. "I don't see him. They met on the trip over to America," she says. "He helped translate Yiddish to German officials for Great Aunt Miriam. Stopped them from sending her back to Russia. Grandma and he got acquainted on the ship. Turned out he was living with his brother on Orchard Street, down the block from your great grandparents."

I am stunned by Mom's story of how Grandma Ethel and Grandpa Phil met. It is more information than I've gleaned in the past seventeen years. I guess the photos are making her nostalgic. I wait for her to say more about her father, but she doesn't.

I pull another photo out of the box. "Boy, in this one Grandma's dressed in an embroidered blouse and, well, a dirndl skirt, like the peasant look."

"Let me see," Ruthie says impatiently and adds, "it's the real peasant look!"

"Who's that?" I put the photo on the table.

"I've absolutely no idea," Ruthie says as she takes hold of it and studies the young man's features. He is wearing a Russian cap and bunches of curling hair stick out from beneath it. He also sports a beard. Behind them are overarching, towering trees, filled with heavy drooping blossoms. Their hands are touching and they look very young and, well, innocent.

Ruthie turns the photo over and on the back is written, "Odessa 1914."

"Must have been someone she knew in the old country, right before she left Russia."

"A friend or a sweetheart?" I ask, curious.

"Grandma never mentioned a boyfriend back in Russia. She was very forward thinking about a new life here. I doubt it was anything serious. What do you have left to go through?" Ruthie says, glancing down at the box.

"These letters, but they're not in English. This one is set up like a poem."

"Yiddish," Ruthie says. "How about you find someone to translate them?"

"Okay," I say doubtfully, not knowing how I'd accomplish the task. I feel like a character in one of those fairy tales given something impossible to do.

"What about these trinkets," I add, pulling out a small round pin that has a mosaic of flowers. "Wait," I say, and look back at the photos, shuffling through them quickly. "Grandma's wearing this one." I hand the picture from Odessa to Ruthie.

"Yeah, it's pinned to the peasant blouse. You want it?" Ruthie asks.

"Yeah," I say, feeling there's something special about it, although it's probably not worth much except for its connection with Grandma Ethel's life in Russia.

Surprisingly, I find that a friend from high school, Alicia, who is good with languages, is studying Yiddish. I bump into her in the hallway between classes and we agree to meet in the library, fourth period, so we can talk. When I arrive, my friend is seated at a table in the corner, far away from the librarian's desk.

Alicia is a much more knowledgeable Jew than I am. Though she attends *Shul* irregularly, she is steeped in Jewish culture. She is amazed that from before the beginning of recorded history, before the Bible, a band of nomadic people travelled the deserts of the Middle East, pledging their lives to follow this one God. "Despite our periodic decimations, like some eradicable weed, we've stuck around, scattered throughout the world, popping up here, there, and everywhere." She feels it's important not to let the Yiddish language die while Jews are still in the world. "Yiddish," she says, "is one of our flowering stalks." She finds it miraculous that Hebrew is again a spoken language, the official language of Israel.

I hand her Grandma's letters and she asks if I know anything about them. "No," I reply. "You're the detective. I know zilch about Grandma Ethel's life before she came over." *Actually,* I think to myself, *with Mom's recent revelations about Grandma, I don't know much about her early life in America, either.* "She wouldn't talk about the old country."

"Same here," replies Alicia. "I wish I'd interviewed Bubbe before she passed away, but I was only eight."

"So much history, centuries and centuries of it lost, as if it never happened," I say, my voice raised with emotion. "Like there was nothing before America. As if they were plopped down out of nowhere, grafted onto a new tree, a new land, a new continent."

The librarian comes over and asks us to quiet down. "Sorry," we say. "We're working together on a paper." She gives us a sharp disbelieving look, then goes away.

Alicia continues, "I guess the religious ones believe the Bible is their history."

"Sure, but it stops way before the modern era."

"There are histories of the Jewish religion from the Middle Ages, written about Torah, Talmudic studies, Midrash. But they aren't sociology," she says.

"That's what I want to know, how they lived, what they felt, what they ate, what they wore."

"A lot like the surrounding cultures—until, that is, they were expelled. A lot of expulsion went on between centuries of semi-acceptance. From England, from France, from Italy, from Spain, from Portugal. They kept traveling east. I think life was shot through with uncertainty. Not like America."

*No, not like America,* I think. "Tell me what you know about the Russian-Polish Jews."

"Well, after fleeing expulsions in Western Europe, our ancestors finally got to Poland. The rulers accepted them for what they could bring to the society—banking, trades, skills, merchandising. Then, in the eighteenth century, the surrounding countries carved up Poland, and Russia swallowed up most of the eastern section. Catherine the Great didn't know what to do with the newly inherited Jews. She believed Jews had a deleterious effect on the Christian peasants. From then on, it was known as the 'Jewish problem.' To solve it the government resorted to forced conversion, control, and restriction."

Suddenly the librarian reappears. "This is your last warning," she says.

"We promise," we both say, but she isn't buying it.

"Next time you're out." She walks away. We roll our eyes and say under our breath, "Dragon Lady."

Alicia continues, "Each Czar had his own policy, rules, and laws regarding the Jews. At one point, they were conscripting ten- and eleven-year-old Jewish boys into the army for twenty-five-year terms, in hopes of forcing them to abandon their religion and accept conversion, or in hopes of them perishing.

Jewish families would maim their own children to keep them from this inevitable death sentence. Jew taxes were levied on top of the ones everyone paid, which drove many into poverty. The virtual imprisonment in an area called the Pale of Settlement, and prohibition of owning farmland, herded them into small towns where one Jew competed with another who was as bad off. Expulsion from the cities, where more opportunities would have been available, and the periodic outbreak of pogroms while local law enforcement turned a blind eye, added to their miseries."

"You know a lot of history of the eastern European Jews."

"Not as much as I'd like," she says with a bit of modest pride.

"Oh no," Alicia says as she looks across the room. "Here comes Dragon Lady." We beat her to the punch as we get up and leave. The bell for next period hasn't rung, so we continue talking in the hallway.

"So, you'll try your hand at the letters?" I ask.

"With great interest. Especially this one." She holds it up.

"Yeah, I'm curious about that, too."

"It might be a copy of one of the Jewish poets from that era."

"Would you recognize it?"

"Probably not. Maybe my Yiddish teacher will know, or know other Jewish literature professors who would. We could always contact the *Forward*. It's published in English as well as in Yiddish."

"I remember my father saying how my Grandpa read that paper, which had stories written by Sholem Aleichem and Isaac Bashevis Singer, all in Yiddish."

"Yeah, the paper might be a good resource if we get stuck."

A few weeks later, Alicia tells me she's made headway translating one of the letters. It's written to someone named Marta. Oddly, it is *from* Grandma Ethel, not *to* her. Either it was never sent, or it was returned to Grandma. We sit together in study hall and go over the letter.

*Dear Friend,*

*I hope I may call you that dear, dear Marta. My letters have been returned to me and I am desperate for some news about you and Jacob. This blackness of not knowing has swallowed me whole and I fear the worst for both of you.*

*If only I had a shred of news about your fate I might risk returning to Odessa for a while. As it is, I leave in two weeks with my family for Minsk to secure our train tickets to the boat in Bremen. I no longer know anyone in Odessa, my aunt* travels with us to America. I have no personal funds to sustain me, no papers, no place to stay, unless you are able to take me in?

I pray for your safety and Jacob's eventual deliverance.

My life hangs in the balance.

Your friend,
Ethel

"Well, who the heck is Marta?" I ask, whispering, so the study hall monitor won't throw us out.

"Maybe another cousin from Odessa?" Alicia suggests.

"Wouldn't seem to make sense," I say. "I'll ask my mother and anyone else alive who might know. I wonder who the guy is. More importantly, why does Grandma Ethel's life depend upon news about these two people?"

It takes Alicia a few weeks to come up with more translations. She comes over after school so we can talk freely. She says she has a lot to show me.

"Boy, these letters are rife with mystery," she says.

Though eager to start, I ask her if she wants soda.

"That stuff will rot your teeth," she replies. "How about tea and something to nosh on?"

"Honey cake?"

"Oh, yeah! Fire up the samovar, put the tea in glasses and we'll time travel back to Russia," she says.

We settle ourselves in the playroom at the card table. The tea is in cups.

"I want to warn you these letters are intense. Ominous, I'd say." Alicia starts.

"Come on," I reply. "Don't leave me in suspense."

She takes the translations out of her notebook and puts them on the table.

"I worked on them in chronological order. Here's the next one."

Dear Marta,

I have not received any letters and I must assume this means terrible things for both of you. If I could get my hands on something to sell, I would hasten back to Odessa and search for you, starting at the café in the Jewish Quarter. Remnants of your Bund group, or those who are familiar with it, must still be there.

*If only I could get back to Odessa, I might be able to sell my hair, as I know it is worth something to the wig merchants. That might sustain me for some time. But I have no funds here unless I steal them from my family, which, forgive me, I cannot bring myself to do. All is needed for the trip to America and anything of value has already been sold.*

*In times such as this, one can only turn to the Almighty. I commend you both to His keeping, for I feel that only some greater strength can help you now.*

*Ethel*

"Their Bund group?" I ask Alicia.

"A Jewish Workers' party, before the 1917 Revolution. I think it would be similar to a trade union. It organized skilled workers to give them bargaining power. As you can imagine, the Czarist regimes were not well disposed towards them. Possibly, that is what the letters are talking about. I mean Jacob and Marta must have been involved with the Bund and a crack-down occurred."

"Makes sense," I say, thoughtfully. I read out loud the next letter.

*Dear Marta,*

*Only five days remain before my family leaves. I cannot sleep and my mother has noticed my state. I go out for walks to the outskirts of the town so I can bemoan this horrible fate that has befallen you and Jacob. My confused grief has no outlet otherwise. Of course it is nothing compared to your situation. If only I understood what has happened to you. It is this not knowing that eats away at me.*

*My mother tells me I must garner my strength for the coming journey. She is worried about my strange behaviour. I am silent as a stone with her and the family. She tells me that America will be the fulfilment of all our dreams. Papa and Samuel await our arrival and I need not fear the future, but welcome it with open arms.*

*Of course I dare not tell her the truth about what has happened to the two of you. My heart lies broken and bleeding because I may never know your fate. My tears do not help you. I wish only, now, that you will be able to lessen the blows that Jacob most likely endures. I know dear Marta you are capable of helping him. All my strength goes out to you.*

*I think this is the last letter I will write. If you had been able, I know you would have sent me news by now.*

*My love to you always,*

Ethel

"Whoa, heavy. This is the third time I've read the letter since translating it and it gets me every time," Alicia says, shaking her head.

"Poor Grandma," I reply. "To be cut off from friends she cared about so deeply. To have to live under an oppressive and violent regime. I don't know how she coped with such pain." I wonder to myself what the rest of the story is, and if it may figure in some way with Grandma's bouts of drinking.

"Yeah," says Alicia, "to be caught in the throes of historical forces. It's the stuff of drama. Wait till you read the poem. I don't think it's by any published Jewish poets, although I can't be sure. I haven't checked with the literature professors that my teacher knows."

"Why don't you think it's a published poet?" I ask.

"I don't know. It seems tailor made to your grandmother. From what you told me it matches her physical description. Here, judge for yourself."

*You Startle Me to Life*
*Grey eyes like the first streaks of dawn,*
*The velvet light that ushers in the rising sun.*
*Hair unbound, loose upon your shoulders*
*Flows like the greatest*
*Of the earth's rivers, if only it swirled*
*In burnished gold.*
*Lips, astir with words, glisten like pomegranate seeds,*
*Or ripen slowly like fruit on the vine, now*
*Blushing pink, now deep in fragrant red, to rival*
*Any flower's petals come spring.*
*Your hands fly through the air like milk white doves*
*Coming at last to rest in the nest of your lap.*
*Your whole self, a gazelle that sprints in joy*
*And peace, suckling beside its mother in green fields.*

"The thing is," Alicia says, "it echoes imagery from the *Song of Songs* in the Bible. Whoever wrote it knew that poem."

"What's the *Song of Songs* say?" I ask.

"It's something you could study, it's all symbolic of the Bride and Bridegroom, as body and soul coming to God. The thing is, it's very *hot*."

"Sexually?"

"Yeah. How the heck it gets past the religion police I have no idea. I brought you some sections of it that are pretty steamy. Here." Alicia hands it to me.

*Thy navel is like a round goblet,*
*wherein no mingled wine is wanting:*
*Thy belly is like a heap of wheat*
*set about with lilies.*
*Thy two breasts are like two fawns*
*that are twins of a gazelle.*
*Thy neck is like the tower of ivory....*
*and the hair of thine head like purple;*
*The king is held captive in the tresses thereof.*

*How fair and how pleasant art thou,*
*O love, for delights!*
*Let thy breasts be as clusters of the vine,*
*and the smell of thy breath like apples;*
*And thy mouth like the best wine,*
*that goeth down smoothly for my beloved...*
*Let us get up early to the vineyards.*
*Let us see whether the vine hath budded,*
*and its blossom be open,*
*and the pomegranates be in flower.*
*There will I give thee my love.*

"Wow! It's practically X-rated. I mean in a good way. So sensuous," I say.

"*And* sensual!"

"Yeah. Look at this." I hand Alicia the photo from Odessa. "What do you think?"

"Well, he certainly looks the part of a Yeshiva boy. The beard, the glasses, everything about him, but no side locks. You think that's the guy referred to in the letters?"

"Yeah. But why no Marta in the photo?" An idea strikes me. "Maybe some weird ménage-a-trois?" I say.

"Boy, your Grandma's pretty amazing. Well you know there was that Russian 'free love' advocate around the first part of the century, Emma Goldman."

"The strange thing is, the more I learn about Grandma's life, the more I think a lot will never be known."

"Silent as the tomb, huh?"

"I'm afraid her secrets might have gone with her."

In the following few weeks, we have final exams. Alicia says she can't do any more translations until after the summer. She's going to a language immersion program in Barcelona for eight weeks.

"I'll come back dancing the Flamenco with a Latin lover in tow," she laughs. "Then I'll translate the rest of the letters for you."

"I only have three more," I plead.

"Sorry. Intriguing as they are, I won't have time," she says. "Have to put first things first."

While I'm stuck in the suburbs, summer drags on. I show Ruthie the translations. She becomes thoughtful and teary-eyed.

"Grandma never spoke about Russia. I think when she arrived in America she made a determined break with the past. Whatever was left back there was no longer a part of her life. I never suspected she was involved with the social movements in Russia."

When Alicia returns in September, I go to the little steamer trunk box to retrieve the last three letters. They're gone. I ask Ruthie if she's seen them.

"No, pumpkin," she says. "Maybe you misplaced them. If you left them lying around, Almeda may have thrown them out by mistake."

*That sounds*, I think to myself, *like the eternal accusation that hangs over the heads of all hired help. It doesn't ring true.*

Whatever happened to them, I feel as bereft as I was at thirteen when my little dog, Sugar, bolted from the transport van on the way to the groomer's shop.

No amount of tears, searches, or advertisements ever led to her return. A hollow emptiness, a feeling of desolation overtakes me. I can't believe the letters are gone. I continue to search for them, but eventually they slip from my mind until decades later when Ruthie passes away.

# Chapter 10
# A Day of Celebration

I am 21 and I am celebrating my college graduation. I've made it through the four years, working hard sometimes, sometimes not. I haven't quite made the grades I'd hoped, and I've sometimes failed to take courses with the best, hardest professors for fear of not doing well enough. Fear and insecurity are still my constant companions. They dog my every step. However, I've finished and gotten through those four years. I have arrived at my diploma.

Things haven't always been easy. After freshman year, I have a period of mental paralysis when I can't seem to finish, or even start, any term papers. I take a semester off, finally tackle them, and make it back to campus.

Then, in my senior year, I face a bigger hurdle. My interdisciplinary creative arts major requires that I write a thesis on the philosophy of art. I try to draw a connecting line through all the arts I've studied, but I fail to find an overarching concept. The paper dissolves into perceptive pieces of the puzzle without a unifying theme. The professor gives me a stern lecture about lack of focus and a grade of "C."

That less than stellar ending of my college career happened over a month ago. Today, I will put it all behind me with an unqualified celebration of making it through those years of hard work. I tell myself *I've done it. I've graduated. Nothing can take that away from me.*

I decide to honour the passage of this milestone in my life at a dinner with my family at an upscale restaurant. Then it comes to me, a really splendid idea: all of us spending a day at a local Hilton, using their spa and pool, and then dining at their candlelit restaurant. Everyone—Bennie, Ruthie, Samuel, and Violet (Samuel's Southern born, blonde, *shiksa* girlfriend)—loves the idea. (Merri is on vacation in Greece.)

We are all pampered from head to toe in the spa. Wearing towels and fluffy terry cloth robes, we go from steam room to sauna to massage table. Finally, the men and women emerge and are reunited at the indoor pool. This is like a giant greenhouse with a glass roof and a jungle of exotic hanging plants.

After all the pampering, I am relaxed, happy, and all aglow physically in a way I don't remember ever experiencing before. As I dip into the pool, the coolness wakes me up and refreshes me. I love the feeling of my body moving through the shimmering water. I am a little girl again, splashing about from one end to the other. I take to the element like a dolphin arching up in joy. Then I resolve into steady, long gliding butterfly kicks and breast strokes, feeling my limbs completely extended and rhythmically pumping along in a meditative state of timeless motion. Finally satiated, I start to climb out of the pool, up the silver ladder from the deep end.

Ruthie and Violet are nearby on chaises lounges, stretched out for catnaps. Bennie and Samuel are at the other end of the pool standing around and talking. Whatever they say echoes off the glass roof and walls as if amplified like a stage whisper. My body is emerging from the pool, my back toward them. I climb slowly up the ladder as my father says in a clearly audible (has he raised his voice?), nearly guttural tone, "Doesn't Lillian have a nice ass?"

A wave of shock runs through my body like an electric current. With one sentence, he has shot me down. All my joy drains from me as if my veins have been cut and I am bleeding out. I am stung to my core and feel defiled, covered with grime I cannot scrape off my soul.

Without thinking, I turn around to see Samuel, his head jerking back as if he has been struck, eyes aghast. Like a deer caught in headlights not knowing what to do, he says, "yeah" in a hurried voice as he swallows hard.

The two most important men in my life have dealt me a mortal blow. I feel like a glass figurine crushed beneath a boot. I collect myself with great effort. I cannot keep the hurt outside of me. The only way I can hold myself together is to begin thinking. I decide this is a defining moment. It is as if I've seen the monster at the centre of the labyrinth of my life. The fact that my father wishes to hurt me, to demean me, to wound me, to destroy my happiness, devastates me most of all. I breathe in this knowledge as if it is a cloud of poison gas.

I am able to excuse my brother as an unfortunate bystander who doesn't do the right thing. Not so my father. If what I am thinking is correct, I can no longer have anything but a superficial relationship to him. I cannot trust him to care for my joy or my love or my sorrow. Even after those four years of college, he does not respect me for my effort, but sees me as "a piece of ass." Any connection to him is tainted by this experience.

I am unable to speak. I do not say anything to Ruthie for fear she will make excuses for Bennie and exonerate him under the banner of his being "an idiot." Probably they will start a fight about it in public, either at the pool or at dinner in the restaurant. Things will go from bad to worse. I do not let myself acknowledge the fact that everything *is* as bad as it can get. My reasoning is all cock-eyed. I cannot face reality. I tell myself if I make a fuss, or tell what has happened, it will ruin the day.

All I can do is refuse to speak. I withdraw into myself. At dinner I simply stare blankly at them and then turn away and engage Violet in conversation. It is okay to talk with her. She has never betrayed me. My mother asks if I am enjoying my duckling. I look at her for a second, then look down, and turn away saying nothing. She asks me if I want to taste her rib eye. I do not answer. Instead, I turn to Violet and ask about her entrée. My brother says I'm a good, strong swimmer. I look at him and say nothing. He seems flustered by my silence.

My father teases me about how expensive the hotel is. He laughs and says it's good I don't graduate from something every year. After a time, they simply give up and talk among themselves as if nothing is out of the ordinary. No one asks, "What's wrong? What's the matter? Why don't you talk to us?" This upsets me even more. It is all I can do to remain frozen, all my emotions pushed down and blocked off.

I feel like a character in a Greek tragedy. Everything—my life, my day of celebration, my future—is a heap of ashes. I am a lump of suffering human flesh. When I get into the back seat of the car to go home, my tears flow quietly over my cheeks. I stifle sobs and know that this day has become another in a succession of memories that will haunt me.

Days later, when I think at length about what happened, I realize why, aside from the hurtful crassness of my father's remark, the episode hits me as hard as it does. Really, it is so simple I wonder how I overlooked it at the time.

As I grew up, my father's attention to my body was more and more hurtful. At age seven, he took the humiliating 8 mm shot of me naked, tinkling in the stream. Another time, when I was eight, out on the lawn in the summertime, running through the sprinkler, he teased me about wearing a top. He said I had nothing to cover up. He tried to convince me to take it off. His words dampened my spirit. I knew that babies and very young children go around without tops, but not someone my age, especially when in public. The fact that I was outside at the time saved me from coercion. I did not acquiesce, which is what happened all too regrettably in an incident two years later.

One afternoon, around age ten, I was in my parents' bedroom talking with my father. He started telling me how cute I was. "You're growing up too fast," he said peevishly. He began tickling me and tossed me onto the unmade bed, pulling up my top enough to bare my belly. He made a "poofy" on my stomach. That started me giggling. However, the physicality of being picked up and thrown onto the bed scared me. I started to get up, but my father pushed me back down and made another "poofy."

"You're still my little girl. When you were a baby you had such a cute *tush* I had to bite it every chance I could get. I called it '*tushie* pie.' Better than apple or blueberry, and you know how I love those pies."

Here my father said, "Mmm, delicious! Let me take a bite now before you grow up anymore."

The thought of what my father wanted to do went through me like a searing pain. A wave of nausea came over me as I scrambled off the bed and stood on the other side of the room, shaking my head, "no." I was rooted to the spot with fear and rising panic. *Why can't I get my legs to work and carry me out of the room to…anywhere?* Strange as it sounds to my adult self, my father wasn't letting me go. He was still talking.

"Oh, come on, don't be so stuck up now that you're older. You're still my little girl. Just pull down your pants and let me take a bite. Ruthie," my father suddenly called out to my mother who was in the adjacent bathroom.

"What is it?" She called back.

"Lillian won't let me take a bite of her *tush*."

My mother appeared in the bathroom doorway clad in her long line brassiere, corset, and panties, with a wand of mascara in one hand and a tissue in the other. She must have been getting ready to go out.

"You're turning into a real sourpuss now that you're getting older," my mother said. "Nothing is wrong with it," she continued as though she was talking about the weather. "He's your father. You know him. He just loves you so much. Would you feel better if I were in the room with you?"

Now I began to feel dizzy. I always did whatever my mother asked of me. That was the way things were. If Merri lost something like her sweater, I was asked to give her mine to solve the problem. If the basement room wasn't set up yet for the new maid, the new maid slept with me in my bed without anyone asking how I felt about it. If Grandma was alone in the afternoons, I was supposed to keep her company, never Merri or Samuel. It felt like the only way they would love me was if I sacrificed myself to their needs.

I was feeling emotionally overpowered. I couldn't say "no" to both my parents at the same time and risk their combined disapproval. Their approval was like air to me. I couldn't seem to go without it. And some part of me desperately needed to believe that they really did love me—no matter how sick I felt about what they were doing. Like a prisoner without any rights, I lay down on the bed and pulled my pants down. I felt my father staring at my backside like it was a target.

He went, "Mmm," then bit me so hard I cried out.

"Ouch!"

"See," my mother said, "not so bad."

No one said anything more to me. My mother went back to the bathroom to finish her make-up. My father went downstairs to read in his easy chair. No one thought anymore about it except me, and I would think about it for the rest of my life.

I pulled up my pants, got up from the bed, and went into the other upstairs bathroom. *These are not real parents*, I swore to myself as I started to cry. Real parents would never do this. Never, never, never. But I kept crying just the same as if they were. They were the only ones I had and I was too young to solve the bitter hurt that lodged in my chest. I was too young to run away. Too young.

Over time I forget what happened. It goes underground and festers for years. When I hit puberty, I simply freeze up whenever anything to do with a boy comes up. I can't kiss one in innocence. I don't feel innocent. I feel soiled.

Years later in analysis the incident occupies hours of therapy. Each time it comes up, I feel guilty, as if it had been my fault for not protesting, for not running out of the room, for acquiescing against my own heart. The event is a stain on my soul that I can't wash out.

When I ask my analyst why it is so monumental, he says, "Because it hurt you, your pride, your sense of self. It was a strangely tangled, mixed up act of shaming and sexual domination cast as a supposed act of love. It's very confusing. The fact that both your parents were involved had a double impact."

When I am much older, the graduation incident appears tragic not so much for my father's remark—by then I had figured out he said it because of his own feelings of diminishment, that his daughter had a college degree and he hadn't even graduated from high school—but tragic because, at age 21, I was reduced to such painful trauma for a nasty remark aimed at lowering my self-esteem. I had let myself be a target for his words, which were aimed at what was in truth a lovely part of my body. I had since learned the Greek term meaning beautifully proportioned buttocks, or "*callipygian.*" I had a *callipygian* backside.

In reality, his comment is a projectile that does no harm to that beautiful target, but like a bullet, pierces my heart. For weeks I bleed profusely from the wound. For years, I turn the anger inward. I go over the graduation incident and upbraid myself for not protesting my indignation. For not unleashing my anger. For not confronting him. I was not assertive then, or now. Merri would have handled things differently. She would have challenged him on the spot. It might have escalated into a fight—something I cannot do in public or even at home. She would have stood up for the truth of her own heart. The day might have become a memory of ruin, but it was, in any case.

All the painful events regarding my father spill over into my adult life. I pick men who end up hurting me. Men who are button-pushers. Men who are passive-aggressive. They are withdrawn, silent, withholding, or else they lash out in a covert way. And really, I don't think they are aware of the pattern. The men have their own emotional scars, sustained long ago. Like me, they are trapped within a labyrinth of pain. I am the poster child for tortured relationships. The joke about two porcupines trying to make love comes to life.

The years pass and a stable relationship with a man is never in the cards (reminding me of Grandma Ethel). I simply accept the fact that my life is not made for intimacy. I give up struggling and receive in exchange a quiet and peaceful life. A life that suits my temperament.

# Chapter 11
# From Another Century

At age twenty-five, after living in Connecticut where I graduate from college and then work four years at a portrait studio, I move to New York City. I find a cheap apartment on 10th Street off 1st Avenue, in easy walking distance to the Lower Eastside. Ruthie bemoans the location, saying it's where the family started out, poverty-stricken, after arriving from Russia.

"Your grandmother is turning over in her grave," she says.

I can't tell if she is seriously upset or finds some rueful irony in it. I couldn't be happier.

I walk the streets for hours going up and down the neighbourhoods, over to Grand Street and Rivington, Essex and Canal, Orchard and Mott. I recall Grandma Ethel's descriptions of the way it was, crowds of pushcart vendors selling everything from pickles to corsets, knishes to pots and pans, sidewalk thick with old world immigrants, greenhorns garbed like peasants, children playing stickball, and horses dropping their manure in the streets. Because of her asthma she could hardly breathe the stifling air of the summer days.

On hot nights the family took their feather beds out to the fire escapes, a poor man's "balcony." I knew from books the air was not fresh. It re-circulated from the lungs of 200,000 bodies, sequestered in a twenty-block radius, one of the densest populations in the world. To sleep on their makeshift porches was like sleeping with tens of thousands. The coal smoke from their stoves added a layer of soot to clothes, dishes, lungs. By day they saw only small strips of sky between the crowding of buildings. At night, they were lucky to glimpse a star.

When I am a girl, the family occasionally makes the trip from Westchester down to the Lower Eastside where Orthodox Jews run stores, closed on Saturday, open on Sunday, that sell everything below retail. Each neighbourhood specializes in different merchandise: Clothing stores all in one set of blocks, bedding and linens in another, then shoes and handbags, lighting fixtures and furniture. The goods are of uptown high quality and have been bought as seconds or overstocks, with imperfections that don't mar the overall appearance or function. Name brand items are plentiful.

Everybody tries to out-price the surrounding competition. It is an Old-World bazaar where bargaining is a pastime enjoyed by buyer and seller alike. Much theatrics goes into it, and a lot of fancy footwork.

Ruthie is a bargainer par excellence. Her major ploy is to *kibbitz* with the sales lady while she piles up a mound of goods. This gives the clerk the anticipation of a big, fat sale. Ruthie adds all the prices up in her head, and then offers a lesser amount for the whole lot. The woman will impugn the price for a while, look at the huge pile of merchandise, repeat several times, "I should die tomorrow if I let them go so cheap."

And then often gives in saying, "Okay, okay, you're a smart Mrs." That usually nets Ruthie one to three items free.

Of course, Bennie goes crazy. Especially at the sight of a lot of clothing. He rants about the fact we have tons of clothes stuffing our closets and over-flowing our dressers. He is apoplectic whenever we cry out that we have nothing to wear. For him the arithmetic is scientifically simple. For us it is veiled in the mysteries of femininity and a culture of ever-changing fashion.

Grandma Ethel didn't exactly shun a trip to the Lower Eastside, but she was strictly an uptown customer at that point in her life. She had done her time in the old neighbourhood. When she was with us, we often stopped at Yonah Schimmel's Knishery. With a misty look in her eyes, Grandma would nosh on a kasha knish and sip through a straw Dr—somebody's—Celray Tonic. I couldn't tell if she was reminiscing to herself or was made sad by visiting her early life. As the years went by, she grew too old to go on our whirlwind tours of the shops. She needed to rest and get off her feet at regular intervals. I think the trips became a burden to her physically as well as emotionally.

Nearer to my apartment, literally down the block, is the 2nd Avenue Deli, another fixture of New York Jewish life. For over seventy-five years people have savoured their fare: stuffed derma, gefilte fish, chicken soup with matzo balls, beef *flanken*, brisket, roast beef or corn beef sandwiches. The tables are crowded with pickle and relish dishes, a breadbasket with onion rolls and black bread, all free for the price of a lunch or dinner. In old-world style, they bring your tea in a glass with a metal spoon.

When I eat at the Deli, I take pleasure in smelling the aroma of my hot pastrami sandwich on crusty rye bread with spicy mustard. As I sip my tea, I wonder if a young Ethel ever sat at one of these tables. What were her favourite dishes? *Matzo brie*? Cherry blintzes? Potato latkes? Was it a luxury to eat out? Could she afford it? I think about her first year in America: a new country and language, a husband she marries within two weeks of landing, and Ruthie seven months later. By the end of the year she finds her way into a lucrative job.

Because of her beautiful hair, she dazzles in a job selling hairpieces. For women not equally blessed, they now have the opportunity to shine. Every lady wants the same luxury of hair gracing *her* appearance. Before long Ethel is traveling to department stores up and down the East Coast, working on commission, and putting away savings because her husband Phil is bringing in less and less from his truck routes. Eventually she discovers he is gambling away his earnings and, on top of that, has a few women friends on the side. Within three years after the birth of their son Max they divorce.

One afternoon I wander over to Washington Square Park, where New York University has bought up the surrounding neighbourhood. At Greene Street and Washington Place, nestled among college buildings, I spot a plaque commemorating the Triangle Shirtwaist factory fire. I know the story. The fire killed 146 Jewish, Italian, and Irish immigrant garment workers. The emergency doors on the factory floor were routinely kept locked, supposedly to stop the women from sneaking out with goods, and to prevent them from taking breaks.

When the fire struck, fuelled by all the ready stock of cloth, the bosses ran out to save themselves and left the workers to be burnt alive. Many women huddled by the windows and jumped to their death to escape the inferno. The fire department ladders couldn't reach up to their floor of the building, and the fire department nets were useless. Bystanders watched in horror as the women fell like scorching meteors, instantly killed as they crashed into the pavement below. When the fire was finally out, they found the burnt bodies of the women who did not jump. One was in a macabre position, her charred skeleton still seated before a sewing machine.

The terrible irony of the fire was the recent legislative defeat of safety and workplace laws that would most likely have prevented the fire and loss of life. The entire nation mourned the tragedy. Out of the flames of death, a new movement arose that passed building safety, fire, and labour laws.

One night during high school I had watched a documentary with Grandma Ethel on the Triangle Shirtwaist fire.

"Do you remember it?" I asked.

"In a manner of speaking," she replied. "It happened in 1911, before I arrived. I knew a girl, Sophie Rosenberg, in our tenement. Her sister Yetta died in the inferno. The fire was so hot and the smoke choked them. They started jumping, some holding hands. They couldn't suffer the heat any longer. Precious young women dropping out of the sky to their death." Tears came to Grandma's eyes. "Of the 500 people who worked there, 146 died in the blaze, others suffered severe burns and other injuries—not to mention the horrible memories that haunted them the rest of their lives. What *Gehenna*!"

"What's *Gehenna*?" I asked.

"Hell," Grandma replied. "Terrible, terrible. Families came by for days trying to identify their daughters, mothers, sisters, aunts. The bodies were horribly disfigured. The only way Mrs. Rosenberg could tell it was Yetta was by a gold locket she wore with a picture of her fiancé. Oh, oh, oh," Grandma said in a pitiful tone. "I remember poor Yetta's mother. She never got over it. She was forever in a daze, her hollowed out eyes red with weeping. She wandered about the tenement and streets a lost woman."

In the neighbourhood of my apartment, I find the Orpheum and Thalia theatres. At the turn of the century they were Yiddish theatres that played the *Jewish Hamlet*, the *Jewish Doll's House*. Had Ethel ever been in the audience?

Once Grandma talked about the movie houses, the Nickelodeons that played the newest silent films that were all the rage.

"For five cents you got admission, for two cents more a bag of peanuts. Peanut shells everywhere you stepped." She laughed. "Special nights they'd have a lottery. You could win a whole chicken or a fancy box of chocolates. Between acts the pianist would play while people walked up and down the aisles and socialized."

"What were the movies like?" I asked.

"Slow to tell a story by today's standards," she smiled. "But they were so different from everyday life. Romantic. And oh, the stars! I loved Theda Bara and Valentino."

"What did you like about Theda?" I asked, thinking of the boring silent films I'd seen.

Grandma's face warmed at the thought. "She was really the daughter of a Jewish tailor from Ohio. But Hollywood made her father a European artist and her mother an Arab slave girl who gave birth to her in the desert beside the Great Pyramid. It was a publicity story because she was playing Cleopatra." We both laughed.

"One of her pictures, based on a vampire story, started people calling sultry, sexpot women 'vamps.' So exotic and smouldering in her looks. She had a curvaceous, full body, like a real woman's body, not like those straight-figured girls, Mary Pickford and Lillian Gish. She was what you call a hussy. In her films she came out on top, instead of being punished by some dismal fate for using her womanly wiles, or waiting for a man to rescue her."

"You admired her movies?"

"I did. I had a sense of freedom watching them. As if I could triumph over the odds and the men, too."

I wondered what she meant about the men, but I didn't ask.

"What about Valentino?"

"Same difference, a sexy man. What allure! Smoky eyes and sensuous lips. He'd give a look and you just wanted to swoon. Women did, all over the world."

I begin photographing the Lower Eastside, to document the neighbourhoods and buildings, the people on the street and in the stores. Not much has changed since the turn of the century. The Orthodox Jews never really left. Most aren't artisans any longer—the watchmaker, the shoemaker, the tailor, the jeweller—but they still are the storekeepers, the merchants selling the same goods. Here and there the streets are made of cobblestone. On the large thoroughfares, Grand and Canal, push carts dot the streets selling hot dogs, knishes, sodas.

Orthodox families stroll past, wives dressed to the nines wearing coarse hair *sheitel* wigs, the little boys in velvet *yarmulkes* and *peyos*, and the little girls with mounds of curly hair. Even in the summer heat the fathers wear fur-trimmed hats and long black coats. The sidewalks are packed with people looking for a bargain. At half the price, you can buy designer seconds and look like an Upper Eastside woman who shops at Bloomingdales. Even your sheets can be Pierre Cardin, your towels Calvin Klein, your shoes Italian leather knock-offs. The immigrant instinct to get the most at a fraction of the cost is still alive.

One day I come across the Tenement Museum of the Lower Eastside on Orchard Street. In a downstairs gallery is a traveling show of clothing, household and religious items, and artifacts from the Pale of Settlement in Russia. Behind a glass case are Jewish peasant dresses, lovely "holiday" aprons embroidered with silver and gold thread, tortoise shell hair combs, Sabbath pearls, leather boots, heavy winter coats. In another are displayed ivory Torah pointers, silver Sabbath candlestick holders, decorative paper silhouette pictures of everyday people, houses, and landscapes. On the walls are photographs of Jewish *shtetls*, market squares, wooden houses.

I wonder if Grandma handled similar objects in her home in the *shtetl*. Had she clipped up her hair with a comb, fastened pearls around her mother's neck for the Sabbath, worn a fancy apron on holidays? I can see her going about her busy days helping with the daily chores of cooking, tending vegetables, washing clothes, caring for her younger sister and brothers. How different a life she had lived a century ago in another corner of the world. A world that was left behind, laced with memories and, perhaps, sorrows.

Grandma's early life has always been a mystery to me, hidden behind silences. After seeing the exhibit, I feel a small piece of the puzzle is restored. I can picture her, where she lived, what she held in her hands, the clothes she wore. For some reason, I feel she had left behind something of importance in that land. She had tried to assuage the loss with husbands, drink, and prosperity with its attendant luxuries. None of these had replaced that early life, that home, that person she had once been. Something, or someone, was irrevocably lost.

The second, third, and fourth floors of the museum are in restoration as authentic tenement flats from the turn of the century up through the '30s when different waves of immigrants flooded into the Port of New York: the Germans, the Irish, the Eastern European Jews and Slavs, and finally the Italians. The ceilings are pressed tin, the walls have dark wood wainscoting. There are large iron stoves for cooking and heating, with wood and later coal. Kerosene lamps were used for lighting before electricity was installed. Outhouses were down in the courtyard until they were replaced by toilets in the hallway of each floor.

The museum has the registration book for the building with the names of all the tenants from 1903 to 1933. I find two Kaplans listed in 1914. Grandma's maiden name. I imagine a teenage Ethel, honey-gold hair and grey eyes, living in the building, getting up each morning and going out to look for work. She steps across the same streets I do now, sees the same sky at daybreak, the same stars at night.

Eventually, the family travels far from the Lower Eastside: up to the Grand Concourse in the Bronx, out to Brooklyn's Ocean Avenue near the museum and

Botanic Gardens, then Long Island, and finally, Westchester. Yet here I am, back where it all started.

I am fascinated by the exhibit. A map on the wall shows the demarcation of the Pale of Settlement in Western Russia. The place that Grandma had never talked about. The crucible that prompted several million Jews to uproot themselves and journey halfway across the world to a foreign land. I am the recipient of that legacy. I am the holder of that dream. The beneficiary of that desire to live a better life, in a better place.

Standing before that exhibit, I realize I owe my ancestors everything. What had their dream given me? A life of safety without the threat of annihilation. A life of myriad freedoms. A life filled with luxuries beyond the struggle for mere subsistence. I wonder how my family would have fared if we'd stayed in Russia. Probably we'd all have died in the concentration camps in Poland. Or in mass graves of the Soviet slaughter. An even greater love for Grandma Ethel and Great Grandma Sarah and Great Grandpa Elias fills my heart.

Over two millennia ago we Jews started out in the Middle East, eventually found our way to Europe, were expelled, and pushed east until the time of going west to America. Through the centuries we have travelled to every corner of the globe. Go anywhere and you will likely find an enclave of Jews. An intelligent people, a hard-working people, a hyper-vigilant people, always alert to possible extinction and political disaster, sometimes joyous, sometimes melancholy, whose hearts are steeped in the history of exile and slaughter.

In a sense, we are all spiritually homeless. I am too. When will this diaspora ever end? Will we ever settle once and for all? Is Israel our one and only home? Or can we ever be part of the permanent fabric of America—supposedly the greatest land of migrations, for all people, from all places, for all times.

Perhaps America will be my answer. Perhaps America can be every outcast's answer. I dearly hope so.

It is no accident I will become the photographic chronicler of those outcasts of society, the homeless—"the wretched refuse" of New York's teeming streets.

# Chapter 12
# To Shul or Not to Shul

I am thirty-five, walking with Merri along the edge of the Atlantic on the beach at Fire Island where my sister and her family have a house.

"So..." Merri says.

"So?" I reply, fearing where that tone of voice will lead the discussion.

"Won't you come to *shul* next week when we're back in the city? You might meet some guys." Her words linger in the air, as if attesting to the benefits of being observant. Merri's Judaism has blossomed. She finds it a comfort and a guide in her daily life now that she is married with two children, ages three and five. At the moment they are in the hands of the *au pair* for post lunch naps.

Eight years ago, single and thirty, Merri left her corporate culture for more satisfying work as a fundraiser for a Jewish charity. At the time she said, "It's meaningful work that makes a difference in people's lives, and you can't imagine the number of Jewish holidays: celebration of the harvest, celebration of the Torah, celebration of the spring—celebration, celebration, celebration! I get off at three every Friday in the winter. It pays to be Jewish." She laughed light-heartedly about the perks of her new job.

And more perks materialized. Merri, who is both forceful and diplomatic, able to make others laugh and enjoy themselves, was meeting the most wealthy and well-connected mothers of New York Jewry as she pressed for charitable contributions. And she was also meeting the bachelor sons of those philanthropic mothers. Merri became "the pretty and dynamic Jewish girl" who needed a nice Jewish boy to complete the picture.

This scenario worked its matchmaking magic. A little more than a year later, Merri stood under the *chuppah*—the flowered bridal canopy—at the Pierre Hotel. Now she is living the fairy tale—a wealthy husband, two children, a seven-room *pied-à-terre* in New York, and a house at the beach.

"Don't you see," Merri says as she stops to look at the horizon, then turns to me and plows on to make her point, "if every Jew acted like you, intermarriage would, in a matter of two generations, obliterate our culture."

*I suppose she has a point*, I think to myself. However, little does Merri know that I'm guilty of an even deeper sin: I intend to foreswear marriage altogether. I realize this is not the moment to confess that to Merri of all people. She is the champion of every societal norm. Better, I think, to respond to the current charge of failure to serve my faith.

"I know what you say is possible today in America but," a flicker of anxiety comes into my voice. An instant later I regain the courage of my conviction and continue, surprising myself with the words, "that's just the point. The world would be a better place without religion. What's been the greatest impact of religion in human history? Devastation, destruction, prejudice, hatred, war, and cruelty."

"That's absurd!" Merri replies in a voice that contains everything from dismissiveness, to passion, to antagonism.

It occurs to me that those qualities are the key to Merri's success in life. I am dazzled by how many strands of energy run through Merri's personality to help her make her mark in the world. She has a sure-headedness guided by conviction, along with a sturdy feistiness.

I give up trying to get my point across. I feel ineffectual, as I often did in childhood. I recall one of Grandma's favourite sayings, which also characterizes Merri's way of being in the world: *Never go to the tail of the dragon when you can go to the head.* Grandma Ethel had the *chutzpah* to meet her challenges head-on, make money, and fight if she needed to. Merri has not only inherited our grandmother's honey-coloured hair and mystifying grey eyes, but her take-charge personality as well.

"You're confusing human action with religion—the worst traits of mankind played out through history, twisting theology to selfish, bloody ends. Why do people blame God for everything bad that people themselves do? We were put here to choose. Don't forget Judaism was the first religion to enshrine God's way on those tablets Moses brought down from Mt. Sinai. They gave the world morality, peace, and justice. *Those* are God's commandments."

In our vigorous walking, we reach the lighthouse at the point of the island. Merri plops down on the beach, shields her eyes from the bright afternoon sun with her left hand, and dips her fingers into the sand with the other.

A lot of what she says is valid, except "God's way" was not very peaceful. She ignores the conquering warrior culture of our ancestors. They fought the inhabitants of the land God had promised to the Jewish people: *Oops, sorry! We'll have to throw you out of your homes and kill you to fulfil God's covenant with our people.* I decide not to raise this point with Merri.

"Let's head back," she says. "The kids will be waking up soon."

We walk along in silence for several minutes.

"You may have a lot of what you think are good reasons, but basically," and here Merri stops walking and turns to look me straight in the face, "I think you're afraid. I think that's what's behind your denial of your Jewishness."

I do not reply. I know that fear is not the only reason for my views on religion. But within my heart, I also know there is truth in what my sister says. I have to admit, at least to myself, I am afraid of the many ways the world might see me as a Jew. Stereotypes abound: cheap, showy, cliquish, money grubbing, crude, uncouth, liars, and Christ killers. Even success is twisted in some people's views to be an evil conspiracy to take over governments, if not the world. Our history is a monument to fears realized.

"I can always tell when you're afraid," Merri says. "As a little girl your chest would sink down and you would look distracted, retreating from whatever was happening." She takes a deep breath. "You're wrong," she continues, "In unity is strength, not vulnerability. You isolate yourself and are cut off from centuries of tradition. Fear isolates. Love liberates."

We start to walk back to the house.

I can't find fault with her conclusions. Neither can I find the courage to live life boldly, as Merri does. She dares the world to make snide remarks about her Jewish heritage, or try to belittle her successes. I, on the other hand, shrink from such confrontation.

The fear concerning my Jewishness starts early in my life. Perhaps it is some genetic inheritance; the biology of ancestors who ran for their lives from one land of persecution to another, who lived and ate their dark bread of fear from day to day. The never-ending history of slaughter and destruction followed them to every fleeting refuge.

My mind flashes back to age nine or ten. I saw a documentary on educational TV showing the skeletal remains of the dead and the living in the camps. The documentary taught me that, not so long ago in the sweep of history, things went horribly wrong for the Jewish people. An ever-repeating pattern lived down through the centuries. Is something going to befall me one day for being Jewish? Here in America? Is it possible? No, I think, America is different. Land of the free, home of the brave.

But I am not brave. I'm a nine-year-old bookworm, plain and gawky with huge eyes, soon to be framed by glasses, and a beak of a nose amid an ocean of brown curls. My dangerous heritage is written all over my face. I am a little rabbit of fear who only knows how to freeze. I live small, hidden from the world.

My nine-year-old self watches, as though frozen to the spot, the walking skeletons of the camp survivors, every rib and vertebra poking through tautly stretched skin. It is a horror movie of emaciated, spectral beings, still somehow alive. But it is not a movie, it is real. It is a film General Eisenhower has ordered to be made to document the German atrocities of the death camps. The survivors' bodies are composed of bare twigs, their eyes are wells of darkness. Their mouths twist in macabre echoes of smiles from some long-ago memory.

The film shows piles of the dead, some stacked in wagons like rigid rags of bone. They were to be transported to the ovens in a jumble of inhumanity—a foot sticking out here, arms askew there, a shorn skull hanging down. This film of their last goodbye fills my mouth with the taste of ashes.

America's army rescued the remaining prisoners, as guards and commanders deserted their posts. America the good had triumphed. My America.

Forever after, nothing could scour those images from the backs of my eyes. My retinas captured their meaning and my brain stored the film's final pictures—piles of innocent eyeglasses, shoes, wedding bands, and gold teeth scavenged from the dead.

Why is it that after the documentary I feel guilty, ashamed? Of what? Of simply being Jewish and being treated that way by the world? Am I a self-blaming victim? In my flesh and in my bone, I am afraid for the world to know I am a Jew. An existential blanket of fear and shame covers me and its poison seeps down into my psyche.

I realize I am lost in the past, not having spoken to Merri for at least ten minutes. I let go of the terrible images and rouse myself back to the present as we walk on this serene day, bathed in sunlight and the sound of the sea on this barrier island.

"So?" Merri reiterates. "To *shul* or not to *shul*? That is not such a big question, now, is it?"

"I'll think about it," I reply.

"That's your problem, you think a thing to death. Take a leap of faith, why don't you?"

As usual, the conversation ends in a stalemate. I walk on in silence and Merri sighs.

# Chapter 13
# Seder at Merri's House

I am thirty-nine, seated with my family at the Seder table, no husband or boyfriend by my side. We are all satiated from our holiday meal: A sumptuous brisket made by Ruthie that is tinged with the taste of apricots and plums, and falls apart in delicate shreds at the touch of a fork; a turkey laden with wine-braised giblets and rich gravy cooked by Merri; a roast beef sitting in its bloody juices brought by Marge, Samuel's Catholic wife. Each family will carry away a portion of the leftovers at the end of the evening. The children have eaten at the kids' table set up in the adjacent living room. Coffee is brewing on the counter next to a steeping pot of tea. Plates of desserts—honey almond cake, chocolate marbled sponge cake, raspberry *rugalach*, chocolate dipped vanilla cookies, and a large bowl of fresh fruit—wait in the kitchen until everyone recovers from the feast. Belts are loosened, buttons are opened as everyone breathes a collective sigh of gratification.

Merri looks thoughtful for a minute or two, then says, "What would happen to the Jews, especially the American Jews, without the practice of our religion? Without our religion, what are we?"

"We'd still be Jews. We'd still have our culture and our heritage. Capitalism can't wash that out of us," replies her husband Richard.

"Leave capitalism out of this. It's doing just fine," retorts Merri.

"We'd still have our culture!" He insists, slapping the table.

Merri squints her eyes at Richard and says, "I'm talking about God."

The faces of all the males go blank. The consensus is that keeping the major holidays is good, even significant. The God question is another matter, to guess from their cynical looks.

"How can you believe in that God mumbo jumbo? It's a throwback. There's no God, Jewish or otherwise," says Samuel.

My instincts prompt me to scoop up my camera. It is my alter ego and never far from my side. This will be a heated debate and I want to document it—facial expressions, body language, all of it. I start clicking away. Nobody seems to notice or care.

"What about the still, small voice within?" Ruthie offers.

"You believe in voices? 'God told me to do it,' the cry of the insane and deranged!" counters Samuel with a look of disgust. The camera goes click.

"What about the six million?" Bennie calls out from the living room couch where he's reading the paper. "How could God let such a thing happen? Considering He's God and all powerful." I get a long shot of him from the table.

"You're blaming God for the actions of men. God created us with moral choice. Otherwise we would not be made in His image. There is such a thing as free will," Merri declares. I catch her ramrod stance. She begins placing the dessert platters on the table. The coffee stops brewing and clicks off. Ruthie gets up to help with the cups and saucers.

"Are you implying that those who went to the gas chambers had made a moral decision that led them there?" Bennie says, slamming down his paper. I record the look of consternation on his face.

"Maybe that's what happens to Jews who assimilate," Merri states boldly.

"Oh, don't even go there," Samuel says through clenched teeth. He gets up from the table and joins Bennie on the couch. "It's a sacrilege to say they deserved it for abandoning their faith!" I get a shot of father and son sitting defiantly on the edge of the couch.

"God forbid! That's not what I'm saying," says Merri, her hands spread wide in exasperation. I shoot her pose.

"What then?" asks Richard.

"What I'm saying is, one takes the risk of being mistreated by the dominant culture. The one thing that makes us strong, has made us strong for centuries—able not just to survive but thrive—is our faith." Merri sits down at the table and continues. I capture her expression as she exhorts. "In unity is the ability to overcome defeat at the hands of men and governments. What we've learned is that however safe and secure we seem to be in our chosen land, time and again the savagery of mankind breaks out in tough times and Jews invariably become targets. All I'm saying is abandon God at your peril."

"Why did God allow the slaughter of the Jewish people?" Bennie asks rhetorically. "I'll tell you why. Because He doesn't exist." Bennie resumes reading the paper.

"There's a story about Rabbis in a concentration camp having a debate about God," says Richard. "Does He exist? Doesn't He exist? Is He all-knowing, all-powerful? If He is, they vote to condemn Him. Who could countenance such atrocities? When they finished the debate, they all said, 'Let us pray'." I catch Richard's "can you believe it?" expression.

Merri puts the coffee pot and teapot on the dining room table. "You know," she says, "the history of Jews is an amazing thing. Jews gave the world monotheism and the ten commandants, a code of laws, and a sense of justice. A God with whom we question, debate, confront, contend."

"Yes, that's true," I say, surprising myself and putting down my camera. "Before that, what were there but gods and goddesses whose lives were soap operas, or spirits inhabiting the natural world that had to be appeased and propitiated?"

"What emerged," Merri says, "was a God who commanded a rational justice and a moral code of behaviour, the 'shall not's' of lying, stealing, killing, adultery." Merri starts pouring coffee and dispensing tea. She cuts the dessert cake. By now everyone has rejoined the table.

"What's so great about monotheism?" asks Richard. "There's still your God versus my God."

"It's a God who is not restricted to time or place, who exists with you wherever you go, and lives in your mind and heart," says Merri as she passes along the cake platter.

"At least," I add, "if each tradition concludes there's a single God, maybe they'll start to understand it's one and the same God."

"No," says Merri emphatically. "The Jewish God is *the* God. The God of Abraham, Isaac, and Jacob. Not Christ Messiah or prophet Mohammed."

"Although," I reply, "Abraham is considered to be the Father of all three faiths. More than one path leads to the top of the mountain."

"It's a different mountain. They aren't equivalent," insists Merri as she sets down her fork.

I take a sip of my tea and sigh inwardly. I wonder, *why not the same mountain? It would bring about peace. There'd be empathy and compassion for each different faith.*

Bennie is dunking the cookies into his coffee and slurping them up. "The chosen people. Ha! Think of that," he says.

"Chosen for what? To be persecuted throughout history?" He asks derisively. I get a photo of him dipping a cookie.

"Chosen to keep God's laws," interjects Merri.

"Pogroms and autos-da-fé," continues Bennie. "You kids don't know how good you've got it. You should thank your lucky stars your grandparents made that miserable journey to America. The start of a new life in a new country, in a new century. Finally, a place we can live in peace. Imagine if we'd stayed in the old country. If the pogroms didn't get us, Hitler or Stalin would have. When you think of it," he adds, "it's sort of a miracle we're here." His words make me think of Grandma Ethel.

"Doesn't it make you wonder at the twists and turns of history and fate? That out of the greatest devastation we've known, we're back in Israel after 2,000 years?" asks Merri.

"Oh, please! That's not fate, that's bitter irony," retorts Samuel.

"That's a literary term. I'm talking about physical reality," she says.

"We're a hardy weed, that's all," he says and pushes away his dessert plate. "Even after decimation a few seeds scatter in the wind and find some fertile soil. We reinvent ourselves in a new land. No matter," he continues, "we're condemned. Condemned for being too foreign, too hardworking, too religious. Condemned for trying to assimilate. Condemned for not trying to assimilate. Condemned for one thing or another."

"Hopefully, we won't be condemned in America beyond the usual anti-Semitic grumblings. This has been our golden land from the start," Merri says. She goes over to the bookcase and pulls out a large tome. "You've got to listen to what George Washington wrote in reply to a cordial welcome from a Newport congregation. We began here as full citizens, not as the usual 'Jewish problem'."

What she reads fills a gap in our knowledge of American history and quietly stuns the room. "Washington writes, 'All possess alike liberties of conscience and immunities of citizenship…For happily the government of the United States, which gives to bigotry no sanction, to persecution no assistance, requires only that they who live under its protection should demean themselves as good citizens. May the children of the stock of Abraham who dwell in this land continue to merit and enjoy the good will of the other inhabitants, while everyone shall sit under his own vine and fig tree, and there shall be none to make him afraid."

"The Dutch of New Amsterdam had no such sentiment or leadership," says Samuel. "Peter Stuyvesant wanted to bar Jewish immigrants from their settlement."

"But capitalism saved the day," adds Richard with a self-satisfied smile.

"That's right," says Samuel, nodding at Richard. "Jewish investors in the Dutch West Indies Company forced Stuyvesant's hand." Samuel leans back, sighs, ponders a moment, then nods toward the history book Merri is still holding. "Too bad Washington didn't express a similar sentiment towards another group of people. It would have saved untold thousands of American lives later on."

"If he had," says Richard, "the country as we know it never would have come together. The slave states would never have agreed to join."

"You see," says Bennie, "politics, politics. Someone's always ostracized."

"Persecuted," snaps Samuel.

After Samuel's words I remember a photo exhibit I recently saw at the Museum of the City of New York. Photos, real photos of lynchings in the South. One from the '30s, of bystanders gawking at the hanging, half-charred body of a black man. It had been sent as a *postcard* with a message on the back about "our barbecue" last night. The pictures are added to my internal gallery of photos of the Jewish Holocaust. There is no dearth of human calamities perpetrated by other humans. *We* are the monsters we project onto others.

Then, too, despite Washington's words I recall that Jews were lynched in the South as well (Leo Frank comes to mind). I also recall the "soft" prejudices: inability to get jobs in certain professions, exclusion from civic organizations, and quotas for Jews at American universities. Some of these probably still exist; I have no illusions about our "modern" times.

Though dinner is over and done with, we stay arrayed around the table.

"Israel has to be protected," Merri says, absent-mindedly straightening out a wrinkle in the tablecloth. "The U.S. should take the lead."

"The U. S. has and does," says Richard, "for its own reasons."

"But this administration has let the ball drop and their support is actively needed."

"Are you saying the Palestinian people have no rights?" charges Samuel. He is leaning back precariously on the chair's two back legs. Though the photographer-me wants to document what's bound to be a lively interchange, the sister-me doesn't want to see my brother and sister blow the holiday celebration out of the water with an argument. Silently I wish peace to reign.

"The Palestinian people," says Merri, rising to the tone of challenge in Samuel's voice, "have been left high and dry by all the other Arab states, who've never come to their aid, or invited them into their countries."

Samuel leans forward in his chair. "The Palestinian people are there and have always been there. It's an irrefutable fact that's not going to change and needs to be dealt with."

Merri fires back, "Statistics show that many of the Palestinians now in Israel came late in the day from various Arab countries as migrant workers to the citrus industry. The boom in construction because of Jewish immigration also contributed to an influx of Arab workers. The land was not stolen from the resident Arabs, they sold it."

"The reality is the Palestinian people are trapped." Samuel sits back in his chair. "Their poverty and lack of education only make things worse. Ignoring these realities has led to the terrorism we all abhor. Ignore these facts at everyone's peril."

"Israelis are not ignoring the facts, but they are trying to protect themselves from the violence. The checkpoints exist for that reason."

"They make the Palestinians' lives more miserable and humiliating on a day-to-day basis," responds Samuel.

Ruthie comes in from the kitchen and says, "Now, now hush up and stop fighting."

"With Jews like you, Samuel," says Merri, "who needs enemies?"

For a moment or two everyone is silent. Then Merri says, "Israel knows there has to be a two-state solution. But when they proffered peace and 90% of the disputed land, they were rejected out of hand. The Arabs want Israel destroyed and will bide their time until neighbouring Arab nations oblige them."

During this speech Ruthie slips back into the kitchen and comes out again. "Enough, Merri," she says. "This is a holiday gathering. Stop fighting, you two, and make up. It's not the time or place," she says, brandishing a rolling pin in a comical stance. I get a perfect shot. She pantomimes slugging each one of her fighting children over the head. And I get shots of that, too.

"Ma, you're wrong. It's exactly the right time and place," says Merri, who always gets the last word in any fight.

"Now calm down and come here," Ruthie says and drags Samuel over to Merri. "Kiss your sister. And you, Miss know-it-all, give him a kiss back."

And I get shots of those as well.

* * *

A year later, the photos I took of our Seder, and as much of the discussion as I can reproduce from memory, are on display at the International Centre of Photography along with other photo documentation of ethnic holidays—Irish, Italian, Puerto Rican, Polish. I call ours, "A Difference in Point of View."

Reviewers praise the show in general, and especially my laying bare the different voices in the Jewish community. Nonetheless, for a few weeks I am anathema in the family. Eventually I am forgiven by everyone but Merri. She believes family loyalty is paramount. However, she too softens when some newspaper columnists support her position and she attains a short-lived notoriety.

The show brings me more than just praise. An old boyfriend from summer camp resurfaces. At age forty my life is about to begin.

# Chapter 14
# Life at Forty

At the opening night of the photo show documenting the seder from a year ago, I am both excited and worried. It is a milestone in my career. But I'm not sure what the reviewers will think.

Out of the woodwork come all manner of old friends and photography colleagues. This is a decidedly mixed blessing. It feels like a high school reunion, something I've dodged for years because I don't want to be reminded that I've failed at "life." That is, relationships. I've never found anyone I could mesh with for longer than a few months. I have a penchant for picking men like Bennie: charming but fatally flawed men who push buttons, trigger fights, cause scenes in public.

Eventually, I realize that even normal guys scare me. I don't want to get stuck in something that replicates my family's constant upheavals and fights. I'm too brittle, I conclude, to adjust to even the natural friction of intimacy. I'm still the lost little girl retreating from storms to the calm of her own room. But there I won't have love and companionship and a family. Just a career to curl up with at night.

And in five minutes that all changes. I see a tall, dark-haired, slender man wandering through the exhibit. My eyes keep returning to him. Something about him is familiar. When he stops at the gallery guest book to write a note, or sign his name, I saunter over as casually as I can manage.

"Like the show?" I ask.

He looks up at me with deep glacial blue eyes.

"I know you," I say, not knowing how to finish the sentence.

"Of course, you do," he replies with a half-smile. "You were my first girlfriend."

Frozen in place I think, *And I want to be your last*. I glance down at the guest book. *Brian Strauss. Oh, no*. I think to myself. *Summer camp*. "Is it really you?" I say, unable to catch my breath.

"Yeah. Your one and only. When I read the piece in *New York* magazine I wondered if you could be *the* Lillian Greene. And you are."

Old camp memories flood through my mind: Brian kissing me under the pine trees, Brian teaching me to sail a sunfish. Brian dancing with me on the last night of camp. I laugh out loud remembering Brian trying to cop a feel by awkwardly plopping his hand on my chest when he walks me back to my bunk.

"What?" He says, smiling inquisitively.

"Remembering old times," I say without explaining. Then I recall how I insensitively ended the relationship when Brian came to visit me after the summer was over. I ignored him. I'd decided he was too much of an egghead.

Merri had given him a ride back to the train station. She said he was quiet, "sort of depressed. What did you do to him?"

"Oh, the summer ended, and so did he. He's so…cerebral."

*Boy, was I wrong*, I say to myself. "Sorry about the way I ended things," I say, smiling sheepishly.

"Who remembers?" He says. "We were fifteen. Promise you won't do it again?" He adds with a devilish smile.

"Promise," I say, laughing. "So, tell me about yourself. What do you do? Rocket scientist?"

"Half-right. Research scientist. Medical research, cancer."

"I'm impressed. You were such a brainy guy." Before I fall too deeply into 'like,' I think to myself, *I'd better check out some of the facts*. "Single, married, divorced?"

"Separated," he says and adds, "Two kids, a little princess just turned six, and a wild-child of a boy, four."

"You sound proud of them."

"Yeah, I am. Aside from my work, they're the best things I've ever done."

Somewhat curious, I say, "Sorry about your marriage."

"Don't be," he says and leaves it at that. "So, single, married, divorced?"

"Early on I came close a couple of times, but no golden ring. Lately it's been one disaster after another. Relatively short-lived, thank God. You know, as they say, all the good ones are taken." I smile at him and he smiles back. We're both silent for a moment.

"Well, your photography show is fantastic. It takes difficult subjects for American Jews and humanizes them. The photo of your mom with the rolling pin is priceless. Did you catch hell from your family?" He asks, gesturing at the display.

"For a while."

We're silent for a minute or two.

"Well, I don't want to take up more of your time. This must be a big night for you."

"Thanks for coming," I say, almost wistfully. "It was good to see you."

He turns to leave, then turns back.

"What?" I say.

"Would you like to go to dinner some time?" He asks tentatively.

"Yeah. That would be fun."

He takes my number. "I'll give you a call," he says and turns to leave.

Those last few words put a tiny fright into me. My mind is fractured in a million different directions. Am I afraid he will call, or afraid he won't? If he does, will I recoil because I suddenly feel unaccountably trapped and suffocated? I've done this before. And what if he never calls? Why do guys say they will, and then never follow through? I'm spinning out of control, I tell myself.

Brian walks to the door, then turns around and gives the "thumbs up" sign before exiting.

And he calls. He calls, he calls, he calls. We have long, relaxed conversations about everything from philosophies of art to the Marx Brothers, to gene splicing, to outer space. Autumn is ravishing the trees outside on the New York City streets, but for us its spring. Everything old is new again, fresh and full of possibility. This is all before our first dinner date. My therapist advises me to keep my head on straight. I giggle like a fifteen-year-old schoolgirl in response.

For three weeks we are a whirlwind of activity—going to art museums, sushi restaurants, classical music concerts, movies, Broadway shows. I finally know what it's like to "have a life." Before, I was a loner. My boyfriends were loners. We stayed in all weekend and did nothing but get on each other's nerves. Brian and I are taking in the world.

All those weeks we do not so much as touch. It's like we both are on an electric current running through us and are afraid of causing an explosion. The first time we hold hands, walking out of Zeffirelli's *Romeo and Juliet,* I see in my mind's eye that space between Adam's finger and God's on the Sistine

Chapel ceiling. My eyes well up with tears that I quickly wipe away so Brian doesn't see.

A brisk wind comes up and whips across the avenues.

"Are you cold?" Brian asks. "Let's go to the Russian Tea Room."

It's a famous restaurant I've never been to. I don't mention this to Brian, or the fact that it's where my father proposed to my mother. I don't know whether this is a bad omen or a good one sent by Grandma Ethel's spirit.

Luckily, it's before the Carnegie Hall concert next door gets out and we are seated right away in a snug, red leather banquette, in our own corner.

"Caviar and tea," Brian tells the waiter, then turns to me. "Let's do something special next weekend, it's not my weekend with the kids. Let's go upstate and see the leaves turn."

"Yes. I'd like that. I haven't been out of the city in months." My mouth is busy making conversation and my heart is thumping in my chest. We haven't yet had our first kiss, but right on cue Brian leans in and guides my face towards him and slowly softly brushes my lips against his. The sweetness on our mouths makes me think, "*Nectar, nectar of the gods.*"

"I'll rent a car."

"And I'll find an inn?" I volunteer.

"That would be perfect—if you're sure."

"As sure as the falling leaves," I say and slip my hand into his.

Next weekend the drive out of the city and suburbs is a revelation. Every few miles I breathe deeper, my neck muscles relax, I slough off layers of old emotions, old Lillians, old lives, old regrets and dissatisfactions. Alongside the parkway more and more trees are turning jewel-like colours: scarlet, orange, yellow, plum. Artist palettes of colour swirl by. I shoot stop action photographs out the window that I know will be a burst of surprises, abstract expressionist canvases of colour.

We are headed toward the Sunnydale Inn, three hours north of the City. It sits on a reserve of land crisscrossed with hiking trails and abuts a three-mile-long body of water. We stop for lunch on the way and check out some antique stores. Arriving just at sunset, we stand on the Inn's large, covered, wrap-around porch and watch the white clouds burst into crimson and pink over the blue waters of the lake. The weekend is all before us. For the first time in a long time I feel whole and blessed.

We dine in the Inn's restaurant, candles and flowers set on each table's white linen. Brian orders a bottle of pungent, red Burgundy and the Chateaubriand for two. He talks of his latest research project with recombinant genes.

"Shall I call you Dr Frankenstein?"

He laughs. "Yes nurse, please do." He raises his wine glass and says, "A toast to this weekend and all sorts of re-combinations."

I laugh. I feel flushed from the wine, the food, the close proximity to Brian.

We order one piece of black forest cake and the waitress gives us two forks. *Oh no*, I think, *not the obligatory feeding each other scene.* Beneath the veneer of my ostensible happiness, I am growing more and more anxious as bedtime approaches. I don't trust myself not to jab Brian in the cheek with my fork while aiming at his luscious mouth. Fortunately, this idea of what sometimes passes as foreplay does not occur to Brian, and I inwardly relax. Brian refills my glass with wine, and I dutifully drink it all in hopes of its calming effect.

"Let's go out on the porch and get a bit of air," he suggests. He clasps me firmly by the hand and leads me outside.

An elderly couple sits on the porch swing.

"Lovely night," says the man, addressing us.

"Lovely world," replies Brian.

"Smell the bit of wood smoke?"

"Yes. Birch?"

"Maybe so, maybe so," replies the man. "Now let me guess, you've been together twenty, twenty-five years?"

"Now Albert, don't be nosy," his wife says.

I laugh. "We met twenty-five years ago, but we've only been together four weeks."

"So that's why you've got the glow."

"Albert!"

Undaunted by his wife, or possibly his mistress for all I know, Albert winks and says, "Let's leave the love birds alone." As they get up to go indoors, Albert turns around and says, "Make the most of it. It all passes like a dream. Like those twenty-five years of yours. Hold onto the glow, it can lead you home."

We exchange names and bid each other good night. Without thinking, I plop down on the swing. "Well, that was enigmatic."

Brian stands at the steps of the porch, looking up at the night sky. "There's Orion, and the Big Dipper," he says. He comes over and sits next to me. He seems pensive.

"Penny for your thoughts?" I say, though I know I'm opening a Pandora's box.

He doesn't answer directly, but says, "How do you always know when I'm far away?"

"Not sure," I say. "Either it's a talent, or a curse, or both."

"I feel guilty."

"About?" I know the answer, but I need him to say it.

"You know. Joanna, the kids. My family. When we had the children, we became a family. Not just a couple. A working unit. I was the provider, the protector, the Papa. It meant—means—a lot to me. I haven't told you about my family growing up. When I was eleven my fourteen-year-old sister started having problems. We thought she was a teenager acting out. Long story short, she had, has, schizophrenia. She calls me once a year or so. Is part of an Eastern New Age sect that takes excellent care of her. All those years when we didn't know what was wrong, the problems shattered our family. We were in constant turmoil." Brian goes silent, leans forward with his elbows on his knees, his hands holding his head.

"So, you don't want to do that to your family," I say softly.

"Yeah. Exactly."

I wonder whether the current situation really does match what Brian had experienced growing up. I imagine that Brian and Joanna separated because of painful unhappiness or unworkable problems. Under those circumstances, so different from Brian's own childhood, staying together might be more detrimental to the children than splitting. However, Brian hasn't told me enough yet about his marriage for me to point that out, if it is true. Besides, there's no denying the fact that at age four and six, divorce is shattering to children.

"I'm sorry," Brian says. "I wanted this to be a beginning for us."

"It's all about getting to know each other. That's what we're doing."

"Thanks," he says and sits back and takes hold of my hand.

Reality has knocked the passion out of us.

"Let's go to bed and get up early and hit the hiking trails." Brian says.

In the bathroom, I change into a quaintly old-fashioned flannel nightgown in keeping with an Inn, not the silk negligee that I thought I'd be wearing tonight.

Brian folds me into his arms and we fall asleep. We wake up still holding each other.

The sun and bright blue sky, crisp air, and turning leaves lift our spirits as we troop through the woods in the morning. I do less photo taking and more just taking in nature. An earthy smell pervades everything. By noon we reach a raised plateau of granite, probably left by retreating glaciers during some ice age. It gives us a 360-degree view of the surrounding forests. Like a crazy quilt pattern, the patches of coloured leaves spread out beneath us and define the varying species of trees: sugar maple, oak, birch, pine, sycamore. I take photos, thinking I'll assemble them in a sequence that can replicate the panorama of nature surrounding the viewer.

We take off our jackets, eat our bagged lunch, and lie back against the warmth of the rock. We hear birds singing and wind ruffling through the trees. The most astounding aspect is the overarching natural silence that soaks into one's body and soul.

"Come here, woman," Brian says and pulls me close.

I am content. Filled with a drowsy awareness of time ticking itself into eternity. Nothing more need happen. Everything is as it should be. My mind is resplendently empty.

We pass the afternoon retracing our steps and spend sunset on the dock at the edge of the lake. Trees in all their splendour frame the blue water, rippling with rows of silver scallops breaking against the shore.

"Let's star gaze tonight," Brian says as we head indoors to clean up for dinner. But stargazing never happens.

When I am in the tub, Brian knocks at the door and asks if he can come in. "I want to *see* you," he says, his voice filled with innocence and eagerness and youthful desire.

"Yes," I say, "but you'll have to join me. I don't want to be the only naked person in the room," I say, laughing.

So, he does. And, as they say, things progress from there. It is magical.

\* \* \*

For the next nine months we have non-stop fun and get to know each other better. Brian is, if not religious, at least somewhat observant. He goes to *shul* some Friday nights; he keeps all the major holidays, but not the Sabbath. He's sort of a patchwork. It turns out, one of the problems between him and Joanna was that she'd grown away from religion. Brian wanted the children to be brought up with Jewish traditions. I'm not sure where that leaves me. He hasn't invited me to go to *shul* with him.

We haven't talked about it. I haven't met his children. I'm not sure what this means. So, although everything is going along great, and life couldn't be better, I have a rising sense of anxiety. Something has to change, either grow or diminish, and I don't know which it will be. I go into scared rabbit mode—I don't talk to Brian about my concerns, don't deepen our intimacy, and emotionally freeze in place hoping everything will continue to be okay.

On a Saturday night, we are about to go out to dinner when the revelation comes tumbling out of him.

"I've got to take a break from us," he says quietly. "Because of the children. I owe it to them to try one more time."

*Here it is*, I say to myself as I'm overcome with astonishment. *My fears realized*. I fall like a dead weight into a chair, comprehending we're not going to go to dinner—ever again.

"This is a hard thing to say, but if you hadn't come along when you did, I might have gone back to them. It was something I'd been considering."

Joanna had called. She wanted to try counselling, again. They agreed to see a new therapist, once a week together and once a week individually.

Joanna had agreed to yield some ground on an important issue. Previously she had wanted to go back to school for a Master's in Education and Brian had objected. With his son still in preschool, he thought it was too early. He didn't want a nanny bringing up his son. Until the children were older, he wanted a traditional home life. (I thought perhaps this related to Brian's childhood and the disruption his sister's illness had caused.) Now Joanna was willing to compromise and wait a few more years if Brian would agree.

With a pitiful look on his face—for him? For me? For the whole situation? He gets up to leave. "I'd still like to call you and talk," he says, as if bewildered, realizing for the first time our relationship is over.

"No," I practically yell at him. "That's not okay. I don't want to be caught in the middle of this. You have to be sure of what you want and don't want before you call me again."

And he doesn't. I keep busy. It's summer and I take a share with another woman in a little cottage on Fire Island, alternating with weekends in the

Berkshires in a large house. Emotionally subdued, I'm not ready to meet anyone new. Most of the time I feel it would be a futile exercise in self-punishment. Somehow, I am relationship cursed and I blame it on Bennie. If only he had been a different father. Someone straightforward, uncomplicated. Someone who was kind. Someone who didn't push buttons. What was I to do? He was the father I'd had. There were no do-overs in this game.

I spend my time reading and taking photos. All the love and peace I felt with Brian is metamorphosed into forest and ocean pictures that people call "otherworldly": fairy kingdoms filled with invisible sprites and sylphs, water spirits and God-like nature forces. I shoot close-up mosses and mushrooms suggesting a fantasyland where one can disappear from the real world. I shoot the ocean at dawn and dusk when the gods of the sea, land, and sky stroll through the human world robed in iridescent garments of amethyst and magenta, rose and scarlet, peach and tangerine. I write a proposal for a coffee table book called *Forest and Ocean*, but those contracts are the hardest to get, rarer than the Dodo. I don't hold my breath.

Back in the city after the summer ends, I revert to my mainstay, street life. I find a new subject: Surreal photos of fashion mannequins in store windows—representations of women caught in all stages of dress and undress in a variety of tableaux. Women with dismantled parts, arms and legs lying by their sides; women disguised in elaborate costumes and headdresses; women provocatively clad in red leather with devil-horned caps; women in short bridal dresses and net veils crouching in grass littered with naked babies.

I play with the reflections of the street overlaying the glass of the storefront windows, amid images of maimed and disguised women. I "sign" the photos by capturing my own image on the plate glass window, like artists through history who put themselves in the foreground of their paintings. I call the collection "The Advertising of Women."

With a portfolio of my most recent works, I go to galleries to see if I can generate some interest. Certainly, my work has enough variety to please different tastes. Finally, at a hole in the wall in the East Village, where gentrification is taking over the tenements, I get into a group show. I had taken shots of neighbourhood life, documenting the punk rock trend of Mohawk hairdos, safety pinned clothing, and facial piercings.

The photos are raw and energetic, yet catch the vulnerability of the human features underneath, giving a push–pull sensation: Are they rebels, or only kids made up for Halloween shock value? One I particularly like is a girl with blackened eye make-up, looking like a raccoon, wearing a ripped tee shirt with *SEX PISTOLS* written across it in lightning script. She looks like she can't believe someone wants her photo. Behind the façade, she's breathtakingly fragile.

It gives me a new appreciation for my own fragility. How could Brian do that to me? Lead me on as though committed, then turn around and walk out on me? According to my therapist, I should have known I was in a danger zone. Why hadn't my therapist warned me, I wanted to know?

"Because," he says, "you're a big girl." He can't save me from making my own mistakes. I have to learn from my experiences.

I wonder why I am paying him so much, and whether a female therapist might have given some motherly advice to proceed with caution?

"Brian," he goes on, "was only separated." There was no stability to that situation, and he had children, always a complicating factor. "You're a smart woman, you're able to see these things for yourself."

*Obviously*, I say to myself, *I'm not smart about relationships! That's why I'm in therapy*! Besides, I was too busy having a "life" for the first time in my life to notice. Perhaps a word of advice might have prepared me for what happened?

I leave therapy feeling confused, betrayed, and guilty, as if I'd caused the catastrophe with Brian. *That doesn't help me at all*, I say to myself. I come to a startling realization: I've seen this analyst for twenty years and I'm still on first base; it isn't working. I make the decision to end therapy and fly solo for a while. If I see a therapist again, I'll choose a woman.

The group photography show opens, and I feel proud of myself. No regrets. No pain about therapists or boyfriends. I'm okay on my own. I'm a full person. The photos of the punk rockers receive a complimentary notice in a downtown paper. The *Sex Pistol* girl with the vulnerable eyes sells to a young collector. He says he has an ache in his heart whenever he looks at her. I haven't been this happy for a long time. I don't need anything more in my life. I'm single and I'm forty, and, perhaps, I was never meant to have a traditional life. Yet I'm blessed with a full one.

A few months later, my mother calls me about Bennie's upcoming birthday. He's turning eighty. She's planning a surprise party at a restaurant.

After Bennie ruined my college graduation with his offensive remark about my backside, I swore off celebrations related to him. I never call him on his birthday or Father's Day. When I see him at the usual holiday dinners at my sister's or brother's homes we hardly speak.

"Lil, you have to come, it wouldn't be a celebration without you." Ruthie says.

"No."

"Why are you so hard on him?" She continues.

"So, I'm the one who's hard, huh?" I reply.

"You know he loves you. Probably more than anyone else."

"He's got a sick way of loving people."

"That's just your father. He's old, Lillian. He won't be around forever. Please, Doll, you're the sweetest kid, but about this you're wrong."

"Who's the one that's done wrong? All he's ever done is ruin things. I was always cut to shreds by how he loved me."

"Don't go to your grave with regrets, Lil. Your father did his best. He doesn't have a loving nature. But you were the apple of his eye. Don't shut him out anymore."

"I'll think about it," I say, mostly to end the discussion. I don't intend to think about it.

But over the intervening weeks, I do. *Time for me to grow up*, I say to myself. My resentments, my feelings of unrelievable tragedy woven around Bennie's transgressions, I realize, are not who I am anymore. They're the old Lillian. And I think about the saying, "Life begins at forty," and like the sound of it. The true test comes the night of his birthday.

The dinner is, if not a surprise, clarifying. He might not have changed, but I assuredly have. I am not a little girl, I am an adult. I don't *need* his approval or praise; I don't need him to be proud of me. A small part of me still wants those things—I'm tempted to talk about my recent success with the show—but after a lifetime of trying, I know he will likely be true to his spots and lash out if he feels insecure or diminished. Then I feel sad, not for my long-sustained injuries—I realize despite them, I am whole—but for all the love he has missed.

# Chapter 15
# Ruthie's Denouement

When I am forty-one, Ruthie's physical decline happens quickly and is unforeseen. By then, Ruthie and Bennie are semi-retired. All the real estate has been converted to rental properties. Although they still personally collect the monthly checks, they hire a super to take care of the buildings. This leaves them with a stretch of three weeks a month to go on trips.

Something Bennie always said he wanted to do in his life was sit in St. Marks Piazza in Venice and sip an espresso in an open-air café like his favourite Baroque composer Vivaldi. Ruthie agrees, agog with images of antique furnishings she might not be able to collect, but at least could admire. The only thing holding her back is her insides, falling out. A fallen uterus is giving her pain and a pessary is put in. What no one suspects, before they leave on their whirlwind seven-day tour of Italy, is that the device will cause an infection.

Not understanding what is wrong, Ruthie experiences ice pick jabs of pain in her female parts that worsen when she urinates. Like a sturdy Russian peasant, she bears the pain without complaint; she thinks, perhaps, the change in diet and the fast-paced tour have given her a bug.

When she returns home, she is exhausted, with a dazed, disassociated look on her face. Right away she goes to the doctor who puts her on antibiotics, takes out the pessary and suggests surgery. Take out the uterus. Not needed anymore, says the doctor. Fastest way to solve the problem. Ruthie and Bennie concur.

"What do I need it for, anymore?" Ruthie asks. Only, she feels at a loss afterwards and can't explain why. She finds herself tired and in bed most of the time. Incontinence follows. Although Bennie gloves up and tells her to bear down on his fingers, vaginal muscle exercises don't do a thing to help. On the Internet Bennie finds a surgical technique, hurrah! Perhaps that will do it. The odds are low, only 40%, but Bennie and Ruthie, now the dynamic duo in their old age, bet their money on the surgeons. What no one warns, not the doctors or the Internet, is that at age seventy-nine, the risks of surgery are much greater. For example, there is a possibility of stroke.

And that's what happens. Ruthie experiences a minor stroke that reduces her peripheral vision to nil. Even though she walks laboriously as if she's afraid to bump into things (which she does with regularity), the effects of the stroke aren't discovered (would you believe it?) until one doctor finally notices and questions her about her diminished gait. On top of that, the incontinence surgery fails.

From then on, Ruthie spends most of her days in bed, or (God forbid! according to Bennie, who can't accept the sight of it), in a wheelchair. However, Bennie dutifully changes Ruthie's incontinence diapers without a word of complaint. In fact, he single-handedly takes on her care with no additional help. His devotion is admirable, yet Ruthie quietly complains to me how isolated she feels in the big house without others around. When I diplomatically suggest to Bennie that she have a female home care worker for the stretches of time he is out doing errands, or getting together with his audiophile friends, or going to the library, he bristles with indignation. He can take care of all her needs, he says. So, through stretches of time each day Ruthie is alone.

Ruthie knows she will never rise out of this invalid bed to go on another vacation. She quietly bemoans the fact that these are now the lost years. Lost to illness. The dreams of vacations once relegated to some future time, after their working years, are lost to her now.

Samuel, Merri, and I try to get to Westchester to visit as much as possible, but we all have busy lives. On birthdays and Mother's Days we plan big celebrations to make up for our absences. Merri and Marge cook meals to bring to the house. Samuel plays his guitar and the grandkids sing and give cards and gifts they've made. I usually have a photo show I present as entertainment.

It turns out Ruthie adores orchids—the satiny petals, the rapturous smells, the labyrinthine blossoms, the vibrant patches of colour. The Bronx Botanic Gardens have a display in the jungle section of the hot houses. So, I spend a day with my close-up lens luxuriating in the curves and loops and velvety softness of orchid bodies from an insect's perspective. I blow up the photos, mat and frame them, and hang them in her bedroom for Mother's Day. Now she can be surrounded by orchids.

About a year later, while I am away on a photo shoot, I get an early morning call from Samuel. The unusual hour tells me it is not good news. And, since

Ruthie has been in and out of the hospital for the last six months, I'm prepared for Samuel's words.

"Mom passed away in the early hours of the morning. The hospital called around four."

I silently start to cry.

"I called Bennie and told him." Samuel says, pausing, "I picked him up and we went to the hospital together. Dad was so shaken; it was like in the movies. He kept saying, 'Re Re, open your eyes, wake up, wake up it's your Butchke.' Finally, he dissolved in tears and couldn't speak. I sat him down and said we'd get through this together, as a family."

I can tell my brother is shaken. "Samuel, you did good," I say. But he isn't finished.

"Dad kept sobbing and losing his breath. He was like a child, bereft, unable to understand the world. The whole thing knocked him for a loop, and he didn't want to accept the fact of it. For about a half hour he was unable to respond to my question if he was all right. When he was quiet, I went to the nurse's station to take care of the paperwork."

I am about to tell Samuel I'll be home in twenty-four hours when he continues talking.

"Jeez, in some ways, I was more disturbed by how it demolished Dad. At least Mom was out of pain, and really, I'd been prepared for the end for weeks. Eventually, I brought Dad back to the house. He wouldn't come down to the City with me. Said he'd be fine. Didn't want to sleep in a strange bed, only in his own. He hadn't cried for over an hour, but he looked spent. I thought he'd be okay, and it was what he wanted."

"Yes, best to let him handle it his way. He'll be in shock for a time. Glad you were with him when he needed you most. I'll get a flight out tonight."

I fight back my tears. My heart is in my throat. *That's all Samuel needs, another crier.* Samuel's struggling to be the stable rock he believes everyone needs, including himself. I want to say, "it's okay to cry." Without my voicing this, he lets out a few tears at the end of the call.

"I don't think I'll ever get over that scene. Dad telling Mom to wake up and open her eyes."

When I call Dad later that day, he is crying on and off. He tells me how he and Mom first met. "We bumped into each other at a classical concert. Mommy was double dating with a girlfriend. I was out with someone they knew. We hardly spoke, but I got her alone for a moment and asked for her number. Her eyes sparkled and glowed. I called her the next day and asked her to dinner. She was so beautiful and slender as a doe."

This story brings a smile to my face.

"What was the date like?" I ask, entering into the spirit of his reminiscence.

"We went on the train to Coney Island. I remember the sound of the waves as we went along the boardwalk. Reminded me of Shostakovich. Long quiet undertows of suspense building up as the water drew in and out of the sand. A whole symphony under us. Before we left, we had a photo taken."

Immediately, I think I know what photo he's talking about. Dad wearing a suit and wide 1940s tie, and Mom with a lovely dress hugging her bosom, a rhinestone pin, vertical, at the cleavage, her hair slightly windblown and in waves. Even then, Dad didn't smile for photos. He looked deep and mysterious. The only thing betraying his feelings: their intertwined hands that are pulled slightly towards his side, as though holding her to him.

I never knew the photo was taken at Coney Island on their first date. That explains the painted backdrop. It was from a photo booth at the amusement park.

"I'm looking at it right now," Bennie says. He repeats in a strained voice "how beautiful she was, how beautiful she was." And starts to cry heavily, struggling with his emotions.

"It's okay, Dad," I say. "It's okay to cry."

"But I already cried so much this year," he says, as if he should have gotten beyond it, or had no tears left. And he starts to sob.

"It's okay, sweetheart, it's okay," I say and wait for his emotion to run its course.

My mind thinks about the past year, all of Ruthie's hospitalizations and continued decline, and for the first time I realize the toll it took on Bennie. I think of her worsening senility; how, like a child, she would repeat a question as if you hadn't just answered it. A few months ago, Ruthie told me about a doctor visit.

"He asked me what day it was and the year. He wanted to know the president's name. I couldn't remember. Said to him I think it's Tuesday, but I don't know the month."

"That's fine," I replied as reassuringly as I could. "Half the time I hardly know what day it is, myself." I was saddened and wondered how aware she was of her limitations. I didn't want to cause her any embarrassment or strain, so I let the conversation drop.

"Dad," I say now, "you and Mom had a lifetime journey together. It was wonderful to see how close you'd grown. In these past few years you took care of her in ways most people couldn't or wouldn't. You fed her, kept her going, cleaned her up every day she was bedridden."

"That was nothing," he says emphatically. "So, I changed the dapoo, like a baby. I changed the dapoo. That's all," he says as if his daily efforts to keep her comfortable and clean from her urinary and bowel incontinence were only a minor detail and not an act of love and caring and devotion.

A new cascade of tears comes as he says, "They wouldn't let me feed her anymore. I wanted to feed her. That's what I do. They said, no. Why wouldn't they let me? She hadn't eaten."

"It's okay, Dad. They were feeding her intravenously. They didn't want her to choke on food."

"But she enjoyed it so much," he says, crying harder.

"Her body was getting ready to leave," I say quietly. "To make the transition."

After a time his crying subsides.

"You took good care of her all these years, Dad," I say.

"I tried," he says.

"You did, sweetheart, you did."

"I get a gold star for effort?" He asks.

"Dad, you've got gold stars right up on your shoulders. You're a Four-Star General."

He sighs into the phone, and lets out a little laugh.

In accordance with Jewish custom, Ruthie is buried two days later in a Jewish cemetery in Brooklyn where she and Bennie have side-by-side grave sites. It is the same cemetery that Grandma Ethel was buried in nearly three decades ago. We stop by Grandma's burial plot and leave small rocks on the headstone to show someone has visited.

# Chapter 16
# Benny at the Hospice

I am forty-three. (Ruthie passed away a year and a half ago). On the last visit I make to the hospice in Brooklyn, Bennie is excruciatingly weak. Sometimes he can barely support his voice with his breath. He is dying of congestive heart failure. He asks me to read to him from one of his books.

"Glasses broke," he says. The rest comes out in drips and drabs. "Believe it? Frame snapped last night." He points to the glasses that lay on the nightstand. "Everything's breakin'," he mutters in a tone of child-like exasperation. Someone had tried to fix them with first-aid tape, but they wouldn't sit properly on his nose and made him queasy.

Bennie's eyes are slightly crossed, with the same eye muscle ailment that afflicted his mother when she got older. He had corrective surgery done a few years prior. I pick up the book, one of his favourites, Somerset Maugham's *Of Human Bondage*. He says he doesn't remember it. I begin to read when he stops me.

"Had a dream about Mommy," he says in a stronger voice than a few moments before. "She floated through the window. Young and beautiful again. Couldn't resist her. We made love," he says without embarrassment. His words end and his face lights up with a huge smile. Then he closes his eyes.

His eyes flutter open and I'm about to return to reading the book when he says in a halting, breathy speech, "When I'm forgotten—"

"You won't be forgotten," I interrupt with a shaky voice that I can barely control.

"Day will come we're forgotten."

"Yes," I say.

"When I'm forgotten, stars will still be in the night sky with their light, faint because they're far away. Stars are like love," he continues, "last millions of lifetimes."

I am touched by his startling words. I recall how he never had the time—between the gruelling everyday schedule of work and our family's needs—to set up the telescope that collected decades of dust in the attic, sitting beneath the roof glass he had the builders install so he could study the stars.

One night long ago, he took the three of us kids to see the Perseid meteor showers. He woke us up in the middle of the night. We were still in our pyjamas, but wrapped in blankets, as he drove us to the town's reservoir at the top of a steep hill.

I must have been only four or five, so he held me in his arms and told me to look up at the sky and see the sparklers that the universe was sending us tonight. He told me to look at the colours of the stars—the red and blue and white light—that were falling down from space to reach us here so far away. When I was older, Samuel told me that Dad had said we were looking through time, and human history, and the clock face of existence.

Bennie's eyes close again so I put the book down and close mine, too, to rest for a moment. Memories of Bennie and me come flooding back.

I recall an adventure I had with him in my teens, when I got into an outdoor art show at the Brooklyn Botanic Gardens. Bennie helped me build a free-standing display, drove me to Brooklyn, and sat himself in a folding chair under a blossoming apple tree. He quietly started reading sections of the Sunday *New York Times*. He looked as if he were in his reading chair in the living room at home, the spent sections in a sea of paper on the grass around his feet.

That day at the Garden, he looked so totally absorbed in reading that the world around him—the people strolling from one exhibit to the next, the incessant murmur of voices, the buzzing of bees from flower to flower—were blurred into nonexistence. He was the "still point of the turning world." I could not help but love him, no matter the painful memories that crowded my mind and spun around and around with old disappointments. He was my father and more special to me than anyone. I could not help but love him even though he had broken my heart time after time.

When the show was over, I'd only sold one photo. I felt a little silly. Bennie didn't seem to notice. He helped me get the display back in the car and, before going home to Westchester, he asked if I wanted to see his old neighbourhood in

Brooklyn. I was elated. An adventure to see his old haunts! Usually, no one could get him to talk about his childhood. We all thought he didn't have any memories of it, but now he was taking me to see the "ancestral" land.

As we drove down Flatbush Avenue, he told me how, sometimes after school, he'd ride his bike to Nedick's and get an orange drink and a hot dog on a mustard-smothered bun with relish and sauerkraut. He said that nothing, not his favourite pot roast cooked to a gooey, shredding perfection, nor any butterfly-cut steak at a fancy restaurant, ever tasted so good. I tried to picture Bennie as an eight-year-old steering his bicycle with one hand and clutching his grilled-to-perfection frank with the other, nibbling away at it to prolong the pleasure as he whizzed along the sidewalk. I imagined him stopping at the Brooklyn Library with its Greek architecture and high-ceilinged splendour to get another book by Jules Verne or Robert Louis Stevenson.

As we slowly drove along the streets to East New York where he grew up, the neighbourhood changed to another ethnic flavour. The streets swarmed with people. Children were playing stickball among the passing cars along with others playing on the sidewalk. On every other corner sat a church with a colourful name like the Tabernacle of the Holy Spirit, the Hall of the Mighty Israel, the Glory Seat of Jehovah.

We arrived at a square-shaped park bordered on all sides with six-floor walk-ups. I thought Bennie would point out where he had lived, but instead, he drove around the park and told a story about a building at one corner where the Parks Department had shown educational films. He spoke of glowing red furnaces of molten iron and rivers of liquid metal flowing into molds in one of the industrial films he saw. He made it sound like the abode of the gods, as if he had witnessed Vulcan at his forge crafting winged shoes and mechanical horses.

"Looks so small to me now," he said, speaking of the modest brick structure where his imagination had once ranged wide as the universe. He went quiet for a time as we cruised slowly through the adjacent streets. When we reached a corner, he made a right turn and looming up before us was a large building. He stopped the car. I could see over the triple-doored entrance the words "Alexander Hamilton High School" chiselled in stone.

*My God*, I thought, *my father was once a teenager walking through the halls of that building, carrying textbooks, writing papers, taking exams, experimenting with science projects.*

I had always wondered if my father had finished school. Ruthie had gone to college for a year before having to get a bookkeeping job to support herself. My father had always been tight-lipped about his education. He was an incessant reader, knew most of the classics, knew all of classical music and could whistle the melodies, was well versed in the sciences. But I had the suspicion that he never graduated from high school and kept it a secret because he felt embarrassed. When the Depression hit, he would have probably been sixteen. His folks owned a candy store and perhaps they needed his help.

I wondered what he was thinking about as we sat in the car looking at his high school. For some reason I couldn't bring myself to ask.

"Yes-siree," he finally said. "Alexander Hamilton High's still there, believe it or not."

After this reverie I open my eyes in the hospice. It looks like Bennie is asleep. The sight of him resting peacefully brings back another memory.

After our reconciliation, Bennie noticed me reading a book about near death experiences and asked me what I thought of it. I said it sounded pretty convincing; did he want to borrow the book? Yes, he did. Just at that time, the author of the book came to town to give a lecture. Were Bennie and Ruthie interested in going? They were. After I bought the tickets, I started to worry that it might be upsetting for them to contemplate their mortality.

We ended up having a grand evening! First, we went to a health food restaurant for dinner before the lecture, where Bennie enjoyed making fun of all the food. The only thing he liked was the apple crumb compote that reminded him of his mother's rice pudding. Nice and crispy-crunchy. At the end of the lecture when there were questions from the audience a surprising thing happened.

Bennie raised his hand and said he thought all the research about the dark tunnel, white light, feelings of overwhelming love, the life review were all a good argument for the existence of God. Did the author think so? Everyone in the audience burst out laughing. Bennie looked a little embarrassed. He didn't understand he was preaching to the choir.

When I was young, Bennie and Ruthie would have arguments about the existence of God. Ruthie reasoned that if you believed, and later found out there wasn't a God, you hadn't lost anything. But if you didn't believe and there was a God, boy-oh-boy, were you screwed. Bennie acquiesced saying she was right, and then announced, "I still don't believe." Ruthie threw up her hands, looked at the ceiling and said, "Please God, help him!"

I come out of my thoughts. Bennie's eyes are again open, "How are you feeling?" I ask. "Are you in pain?"

"No," he says matter-of-factly. "No pain. Just discomfort."

Every day he is a little weaker with his heart failing a little more in its ability to pump blood. The diagnosis of congestive heart failure came late. For a year, he had coped with feelings of exhaustion without any substantial help. As a man who had always been a workaholic, he had to let go of his many activities and watch in frustration as life slipped away.

A year ago, the doctor finally realized the problem and Dad went in for his first hospitalization because of chest pain. At the time, he grudgingly accepted his condition with a huge streak of fatalism. On the Internet, I found an alternative supplement used exclusively for congestive heart disease in Japan. I tried to convince him to try it. He simply brushed off the suggestion.

"My ejection fraction is a 17, out of 70," he said. "Nothing's going to restore that to a healthy heart's score. I'm old. The heart's not going to repair itself, with or without supplements. Not possible."

I printed off literature that documented exactly the benefits he was saying were not possible, but he refused to read it.

"Why are you so stubborn?" I asked. "Would it hurt you to try it?" I realized I was sounding like my mother.

Then, more in a tone of resentment than sorrow, he said, "I'm not able to *do* anything."

"You'd rather not try it?" I asked in a quiet voice. I didn't want to argue at cross purposes, but meet him where he was, emotionally.

"Yeah," he said, in a bitter tone of voice, "what would be the point? There's no quality of life."

"Sometimes these things happen for a reason," I tentatively ventured.

"What, to make you suffer?" He asked with a sneer.

I felt helpless. I should have said, "to give us more time to share more moments of love." But I was afraid of what his response would be. Afraid, too, it was a selfish desire on my part, if he was suffering.

Eventually they did stabilize him on medications, and he came home after that first hospitalization. Over the next 6 months, he kept having episodes. He'd call Samuel or Merri in the middle of the night and they'd alternate driving up to

Westchester from the City. One time when Merri got to the house, he was in the kitchen having a bowl of bananas and sour cream, and he refused to leave for the hospital until he'd finished eating. It was enough to give **her** a heart attack!

Finally, Merri, who always knows the best Manhattan professional in any field, from lawyer to doctor to hairstylist, got him to a cardiologist at Mt. Sinai. This doctor really knew what he was doing. He adjusted the medications and Dad resumed an uneventful life, albeit with slowly progressing heart failure.

At the hospice as I sit with him today, he is stretched between fatalism and a strange kind of elation.

"First, glasses break. Can't read anymore. Then y'know what? They won't let me out of bed. Palpitations, they say. I want to take a walk! What, they don't want me to die in their precious hallway? Can you believe it? I say, I'm dying. If you haven't noticed this is a hospice. Idiots! I'm bored," he finally says in exasperation. "The stupidity never ends. Even on the way out."

I notice the TV is on mute. "Can you see the TV okay?" I ask.

"Yeah, CNN. Same stories every twenty minutes. Nothin' else on. Talk shows and soaps. What *dreck*! For the house ladies."

I glance around the room looking for something to occupy him on these last few days of his life. Several books are stacked up on the nightstand. "What's this book about?" I ask as I notice the words *The Genesis of Life*.

"Which one?"

I pull it from under the pile. "The one about the beginnings of life."

"Oh, that. Yeah, theories on how life formed."

"How did it form?" I venture.

"Soupy concoction of chemicals," he says dismissively, "all speculation." He tries to say something but the word comes out garbled. He attempts to wet his lips with his tongue. The talking has dried out his mouth. He doesn't have the energy to reach the water cup on his nightstand so I bring it to his lips. He sips slowly, coughs a little and sips again.

"Never cared for mystery," he continues. "Always thought—explanation for everything, even if unknown. Not so sure anymore—" his voice trails off into strained breathing. His eyes flutter and close and he is silent. I'm not sure if he's fallen asleep.

Then he opens his eyes and goes on with his thought as if he were talking to himself, "prob'ly nothing happens when you pop-off." His jaunty phrase sounds both irreverent and innocent at the same time. "Like falling asleep. All that gobbledygook,"—he says the word clearly this time—"about tunnels and lights, just brain death." He suddenly opens his eyes wide, looks at me with his nearly crossed vision and says with worry in his voice, "Existence is the puzzle. Never understood. I'm sorry," he says in a low voice, "Lived my life one difficulty to the next—squandered so much…" His voice trails off.

I begin to cry and can't speak for a few moments. "Can you forgive my not seeing the love that was keeping me afloat every day?"

He shakes his head as if dismissing the apology. Tears well up in his eyes.

I think to myself, *it has taken me half a lifetime to understand the many confusing guises and forms of love. How complicated and difficult it had all seemed, with so many torturous paths, dead ends, and imprisonments*. I feel suddenly released from all of that, able to finally recognize the simpler truth that is love. *How resilient we are.*

Then I remember what Grandma Ethel had said that night in the Emergency Room—how love was all that mattered, how the important thing was to love each other. I see my heart like a golden charm swinging inside the imprisonment of my body, waiting to be set free like a pure white dove released into the blue firmament of heaven. Love is that freeing agent.

Bennie dozes off; his ragged breathing fills the room with its sound. I bend down to kiss him goodbye. He does not open his eyes. I leave his room quietly. On the way home I think about our last journey, that inescapable adventure. Ruthie has gone ahead and now Bennie is going. One day I will follow. Perhaps there, wherever that is, we will have another chance to live what we have learned.

I think, too, about suffering. That perhaps it has been in its way a purification, burning off everything that is not love, so in the end, we can recognize the love we came in with and can go out understanding. Life has been a teacher, and perhaps a means to find my way back home without any resistance left in the bones; the ultimate experience like a huge wave sweeping me up in its power and carrying me to the last destination.

I call Bennie the following day. When he picks up, I hear a large crashing noise. Has he dropped the phone? Or worse, fallen from the bed? After a few moments my fear subsides as I hear him breathing into the receiver. I start chattering away at him as I listen to his laboured breaths.

"Dad," I say, "Now that you're back in Brooklyn, your old stomping grounds, how about a grilled hot dog with a Nedick's orange drink?" I hear a large exhalation of breath, but nothing more. Is he trying to laugh? Even that is beyond him.

"I'm coming tomorrow. How about some brisket and corned beef on rye with lots of mustard and some coleslaw and pickles from the Second Avenue Deli? Some poppy seed rolls? You can dunk them in your tea. Or honey cake?"

The breathing sounds heavier, but no response comes. The truth is he has no appetite and has begun refusing food. I still bring things hoping they might tempt him. "Well, Dad," I say, "I'll stop yakking at you if you want to rest?" I hear nothing but his breathing.

He hasn't the energy to speak. "I'm going to hang up now." No response comes.

I freeze for a moment not knowing what to do, and then it comes to me. "How about I hang up and I'll call the nurse's station to let them know you need the phone hung up."

There is no response for a few seconds and then comes the word, "yes" in a clear voice, nothing more.

"Love you," I say, "see you soon." I listen to his breathing for a few seconds more.

Benny dies that night, finally released from his worn-out heart and the life he'd lived on this earth for 83 years.

I mourn him more deeply than Ruthie, perhaps because things had gone so wrong in our relationship.

The earliest days, before the disturbing things started, come back to me. When we went for family picnics, he'd take photos, arranging Merri, Samuel, and me from biggest to smallest, or with me in between. One time, without prompting, I made a curtsey, holding out the sides of my skirt, which seemed to delight him no end. He asked me where I'd seen that pose, but I had no idea; I shook my head, raised my arms and shoulders, turned out my palms and beamed a smile at him which he snapped with even more delight.

I remember the rides to the bakery before he'd become disconsolate, distracted, and visibly sad. Then all had changed. Had the marriage failed by that time? Did he regret his love for Ruthie? Had her disturbing behaviour—yelling, screaming, carrying on in the face of life's inevitable stresses and strains—surfaced by then? What could he do but go on? He had a family to support, along with his widowed mother.

As I mourn, I realize he'd been all things to me. He had broken my heart and damaged my spirit. He had also given me the attention and love I'd so much needed in the wake of Ruthie's inconsistent mothering.

How many years it had taken me to assemble the confusing pieces of the puzzle that was my whole father. He had loved me, but sometimes in broken ways. Some part of him was damaged; an unhappy child, choosing part of the time power over love.

In the end, I make peace with my early life. I put to rest the broken child I was, with all my pain, sadness, and resentments.

Part of me dies with my father's death. An old, disfigured me, finally kissed by life to wake from a malevolent enchantment that has kept me frozen in time. I realize we must take the love we've been given and make a life out of it.

Reflecting on Bennie leads me to reflect on Brian. I realize I didn't fully open myself to Brian. Despite his failings, I think he had tried to love me. But there were hidden places in me where Brian's love couldn't go. I had not shared important intimate truths about myself, about my relationship with my father. In the future, if I had another chance at a loving relationship, I knew I would need to share the dark along with the light. I would need to divulge the tender points of pain that sometimes left me moving through the world as only half a person.

# Chapter 17
# Caprice

It is the day before my 44th birthday. Although I'm in for the evening, when my phone rings I contemplate letting it go to voice mail. I don't feel like talking to anyone. At the last moment something prompts me to pick up.

"Hello," I say.

"Lillian?" A man's voice asks.

"Yes?" I ask. The voice is familiar. *It can't be*, I say to myself as my mouth goes dry. "Who is this?"

"It's me, Brian."

I can't think of anything to say except, disbelieving, "Brian Strauss?"

"Yes."

"Uh, Brian…" I go silent. Tears come to my eyes.

"How are you, Lillian?"

"Fine. And you?"

"All right."

I don't know if I want to hang up, or listen to what he has to say.

"Lillian, are you willing to talk to me?"

I don't say anything.

He goes on. "I know how badly I hurt you and I am so painfully sorry for what I did. For these past two years our relationship has haunted me. Through the days and nights with my family you've never left my heart. I've felt like an imposter, a fraud, a thief of time. Both theirs and yours."

"Brian, you can't erase these past few years. I've gone through so many changes. I'm not the same Lillian."

"Are you willing to let me see you? Get to know you for who you are today?"

"Maybe. I don't know. I'm not sure."

"Could we try?"

"Brian, what you did hurt me to my core. It destroyed the trust that was built up over those months we were together. Waltzing back in as if nothing happened doesn't work for me anymore. I was left hanging, and I don't know if I can get past that. You have to be aware of the consequences of your actions. Otherwise, you're just blown this way and that and the future be damned."

The silence between us is profound. I begin to wonder if I'm being too intense about Brian's attempt to reconnect. Maybe I should not crush out-of-hand this olive branch he's extending. Maybe some of my resistance is coming from the reservoir of emotions about my father and not about Brian.

"I'm sorry," I say. "I don't want to act out of resentment.... It would take a delicate balance of who we are now, what we're willing to undertake to see if this can go somewhere strong and true."

I hear Brian inhale deeply and exhale slowly.

"You're right about a lot of things," he says. "I was thoughtless, not thinking seriously about where our relationship was going. When I was seeing you I hadn't truly ended my marriage. I was carried away with the joy I found again. It was thoughtless of me, and I am *deeply* sorry for hurting you."

"Thank you for saying that," I reply. I ask myself if I should end the conversation.

"When I went back to Joanna, I kept experiencing the sorrow of losing you. The sorrow never went away. It made me realize how unhappy I was in my marriage. And how I had damaged what made me truly happy—being with you. My children are up there with you, in the same way."

"Of course they are," I say, realizing the complexity of Brian's emotional situation. "I know how much you love them."

"If you are willing to see me, I know I'll need to build trust with you and take everything slowly this time. And I won't presume anything."

"I'd like to take time to think about it for a few days," I say finally. "But answer me this: Single? Married? Divorced? Separated?"

"Divorced. A year ago today. As you said, don't call until I know what I want. And you? Single? Married? Divorced? Boyfriend?"

"Single," I say. "I'll talk to you soon." And like a river overflowing its banks I start to weep as I hang up the phone.

For the next three months we see each other but don't move ahead with anything physical. I practice asserting my feelings as they come up, letting Brian know where I stand at each juncture of increasing intimacy. We're like a courting couple, but with brains. Excitement is mixed with sober reflection. I see Brian's personality in a much fuller way than I did on the first go-round. Sometimes he's domineering, sometimes extremely considerate and aware of our differences.

Around the fourth month we take the plunge into bed. It's heavenly. We play, we frolic, we're exuberant and sink deep into each other's psyches, as if when we merge there are not two bodies but one whole embraced being. As if our thoughts are not encased in bony skulls but mix like vapor or mist into one consciousness. The experience is exhilarating, like we've escaped our human singularity and exist in a rarefied space created by our union.

Then something happens that brings up the past. This time I recognize the importance of sharing it with Brian, instead of bottling it up inside me.

I am called to serve on Grand Jury duty for a couple of weeks. It takes place in a nondescript room with dirty beige walls and an industrial clock facing the twenty-four jurors. Our wooden seats are fixed in concentric rows that are raked slightly upwards toward the back of the room. It is reminiscent of a small college lecture hall or theatre. The cases, with several playing concurrently, are like dramas.

Most are paper crimes—embezzlements, swindles, overcharges in an asphalt supply business. Each case is a "play," but the scenes are out of order. It is like watching a soap when you have missed episodes. The witnesses are like actors with stereotyped occupations and personalities: The accountant, the businessman, the secretary. They all know they are playing a part; they have rehearsed their lines. Even I have a role to play; I am the observer chosen to decide whether there is or isn't a credible case to try.

It is the third week of service and nothing I've seen so far has prepared me for today's proceedings. At the front of the room is a bare wooden table with one chair at each side, facing forward like a stage set. A young woman wearing a dark suit, carrying a briefcase and a large shopping bag, enters the room from a side door and speaks for a moment with the court attendant. Then she walks to the front of the room, puts the shopping bag down on the floor, and sets the briefcase on the table. She begins to read from a black penal code book she has in her hand.

For a few moments I stare at her blankly, not taking in what she says. We have not seen this D. A. before. She has a delicate face with a finely chiselled nose, sensitive mouth, and large round eyes. Her light brown hair falls softly to her shoulders. She tells us with a clear but subdued voice that after presentation of evidence she will ask for indictment of the accused on molestation and assault charges. Then she turns to another section of the penal book and reads additional information. It becomes apparent that the case involves a child.

When she stops speaking, the room is unnaturally silent. No one turns to confer with her or his neighbour, which is a usual response after introduction of a case. A feeling of dread and shame overtakes me. My eyes are focused straight ahead on the wall in the front of the room. I am barely breathing. An invisible force like the grip of a giant hand is pressing on my ribs. I want to get up and leave, but I know that's impossible.

Within moments, the attendant turns and opens a door at the side of the room. A little girl in bright yellow slacks and yellow play top walks in. She doesn't look at us directly, but gives a sidelong glance from under half-lowered lids. The D. A. guides her to the table at the front of the room. They sit in the chairs, facing us, and the D. A. begins to speak.

"Please tell us your full name and where you now live."

The little girl says her name softly and the D. A. asks her to speak louder.

"Caprice Harris," says the little girl in a louder voice.

"And where do you live, Caprice?" The D. A. prompts.

"With my grandmother."

The little girl bobs her head from side to side as she gives the address, but she is confused and reverses two of the numbers. The D. A. helps her correct it for the record and the little girl flashes a nervous smile.

"Have you always lived with your grandmother?" asks the D. A.

"No."

"Where did you live before?"

"With my mother and sister and brother."

"And your stepfather?"

"Yes."

The D. A. swings around in the chair to face the little girl across the end of the table.

"Caprice, do you know what it means to lie?"

The little girl nods her head. "Does to lie mean to say something that's not true?"

"Uh-huh," says the girl.

"And what happens to you if you lie?"

"You get punished."

"If you were to lie to your grandmother what would happen?"

"I get punished."

"And if you were in school and you lied in school what would happen? What would the school do?"

"I get punished. I have to face the corner."

"And if you lied to the court what would the court do?"

"Punish me."

"And if you lied to God?"

"God punish me."

The D. A.'s voice had gained rhetorical momentum during this litany until it reached a peak of loudness and tension. Finally, the D. A. exhales and lets her body relax into the chair.

We realize this is to replace the usual swearing in.

"How old are you, Caprice?"

"I'm eight."

"And when were you eight?"

"October 2nd."

"Was that 1996?"

"Uh-huh."

"Please try to speak up, Caprice, and answer 'yes' or 'no'."

"Yes," the girl replies in a louder voice.

She is talking in a stage whisper. I can hear her, but I have to strain forward. The room is dead silent.

"Now bringing your attention to that day, the evening of October 2nd at around six o'clock, could you tell us what you were doing?"

We know it is important the D. A. ask the questions in the standard legal form that will be admissible in court if we vote to indict, but it is still difficult to listen to a child interrogated in this way.

"I was in my room."

"And was anyone else at home?"

"My stepfather."

"And your mother and sister and brother were out?"

"Yes, they getting me a present."

"And what happened to you?"

"He say, 'Don't you tell!' 'What?' I say. 'If you tell, I'll kill your brother and sister.' He hit me."

The little girl twists her face and body toward the D. A. in a spasm of pain.

"Then what did he do?"

"He pull down my pants."

"And did he pull down your panties?"

"Yes." She says quietly.

"And did he pull down his panties?"

"Yes."

"And what did he do then?"

"He got on top."

"And what happened then?"

The little girl tries to speak. She looks as if she can't swallow. Grimacing, she doubles over as if she has a sharp pain in her stomach. Rivulets of tears flow down her cheeks.

Suddenly, one of the women jurors gets up from her seat and runs into an adjacent waiting room that leads to the toilet. I bite my lip to stop from crying. Tears are welling up in my eyes. I'm afraid I'll make noise and disturb the proceedings.

"Can you go on? Can you finish?" The D.A. asks softly. "Are you able to go on?"

The little girl wipes her eyes with the back of her hand. "Yes," she says after a while. She sits quietly. She is an adult for a moment, seeing the horror of her situation and the need to move through it. But she remains silent. The D. A. prompts her.

"Is there a name you use for your private parts?" The D.A. asks.

The little girl is silent.

"Where you go to the bathroom?"

The girl sits there without saying anything. You can see a struggle going on inside of her. The D. A. waits an instant before continuing.

"Did your stepfather put the thing where he goes to the bathroom inside where you go to the bathroom?"

"Yes."

We all hope this is the last bit of testimony that is needed of the little girl. But the D. A. begins to pull something out of the shopping bag that is sitting on the floor next to the table. She swivels in her chair and turns to face us.

"Grand Jurors," she says, "these are anatomically correct dolls. One is female and one is male." She turns back toward the little girl. "Caprice, would you take the dolls and show what your stepfather did on the evening of October 2nd, 1996?"

The little girl takes the female doll and lays it belly-up on the table. She lifts the doll's skirt and pulls the panties down part way. Then she lays the male doll on top, also pulling down its pants and panties.

The D. A. asks if we have any questions for Caprice. No one says anything. She nods at the little girl who gets up and walks past us on her way out of the room.

I want to tell her how brave she is, how she has done a very difficult and heroic thing by telling us her story, that she can be proud of herself. Of course, I say nothing. I know I cannot help her directly. Speaking to her might even jeopardize her case. And words seem so small a thing in the face of her pain.

When Caprice is gone, the D. A. reads the medical report. The hymen was unbroken, but damage had occurred at the 4, 6, and 8 o'clock position with rupture of the tissue surrounding the vaginal opening.

The charges are reread and then we vote to indict.

I spend the rest of the day crying, upset beyond all reason. Whether I am crying for the little girl who was abused, or for the little girl inside me, I don't know. At seven o'clock I ready myself to go out to dinner with Brian. When he arrives, I burst out in a new set of tears.

"What is it, Lillian? What's upset you? I'm here."

We are seated on the couch. With a box of tissues on my lap, I tell Brian about the case.

"How horrible," he says. "Such a tragedy for an innocent child. And how difficult for you today to witness the child's story and her pain."

"I can't stop crying. Because I'm also crying for myself. Because it touches on some emotional problems I have. Though it's nowhere near what happened to her, I experienced some emotional and physical violations at an early age with my father." I tell Brian about the home movie of me naked at age seven, and my father "molesting" me with my mother's complicity at age nine.

"How terrible," Brian says, "to be injured that way by your own parents. A betrayal of all trust."

"In my head I keep hearing a remark by one of the jurors, 'Ruined. She's ruined for life.' And the remark keeps boring into my mind like some parasitic worm. I can't let that little girl be ruined. I don't want to be ruined for the rest of my life. I've spent forty years with it ruining emotional intimacy for me."

I am crying too much now to catch my breath, and a new burst of pain issues from my lips.

"You're all right, Lillian. You'll be okay. It's over." Brian reaches out and puts his arms around me. I let myself lean into him and rest my head on his shoulder. He holds me tightly and strokes my arm. "Shush now, it's going to be all right."

Though I am full of grief, it is as if the world of goodness and succour has opened its arms to me, and I let myself be embraced both as the wounded one and as the survivor. Brian kisses the side of my head, tells me I'm safe. After a few minutes I'm calm and can feel his heart beating against my chest.

"I once asked my analyst why those events had hurt me so much, and he said because it was an act of betrayal couched in the guise of a supposed act of love. And it wounded my sense of self at a too-young age."

"Yes," Brian says. "The point is not why does it hurt so much, but that it does hurt so much. You experienced these things at a tender age. And what makes you such a good photographer and artist is your depth of empathy with your subject. You have a sensitive soul, Lillian."

"You want to know something?" He asks. "When I saw you at the photo show after a space of twenty-five years, my first thought was 'that woman has a light inside her that shines forth, a brightness of being.' That light was not extinguished by what happened to you. But the hurt is real; it is a part of you. And it hurts no less because you compare your hurt to another's—that little girl's—which one could say is worse than yours. If you hurt, you hurt. You can't rationalize it away."

"It's like a stab to the heart that he did it on her birthday," I say. "The hurting is twisted and darker than if it had happened on any other day. She will remember it on each birthday. To inflict pain on a day of supposed happiness or celebration holds greater power to injure—a psychic hurt along with the emotional and physical. The cruelty adds another layer of pain, a further damage to the child's ego." I tell Brian of my father's remark on that long ago day celebrating my graduation from college.

"Sweetheart, I'm so sorry you went through that," he says and holds me tighter. "As I get to know you better and learn the story of who you are, it's like a beautiful bolt of silk fabric whose complexity unrolls itself a little at a time in an array of dark *and* rainbow colours. Storms erupt—that's part of you—and subside, and dawn comes to a landscape of what makes up Lillian in all her humanness. I want to get to know all of you—the heartbreak along with the joy."

When night comes, I fall asleep in the arms of a man who I know understands my grief. A man who is willing to go with me into the bitter dregs of psychic violations, the repair of which has taken so much longer than the healing of flesh.

But I also fall asleep wondering why I have suffered so long? As if the wound was buried so deep, like a stiletto in my sense of self, that it could not easily be pulled out—a cut that had wept and never knitted together. In the same way, I fear the little girl's pain will return to her on every birthday. Her grandmother was her healing balm and protector who saved her from further violation. Her mother, sister, and brother are lost to her. She will experience multiple wounds, and I fall asleep with the troubling thought that I'm at a loss to help her.

I wake to morning light and to a liberating thought: I *can* do something for Caprice. Perhaps not for the Caprice of this day and hour, but for the future self that will come to terms with her history.

A book of photographs formulates in my imagination: Portraits of adult survivors of sexual abuse—*The Faces of Innocence*. Contemporary portraits dignifying these people who have suffered grievous emotional wounds, side by side with childhood pictures of them. It will be a book in which they can tell their stories—stories of the suffering child who still lives within them, and stories of their victory over the darkness embedded in their souls. The book will be their testament, a holy writ in their own words. And perhaps these stories will be a touchstone and a healing amulet for other survivors, honouring their journey back to wholeness.

I promise myself I will no longer spend my life constricted by the dark emotions and fears that prevented me from living a full life.

As Brian stirs and wakes, I realize I have found meaning for myself and purpose in what was before only the senseless ruin of innocence. I have found a way to help others and myself.

# Chapter 18
# Grandma's Demise

I am now forty-six. I think more and more about Grandma, and, sadly, too often I focus on her death.

As far as I can remember, the beginning of Grandma's end started with an extended visit from her sister. I did not have a good opinion of Great Aunt Anna, probably because of things Ruthie had told me. Ruthie had had to live with Aunt Anna and her family when she was twelve while Grandma was "traveling for business" (which I later learned was the year Grandma spent in prison). According to Ruthie, Anna had been resentful and stingy during this time.

Two sisters could not look more different than Anna and Ethel. Great Aunt Anna had aged into a stout woman with wiry salt-and-pepper hair and a creased face. Her eyes were like two dark beads cushioned by a fold of skin. She made no effort to converse with me or anyone else, aside from Grandma.

In contrast, Grandma Ethel had a broad, golden face like a field of wheat, the jewel-like grey eyes expansive as a day of stormy weather. Her hair was short, but wavy and well maintained, the colour of thick, sweet honey. Her nose was a bit too large, but preferable to Anna's pinched and diminutive one. Even in old age, it was hard to deny that one was the swan and the other the goose.

Through the years, the sisters had quarrelled repeatedly over issues no one else could ever quite fathom. So it was no great surprise when, around the third week of the stay, Grandma and Aunt Anna had a falling out and Aunt Anna left in a huff. Several weeks after that was when Grandma ended up on the floor of her bathroom.

Subsequently at the hospital, it was discovered that one of the reasons for the fall was an inflamed sore, lurid as a tropical sunset, on the bunion on her left foot. She had accidently banged it against the metal leg of the convertible bed that had remained open those three weeks while the two sisters slept side by side as they had as children. Grandma had not told anyone about the accident, and the bruise had slowly blossomed into an infection.

We were reassured by the doctor's lack of concern. Now that she was in the hospital, they would hook Grandma up to an I.V. of antibiotics and take care of the problem swiftly. The first sign that things were not going well was Grandma's pleas for painkillers. She said the pain was "blindingly atrocious." The nurses increased the over-the-counter analgesics, but this wasn't doing much for Grandma, who began fighting. One day while I was visiting, Grandma erupted.

"Come on now pretty lady, take your meds," said a burly nurse from the Caribbean as she thrust a little paper cup full of pills at Grandma.

"They don't do anything!" cried Grandma in a voice of outrage.

"They will if you just take dem, my lady," responded the nurse in a mechanical voice that soon gave way to impatience. This was taking up her time.

"No, you hyena," snarled Grandma. "I want the doctor. Tell the doctor I want to see him."

"Doctor's not here. Now take your pills," replied the nurse like she was talking to an unruly five-year-old.

"You have no idea what you're talking about," slurred Grandma between gritted teeth. "You bitch!"

I felt myself shrink to a speck on the linoleum floor.

"You're worse than those bastard doctors! You think you can force me? You know less than my little finger." She swivelled her pinkie in the air.

I was standing by the hospital room window, watching the tiny cars moving on the street below and cringing with embarrassment. I had been a "good girl" for most of my 17 years and I could not stand confrontation of any sort, justified or not. If Merri had not been away at college, I'm sure she would have backed the nurse into a corner and found out where along the chain of command the problem was located. I, on the other hand, just wished Grandma would be quiet. *Why does she have to make such a big deal out of it*, I thought. I'm ashamed to admit it, but at that moment I had little sympathy for her pain.

Aside from my youthful insensitivity, I was horrified at the spectacle of what was fast becoming Grandma's demise. I didn't want to believe that at the end people were reduced to creatures yelping in pain. What I wanted was for Grandma to suffer stoically, nobly, as I thought I had done for most of my short life, without so much as a whimper.

But that wasn't Grandma Ethel. If she didn't like something, she let you know fast. She couldn't care less, sick or well, whom she might offend or how she might appear. Now I envy her marvellous self-assuredness, but then, her howling was beginning to pierce my own repressed suffering. I wished the whole problem would just fade away.

And in a manner of speaking, it did. The infection kept spreading, and the doctors advised that her foot was beyond saving. They feared her entire body would become fatally septic if the foot were not amputated immediately. Ruthie reluctantly acquiesced.

By now, Grandma was floating in and out of lucidity, calling me Merri and sometimes Ruthie. She was asking for her son Max, whom she was speaking with on the phone every day. She was confusing Samuel with Bennie and vice-versa, though Bennie, after ten- to twelve-hour days at the car wash, only came on Sunday.

Within a few days the amputation was performed. Had Grandma been told the fate of her left foot? If she had, the awareness had slid away from her. Her decline into illness had been momentarily halted. Grandma was rallying, yet she complained more and more about the pain in her left foot. She was so wrapped up and bandaged that neither she, nor anyone else, could have known from a visual inspection that she was short that appendage. Her pain complaints were still vociferous and accompanied by little cries. It bewildered me no end until the phenomenon of phantom limbs was explained to me.

After a few days of convalescence, Grandma left the hospital and came home. She still didn't realize what had happened to her. All bandaged, she was put straight into bed. When the family doctor came, she complained of some pain in her foot, but she also said, "it's much better, thank you, dahling."

She added that she liked the doctor's "bedroom manners" and we all laughed and said, "Grandma, you mean bedside manners."

Grandma responded by rolling her eyes and saying, "Oh boy, do I."

A hired nurse took care of her during the day as she again faded in and out of reality. Nightly, we gathered around Grandma and the TV set as if it were some tribal ritual that preserved our kinship and our values. It was our way of easing Grandma in her rite of passage. We could do nothing else.

Grandma's return to the house lasted a few weeks. Then she started blacking out and had a mini-stroke. We got her by ambulance to a much closer, new hospital where the nurses and doctors walked and talked very quietly, very carefully. Nurses would glide into the room in a halo of white. Their faces were soft, their voices were soft, their personalities soft as angels. Unconsciously they knew their mission: to soothe, to sedate, to alleviate. The gleaming linoleum rang with gentility. There would be no screaming or cursing here. But I wasn't sure if Grandma knew what was happening to her.

She became blissfully or, depending upon your viewpoint, objectionably dopey. A child-like demeanour graced Grandma's face and voice. I began to miss the blood-and-guts Grandma who knew how to do battle and take situations into her own hands. The Grandma who innately understood power and dominance. The Grandma who chain-smoked cigarettes, wore movie star sunglasses, painted her nails fire engine red, ate Almond Joy and Milky Way candy bars without a second thought, drank coke and ginger ale and kept a bottle of Cherry Heering in the closet. Who, full of contradictions, consumed wheat germ, V-8 juice, buttermilk, chamomile tea, and the bitter seed inside the apricot pit all because "They're good for you, dahling."

I wanted that Grandma back, the one who defied classification, the one who would break you up with a roll of her eyes and a shrug of her shoulders. The one who sometimes laughed so hard at her own jokes, she couldn't get the punch line out. The one who made a fortune in real estate after escaping the oppression of Imperial Russia. The one who challenged you to find anything unbecoming about her while assuaging unspoken sorrows with drink.

I wanted the Grandma who was brazen and soulful, life affirming and distraught, inspired and stricken, because that was the real Grandma Ethel—the one who was a living fire and an inexplicable mystery. Who was as multifaceted as every one of Shakespeare's triumphant or doomed heroines from comedy or tragedy. The woman who had lived her life full-tilt forward and yet was as sensitive as a bone china cup.

Somewhere between the amputation and the convalescence, Grandma Ethel had disappeared down a corridor, and I couldn't find her. In her place was a manageable, innocent child.

One night at visiting hours, somewhere into the third week of this hospital stay, Ruthie and I sat watching Perry Mason along with Grandma, who lay swaddled in her bed sheets. Every few minutes, Grandma asked Ruthie questions about what was happening in the unfolding story on the TV. Even the jazzy saxophones of the theme song got no rise out of her, no come-hither smile or dancing shoulders. Ruthie was explaining who were the bad guys and who were the good. Grandma kept confusing one actor with another. But then she flashed a smile and said that Perry would save the client once more and that her husky boyfriend would uncover the *real* villain. (This was before I knew about Grandma's stint in prison and the "bum rap" she had gotten from the publicity-hungry D.A.)

A nurse came in to give Grandma some medication. Grandma stretched out the palm of her hand and took the pills, slowly sipping from a paper cup. The nurse fluffed up the pillows and then grasped hold of the corners of the bed sheet and shook it up in the air so it billowed out like a sail, suspended for a moment between heaven and earth. Then it descended slowly, covering Grandma and the bed.

Visiting hours were over and Ruthie and I kissed Grandma on opposite cheeks while she made smacking sounds with her mouth and waved us out of the room with one of her fingers, bending it up and down in a goodbye. At the last moment she called out something about not wanting the "Yeshiva boy" to visit, and then went silent.

Early the next morning the phone rang. I heard Ruthie speaking in a low voice. Then she came down the hallway, stuck her head in my room, and said Grandma passed away overnight. Ruthie turned away and shut the door. She went into Merri's room, which had become hers now that Merri was back at college. I heard her close the door behind her, and fall heavily onto the bed and burst into tears. Sitting in my room listening, not knowing what to do, I began crying quietly to myself.

# Chapter 19
# A Riddle Solved (Partly)

It's two years now that Brian and I are together. We're shedding our separate apartments and moving to a house in Riverdale, along the Hudson River at the northwestern edge of the Bronx. We've talked of marriage, but we haven't come to any conclusions. Brian is concerned his children may find it upsetting. They spend alternate weekends with us and we go on day trips upstate, or visit the Museum of Natural History, the Planetarium, see the ballet or the newest Disney movie. His daughter Rachel is almost twelve and is a budding collector of rocks and scholar of butterflies—she doesn't want to kill them, though, she says and adds emphatically, "Their lives are so short as it is." Brian's son is ten and already an accomplished violinist. With a little coaxing the boy will play the Vivaldi A-Minor Concerto. He becomes quite focused, yet entranced, when he performs for us and blushes shyly afterwards when we clap and compliment him.

The children are navigating a time of transition, as Joanna has begun dating. We try to give them a home that is stable and consistent. When they are with us, we celebrate Friday evening Sabbaths with the lighting of candles and a traditional dinner.

I have even taken to baking *challah* on Friday afternoons. If Rachel arrives early enough, we do it together. I think of all the generations of women, my family and hers, who have performed this sacred task. Sometimes I imagine Grandma Ethel as a girl in her Russian *shtetl* home making *challah* on Fridays, Great Grandma Sarah holding one end while Ethel twists the three strands of dough into a braid like the braid she wears over the crest of her brow. Then they bake the golden loaf with egg-yellowed crust so the sweet flavour of the soft bread, drizzled with honey, graces the Sabbath dinner. I can see Great Grandpa Elias blessing the bread then pulling it apart for the family to savour.

More and more I see how our lives are braided together. We are separate yet intertwined, like the strands of the *challah*. We are consecrated by life to live together, to feed one another's souls as the *challah* feeds our bodies and spirits on the Sabbath. For now, in this century, in a place called America, we are safe; no longer escaping danger, enemies, pogroms, wars, camps. Though I am a secular Jew, I feel the importance of taking the time each week to acknowledge the good in my life and the gift of life itself. My ancestors' lives were filled with grave difficulties—persecutions, expulsions, hatred, and death because of our Judaism. Some still suffer these things today. I have been fortunate to have grown up without those dire burdens. But I can honour those who bore them.

So, as a family, whether it is two, or four, or more of us, we celebrate this goodness we have been given and share this love with each other. And with those we cannot love, we try to extend our compassion and empathy.

Sometimes the braids of *challah* remind me of Grandma Ethel's antique hair braid, grown in the Old World and shorn off in the New, braiding together the oppression and catastrophe of her early life in Russia with the success and sadness of her life in America. Did she save that braid because it reminded her that her life, with all its light and dark, was braided together with the lives of those she loved?

The disappearance of that braid still spooks me sometimes. But then I think that maybe we—Merri, Samuel, and I, Ruthie and Bennie too—have become the braid. Have the strands of Grandma's life—fear and loss in the Old World, safety and comfort but still loss in the New—have they intertwined to help make us the mosaic of light and dark that we are?

And why just the five of us? What Grandma Ethel said that night in the Emergency Room—that love is the only thing that matters in the end—I see now, has a much broader meaning than I at first realized. I had thought it referred to an individual's life and the lives within a family. I see now the world is forever in that Emergency Room looking for life-and-death help. And we are all the family of humankind, all braided together. Yet I also know, though love is the answer, the way is full of work and daily struggle.

Something startling happens this year. While cleaning out Ruthie's things from the Westchester house a few years ago, Merri came across some papers in Mom's jewellery box; papers in Yiddish in Grandma Ethel's handwriting. At the time, Merri never mentioned them to me. Now she is cleaning out her files and comes across them again. She asks if I know anyone who can translate Yiddish.

My heart jumps, remembering the mystery of the missing papers from Grandma's closet years ago.

"Not only do I know someone," I tell her. "I live with the greatest Yiddish devotee of the century. He likes to read *Sholem Aleichem* in the original."

When I ask Brian to take a look, he's excited.

"I've never seen an original document in Yiddish before," he says. "This will be fun."

As might be expected, Brian's scientific personality is nothing if not meticulous. He won't satisfy my immediate curiosity with an off-hand translation, but wants to sit down with his dictionary and go over it with every attention to detail.

It's easy to see one is a letter signed by Grandma and addressed to someone named Marta. No envelope. So we wonder if Grandma never mailed it, or whether it was returned as undeliverable.

By the end of the week I am impatient with Brian. Yes, he's translated one, but he doesn't want to show me until they're all done. Because they may shed light on one another and alter the overall meaning. He'll finish them this weekend.

When Sunday finally comes, I'm beyond curiosity and into mania.

"*Nu, Nu?*" I say as Brian lays out the papers. He starts off hesitantly.

"I'm not sure if this, which appears to be a letter, was sent, or returned. It's undated, and may only be a sort of testament to your grandmother's feelings, a commemoration of her love for someone."

I feel my body tingling in anticipation of a story of love that Grandma Ethel lived through in Russia.

"Your view of who you've always been may be upended," Brian adds.

"Okay, okay, don't keep me in suspense any longer." I say, feeling on the edge of a precipice, wondering if I will ever be the same after reading these pages.

"I put them in, as far as I can tell, their logical order."

*Dear Marta,*

*Thank you beyond all [measure? limits?] for your letter about Jacob's imprisonment. His misfortune is difficult to bear, but at least he survived at the hands of the secret police and his internment is limited to three years. In its way, the news is far better than my [dire?] imaginings. I cannot express my gratitude enough for all you are doing. Please let me know when you are settled in Siberia and I will send more money. I agree it is worth attempting* to *[ease?] his time there if the guards prove to be [amenable? to bribes?]*

*I hope you will forgive me for what I am about to tell [divulge to?] you. No one's ears are meant for this secret. I only hope you will understand.*

*My belly is ripe with the [fleeting?] love Jacob and I shared. I would want him to know I carry a part of him with me into a new world, free of danger, undue hardship, and imprisonment.*

*Perhaps I am [too much?] innocent [naïve?] to think this may bring you happiness as well, since we both share the love of the same man.*

*He is lost to me and you are his life now. But I wanted to give you this news, in hope you would be willing to share it with him [someday?], when he is once more free and your life [together?] is secure.*

*I cherish his love, although lost to me, a part of him will live forever within my [very?] being, and in the [very] bones [sinew?] and heart of our child.*

*Blessings upon you, take care of yourself,*

*Ethel*

I look up at Brian with tears in my eyes.

He puts his arm around my shoulders and asks if I'm okay.

"I don't know. I think I'm in shock. I never imagined," I say. "Who could've? My lineage, my history, my very body, no longer what I always thought they were. And Grandma, poor Ethel, to be caught in the throes of historical forces, to live with that secret burning in her heart. Do you think he was a 'revolutionary'?"

"Some sort of dissident, I imagine. A lot was going on in Russia just before the 1917 Revolution. Are you ready for the next piece?"

"Ready or not, here I come," I say blowing my nose.

"This one seems like a journal entry; perhaps a fragment of a letter."

*Our child is a perfect blend of our two physical natures—your pale, freckled [complexion?] and with [startling?] sea green eyes, all crowned from birth with a halo of strawberry curls. She is truly a child with a new future in a new land. Her look is sometimes serious with your [pensiveness?], and her laughter is filled with the delight we shared in each other's arms. Your [legacy?] lives in a land of freedom and peace.*

*One day, perhaps, she will know of her [unusual? remarkable?] father. But not for a long time. My lips bestow on her your kisses that travel through [space and time?] to reach her.*

"That's definitely Ruthie! She always said she had red hair as a baby. I used to wonder who she inherited it from."

"Now you, kinda, know."

"Yes, this knowing opens a huge geography of the unknown. Grandma, an illicit love affair, the hiding of a secret of a birth, and a Russian Revolutionary. The stuff of romantic novels."

"Sweetheart," Brian says softly, holding me in his arms, "I'm afraid it doesn't have a happy ending."

"What?" I say, coming out of my state of confused wondering. Brian hands me the last paper. He places his arm around my shoulder and I read.

*Dearest Jacob,*

*I write this knowing your eyes will never see me or your child.*

*Marta wrote me of the typhus epidemic at your work camp. She could get you no medicine or care of any kind. After two weeks of sickness, you were sent out to the forest on a work crew to [fell?] and saw timber. Struggling with fever, you [collapsed?] in the snow. Your body was pushed aside and left to freeze as the ground was too hard to place you within it for comfort.*

*Your sightless eyes are now witness to the blue of the heavens, the grey of storm, the [obliteration?] of falling snow, until spring arrives and wildflowers grow up around your bones, within the fertile earth of your body.*

*Blessings of God be upon you. Love encircle you. Return to the dust from which you were made.*

*I will hold you within my heart forever,*

*Ethel*

I begin to cry again. But then a thought hits me. "Oh, my God, oh my God, the photo and the poem!"

"What photo?" Brian asks.

"I know who Jacob is," I say, as I run upstairs to get the box of memorabilia from my closet.

Brian is understandably bewildered. I show him the photo of Ethel with Jacob, the photo we found in Grandma Ethel's closet after she died.

"See," I say and turn the photo over to show him the writing on the back, "Odessa, 1914. That must be him because Ruthie was born in 1915. And with it we found this poem which describes Grandma Ethel perfectly." We are both stunned into silence.

"I can't imagine a more tragic ending to a story," Brian says.

"I can," I say. "Now Grandma's life makes sense. Jacob is the puzzle piece that explains everything. Her secret sorrows, the passionate sadness she had to assuage with periodic bouts of drinking; the three impossible husbands; the countless boyfriends; maybe even the sublimated drive for success and the self-indulgent luxuries."

"From what you've told me of Grandma Ethel, she was a dynamic, self-directed person. She never gave up on life and seemed to celebrate it, too. She was a multifaceted human being like most of us. And, she accomplished a great abiding feat: she established your family in a land of safety and prosperity and freedom."

"Yes, you're probably right," I say, hugging Brian around the waist, and leaning my head against his chest. "Probably right. She gave her best to this new land and I'm grateful beyond measure."

At the end of her life Grandma Ethel delivered a message. I know now her whole life was a message. One that took most of my life to understand and accomplish: In the end the most important thing is the love you give and the love you receive. Though so much else is also important, without those it is an empty life.

# Epilogue

As soon as she woke, Ethel knew where to go. In the *shtetl* she lifted herself up the ladder to the roof of the synagogue. It was as she remembered it that Sabbath long ago. The mothers were busy portioning out food to their children. Soon they would be settled on their improvised beds for the night as they waited for the spring flood to recede from the lanes around their wooden houses. The Rabbi and men were *davening*, rocking precariously back and forth in their ecstasy of prayer to welcome God into their hearts and His Holy Time on the earth. This night was like a celebration, a time when the congregation was a little closer to God's Heaven. Under the night sky they could feel the infinite and the eternal all around them, sweeping them up in a rapture of Divine Being.

Ethel's elderly self glanced up at the bridal canopy of stars in the firmament overhead. *How was it possible,* she wondered. Of course, in God's Time anything was possible. God's Time was miraculous, the same as one's inner world. Life was breathing into her again.

Then she felt someone take her hand. Looking down, she saw the young boy with copper curls like a halo, and soulful eyes, deep set and piercing sharp with intelligence and love. Jacob was lying next to her under the dark blue expanse of the sky. The little girl Ethel had once been was waking up from a three-quarters-of-a-century dream. It had all happened, of course, but it was no longer real. This was real, where her heart had been waiting, where a young boy and a young girl were dancing with their eyes.

Jacob lifted their clasped hands and pointed at the night sky. He was telling her the stories of the constellations. She did not need to hear his words, though she cherished each flaming utterance he first spoke in Yiddish, and then, Hebrew. His words were the stars that composed her soul. All she had lived through were the stories the stars told, if you could read them as he could.

Her great failing—her lack of courage in Russia—was transformed in America. In America, out of necessity, she had to be courageous, to face the difficulties of survival, to learn a new way of life, to fill the emptiness inside with the fruits of desire. In America, people admired her success. She had achieved many things—wealth, marriage, family, and grandchildren. Yet part of her had always been here, next to Jacob, the universe of the night sky their habitation.

She hadn't known it at the time, but he had been all things to her, the most bitter and the most joyous. Joined with him again on this rooftop she realized he had taught her how to open her heart, and how to love. He had done it magically by staying inside her like a ravenous child, eager for life, enabling her to take on living after his loss. He was the only person she had loved fully, with her whole heart, without reservation, without judgment, with every part of herself. And she had been loved back the same.

"Loving" was the gift. Just that. It was as if her soul had been turned to gold by it: a spun gold of delicate yet indestructible filaments, like some enchantment that had, instead of imprisoning her, set her free. Only she'd never realized this. She had only seen with mortal eyes the ripping and tearing of her heart.

Surprisingly, she felt both enlarged and contracted at the same time. As if those filaments of love had exploded outward in infinitesimal sparks. As if her being was in all those uncountable flickering lights, and in all the things of the earth. As if she was part of the blood red petals of the evening rose, and part of the milky yellow moon setting at dawn, and part of the black shadow of eclipse falling on heavenly bodies. As if she was in the sparkling of the coloured stars and in the spinning of the deep blue galaxies. That was what Jacob had done to her heart. Ignited it into endlessness. Not torn it to pieces.

On the other side of suffering was God. Not the God of the Bible. Not the God invoked in temples and churches. Not the God that one prayed to for things. The God that was Life itself. The quickened substance that touched all things. Made them come alive. Made them feel and grow and experience. And eventually made them die; another mystery that Jacob had unlocked for her without his knowing it.

Side by side, they lay on the roof of the synagogue, fingers entwined, and watched the eternity of night cover them with a blanket of stars.

CPSIA information can be obtained
at www.ICGtesting.com
Printed in the USA
LVHW052310240723
753137LV00004B/134